RUTHLESS

A Born Assassin, Book 3

JACQUELINE PAWL

ALSO BY JACQUELINE PAWL

Defying Vesuvius

A BORN ASSASSIN SERIES

Helpless (prequel novella)

Nameless (prequel novella)

Merciless

Heartless

Ruthless

Fearless

Limitless

A Born Assassin Series Omnibus

THE LADY OF INNISLEE SERIES

Court of Vipers

Copyright © 2021 by Jacqueline Pawl

All rights reserved.

No part of this book may be reproduced in any form or by any electronic or mechanical means, including information storage and retrieval systems, without written permission from the author, except for the use of brief quotations in a book review.

1

MERCY

A heavy book slammed shut, shattering the silence of the infirmary and causing Mercy to jump. She sat atop Alyss's worn desk, Tamriel slumped in the chair beside her. He leaned back and rubbed his eyes with the heels of his palms. "How long do you think it'll take us to figure out the cure? We've been reading for hours, and we haven't seen a single mention of Cedikra."

Mercy shook her head, trying to clear the fatigue from her mind, her body. She folded the sheaf of notes she'd been attempting to decipher for the last hour and tucked it into her pocket. Even after falling ill, Alyss had worked obsessively on potential treatments for the plague, and it was clear now how quickly the disease had ravaged her mind. The healer's scrawl was nearly illegible, the words small and cramped, crisscrossing one another until it was impossible to tell where one sentence ended and the next began. Even so, Alyss had studied the plague longer than anyone. There had to be something useful in the mess of ink—if only Mercy could find it.

"There must be something here," she said. "Pilar saw the cure in a vision, and so did Cassius. We have to keep looking."

Tamriel didn't look convinced, but he nodded, trailing his fingers along the cracked leather cover of the book in his lap. Neither of them spoke of the revelation they'd discovered the day before: visions didn't always come true. Cassius had sworn to Ghyslain that the prince would die on the journey back to Sandori, but Calum had altered that future by jumping into the path of the arrows meant to end his cousin's life. That meant everything they had done might be for naught. All the guards who died in the Howling Mountains and in the Islands might have given their lives for nothing. Mercy and Tamriel could labor over the cure for weeks, for months, and fail.

Mercy picked up the lantern beside her and hopped off the desk. She traced the spines of the books stacked beside Tamriel, the gold lettering shining in the light of the lantern's dancing flame. The pile stood taller than she and consisted of every medicinal and herbalist manual they'd found in the castle. The stack beside the hearth was much smaller, but growing by the hour as they scoured—and rejected—more and more books. Not a single one had mentioned Cedikra, or any plant remotely similar.

Keep looking, whispered the voice in Mercy's head. It wasn't the same voice she had heard before; it wasn't Liselle. Her sister had been worryingly absent since they left the Islands. She'd claimed that Firesse was trying to banish her to the Beyond, and the possibility that the First may have succeeded caused Mercy's stomach to tighten with fear.

Desperate to take her mind off her troubled thoughts, Mercy plucked the top book off the pile and handed it to Tamriel, then took the next one for herself. "Your father sent for healers to help Niamh, didn't he?"

"Yes. Any healers who can be spared from the infirmaries should arrive by tomorrow night."

Mercy's gaze drifted to the nearest cot, guilt and grief washing over her at the sight. Alyss had lain there for Creator only knew how long, waiting for Mercy to uphold her promise and end her misery. Eventually, Mercy had, but only after being released from the cell in which she'd been locked for nearly a week. If she had arrived a day or two later, she would have found a lifeless husk in Alyss's place. The thought sent a shudder down her spine.

She'd seen enough death to last a lifetime. Simply riding down the streets yesterday morning had been painful. There had been so much curiosity and hope on the people's faces at their prince's return, but Mercy knew the death toll would continue to climb in the days to come. The plague had already weakened the city, which could prove catastrophic should Firesse attack the city. Mercy had no idea what other tricks the girl had up her sleeve.

The First was insane. She had dabbled in forbidden powers to pull Liselle from the Beyond to torment Ghyslain. She had enabled Drake Zendais to possess Calum and murder Odomyr—a man who had been like a father to her—on the sacred night of *Ialathan*. She was the reason Calum could very well be dead.

No, he can't be dead yet—not until I see him pay for his crimes.

"Hey," Tamriel said softly, rising and pulling her into an embrace. She buried her face in his chest, breathing in the scents of old books and woodsmoke on his clothes. He leaned back and peered down at her, brows furrowed in concern. "What are you worrying about now?"

"Nothing." *Calum*, she didn't say, but he read the truth on her face. His expression darkened.

"Wherever he is, I hope he is suffering for his treachery," Tamriel growled. "When this is over, we will find him, and he will face justice for his crimes." He pulled one of Mercy's hands from the book she was holding—she'd been absently worrying the corner of the cover—and laced his fingers through hers. "Let's not think about him now."

A knock at the door startled them. The hinges squeaked as the door swung open, and Niamh and Nynev rounded the row of shelves a second later.

"Find anything?" Niamh asked, her words lilted with her slight Cirisian accent. She took in their rumpled clothes and the books discarded by the hearth. "How long have you been down here?"

"What time is it?" Tamriel asked.

"Eight in the morning."

"Oh. About four hours. Maybe five."

"You should've woken us. We'd have helped you." Niamh slipped past her sister, grabbed the top book from the pile, and started toward the nearest cot. When she noticed the stains on the sheets, she scrunched her nose and instead sat cross-legged on the floor.

"After all that riding, you deserve rest," Tamriel responded. "I appreciate what you're doing for my people. You're risking your lives by leaving your home, and I swear that I will make it up to you."

Niamh grinned. "It's easy to risk one's life when one is unable to die."

Nynev snorted. "Just remember that I'm here to watch out for her," she grumbled, pointing at her sister, "and not to help you. We're leaving the second this plague business is finished."

"I would expect nothing less."

The huntress bristled, glaring at Tamriel. "What is that supposed to mean?"

"Simply that I don't blame you for wanting to leave. Our

problems are not your concern. Nevertheless, I'm grateful for your aid."

Niamh shot her sister a warning look, and Nynev thawed, conceding a shallow dip of her head. "Helping us rid the Islands of Firesse's evil will be repayment enough. She is too young and angry to realize that nothing good will come of drowning the world in more blood."

"Exactly." Niamh turned to Mercy. "But back to the plague. What treatments have you tried already?"

"Lots of tinctures and poultices—none of which had any effect. Tabris has already figured out that most parts of the Cedikra is poisonous, so it's a matter of figuring out which plant can neutralize the toxins. Oh! The Pryyam salt." Mercy crossed the room and searched the shelves until she found the right bottle. The lavender crystals within sparkled in the light as she held it up for Tamriel and the others to see. "Alyss ground this into the priestesses' skin after they washed. It was excruciating, but it seemed to draw out the infection from the blisters—at least for a little while. Perhaps mixing it with Cedikra could help."

"Maybe," Niamh agreed, but her expression was doubtful. She wasn't a healer by any stretch of the term; her knowledge of medicine began and ended with what Mercy had taught her during the ride to the capital. What connection she had with the cure, not even Cassius knew. "We won't find the answers we need simply by talking about it. There must be some mention of Cedikra or Fieldings' Plague in the books." Her lips parted into a crooked grin as she opened the book in her lap, the leather spine cracking. "Five aurums to whoever finds it first."

THREE HOURS AND A DOZEN BOOKS LATER, THE WAGER HAD yet to be settled.

Niamh sighed and set aside the tome she'd been reading, then picked up a poker and began to stoke the hearth's dying fire. "Well, I've found a fat lot of nothing. You?"

"No."

"Nope."

"Nothing."

She frowned, creasing the vine tattoos swirling around her forehead and cheeks. "That's...not ideal."

"You think?" Nynev shut her book and grimaced as she massaged a crick in her neck. She scowled at Tamriel. "I don't know why you think my sister can help with this cure—vision or no. Neither of us has any experience healing. In fact, the only one of us who can heal is—ironically—the assassin."

"I can sew wounds and treat minor ailments. Diseases are entirely different." As she spoke, Mercy ran her fingers along the long, puckered scar on the inside of her forearm, a reminder of the day Mistress Trytain had carved open her flesh and forced her to sew herself up.

"Okay, so none of us has any idea what the hell we're doing," the huntress responded. "That bodes well for the people of this city."

It had taken them three days to ride from Xilor to Sandori. Each day, more people fell sick, the Cedikra grew closer to ripening and rotting, and the threat of Firesse's attack loomed nearer. Mercy wished Mistress Sorin were here. Perhaps she would know what to do. The Guild's healer had been one of the few good people in Mercy's childhood; the infirmary had offered a welcome respite from the cruel apprentices.

"Stop," Tamriel whispered, laying a hand atop Mercy's. Under her sleeve, her old scar ached. Without meaning to, she'd rubbed it raw. The prince turned to Nynev. "We'll keep looking—"

"Admit it," Niamh suddenly snapped. "We're not remotely suited to cure anything." She tossed the iron poker aside, and it clattered loudly on the stone floor, leaving a streak of black soot in its wake.

"*Mo dhija?*" Nynev asked. *Sister?* She appeared as surprised by her sister's outburst as Mercy and Tamriel were; Niamh had barely said ten words over the course of their ride to Sandori.

"How can this be anything but a waste of time? I don't understand half the words I read in these gods-damned books. How—*How*—can you expect me to save all your people? How can you put that on me?" she implored Tamriel, her eyes wide.

He crossed the room and crouched before her, the hearth's flames limning him in gold. He waited until she met his steady gaze to say, "I know you can do this. *You can.* We're all here to help you. Whatever you need, we'll get it." In his voice was none of the uncertainty, none of the fear, from before. He'd be strong for her, Mercy knew, just as he'd been strong for his people, for his father, for years. Niamh needed to know he believed in her.

"He's right," Mercy added. "We'll figure it out. It's all a part of Cassius's vision, remember?" They'd not yet told the sisters that the visions could no longer be trusted. Perhaps they never would. Niamh didn't need any more stress than she already bore. "The healers will be here soon to work with you on the cure."

"But what if—" The sudden rumble of Niamh's stomach cut her off, breaking the tension, and she shot them a sheepish grin when they all laughed.

"The cooks must be preparing lunch," Tamriel said. He helped her to her feet and looked to Nynev. "Why don't you go to the kitchen and see what you can find? Mercy and I will meet you there in a few minutes."

Niamh opened her mouth to speak, then hesitated.

"What's wrong?"

She blushed. "The elves. The...slaves. They stare at me."

Nynev rolled her eyes and tossed her book aside. "We're Cirisian. Of course they're going to gawk."

"It doesn't bother you?"

"I don't *let* it bother me. Come on, let's go." Nynev grabbed her sister's arm and dragged her out of the room. The door softly clicked shut behind them.

"Why did you want to stay behind?" Mercy asked as she rolled her neck, stiff from so many hours bent over a book.

Tamriel offered her a devilish grin, crossed the room, and kissed her. One of his hands cupped the back of her head, tangling in her wild curls. His other hand slipped around her waist and tugged her close. "Must I have a reason beyond wanting to steal a little time alone with you?" he murmured as he pulled away.

"I suppose not." She followed the curve of his lower lip with her thumb. Tamriel reached up and caught her fingers, splaying her hand against his chest, right over his heart.

"I love you," he said, his dark eyes full of desire, and Mercy's heart swelled. It was hard to believe that two weeks ago, he'd been glaring at her, his gaze burning with hatred and betrayal.

"I love you, too." She linked her fingers behind Tamriel's neck and guided his mouth down to hers. "I love you," she repeated between kisses, "more than I ever thought myself capable of loving anyone."

"I've never thanked you for...everything." He met her eyes and shot her a breathtaking smile. "For protecting me. For standing up to my father. For being the amazing, stubborn, fiercely loyal warrior you are. And...for not killing me, of course."

She laughed. "I'm especially grateful for that last one—even if killing you would have made my life a hell of a lot easier."

"We're going to make it through this, aren't we?"

"We are." She hugged him tightly, her eyes fluttering shut as the warmth of his body seeped into hers. After so many years of training in the Guild, of trying to fit in where she didn't belong and was not wanted, she'd finally found home—with him. *This is where I belong. No one—not Firesse, not Calum, not any of the Daughters—will take him from me,* she vowed. *I will not give up this life for anything.* "We've made it through worse," she said, her words muffled by the fabric of his tunic.

Tamriel's breath tickled the tip of her ear when he whispered, "That we have, my love."

2
MERCY

Mercy and Tamriel were halfway to the kitchen when shouts echoed down the hall. They were distant, the words distorted and indecipherable, but the panic and anger in them were unmistakable. They froze mid-step as another wail filled the corridor.

"What's happening?" Mercy asked. "Who is that?"

Tamriel cursed under his breath. "I have an idea. Go on to the kitchen—I'll be right there."

He started toward the source of the cry—somewhere near the great hall—and, of course, Mercy followed. She made it all the way around the corner and halfway down the next hall before the prince glanced back and caught her walking soundlessly a few strides behind him. He let out a huff of exasperation. "Fine, then. Come if you like, but stay out of sight."

She grinned at him. He rolled his eyes.

"You're too stubborn for your own good."

"You like that about me." She trailed him down the next few halls, until the large doors to the great hall appeared before them. The shouts drifting from within rose again, followed by the soft *whump* of flesh striking flesh, and a grunt of pain.

"I like it when it's not directed at *me*." Tamriel smoothed his tunic and straightened his shoulders, a mask of cool detachment sliding over his features. In those few tiny adjustments, he transformed into the regal Crown Prince she had met so many weeks ago. He brushed a bit of dust off his sleeve, then strode into the great hall.

Before the massive doors swung shut, Mercy slipped into the room behind him, her new, supple leather boots silent as she slunk to one of the ill-lit corners of the room.

The king stood in the center, flanked by guards. It took her a moment to realize that the sobbing lump of fabric crumpled before Ghyslain's feet was Elise. The serenna was kneeling on the floor, surrounded by three guards in full, gleaming suits of armor. Her cheek was red and swollen; one of the guards must have hit her to stop her wailing. Mercy watched Tamriel step around Elise, ignoring her completely, and exchange quiet words with his father.

The doors on the opposite end of the hall flew open so hard they cracked against the wall. Seren Pierce stormed through the doorway, his face splotchy with rage.

"How *dare* you?" he roared when he saw his daughter. "I demand to know the meaning of this!"

"Calum tried to murder my son," Ghyslain responded evenly, not even sparing his advisor a glance. "Your daughter helped him forge the assassination contract, and she will be kept in the dungeon until the council's investigation into her guilt is concluded."

"Her *guilt?*" Pierce stormed toward the king, but, at a flick of Ghyslain's hand, two of the guards leapt forward and restrained the seren. A vein throbbed in Pierce's forehead as they forced his arms behind his back. "My daughter is guilty of nothing."

Elise looked up at the prince, then the king, with wide, terrified eyes, her head bobbing up and down—rather chicken-like, Mercy thought with a wry smirk. "It's true! I have no business with the Guild! I wouldn't even know how to contact them if I wanted to. Please, Your Highness, Your Majesty, you must believe me!" she wailed. "I didn't *do* anything!"

Mercy's lip curled in disgust. *Pathetic coward.* No wonder she and Calum had fallen for each other.

Tamriel leaned forward, his features contorted in anger. "I know Calum bought the contract. I've seen it. I know that you helped him fake it."

"If you're looking for someone to punish, lock up the Assassin instead," Pierce snapped. "She's the one who attacked you and carved you up like a roast pig. Where is the little wretch, anyway? I know she's in the city."

Mercy reached for the daggers sheathed at her hips, wishing she could show him how easy it would be to carve *him* up.

Tamriel turned on him, his voice low and deadly. "Do not bring her into this."

"Why didn't you give her the hangman's noose the day the guards found her standing over your son with his blood on her hands?" Pierce snarled at Ghyslain. "Do you still have a soft spot for her kind? Or have you simply gone so mad that you can no longer tell friend from foe?"

"Father!" Elise gaped at Pierce. Mercy had never expected the mousy little man to be brave enough—or stupid enough —to speak to his king so brazenly.

"You know the law, Pierce," Ghyslain said, ignoring the slight. "She'll be held here while the council investigates. In a few days, you may attend her trial and watch her plead her innocence." He waved a hand to the guards. "Take her away."

"No!" the seren shouted.

The guards seized Elise's arms and pulled her to her feet. She shrieked and tried to fight them, but their grips didn't waver. Her tears left dark streaks of makeup down her flushed cheeks as they dragged Elise out of the room and let the doors bang shut behind them.

Once her cries had faded down the hall, Ghyslain ran a hand down his face. "Release him."

The guards dropped the seren's arms. Pierce gave one enraged tug on his shirt and glowered at Ghyslain. When he took a step toward the king, Tamriel warned, "That's close enough."

"What do you think I'm going to do, boy?"

"Mind your tongue when you speak to me, Seren."

"Or what? You'll cut it out like you did that criminal they call Hero?" Tamriel stiffened almost imperceptibly at the mention of his partner-in-crime, but the seren continued, "I will not stand for this. My daughter is innocent. The Creator will see the truth come to light at her trial, I assure you." Pierce shot a withering glare at Tamriel. "The nobles have always wondered about you, Your Highness," he sneered, the honorific dripping with contempt, "but it is now clear that you follow the same foolhardy path your father once walked. Bringing the Assassin back to the capital with you was a grave mistake—one you will soon regret."

Mercy's lip curled, her blood boiling. In the Guild, she would have answered such threats with violence, but doing so now would only prove the man's point—even if he *was* asking for an arrow in his smug face.

Tamriel's voice was dangerously low as he asked, "Is that a threat?"

"Not a threat, Your Highness. A warning."

Ghyslain glared at Pierce. "Your family has grown comfortable and rich from the power I granted you when I bestowed your title so many years ago. Lest you have forgotten, I gave you your place in the nobility. That does not mean I cannot—or will not—take it away." Before the seren could respond, Ghyslain turned his back on him and said to the guards, "Escort him home. Pierce, your services will not be needed for a long while. Until the trial, you are not to set foot on the castle grounds."

Pierce fumed as the guards led him out of the castle.

Mercy stepped out of the shadows the second they disappeared through the massive double doors. "She's lying, Your Majesty. She's clearly guilty."

"Of course she is. But you need more evidence of her involvement in Calum's scheme if you are to convince the council and the rest of the court. You need proof that she voluntarily forged the document."

She frowned. "You're the king. Why the hell do you need the court to approve?"

"She's a noble, and they will always side with one of their own over the crown. I need the court to agree with my ruling if we don't want a riot on our hands when I sentence her to execution." A shadow passed across Ghyslain's face as he spoke. No doubt he was remembering the aftermath of the last time the nobles had acted with such blatant disregard for the crown—when they murdered Liselle in cold blood. "Work with the guards on the investigation and see what you can find. The rest of the city will know of Elise's arrest by supper, I'm sure, and we can't afford any dissent among the nobility when I declare her guilty. We can't fight Firesse if we're fighting amongst ourselves."

"And Calum?" Tamriel asked. "When are you going to tell the rest of the council about his betrayal?"

Ghyslain sighed, pain flickering in and out of his eyes so quickly Mercy wasn't sure if she had imagined it. Had he ever cared for Calum? Or had he simply taken the orphaned boy into his home out of guilt for having his father killed? "Tomorrow morning, when we meet to discuss Elise's arrest."

"Your Majesty?" Master Adan's voice preceded him into the great hall. It was still a shock to see the man who now held Master Oliver's position, to look up from the shining metal armor and not see Master Oliver's stern face, his broken mess of a nose. "Two healers have arrived."

"Excellent. Escort them to their workroom and introduce them to Niamh and Nynev." Adan left, and Ghyslain turned back to Tamriel and Mercy. "Are you any closer to figuring out the cure?"

"No."

"I'm sorry."

Mercy nearly burst out laughing. Ghyslain hadn't had any qualms with hiding the cure from everyone when he thought it would prevent Tamriel's death. He would have let thousands people die if it meant saving his son's life. Then again, if she had known about Cassius's vision before they had left for Cirisor, she would have begged Tamriel to stay behind as fiercely as Ghyslain had.

After the king excused himself to attend his duties, Tamriel turned to her. "Now do you see why I didn't want you to witness that? You heard what Pierce said about you. Compared to what the nobles say about Liselle, that was tame—but it's only going to escalate the longer you're here. I'm terrified they're going to hurt you. What if they do the same thing to you as they did to your sister?"

"They can try." She sidled closer to him and purred, "But you're not ridding yourself of me that easily, Your Highness."

"You're tough, Mercy, but you can't keep your defenses up all the time. The nobles—"

"—sit on their asses all day, drinking wine and growing fat. I'm not my sister. I know how to fight, how to defend myself. Firesse, Lylia, Kaius, and Faye couldn't tear me away from you. Do you think I'm going to let some silk-swathed noble do it?"

She smiled, and some of the worry on Tamriel's face disappeared. He slipped an arm around her waist and pulled her close. "I think you're more likely to run them through with your precious daggers than let them tell you what to do."

3
CALUM

Every minute Calum spent trapped within the prison of his mind, watching through eyes he couldn't control, lasted an eternity. Ice-water still flooded his veins, the sensation as foreign and numbing as it had been when Firesse had first allowed Drake to possess him. The tentacles that accompanied Drake's presence still poked and prodded Calum's mind, tasting his memories, his thoughts, his desires. Sometimes, when Calum remembered the feeling of his dagger puncturing Odomyr's heart—when the First's warm, slick blood had poured out, coating his hands—he heard his father's laughter rumbling through him.

This was the Creator's punishment for his sins, he'd decided—for betraying Tamriel, for agreeing to trade Mercy to the Guild. Perhaps he really had died from those arrow wounds in Xilor. Or perhaps his wounds were still infected and this was nothing but a terrible dream, a mirage created by his fevered mind.

Don't be melodramatic, Drake whispered, the words slick and cool as silk. *This is real—it's all real—and when we return to the capital, we're going to show that elf-loving fool of a king what a grievous error he made when he destroyed our family.*

You have no one to blame for your death but yourself, Calum shot back. *You're a monster, a despicable—*

Careful, son. I'm the only reason you're alive right now. Without me to relay the information trapped inside your head, Firesse would have no use for you. So how about a little gratitude for the man who sired you?

Go to hell.

"Keep practicing!" Drake yelled with Calum's lips, Calum's tongue, Calum's voice. He rose from the tree stump atop which he'd been sitting and scanned the Cirisians around him. They were clustered in groups of twos and threes throughout the clearing, sparring with swords they'd stolen from the Beltharan and Feyndaran forces and had later blunted for practice. They were working through drills Drake had demonstrated for piercing the gaps in Beltharan plate mail.

In the few days since Calum, Kaius, and Faye returned to the Islands, the land had been transformed into a military training ground. Half of the fires throughout the camp were now being used to heat and sharpen the Cirisians' swords and forge new arrowheads. Drake had even pitched in for some of the work, tapping into Calum's memories of his apprenticeship in Myrellis Plaza and his travels with the Strykers to copy the weaponsmiths' techniques. He was clumsier and more careless than Calum was, but his repairs would be sufficient until the Strykers arrived—*if* they arrived.

The day of Odomyr's death, Firesse had sent messengers to the other clans announcing her intent to declare war on Beltharos. In the week since *Ialathan*, her ranks had swollen considerably. Lysander, Ivani, and Amyris had already pledged their fighting-aged clansmembers, and the elves from Odomyr's former clan were more than ready to take their revenge against Ghyslain and his citizens. There were nearly a thousand elves spread across the land surrounding Firesse's camp, and more Cirisians arrived each day. Calum was shocked at how many elves lived in the Islands; Master Oliver's reports had estimated their population to be in the low hundreds. Ghyslain had no idea the true size of the force coming to destroy his capital.

Calum struggled against the invisible bonds shackling him within his mental prison, making him a stranger in his own body. Simply wiggling his pinky toe or twitching a finger would be good enough. All he needed was a sign that he still had some modicum of control over himself. If he could do that, maybe one day he'd be strong enough to overpower Drake.

It won't work, Drake crooned, sensing Calum's fight for control.

He kept focusing on pushing those mind-tentacles back.

Nothing.

Drake marched across camp and strode into Firesse's tent without asking permission, blinking until his eyes adjusted to the sudden darkness. The First was seated beside Kaius on the cushions littering the floor. They were bent over a weathered map of Beltharos, notes scribbled in Cirisian along the margins.

"He's trying to take control again. Fourth time this week," Drake said in lieu of a greeting. Without waiting for an invitation, he planted himself on one of the threadbare cushions. He folded his hands in his lap, his lips spreading in a sly, very un-Calum-like smile. "There's no doubt he's my son. It's comforting to know that my blood instilled in him a little bit of a spine, because the worthless whore who bore him certainly didn't."

Don't say a word about her, Calum snapped. He'd never met his real mother—he hadn't worked up the courage to approach Dayna after catching a glimpse of her at *Ialathan*—but he'd be damned if he let the monster who forced her to bear his child speak ill of her.

Firesse studied him, her frown tinged with unease. "Nothing too bothersome, I hope?"

He flashed her another grin. "Of course not."

Kaius murmured something to her in Cirisian, glancing first at Drake, then at the map.

"Right," Firesse said, nodding. "We were about to call you in, actually. Calum and Kaius sent several letters during their ride to Xilor—one to the Guild, and a few to the Strykers. Provided they received the letters in time, the Strykers should arrive two days from now. You will ride out to meet them."

"Very well. Have you news of the Assassins?"

"Not yet."

"It's highly unlikely that the Guildmaster would risk a letter being intercepted by one of the king's men," Kaius interjected. "We must merely wait for the Daughters to arrive."

"She won't cast aside the opportunity to complete the contract on the prince and retrieve her wayward Assassin," Firesse said, fingering one of the clay beads in her hair. "Plus, with the substantial payment you've offered her..." she trailed off, gesturing to Drake.

Calum felt his father's sudden flash of annoyance at her words. His grandfather had toiled all his life for that money, day in and day out, to keep their family among the nobility. After his father's death, Drake had done the same. Together, they had built the Zendais name into the noble, respectable house it had remained until its collapse. He would not let that effort go to waste—for his hard-earned money to fill the coffers of the Assassins who had killed him. Alas, Drake had been brought here from the Beyond by the First, and he remained at her disposal until she saw fit to release him.

Drake simply smiled and said, "Of course, the payment. Most of my money is overseas, but my son keeps an account in a bank in the shipping district in the capital. When Sandori falls, Firesse, the money's yours."

He leaned forward and examined the map of Beltharos. "Where shall we attack first?" Then he pointed at a dot on the map, answering his own question. "There. Fishers' Cross. It's hidden on two sides by a bluff, so it'll be easy to ambush. Two dozen men could take it in an hour."

She studied the map, tugging on a strand of flame-colored hair that had slipped free of her braids. "I don't know... For many of the people in this camp, this is their first time holding a sword. Do you think they're ready?"

"We've not gathered them here only to lead them to a slaughter," the archer added.

"Your soldiers will learn more about combat by actually fighting than they will running drills. Not to mention, Tamriel and Mercy know you intend to attack. The king likely has soldiers marching for these Islands as we speak. Strike now, while the easternmost villages are still unprepared." He pointed at the little squiggly line that represented the bluff. "Place a handful of men north of the bluff, and another few south to catch any stragglers trying to flee. Then send in your warriors in the dead of night. I guarantee you, it'll be over by dawn."

Firesse and Kaius exchanged wary glances.

"You'll have to move inland quickly—you won't be able to house all your troops in the eight buildings in town, but the rest can share tents until then. You can resupply in Fishers' Cross before you march on the larger towns."

The words sounded wrong rolling off Calum's tongue. He wished he could push Drake away, that he could scrub away every last hint of his father's corrupting influence on his body and mind. Even if he somehow managed to free himself, though, he knew the memory of being trapped within his own body—unable to move, to speak, to do *anything*—would never fade.

The worst part was, Drake didn't care about the elves. Where Firesse went, he went—and she would lead him straight to the capital. To Ghyslain.

To revenge.

Just as Calum had wanted when he'd bought the contract on Tamriel's life. He'd been a fool for trying to kill Tamriel, he now knew. He'd been a fool for thinking he could avenge his father's murder. He'd been a fool for *wanting* to avenge his father.

"Well?" Drake asked, looking expectantly from Kaius to Firesse. "What do you say?"

"My hunters and Myris's fighters could accompany the recruits," Kaius suggested. "The archers can stand atop the bluff and pick off anyone who tries to flee to the docks."

"Once the Strykers arrive, we'll attack," Firesse finally said. "They'll be a valuable asset in the coming battles. Kaius, I want you and Myris to help Drake train the soldiers. Don't hold back. Have Lysander and Ivani do a full count of our troops. Amyris can do a full inventory of weapons and armor, then help the foragers gather healing supplies."

She stood and led them out of the tent. A breeze swept across the clearing—a breeze Calum should have been able to feel kiss his skin—sending the leaves of the palms and mangrove trees dancing. Across from them, the elves Drake had been training sparred in partial suits of plate mail—what limited pieces they'd managed to pilfer from the Beltharan and Feyndaran soldiers. They'd done their best to adjust the armor to fit their thinner, lither bodies. The sight reminded Calum of when he'd helped Mercy cheat the Trial, working in the stifling underground smithy at Kismoro Keep. Even then, he had known they shared a mother, but he had not chosen to help her out of a sense of familial obligation. He had chosen her because she was emotionless, ruthless, merciless. She'd been fueled by spite and rage at the world around her. He had been envious of her strength from the moment he met her.

So he had chosen her out of all the Assassins.

Look how well that had turned out.

Firesse surveyed the fighters as they trained, her tattooed lips spreading into a grin. "You've taught them well, Drake." Her smile grew, something dark and hungry glinting in her eyes. "Keep the soldiers working this hard, and they'll be ready for battle before we know it. By the week's end, we'll invade Beltharos."

4
TAMRIEL

Tamriel awoke early the morning after Elise's arrest, groaning when he rolled over and realized that, beyond his window, the sky was still dark, shining with bright stars. After dealing with Elise and attending to his other duties, he'd finally fallen into a fitful sleep late that night. He had tossed and turned for hours, his mind plagued with memories of Pilar's red, inflamed skin, her bulging blind eye, and Calum crumpling to the ground in Xilor, an arrow buried deep in his chest.

He stared at the ceiling high overhead, his mind going to the chests of Cedikra sitting in the infirmary a floor below. It was only a matter of time before the fruit began to rot, before their supply ran out, before more of his people fell fatally ill. The last thought chilled him to the bone. Cassius's visions didn't always come true. They could exhaust every resource trying to find the cure, but all their efforts could still amount to nothing. Meanwhile, Firesse was gathering her forces and preparing for war.

At this moment, his father's troops were marching toward the border. The king had dispatched six hundred men immediately after Tamriel had told him what they'd witnessed in the Islands. Even if her numbers had increased beyond the four hundred elves at *Ialathan*, six hundred soldiers would be more than enough to defeat her untrained clansmen. The Cirisians were fierce fighters, but only when they had the advantage of the Islands' wild landscape. They had no experience fighting in the wide-open plains and rolling hills of the fishing district. Even so, fear for his people coiled within him.

Tamriel rose, his troubled thoughts making him restless, and changed into fresh clothes. He started toward the door, stepping over the tangled sheets he'd kicked off his bed during the night, then stopped. After a moment's consideration, he returned to his wardrobe and slipped his sheathed sword onto his belt. The Daughters were still hunting him and Mercy, and he wouldn't be caught unprepared the next time they dared to set foot in his home.

The guards outside his door bowed when Tamriel stepped into the near-empty hall. Unlike the rest of the castle, no red and gold rugs covered the gray stone floors, no enormous gold-framed paintings lined the walls, no decorative suits of armor stood watch. Every bit of decorum in the guest wing had been removed after his mother died. No foreign dignitaries had stayed in the castle in Tamriel's lifetime. They'd all been scared away by the rumors of the king's madness, and as a result, the guest rooms were locked up and forgotten. They'd remained that way until Tamriel's party returned from the Islands. Mercy, Nynev, and Niamh had needed a place to stay, so he'd had the rooms cleaned and prepared for them—including one for himself. It was too soon after the Daughters' attack, too soon after he'd watched his guards die at their hands, too soon after he'd nearly lost his life, to return to his own chambers.

When he started toward Nynev and Niamh's room, one of the guards cleared his throat. "They're not in there, Your

Highness. They went with the Assassin to meet the healers." The tips of his ears flushed when Tamriel shot him a sharp look. "Uh, with Mercy, I mean."

Akiva elbowed the guard. After returning to Sandori, Tamriel had requested the young Rivosan join his personal guard, and Akiva had gone straight to work after his injured leg healed. "Would you like us to accompany you, Your Highness?"

"No, thank you. Remain at your posts. How is your leg faring?"

"It aches, but I'm alive, so I cannot complain overmuch." Grief passed across Akiva's face. Of the handful of guards who had accompanied them to the Islands, Akiva was the only one who had survived. The weight of the men's deaths hung heavily on Tamriel, but he had not known them as well as Akiva had. He couldn't imagine how painful the deaths of his brothers-at-arms must be to him.

Tamriel continued down the labyrinthine corridors and climbed the stairs to emerge in front of the library. He ignored the instinct he had developed as a child—to hide from his mad, grieving father and lose himself in a make-believe world—and marched down the hall to his right. A few minutes later, the door to his father's study loomed before him. Although he had learned not to show it, he'd always hated this room. Ghyslain had often locked himself inside when his grief was the most profound—the earliest years of Tamriel's life. His memories from that time were fuzzy, but his father's wailing sobs haunted him still.

He took a deep breath and opened the door, the familiar scent of woodsmoke rushing over him. The fireplace wasn't lit, but the aroma had seeped into everything: the chairs, the bookshelves, even Ghyslain's massive desk. Tamriel stumbled through the dark room, cursing the maid for leaving the heavy velvet curtains closed, and lit the candles in the gilded candelabrum on the desk. He opened the topmost drawer and shuffled through the papers until he found the one for which he had been searching.

The contract on his life had been written on a simple piece of parchment. He didn't bother to read the paragraphs of elegant, swirling cursive that detailed the specifics of the contract and the payment and whatever else was needed to arrange the assassination of a royal; he skipped straight to the bottom. His father's signature was there, plain as day: *His Majesty King Ghyslain Myrellis.* Every facet was identical to his father's signature, except for one—the smudging. Like his son, Ghyslain was right-handed, so his words never smeared when he wrote. But on the contract, the ink blots from the pen were smeared to the right, dragged by someone writing with her left hand.

Tamriel sighed and dropped the contract on the desk. The differences were barely discernible. Alone, they wouldn't be enough to convince the nobles of Elise's guilt. He could only hope that the guards would find more evidence at Pierce's home.

He traced the signature, struggling to imagine Calum and Elise plotting his murder. After all they had endured growing up in the castle, how could Calum be so cold as to murder his only cousin, his best friend? Was his need for vengeance truly that great? Or was he simply hiding his own selfish desires— to win the throne and Elise's hand in marriage—behind a false demand for justice?

Soon, this will all be over, he told himself for what felt like the millionth time. When Fieldings' Plague was finally cured and Firesse and her band of warriors defeated, he and Mercy would destroy the contract together. They'd pay off the Guild if possible, then watch this terrible deed crumble to ash, severing the hold the Assassins had on their lives. For now, Tamriel returned the contract to the drawer and slammed it shut with more force than was necessary. The flames of the candelabrum flickered and guttered with the movement.

"Are you proud of yourself, you stupid, stupid fool?" he muttered to the empty room. He had no idea if Calum was alive. If he survived his wound in Xilor, Tamriel hoped he would have the good sense to stay far away from Beltharos. As much as he wanted to see his cousin brought to justice for his crimes, he didn't know how he would react to seeing Calum in the flesh. Calum had shifted allegiances so quickly it made Tamriel's head spin. He'd helped them escape in Xilor—had taken *arrows* for Tamriel, for the Creator's sake— and had warned them about Firesse's intentions to go to war, but that didn't exonerate him of buying the contract in the first place.

If he is alive, Tamriel thought as he snuffed the candles and left his father's study, *Creator have mercy on him, for he'll receive none from me.*

Half an hour later, Tamriel arrived outside the council chambers only to find the advisors already engaged in a heated debate. Even through the closed doors, their raised voices spilled out into the hall. Tamriel sucked in a tight breath and gestured for the guard his father had sent to summon him to open the door.

"You think it's right for her to be locked up without a shred of evidence?"

"There must be a reason—"

"—a reason which the king has, thus far, declined to tell us. Pierce said—"

The advisors were so caught up in their debate that, at first, they didn't notice Tamriel's entrance. Landers Nadra and Edwin Fioni were glaring at each other from opposite sides of the table, while the rest of the council members milled about, murmuring to one another. Ghyslain was seated at the center of the table, rubbing his forehead under the band of his diadem.

When the king's eyes at last slid to him, Ghyslain abruptly stood and announced, "The prince has arrived. Now we may begin."

Every pair of eyes in the room swung his way—some expectant, others annoyed. Tamriel forced his face to remain impassive under the weight of their gazes, fixing them with a flat, level stare. Before Calum and the Daughters attempted to kill him, he had never cared much about the nobles' opinions of him. Now, after so many brushes with death, he knew better than to trust in their loyalty. If Calum had had no qualms with having his own blood assassinated, what was to keep the nobles from doing the same?

"You waited for me?" he asked his father, unable to keep a note of surprise from his voice. The king had always been content to give him meaningless jobs around the castle, and he'd certainly never cared whether Tamriel attended council meetings.

"Would you like to share the news, or shall I?'

"...I will." He scanned the faces around him—nobles who had served his father since before he was born. Some of these men might have even helped plot Liselle's murder; Ghyslain had never managed to find everyone involved in her death. "You are all aware that someone tried to have me assassinated. Several weeks ago, three Assassins snuck into my chambers with the intent of murdering me and my guards. Without Mercy's help, they would have succeeded.

"The night of the attack, I fled Sandori with Master Oliver and several guards for my own protection," Tamriel explained, sticking to the story he and his father had concocted—that he had only left to escape the Daughters.

There was no reason to tell them about the possible cure until they knew more about Cedikra and its uses. "I have since learned that Calum was the man who paid to have me killed."

"Calum?" Landers repeated, bewildered. Tamriel could tell from the advisors' expressions that it wasn't the answer they'd expected—or wanted. "How?"

"He and Elise forged my father's signature on the contract. They planned to reveal it to the citizens after my death to frame my father so you would remove him from power, leaving the throne empty. He was then going to petition you for the crown."

Landers scoffed. "If this were true, why would he assume we would place a commoner on the throne?"

"We would certainly give the crown to one of the sons of the nobility over him," Porter Anders said, nodding.

Tamriel clenched his jaw to keep from gaping at them. "You take issue with his *reasoning?* He tried to have me killed!"

"Allegedly." Landers glanced sidelong at Ghyslain, eyes narrowing.

"You don't believe me."

"I'd like to, Your Highness, but have you any evidence?" He leaned in close and lowered his voice. "Forgive me, my prince, but considering Calum is not here to defend his innocence, this story seems like a scheme devised by your father to fool you into trusting him. Isn't the Guild's rule that only a royal can buy a contract on another royal?"

Tamriel fought to keep a rein on his temper. He knew the story sounded insane, but it was the *truth*, for the Creator's sake. He was their prince, after all; who were they to question him? "Shall I go into detail, then?" he asked, his words clipped. When several of the council members nodded, he continued, "Calum attacked me in my mother's house because he thought Mercy was taking too long. He framed her for the attack and, after she was arrested, wrote to the Guildmaster to have more Assassins sent here to kill me. After one of the Daughters snuck Mercy out of the dungeon, she managed to slip away and found my guards and me fighting the Assassins. She fought against her Sisters to save me. She *killed* one of her own to protect me."

The advisors exchanged uneasy looks. A few of them murmured to one another, their eyes flitting to Ghyslain between whispers. Tamriel could tell they weren't convinced.

"Elise does calligraphy," he supplied desperately. "She forged my father's signature. We can show you the contract. She agreed to help Calum because they wished to marry after Calum took the throne."

"Calum wanted revenge for his father's death," Ghyslain added. He stared down at his hands as he continued, "He wished to hurt me. It was a stupid thing to do, buying that contract on Drake, but I couldn't let what he did to Liselle go unpunished."

Landers crossed his arms over his round stomach and peered at Tamriel. "So…your only evidence is a piece of paper bearing the king's own signature, testimony from an *Assassin* of all people, and the fact that Elise does calligraphy? Does that really justify jailing a woman? Especially Elise LeClair, whose family has faithfully served yours for generations?"

Tamriel turned to his father with wide eyes, wordlessly imploring him to do *something*. How could he just stand there and allow the nobles to question him so brazenly?

His father didn't meet his gaze as he sighed, "Leave us."

Tamriel gawked at him, dumbfounded, as the council members bowed and shuffled out of the room. When the last one shut the doors behind him, Tamriel exploded, "*Why* did you let them speak like that? Why won't they believe me?"

Ghyslain sank into a chair, a look of abject hopelessness on his face. "Don't tell me you didn't see it in their eyes. They think I bought the contract on your life—just as I told you they would. It's the logical assumption, and you don't have enough evidence to prove them wrong. They think it's an elaborate lie I created to cover my own tracks, and probably that I bribed Mercy to corroborate the story." He rubbed his temples, at last meeting Tamriel's eyes. "The nobles despise us, Tam. We can only trust their loyalty as long as they have something to gain from keeping us on the throne. They're simply biding their time until we outlast our usefulness. The moment we do, they'll cast us aside and stick a pawn in our place."

Tamriel slumped into the nearest chair, his father's words turning his stomach. "How can we convince them of the truth?"

Ghyslain shook his head. "Unless you find explicit, undeniable proof of Elise's involvement in Calum's crime, there's no way to justify imprisoning her."

Tamriel was out of his seat before his father finished his sentence. "That's what I'll do, then. I'll find something —*anything*—to convince them of her guilt, like you said." He walked out of the room before the king could respond, trembling with anger as he shoved his way through the advisors waiting outside. As he passed Landers, the balding old Rivosan placed a hand on Tamriel's shoulder, stilling him.

"Your Highness, you know this isn't personal, don't you?" he asked. "It is simply our duty to uphold the laws of the land. Despite being king, your father is not above them."

Tamriel shook off Landers's hand and glared at him with such hatred that the advisor actually stumbled back a step. "Lay a hand on me again and I'll have it struck from your body," he growled, low enough for only Landers to hear, and stormed away.

5
MERCY

After two excruciating hours of trying—and failing—to decipher Alyss's haphazard notes, Mercy crumpled up the papers she'd been reading and tossed them onto the desk. Needing to move, needing to do *something*, she walked to the shelves and examined the rows of vials and bottles. The shelf to her right held a familiar sight: the tonics and ointments Alyss had made when she was well enough to work on the cure. She'd left the infirmary a mess—bottles broken on the floor, the contents spilling out across the stone—but a slave must have come in and cleaned it while Mercy and Tamriel were in the Islands. Mercy squinted at the tiny handwritten labels. She recognized some of the recipes from her work in the Guild's infirmary, but others were completely foreign to her.

"What about this?" Nynev asked. She was seated on the floor beside the fireplace, bent over a massive tome on medical treatments. She pointed to the center of the page and read, "Pink laurel, tulsi, aarajalda—whatever that is—and bitter wormwood?"

"That may work. Tulsi reduces swelling and bitter wormwood can be used to cleanse wounds." She stopped and plucked a half-empty vial from the shelf. "Alyss thought the same. Perhaps it would work with the addition of Cedikra, but we need to make sure we don't exhaust our supply on prototypes. Once we figure out the cure, we need enough to cure all the sick in the country."

Nynev cursed under her breath and closed the book, shoving it aside. "Then we have to hope that the healers know more than we do about the plague." She glanced at the infirmary door, clearly wishing she could be with her sister, who had left hours ago to meet with the healers Ghyslain had summoned.

"I'm not one to stake much on hope." Mercy turned her back to the shelves, shoving the infuriating mystery of the cure out of her mind, if only for a little while. "Let's take a walk. If we spend any more time in this dank little room, I'll go insane."

Nynev jumped up and grabbed her bow and quiver of arrows—with which she had not parted since leaving the Islands. She slung them over her shoulder and said, "I couldn't agree more."

As they made their way through the castle, Mercy kept an eye out for Tamriel. She had expected him to meet them in the infirmary after he awoke, but he had either finally allowed himself to sleep in or had gotten caught up in another matter. To her disappointment, they made it all the way through the castle and out the gate without catching so much as a glimpse of the prince.

Myrellis Castle sat atop a slight hill, and from the intersection right outside the grounds, Mercy and Nynev could see all the way down the gently sloping main street to the southern gate of the city. Outside the massive gray walls, more houses and shops spilled over the land, gradually growing farther and farther apart until they gave way to the plains of the countryside. Sterile white infirmary tents dotted the fields in little clusters. There were nearly a hundred tents, each manned by healers and Church priestesses, each containing scores of people suffering from the plague. Death carriages wove their way between the tents and collected the bodies of those who had succumbed to the plague. They'd take the dead to be burned in the massive pits on the opposite side of Lake Myrella, where a constant stream of black smoke rose and stained the fat white clouds hanging over the city.

As they started toward the city center, Nynev gaped at the massive mansions of the Sapphire Quarter. Mercy laughed at the awestruck expression on the huntress's face; no doubt *she* had looked exactly like that when she and Sorin had first ridden into the city. Nynev was so absorbed in the houses that she didn't seem to notice the wary glances the passing humans shot them or the curious looks from slaves who trailed their masters down the sidewalk.

They passed under the arch that divided the Sapphire Quarter from the rest of the town, and Myrellis Plaza spread out before them. It didn't escape Mercy's notice that the bustle of the square was greatly diminished from the last time she'd been here; several of the stores and artisans' workshops were boarded up and abandoned, the doors marked with bright red splashes of paint. Multiple homes they passed bore the same marks on their doors and shuttered windows, but it wasn't until Mercy and Nynev stumbled upon a large crowd gathered before a house that she realized what the markings meant.

A carriage bearing identical red slashes was stopped in the middle of the road, its doors standing wide open. Two masked and gloved men emerged from the house, dragging a rash-covered woman between them. She bucked and tried to escape their grasp, but they were too strong. She shrieked in terror and kicked at one of the men's legs as they dragged her down the steps and into the street. He let out a grunt of pain but didn't release her.

"By the gods," Nynev breathed, and Mercy followed her gaze to the baby-faced girl who had just stumbled out of the house, a threadbare stuffed rabbit clutched in her fist.

"Mama!" she wailed, tears streaming down her round cheeks. She belatedly noticed the crowd and froze at the top of the steps, her face contorting in terror. "M-Mama?"

At the sound of her daughter's voice, the woman let out a sob. Tremors wracked her body as the men lifted her into the carriage.

"Dahliana!" The girl's father burst out of the house and snatched her up, wrapping her protectively in his embrace. She buried her face in his chest when the carriage doors slammed shut, the bolt sliding into place.

One of the carriage workers climbed the steps and spoke to the girl's father in a low voice. The man nodded, then carried his daughter into the house, kicking the door shut behind him.

"Dahliana! Cedric!" the woman screamed, clawing at the small window in the carriage as she watched them retreat into the house.

The other carriage worker rifled through a chest attached to the back of the carriage and pulled out a thick paintbrush and a bucket. He painted one long red slash across the house's front door, climbed onto the bench beside the driver, and gestured for the crowd to part. They obeyed immediately, and the carriage lurched into motion. The clacking of the horses' hooves against the cobblestones was almost completely lost under the sounds of the woman's sobs. Whispers erupted around Mercy and Nynev as the onlookers began to wander away.

"—healers can't do anything—"

"—taking her to be treated—"

"She better not have infected anyone else—"

"Why did they not take all three of them?" Nynev whispered. "Is it not unsafe for them to remain in the city?"

"If they've been living with that woman and haven't been infected yet, they're probably immune. They'll still be quarantined for a few days just in case."

Nynev shook her head and followed Mercy through the throngs of people. "I'm glad Niamh hasn't had time to explore the city and see the damage the plague has already done to your prince's people. She puts too much pressure on herself as it is." Although her expression didn't change, darkness flickered in and out of her eyes as they walked; she clearly didn't miss the way the humans recoiled from them, as if *they* were the ones infected by the plague. She frowned and touched the vine tattoos coiled across her face. "Do you have any money?"

"Some. Why?"

"I'd like to get some makeup—something thick enough to cover tattoos."

"I thought you don't care how people look at you."

"I don't. It's for Niamh. She has spent enough time feeling like an outsider, isolating herself because of who—*what*—she is." At Mercy's questioning look, she elaborated: "After Firesse worked her magic on my sister two years ago, Niamh refused to leave her cave for weeks. She wouldn't eat or sleep or even speak. I think she was hoping that one day she'd simply fade away.

"When starvation didn't work, she jumped off Hadriana's Bluff while Isolde was out hunting. The poor girl returned to find Niamh in a heap of broken bones, but my sister hadn't died. She couldn't—can't. That night, Isolde snuck into Firesse's camp and begged me to talk some sense into her." Pain flashed across Nynev's face. She looked down at her hands, realized they'd begun to shake, and shoved them into her pockets. "I'll never forget the sight of her lying in that cave, disfigured almost beyond recognition."

"How did you make her change her mind?" Mercy asked softly, shocked at how much the huntress was revealing.

Nynev sucked in a sharp breath. "I screamed at her. I called her every terrible name I could think of. I told her she was being selfish, that we hadn't risked everything to escape to the Islands so she could give up. I told her our parents were cursing her from the Beyond for being so weak." She flinched and looked away, biting her lip. "I was awful to her. I hated her for being so cocky when she fought, for letting herself be injured that gods-forsaken night, for believing she didn't deserve the life Firesse had given her. For days, I begged her to return to camp. Isolde and I tried to convince her to move to another clan with us—somewhere they wouldn't question her miraculous recovery. She refused every time."

"Why?"

She lifted a slender shoulder in a shrug. "Firesse's magic had done something to her...changed her in a way I can't completely fathom. She's not entirely my sister anymore—not really. Her soul is trapped between worlds, and she can feel it. She knows she doesn't belong here, but she has stopped trying to force herself to pass into the Beyond. I have no idea how long Firesse's magic will last—if I'll wake up one morning to find a corpse in her place or if she'll still be here long after you and I have turned to dust—and not a day goes by that I don't think about the curse Firesse placed upon her. *I* subjected Niamh to it—*I* asked Firesse to help. I should be the one who pays the price." She scowled, turning her attention to the shops and workshops. "So I try to make her life as bearable as possible. I do my best to ease her suffering because I know she knows who is responsible for the hell she endures every day. Anyone else would hate me for it. Niamh doesn't."

"I can't imagine Niamh hating anyone," Mercy admitted. She remembered the tale Niamh had told them in the Islands, how she had received her monstrous wound in a fight against human soldiers. That woman was worlds away from the one they'd found in the cave. "Honestly, I can't even imagine her being one of Myris's fighters."

"Firesse saw the darkness that bloomed in Niamh's soul after our mother died. She did then exactly what she did to Calum and Drake—she nurtured it, fed it, encouraged it. She knows how to manipulate people into following her."

"A woman with a sharp tongue is often more dangerous than a woman with a sharp sword," Mercy said, paraphrasing Mistress Sorin's words from her first day in the city. She had thought Sorin was trying to be clever, but now, after being deceived by Calum, Elise, and Firesse, she knew how true the statement was.

Nynev nodded. "Exactly."

They walked in silence for a while, pretending they didn't see the houses and stores with boarded-up windows and red slashes painted on the doors. When they found a shop selling jewelry and makeup, they stopped inside and purchased a tin of face paint and a compact of powder for Niamh.

As they started back toward the castle, Mercy caught Nynev studying her more than once. After the tenth time in just as many minutes, she asked, "What?"

"Something's on your mind. You didn't just want to take a walk to get some fresh air," she said, wrinkling her nose as another plague-marked carriage rolled past. "Not that one could call this air 'fresh.' Is the plague what's troubling you? Or something else?"

"It's the Guild. By now, Mother Illynor must know that Lylia is dead, which means she will search for me even more fiercely than before. Illynor won't take the loss lightly. I can defend Tamriel and myself from any Assassin she sends, but if Firesse succeeds in convincing the Daughters to fight alongside the elves, it could turn the tide of the war."

Nynev raised a brow. "You think a few dozen Assassins are that gifted at fighting?"

"We've been trained all our lives to become instruments of death. We may not be soldiers in the traditional sense, but we've spent our lives learning how to kill." Mercy grimaced. If her Sisters joined in the attack, what fate lay in store for her and Tamriel? Betraying the Guild was an insult of the highest degree, made worse now that they'd killed two Daughters. Would they kill her outright, and her prince immediately after? Or would they drag her back to the Keep as a lesson for other assassins about the cost of deserting?

Seeing the fear in Mercy's eyes, Nynev paled. "If the Daughters are truly as dangerous as you claim them to be, may the gods have mercy on our souls."

6

TAMRIEL

The front door of Seren Pierce's house was ajar when Tamriel arrived. Through the gap, he watched Pierce pace the length of the foyer, his fists clenching and unclenching as he muttered angrily under his breath. The sounds of furniture scraping the floor drifted from every room—the guards searching for evidence of Elise's crime. When the seren's back was turned, Tamriel slipped inside and leaned against the doorframe, crossing his arms loosely.

He cocked his head, knowing he should hold his tongue, but too angry to care. "Be careful, Seren. Too much pacing and you'll wear out that fine rug."

Pierce whirled around. "Your Highness," he said, his voice pinched as he tried to rein in his temper. "What a pleasure it is to have you in my humble home."

"Humble?" Tamriel cast a glance at the gold-framed paintings on the walls, the colorful silks and chiffons draped over each archway, the ostentatious navy and gold rug running the length of the hall. "No, I daresay your decorations rival that of the castle. I had no idea you had such an eye for interior design." He bit back a satisfied smirk when Pierce's face flushed purple.

"My wife's influence." The seren straightened and took a deep, calming breath. "Your guards won't find anything on my daughter, Your Highness. She's a good child who has always served your father well."

"As long as you and I agree that the people who tried to kill me must face justice, we won't have a problem."

Tamriel wandered through the house, Pierce trailing a few steps behind him. As they moved from room to room, the guards reported their findings—*nothing*. Every minute, Tamriel's impatience mounted. What if his father was right? What if Elise and Calum had been clever enough to hide every trace of their treachery?

He was so caught up in his thoughts that he didn't realize Pierce had been speaking until the seren paused, waiting for a response. "Pardon me?"

Pierce leaned against the kitchen counter, clasping his hands in front of him. "I was wondering at the wisdom of staking my daughter's freedom on the testimony of an Assassin. You care for her deeply, don't you? I understand that you're young, Your Highness, but affairs of the heart do not last. You should be married to a woman of the court by now —or, better yet, a Feyndaran princess. Not an Assassin masquerading as one."

Across the room, two guards paused in their search of the cupboards and glared at Pierce, warnings in their eyes.

"You don't know what you're talking about," Tamriel responded icily.

"Don't I? Perhaps, my prince, I wish to not see your heart broken the same way your father's was. He was my friend once, you know. I watched him fall for Liselle. That little harlot had your father wrapped around her finger. She nearly destroyed our country, and your darling *Assassin*"—he spat the word like a curse—"will no doubt do the same."

At the seren's patronizing tone, the leash on Tamriel's temper finally snapped. To hell with not making enemies. He seized Pierce by the lapel and pinned him against the counter, the seren's fine shirt bunched in his fists.

"Your Highness—"

"Not. Another. Word," Tamriel hissed.

The guards rushed forward. "Your Highness, would you—"

"You're dismissed."

"Your—"

"*Dismissed*," he snapped. He looked away from Pierce's pale face long enough to glare at the guards. "Ignore my order again and you'll find yourselves out of a job. Search upstairs."

The guards tripped over themselves in their haste to leave.

He returned his attention to the seren. "Listen to me carefully, Pierce. Your slander against Mercy ends now. Your opinions of her character are worth less than dirt to me, do you understand? From here on out, you do not speak to her, you do not speak *of* her, you do not so much as *think* about her. If any harm befalls her, my guards will kick down your door and throw you into the dungeon beside your treasonous daughter. Have I made myself clear?"

Pierce's eyes, which had been steadily growing wider as Tamriel spoke, hardened at the mention of Elise. "I think you should be very careful who you threaten, princeling." He sniffed, somehow still managing to appear haughty despite the fists at his throat. "I'm part of the nobility and the council. Their hearts are with me and my family. If your father wrongfully imprisons her—if he kills her—they'll be clamoring to remove your family from power. The king seems to know that well, my prince. It's time you learned that, too."

Tamriel leaned forward until their faces were mere inches apart. "You are speaking out of turn. Two days from now, your daughter will have her trial. Justice will be done, regardless of the consequences."

"Pierce? Are you down here?" someone called from down the hall. Tamriel released the seren's shirt just as Pierce's wife, Nerida, swept into the room with a whisper of silk. Their family slave trailed her, attempting to pin little flowers in Nerida's long blonde braid as she moved. "Ah, there you are. Your Highness! What a surprise."

"Hello, Serenna." When she bowed, he offered her a polite nod. He smiled at the slave, but she merely bowed and positioned herself behind her mistress, out of the prince's line of sight.

"I beg your forgiveness for my appearance, Your Highness," Nerida continued, either oblivious of or purposely ignoring the tension in the room. She clutched the belt of her black silk robe. "The guards moving everything about has made it quite difficult to dress."

"You look lovely, my lady. For what it's worth, I am sorry for the interruption, but we must be thorough in our investigation," he responded, finding it easier to control his anger in her calming presence. He had always liked Nerida. She was from a prominent upper-class family in the countryside and was, like most people from the farming sector, exceedingly honest, diplomatic, and kind. Seeing her and Pierce together, seeing the affection between them, it wasn't hard to understand why Pierce was such a champion of arranged marriages.

She waved his apology away. "Please. All we want is for the truth to come out." She shot her husband a look as she added, "*Whatever* the outcome."

Upstairs, there was a loud thump and a hissed curse. Nerida jumped and looked up at the ceiling, biting her lower lip. "They'd better not be ruining my Elise's art gallery. Her paintings are more valuable to me than anything else I own."

Tamriel froze, an idea striking him. "I— Ah— Excuse me, won't you?" he stammered as he darted out of the room. He ran down the hall—nearly bowling over a guard who had chosen that exact moment to step out of the dining room— and flew up the stairs.

Three guards were searching through the piles of supplies in Elise's art gallery. All of them snapped to attention when Tamriel burst through the sheer curtain hanging over the archway.

"What have you found?"

"Nothing yet, Your Highness. We'll keep looking." The guard's voice wobbled a bit, and it took Tamriel a moment to recognize him: Raiden, the man whose nose he had broken for insulting Mercy. His nose had healed, but crookedly.

"I might know where to find a clue." Tamriel stepped into the room and—

There it is.

The painting of Calum kneeling beside a merchant hung in the center of the wall, its frame shining under the sunlight streaming through the window. In it, Calum was only eight or nine, offering a handful of coins to the merchant so he could repair his broken wagon wheel. Elise had painted it a couple years ago. Tamriel remembered Calum bragging to him about her talent after she had finished and, sheepishly, shown the painting to him. *Maybe one day she'll paint the portrait of you as our king,* Calum had suggested.

Tamriel stepped back, and his suspicion was confirmed when he realized that the painting was slightly crooked, one side dipping almost imperceptibly to the right. "Take down that painting."

One of the guards jumped up and took hold of the frame. When he pulled it down and flipped the painting over,

Tamriel's heart skipped a beat. A sheaf of folded papers was adhered to the back. Tamriel gently peeled them off, then began reading the first page, dated several months into Calum's year-long excursion with the Strykers.

My love,

These last few months away from you have been bleak, but I cannot deny being pleased with what I have learned in the Strykers' company. We work from sunup to sundown over scorching forges, and Nerran sometimes likes to sing along with the beats of our hammers. I must say, I envy you, for you are not forced to listen to his attempts to deafen the rest of us with what can only be likened to the braying of a sick donkey.

Despite the constant traveling, the work we've been doing is rewarding. Hewlin has taught me how to make scimitars and spears and swords and daggers, how to fold and sculpt metal into something of beauty, as well as functionality. It more than makes up for the nights of sleeping in old tents and lice-infested taverns, wishing I could do more than reread the few letters you have dared send me. I know your father doesn't approve of our 'dalliance,' as he calls it, but you must write me more often, my love. Perhaps Liri could smuggle your letters to the courier?

Soon, we shall move south, to the farming district. It seems some wealthy landowners need new tools, and Hewlin is more than happy to oblige. Some of the men think it's a waste to use Stryker talents on farming implements, but it pays for our travels and food, so they cannot complain too much.

As we head south, I cannot help but consider what we discussed before I left. I wish justice could be served without such dire consequences. I wish Tamriel did not have to be dragged into the middle of this. If we go through with this, I will never forgive myself. But if I do nothing, the man responsible for my father's murder will continue to go unpunished.

Write back soon, my love. As I sign off to endure another night of troubled dreams, I leave you with this:

So much of my life is uncertain. I don't know the woman who gave me life. I don't know my place in the castle. I don't know what will become of us when I return. But I am certain of two things, and they shall never change: I love you, and I shall continue to love you as long as my lungs draw air.

Yours,

Calum

Tamriel sank onto the settee in the center of the room, forcing himself to scan the next several letters. They were all similar to the first—mostly flowery language, declarations of love that Calum would have killed Tamriel for reading, updates on his travels. Almost every one of them alluded to the contract on Tamriel's life. Calum had been smart not to mention it explicitly, but it was obvious that they'd been planning his death for the better part of a year. Tamriel flipped to the last letter.

—will be arriving in Ellesmere within the fortnight. Send the papers and coin to a tavern called Pearl's End. *The owner, Myreese, works with "I." I'll retrieve them and deliver them to her on behalf of the king when we arrive for the Trial.*

My heart is heavy as I write this, but I know it must be done. For my father, for myself, for you... I have no other choice.

Creator forgive me.

—Calum

"By the Creator," Tamriel breathed, numb with shock. He looked up at the guards as he tucked the letters into his pocket. "I need to speak to my father immediately."

Please, Creator, give us a victory, he prayed as Raiden trailed him out of the room and down the hall. *Let this evidence be enough.*

7

TAMRIEL

A few minutes after they arrived at the castle and Raiden left to find Ghyslain, the main doors swung open behind him. Tamriel turned, expecting to see a guard on rounds or slaves running from chore to chore, but instead found Cassius Bacha striding up to him.

"Your Highness," the lord said in a puff of breath. He stopped before Tamriel and bowed, his bald head shining under the light of the chandeliers. "My sincerest apologies for not responding to your father's summons sooner. Murray has taken ill."

Tamriel stiffened, fearing the worst. "She hasn't caught the plague, has she?"

"Thank the Creator, no. Just a fever, but she's been bedridden and it's making her crankier than usual, if such a thing is possible. May we speak in private?" He gestured for Tamriel to follow him into the throne room and closed the double doors behind them. "I must admit, I had not expected to see you alive again, my prince. I am grateful my vision did not come to pass."

"Not as grateful as I, I assure you. That's actually why we

wished to speak with you. I had thought that whatever happens in your visions is certain."

"In my experience, until now, it had been."

"Calum took two arrows to the chest in Xilor—the ones that would have killed me. That means your visions are not certain. *That* means we might never figure out the cure."

Cassius blinked and frowned, wringing his hands. "That is worrying, indeed, Your Highness, but if you think I can explain the Sight to you, I'm sorry to tell you I cannot. I can share with you what little I know, which is what I saw in my dreams. First, about the cure: I drew that strange plant and wrote down that word I saw. Niamh. Did you figure it out?"

"Yes."

"And I was right about the plague infecting Beggars' End first, remember?"

"I remember, but that doesn't help me understand why your vision of my death didn't come to pass," he said impatiently.

"As I said, Your Highness, I don't have the answers. The Sight is weak in my family."

"Have you Seen anything else recently? Any other visions?"

Cassius shook his head again. "Nothing, Your Highness. My Seer blood is so diluted I rarely have multiple visions in one year. Perhaps this year is different because of Solari."

Tamriel snorted. "Years on which a Solari falls are said to be blessed, yet less than two months after the sacred holiday we've had to face an outbreak of plague, an impending Cirisian invasion, and betrayals from every side. If this year is blessed, I'm terrified to see what next year will bring."

"Priestesses of the Church believe the Sight is a gift given to humanity by the Creator. As Solari is a celebration of him, it would make sense that I would receive more visions than usual. Perhaps he has a plan for you." He smiled, dropping a wrinkled hand on Tamriel's shoulder. "All will turn out the way he intends it. Have faith in that, Your Highness."

"How can you say he has a plan when the Church teaches that he is all but lost to us? All he does is sit in his prison and watch us bumble around trying to make sense of everything." Tamriel looked out the window at the back of the room, scowling at the sun shining over the lake. The Church claimed that the Creator imprisoned himself for slaughtering the Old Gods—his brethren. Even *he* had fallen prey to a desire for vengeance. He was no better than Calum. "Does he have a plan for the hundreds of people who have already died from the plague? Is there some divine reason why my people must watch their children waste away to nothing? Why should I worship a god who allows his Creations to endure something so terrible?"

"I wish I had the answers, Your Highness, but we call it faith for a reason. Terrible things have befallen you and your people before, but we always pick ourselves up and keep toiling. We rebuild. We heal."

Unconvinced, Tamriel reached into his pocket and pulled out Elise's letters. "Have you heard the news yet? Calum and Elise tried to have me killed."

"I've heard whisperings. May I?" He took the letters and, after perching his spectacles on the tip of his nose, scanned them, his brows furrowed. His frown deepened as he read. When he finished, he made a sound of disgust and thrust the papers back at Tamriel. "Despicable. Foolish boy. Drake paid his price for murdering Liselle, and Ghyslain pays his penance for sinking to that bastard's level every day he is forced to live without his loves."

"Bacha."

The king's voice preceded him into the room. Cassius pocketed his spectacles and swept into a deep bow. "Your Majesty."

"How are you and Murray?"

"I am fine. Murray is sick but recuperating well."

"I am glad to hear it. What news, Tam?"

Tamriel held out the letters. Surprise and understanding crossed Ghyslain's face when he saw Calum's swirling signature. "You might want to sit down when you read these."

Fifteen minutes later, Ghyslain sat back in the desk chair in his study, his expression unreadable. He shook his head and tossed the letters onto the desk.

"Well?" Tamriel asked, watching his father's reflection in the windowpane. He had been staring out at the waves of Lake Myrella—and the dark smoke from the plague victims' burning bodies beyond—but he now turned his attention to the king. "Is it enough? Will the nobles believe that she's guilty?"

"It's enough." Ghyslain's black hair stuck out around his temples; he had been running his fingers through it while reading. "By the Creator, Tam, you've done it."

"Even so," Cassius piped up from one of the two high-backed chairs before the desk, "this must be approached with diplomacy. The council is angry. They already assume that this is a cover-up for His Majesty." He picked up the papers and squinted at them. "Here, Calum explicitly says '*I'll retrieve them and deliver them to her*'—she being Illynor, of course—'*on behalf of the king when we arrive for the Trial.*' He lied to the Guildmaster about the contract's origins, but it won't look that way to the rest of the council. That, coupled with your cousin's absence, will make them suspicious that His Majesty somehow planned Calum's accident in Xilor so there wouldn't be a witness to his crime."

Tamriel looked to his father. "You admitted yesterday that

you don't need their permission to jail someone. Why must we do so much planning?"

"If I sentence her to death out of what they believe is mere self-preservation, we've just given them a martyr. She'll become to them what Liselle was to the elves."

He threw up his hands in frustration. "Then what do you suggest we do?"

"Speak to the council members in private," Cassius suggested after a moment of thought. He turned to the king. "Tell them exactly what you told me about the plague, the Islands, and Firesse. Leave out the magic but tell them the Cirisians intend to attack. They won't dare to throw the capital into political turmoil while a larger threat is on their doorstep. Turn their selfishness against them. Use it to manipulate them into doing what *you* want."

"If we approach it just right, it should work," Ghyslain affirmed. He glanced at Tamriel. "Why don't you go visit Niamh and check on her progress with the cure? Cassius and I will discuss the specifics of the trial, and I'll fill you in on the plan tomorrow after Oliver's funeral." Tamriel flinched at the sharp twinge of sorrow that hit him at the words, and Ghyslain's expression softened. "Are you ready to see him?"

"It doesn't matter if I'm ready. Master Oliver gave his life for me—I won't disrespect that sacrifice by missing his funeral."

HE WAS HALFWAY DOWN THE DANK UNDERGROUND hallway, on his way to the infirmary to meet Nynev and Mercy, when he heard their voices echoing off the stone walls behind him. They must be coming back from lunch or errands. He paused in the middle of the corridor and waited for them to catch up.

"We did it," he announced when they rounded the corner.

Mercy stopped mid-step. "You mean Elise...?"

"Will be found guilty at her trial. I found letters from Calum talking about my father, the contract—everything."

"Oh, Tamriel." Mercy beamed at him. She closed the distance between them, threw her arms around his neck, and kissed him. "You did it," she murmured. "You really did it."

"Yes," he whispered, breathing in the scents of herbs clinging to her skin. He could *feel* Nynev rolling her eyes at them, but he couldn't bring himself to care. For the first time in what felt like ages, something was finally going right.

"All right, cut it out, you two," the huntress said, tugging at Mercy's sleeve.

She stepped out of his embrace, looking sheepish, but Tamriel merely raised a brow and drawled, "Jealous, Nynev? Should I find you a dashing young courtier of your own?"

She rolled her eyes again and brushed past them, muttering something about finding Niamh. The second she disappeared around the corner, Mercy grabbed Tamriel's hand and grinned at him. A swell of adoration overtook him as he studied her, her wild curls like a mane around her face, her brown eyes glowing gold in the torchlight. She was fierce, strong, fearless—everything Tamriel had wished he were when he was a child, cowering under his covers as his father's grief-stricken moans filled the halls.

Mercy squeezed his hand. "You're staring at me."

He pulled her close, his free hand sliding to her lower back. He smiled at her and guided her backward until she was pressed against the cold stone wall, then dipped his head forward until his lips brushed the point of her ear. "How can I help it when you're so infuriatingly beautiful?" he whispered. An all-too-encouraging moan escaped her when he pressed a line of kisses along her jaw and down her neck.

"A guard could walk around that corner any second," she

said softly, her breath hitching when he slipped a hand under the hem of her tunic. "Tamriel!"

"Let one come—I don't care."

She sighed and, at first, he wasn't sure whether it was out of pleasure or exasperation. She didn't stop him when his fingers grazed the bare skin of her stomach, or when he pushed aside the collar of her shirt and kissed her pale, scarred collarbone. She shivered and arched her back, leaning into him. Her fingers snaked through his hair, driving him out of his mind with desire. "Oh, come here already," she moaned, and pulled his lips to hers.

8
CALUM

The day the Strykers were expected to arrive, Drake left Kaius and Myris to train the soon-to-be-soldiers and crossed the camp alone, eyeing the elves who scurried out of his path. They didn't know about Firesse's Old God powers, but it was obvious his presence disturbed them. A small boy grabbed his younger sister and tugged her back into the tent they had just exited. A woman with ice-blonde braids studied him warily as she cleaned the blade of her sword with a scrap of fabric.

She's pretty—for a knife-ear, Drake whispered to him.

Don't you dare.

Drake smirked as he passed through the tree line and started down the trail to the next island. "You think you're so much better than me, don't you? Such manners. Such *respect* for the knife-ears."

Keep your—my—voice down. What if one of them hears you?

Drake spread his arms wide, gesturing at the thick vegetation around them. "Do you still fear that Cirisian savages are hiding in the trees, waiting to swoop down upon us? Don't act like a child. Even if one hears me talking to myself, what do you think he'll do? Run to Firesse and tell her you've lost your mind?"

Calum didn't deign to respond.

When he reached the shore, his father crossed the water in one of the Cirisians' canoes and started across the westernmost island of the archipelago. He trudged through the underbrush until the vegetation gave way to sparkling white sands and the blue-green waves of the Abraxas Sea beyond.

Drake leaned against one of the thick-trunked palm trees at the edge of the beach, shading his eyes from the blinding reflection of the sun on the water. "Now," he sighed, "we wait and see if your Stryker friends took the bait."

AFTER TWO UNEVENTFUL HOURS PASSED WITH NO SIGN OF the Strykers, Drake threw up his hands in agitation and kicked at a clump of dirt by his feet. As his father's impatience mounted, so too did Calum's anxiety. What if the Strykers didn't show up? What if they never received the letters? Perhaps if they arrived—if they saw him acting strangely—they'd realize something was wrong. They might find a way to free him. He struggled against the ice-water in his veins, the bonds of his mental prison.

"Stop that," Drake snapped.

Am I hurting you? Calum asked, satisfaction flooding him at the thought.

"No, but it's quite annoying—like an insect buzzing in my ear."

He continued fighting for power, for control, but paused when a new approach occurred to him. *What if you just left? No one else is around. No one else would know for hours.* The bridge where he, Tamriel, and the others had crossed from Beltharos was on the western shore of this island—just a few miles northwest of where they were now. Perhaps if he could get Drake alone, away from Firesse and her unnatural powers, he could find a way to fight this possession. Perhaps Drake's strength would weaken the farther he wandered from the girl who had summoned him from the Beyond. *You could run, strike out on your own—*

"And I'd get a few hours' head start before Firesse realizes we're gone and pulls me back. She brought me to this realm, she can call me back to her side whenever she wants. I'm as trapped as you are, boy." He snorted. "Enslaved to a knife-ear, of all things. What cruel irony."

There must be some way you can free us from her.

"Us? You think I'm going to release you after I get my revenge? No, not yet. There's a whole world out there that I've missed out on. I'm not going back to the realm of the dead for a long, long while."

You— Calum began, but he stopped when Drake noticed a blot of darkness on the horizon. In the distance, the small ship bobbed on the waves as it drew nearer, white sails spread wide. When it was close enough for Calum to make out the individual men aboard, he spotted Nerran standing at the helm, waving his arms wildly. As the men steered toward the shore, Calum felt the strange prickling sensation that accompanied his father searching his memories, learning about the year the Strykers had spent traveling together.

Nerran jumped from the ship the second it hit the shore. He splashed through the shallows and met Drake on the beach, immediately embracing him. "It's good to see you, mate," he said, laughing as he slapped Drake's back.

"You, too," Drake responded, forcing warmth into Calum's voice. "I see you received my letters."

"We did. Six of them, if I'm not mistaken." He stepped back and raised a brow. "You are going to explain what's going on, aren't you? Like...what the hell you're doing in the Cirisor Islands?"

"I'll tell you everything on the walk to camp."

"You'd better. Hewlin wasn't happy about leaving, but we insisted we help a friend. Your letters sounded like you really need it. We're supposed to be on our way to Rhys right now."

"He won't mind when he sees how much Firesse is willing to pay for your work. Believe me, it's worth the trouble."

"It had damn well better be worth it," Hewlin grumbled as he made his way onto the shore. Behind him, Oren and Amir worked on lowering the ship's anchor.

"Who are you working for in Rhys? The queen?"

"Something like that."

Drake nudged Nerran with an elbow. "If you see the princesses, put in a good word for me, won't you?"

"Don't you have a girl back home? You know, the one you were always writing to and fawning over?"

He shot Nerran a sly grin. "She wouldn't need to know."

"You, my friend, are incorrigible."

"Don't pretend you're any different."

"Oh, I won't. You all know me too well."

"You're looking better, Oren," Drake said as the other two Strykers joined them. Calum was relieved to see that the sickly, lanky man actually *did* look healthier; his once sallow skin was now flushed, and he had even put a little meat on his bones since their time at the Keep.

"Thanks."

"It's been a while," Amir said, grinning. "After you ditched us, I thought we'd never see you again."

"I couldn't do that to you. You'd have missed me too much." Drake glanced up at the mid-afternoon sky and the clouds rolling in from the west. "We'd better head back. It'll take a while to cross to the next island. Leave the ship here—it'll be too hard to maneuver through the channel."

Hewlin nodded, still frowning. "As you say. Just give us a minute to gather our supplies."

PLEASE NOTICE THAT I'M DIFFERENT. REALIZE SOMETHING IS wrong. I'm not the same, can't you see? The man before you isn't me—can't you tell? Calum pleaded silently as the Strykers followed Drake down the trail to Firesse's camp. *Don't you know me?*

Earlier, as they'd crossed the channel between islands, Drake had explained as much as he'd dared. He'd left out Firesse's magic, of course, but he'd told the truth about Calum's upbringing in the castle and his need to avenge his father's murder.

"So...you're royalty, then," Nerran had said as they'd rowed the canoe across the waves, his surprise at learning Calum's true surname still etched on his face.

"Not royalty. Related by marriage, not blood."

"But...you're rich. Your family was rich, wasn't it? And you never told us?" The hurt in Nerran's voice had cut straight to Calum's core. He and the Strykers had traveled together for a year, sharing meals and tents and jokes. They'd become family—and Calum had lied to them since the day they'd met.

Now, Calum only hoped that they would realize something was wrong with him before they became ensnared in Firesse's misguided war...but Drake was too great an actor. He teased Nerran, Amir, and Oren, even earning a few chuckles from Hewlin in the process. He searched through Calum's memories as easily as flipping through a picture book and regaled the men with humorous stories from Calum's childhood in the castle. In sharing details of the life they'd never known he had, Calum could see their trust in him—in Drake's charade—grow.

Look at me, he silently implored them as Drake began to

explain the history of Firesse's clan and the events leading up to her declaration of war. *Look at me and see that something's not right. Get out—save yourselves before you too become puppets in Firesse's game.*

But no one even blinked twice at him.

"Here we are," Drake announced when they finally reached camp. The forest parted, revealing the massive clearing that housed the troops—hundreds upon hundreds of elves chattering to one another, preparing dinner, working fighting drills, finishing their chores. On the other side of camp, Kaius and Myris continued training the soldiers. As he watched their blades whistle through the air, Calum noted with foreboding how skilled the elves had become in such a short time. Many had pledged themselves to Firesse without ever having held a sword; they'd joined simply because they'd learned of Odomyr's murder at a human's hand during the sacred celebration. It had been the straw that broke the camel's back—and it was the reason most of them were awake before dawn and still training long after the sun had sunk below the horizon each day.

Hewlin stopped dead in his tracks. "You— These elves— I thought— There are so many," he stammered, his face turning as pale as his graying beard.

"Don't worry," Drake drawled as he led them farther into camp. "Contrary to the elves in your nursemaid's stories, these don't bite."

Firesse met them outside her tent, grinning from ear-to-ear. "I see our guests have arrived." She offered them a graceful little bow, the beads in her hair clinking softly, as the Strykers gawked at the slender, delicately-boned girl before them. Since *Ialathan*, she had abandoned her usual Cirisian garb in favor of light leather armor. Razor-sharp hunting knives were strapped to her hips, thighs, and forearms. The leather-wrapped hilt of one stuck out of the leg of one of her boots. "I'm Firesse, First of my clan and leader of this army."

"First?" Oren echoed. His shoulders curved inward when Firesse straightened and fixed her steady gaze on him.

"Head of my clan. These are my soldiers, and you're going to outfit them with all the weapons and armor we need to invade Beltharos. Follow me." She turned on her heel and led them toward the sparring elves, leaving no opportunity for further questioning. "As you can see, we already have some supplies from the Beltharan and Feyndaran forces, but they're few and far-between, and they're not Stryker-made. I need every advantage I can get if we're to win the war. Spears, swords, daggers, maces, arrows—whatever you can make, we'll use. You'll be paid handsomely for your services."

Nerran raised a brow, casting a wary glance at the tattered tents and pieced-together suits of ill-fitting armor. "With what money?"

Drake cleared his throat. "Ghyslain seized most of my father's assets after his death, but a few accounts remain in Sandori and Feyndara. You'll get your money."

"The Beltharans have better numbers, weapons, training, and experience," Hewlin argued. "They'll decimate you in the first battle, I guarantee you. It's hard to collect money from a dead man."

"You don't know what tricks I have up my sleeve," Firesse responded, a mischievous gleam in her eyes.

He exchanged looks with the rest of the Strykers, silently debating the wisdom of allying with the fabled Cirisian savages, then turned his gaze to Drake—studying him, assessing him. Could he tell something was wrong? Could he sense the bloodlust lurking just beneath Firesse's teasing tone? Finally, he nodded, and Calum's hope withered. "Fine. We'll help you, but we can only do basic repairs here. You want us crafting anything new, we'll need a workshop and a forge."

"We'll see what we can do. For now, please rest and eat while I speak to Calum and my generals. I'm sure you must be tired from the journey. Vyla will help you get settled." She called to a young woman in Cirisian, and the elf nodded, gesturing for the Strykers to follow.

Catching sight of Firesse, Kaius shouted for the sparring elves to take a break. He and Myris met them inside Firesse's tent moments later. "The Strykers have agreed to help?"

"Yes, but they need a forge to craft new weapons." She turned to Drake. "Do you remember if there is a blacksmith's shop in Fishers' Cross?"

Before he had a chance to search Calum's memory, Kaius said, "There was a ship repair shop with a forge. It's not ideal, but I'm sure they can make do with many of the supplies until we move farther inland."

Drake nodded. "Good enough for now."

"Are the soldiers ready for an attack?"

"With the help of the archers and Myris's fighters, they'll manage. We've been training hard."

"Good. We've already waited as long as I am willing. The Strykers will have tonight and tomorrow to repair weapons and armor. I want our people in Fishers' Cross by midnight. Kaius, you'll be with the archers atop the bluff, and Myris, I want you on the street below. Keep an eye on the recruits." She grinned. "Tomorrow night, the slaughter begins."

9
TAMRIEL

The day of Master Oliver's funeral was depressingly beautiful. Rays of golden sunlight streamed through the slats of the tall, narrow windows in the Church's vaulted ceiling, illuminating the dust motes in the air and the dark clothes of the mourners seated below. The double doors at the front of the room stood wide open, allowing a floral-scented breeze to sweep through. Tamriel ignored the bead of sweat rolling down the back of his neck as he stared at the two caskets sitting atop the dais.

In one, a guard, Clyde, was laid out in finery far above his station—gifts from Tamriel's own closet—with a gleaming gold medal pinned to his chest. Across the aisle from Tamriel, Clyde's mother sobbed into a handkerchief, one arm wrapped around the slumped shoulders of a girl he assumed was Clyde's younger sister. In the other casket, Master Oliver was clad in full military regalia, his medals strategically pinned to hide the deformity the Daughters' arrows had made of his chest. Plaques dedicated to the guards whose bodies they'd been forced to leave behind—Parson, Conrad, Florian, Silas, Maceo—sat beside the bowl-shaped altar. Piercing sorrow engulfed Tamriel. These men had given their lives for him. He'd do everything in his power to ensure their sacrifices would not go to waste.

The High Priestess climbed the steps of the dais and began reciting passages from the Book of the Creator. As she prayed, she dropped bunches of dried herbs into the altar. "Innis leaf to cleanse you of your sins," she said, her rich voice spilling over the mourners and echoing off the high ceiling. "Ender root to ease your loved ones' mourning. Osha's Grace to guide you safely to the Beyond."

The High Priestess waved a young initiate forward and took the vial of golden oil from her hands. She moved to Master Oliver's casket, dipped her fingers into the oil, and traced the Creator's holy eye symbol onto his pale forehead. She did the same to Clyde, then poured the remainder into the bowl. The initiate stepped forward again and dropped a lit match onto the altar. The herbs inside burst into flame.

"Go now to the Creator's side," the High Priestess murmured.

"And there find peace eternal," Tamriel and the others responded, finishing the prayer. He squeezed his eyes shut as someone in the back of the room began sobbing in great, keening wails. He felt his father stiffen beside him.

Someone touched Tamriel's shoulder, startling him. Mercy, who had not uttered a single word since sitting down beside him, was watching him with concern in her eyes. She eased open the fist he hadn't realized he'd been clenching and laced her fingers through his. He let out a tight breath as she brought their joined hands up to her mouth and pressed a soft kiss to the back of his. She didn't try to ease his grief with hollow words. Instead, she merely let their hands drop down to sit on Tamriel's knee and rested her head on his shoulder.

Once the flames had died and the herbs were reduced to

smoldering embers, several senior members of the guard stepped forward and lifted the twin caskets onto their shoulders, beginning the slow procession out of the Church. Clyde's mother's cries began anew when her son's casket passed her.

"Your Majesty? Your Highness? Are you sure you would like to attend the burial?" Akiva asked from the end of the pew, reading the pain on their faces. He grimaced and shifted his weight off his bad leg. After they'd returned to the capital, Tamriel had offered him time to rest and heal, but the guard had refused. *Master Oliver wouldn't have taken time off,* he'd said through clenched teeth as another guard had rebandaged his leg, *so I won't, either.*

Ghyslain's gaze was still locked on the altar, his mind no doubt consumed by memories of those he'd loved and lost. "Yes, we're sure," Tamriel answered for him. They owed it to him to see his body laid to rest.

"Very well. A carriage is waiting outside for you, Your Highness."

"Thank you, Akiva." He stood and turned to Mercy as the guard limped away. "Are you coming?"

She shook her head, tugging at the sleeve of her black mourning gown. "Go ahead, mourn in peace. I'll see you at the castle."

A contingent of guards surrounded him and his father as they left the Church and climbed into the carriage—Ghyslain on one bench, eyes glazed with pain as he stared out of the little window beside him, and Tamriel on the other. A heavy silence descended upon them, broken only by the clattering of the carriage wheels. As they passed Myrellis Plaza, Tamriel could hear talking, laughing, the sounds of life, echoing off the houses' façades. He looked out the window and watched three young children race alongside the carriage, drawn by the royal crest painted on its side. One caught his eye and waved, shooting him a gap-toothed grin. Tamriel lifted a hand just as the carriage turned the corner and the children fell out of sight.

"Will this grief never end?" his father finally murmured. His eyes were still trained on some distant point, his hands gripping the carriage's bench seat so tightly his knuckles were white.

Tamriel didn't respond. He wasn't sure whether his father had meant to speak aloud or if he was still lost in his memories.

The carriage slowed as they neared the shipping district. The houses here were tall and narrow, some of them so old that they'd begun to lean forward into the street. If Tamriel reached out the window, he could touch them. They passed enormous factories, boarded-up warehouses, and shops and homes marked with the plague. Tamriel steeled himself when he saw a death carriage stopped in the street, two workers carrying a body from its home. Finally, the aged, crooked fence surrounding the cemetery came into view. As the carriage slowed to a halt in front of the gate, Tamriel turned to his father.

"Does it ever become easier? Losing people you care about?"

Ghyslain finally met his gaze. For a moment, the king appeared much older than his forty-odd years: the lines of his face were drawn, and shadows hung in the hollows of his cheeks. For the first time, Tamriel noticed that his father's ebony hair had begun to gray around the temples.

"I wish it did," Ghyslain said, then climbed out of the carriage.

They lingered at Master Oliver's graveside long after the final spadeful of dirt fell. The gray headstone stood out starkly against the chipped, mossy gravestones surrounding them.

OLIVER RYEVOSS
Master of His Majesty's Guard and Army

Sorrow carved a hollow in Tamriel as he gazed down at the headstone. Oliver had been so much more of a father to him than the king. He'd been warm, unwavering, calm in the face of Ghyslain's fits of madness. Even more importantly, he'd been a brother to the king. Oliver had been Ghyslain's most trusted guard since his coronation, Tamriel knew, and although the stoic guard had tried to keep their relationship strictly professional, a fierce friendship had grown between them.

Ghyslain knelt in the dirt and traced the words etched into the gray headstone. When he reached the date of Oliver's death, he paused and looked up at his son. "You were preparing to steal my throne the night Calum attacked you in your mother's house."

Tamriel stiffened. When he didn't respond, his father continued, "You were going to meet with the nobles and convince them to help you depose me. Don't look so surprised. Calum isn't nearly as sneaky as he thinks he is, and there *are* a few nobles in the court who are still loyal to me."

"I..." Tamriel hung his head, shame filling him.

Ghyslain sighed and ran a hand down his face as he stood. "The nobles think I am so desperate to keep my throne out of ambition, or pride, or some need for power, but they mistake their own selfish desires for mine. I never wanted to be king. I know my duty to my country, but I've never enjoyed ruling. Even so," he said, his dark eyes pinning

Tamriel in place, "I promised myself the day you were born that I would never abdicate. All I have ever wanted was to keep you from becoming king as long as possible."

He recoiled, stung. "You don't think I could handle it?"

"No—that's not it at all. When I was a child, I saw first-hand how running the kingdom destroyed my father. He met with courtiers, foreign dignitaries, noblemen, and advisors constantly. He held court daily. He went out of his way to visit his people, to speak with them, to rule them justly. He was all heart, and it killed him when he was only a few years older than I am now.

"For the first two years of my reign, I tried so hard to be like him. I tried so hard to be the king he wanted me to become," he murmured, his voice raw with pain. Tamriel knew what had changed—he'd been born, killing his mother in the process, and Liselle had been ripped away by the people his father should have been able to trust the most. His whole world had crumbled around him that one horrible day. "So even though it's selfish to keep the throne to myself, I've never even *considered* giving you the throne, no matter how much I loathe it. I can't watch it claim the life of anyone else I love."

"It won't—"

"It will, Tam, because you're just like your grandfather. You care so much for our people, and I am too weak to watch you destroy yourself serving them." He cast one final look at Master Oliver's grave, then started toward their waiting carriage, Tamriel close on his heels. "I have no doubt that when the time comes, you will be a wonderful king. But for your sake, I hope your rule does not come for a long, long time."

10
MERCY

After Tamriel and the king left for Oliver's burial, Mercy walked into the hallway at the back of the Church, peering into every bedchamber she passed until she found the priestess for whom she had been searching. Lethandris was kneeling in the middle of her room, her head bent forward in prayer. She jumped when Mercy hissed her name.

"Mercy? I haven't seen you since Pilar...since her passing." She stood and waved Mercy inside, gesturing for her to sit on the single rickety bed against the wall. "I presume you did not come for a social visit. How may I be of service?"

"I need to know more about your people—your myths, your lore, your sacred rituals. Anything you can tell me. A First named Firesse began gathering an army after she took the prince's cousin hostage. She plans to lead them straight to the city gates." Mercy explained the events of the past few weeks and, as she spoke, Lethandris's expression slowly shifted from disbelief to horror, and—finally—to fury.

"She *dared* to kill another First on *Ialathan?*" she seethed, pacing the length of her tiny bedroom. "That festival is our most sacred night of the year. *Fasta-va shithe,*" she cursed, spitting the words.

"Please, I need you to tell me everything you remember about Cirisor. I need to know what her strategy might be and how she came to wield Myrbellanar's powers." Beside Niamh and Nynev, Lethandris was the only other person Mercy knew who might have some insight into Firesse's strange powers. Plus, she had access to the Church's library and sacred documents—resources even the prince didn't have. There had to be something useful in the vaults under the Church.

"I'll tell you what I can, but I don't know anything about the powers you claim she holds. I've heard the legend of Myrbellanar, of course, but that's all it is—a legend."

"I know an angry little elven girl and a few ghosts who would strongly disagree with that statement."

The color bled from Lethandris's cheeks. "I may be able to find more information about Myrbellanar and the other Old Gods in the library. Give me a few days to search, and I'll send a message once I've found something."

"Thank you, Lethandris. Truly."

The priestess shook her head and smiled at her. "You tended to Pilar and eased her suffering, and for that, I consider you a friend. Your thanks are unnecessary."

The next morning, pounding on Mercy's door startled her awake. "Come on!" Nynev shouted through the wood. "The trial begins in half an hour!"

Mercy opened the door to find the sisters standing side by side in the hall, clad in simple linen shifts. Niamh's was the pale blue of a robin's egg, striking against Nynev's deep burgundy, but the most shocking sight was the lack of tattoos on the former's face. It was like finding a beautiful mural suddenly painted over a dull beige. Niamh self-consciously touched a hand to her cheek. "It's a bit strange to see it blank, isn't it?"

"When was the last time you saw it like that?"

"Eight years ago? Ten?" Niamh swept past Mercy and began rifling through her wardrobe. Her sister sprawled out on the bed.

"I can see up your dress," Mercy said to Nynev, smirking as she closed the door.

"Lucky you."

"You should wear this one." Niamh pulled out an emerald gown the guards had retrieved from Blackbriar upon their return to the city. The silk shimmered and rippled in her hands, as fine and fluid as water.

"We're going to court, not a ballroom dance."

"Fine. This one?" She held up a knee-length champagne-colored dress. The bodice was fitted and sleeveless, embroidered with tiny flowerbuds and glittering with crystals. "Oh, you will look so beautiful!"

Mercy poked the girl's side until she huffed and stepped back, then grabbed her usual black tunic and pants. "*These* will do. Wrapping myself in silk isn't going to protect me from the court, or make them forget who I am. *Those* will," she said, nodding to her daggers, sitting in their sheaths atop the vanity table. "I'm not masquerading as a royal anymore."

"If I have to wear a dress, so do you," Nynev said, rolling off the bed. "You stand out to the nobles from your ears alone. At least if you dress like them, you'll blend in a little. Go in looking like you're ready for battle and they'll make you fight for every last inch. They'll respect you more once they stop seeing you as some uncultured Assassin and start seeing you as a player in their silly little games."

"I don't care about their respect. All I care about is curing the plague and keeping Tamriel safe."

The sisters shared an amused look, some unspoken agreement passing between them. Niamh carefully returned the champagne dress to the wardrobe.

Mercy backed up a step, sensing an ambush. "I'm guessing I'm not going to like what that look means."

"No, you're not," Nynev said. Then they pounced.

Nynev had been right, Mercy realized as they joined the current of nobles ambling into the throne room a short while later; no one looked twice at them as they made their way to the front of the room. All around them, whispers filled the air. The courtiers speculated about the king's evidence and what the punishment would be if Elise was found guilty. *Hangman's noose,* Mercy thought, *or the executioner's blade.* Treason could be answered by no lesser punishment. She, Niamh, and Nynev found an open spot by the foot of the dais just as two guards dragged Elise in.

Her hands were cuffed behind her back, and the chains jangled loudly with each step, startling the gathered nobles into silence. Even after three days in the dungeon, the Creator-damned girl still had the gall to look lovely. She held her head high and her shoulders back, proud despite the stains and tears on the hem of her dress. She didn't look like a criminal. In fact, she looked exactly as she had doubtless intended—a scared young woman, a daughter of nobility, framed by a king desperate to protect his claim to the throne. Mercy could tell by the pitying expressions on several of the courtiers' faces that the ploy worked, and it disgusted her.

The guards ordered Elise to kneel before the dais. She obeyed, trembling, and trained her eyes on the empty throne. Her hands clenched into fists behind her back.

A moment later, Ghyslain strode in, followed by Tamriel

and Master Adan. The crowd bowed as the king settled upon his throne, his son behind his left shoulder and the Master of the Guard behind his right. Even though they stood directly in his line of sight, Tamriel made no sign of having noticed Mercy or the sisters.

"Your Majesty—" Elise began, her voice tight.

"Serenna Elise LeClair, you were arrested three days ago on charges of treason, forging His Majesty's signature on an official document, and conspiring to assassinate your prince," Master Adan interrupted, his deep voice booming through the hall. "How do you answer these charges?"

"Innocent! I'm innocent, I swear! I—" She jumped to her feet, but the guards forced her back to her knees. She hung her head, squeezed her eyes shut, and mumbled, "I'm innocent."

Mercy snorted derisively. Several of the noblemen and women around her shot her dark looks, but she didn't care. Her attention was focused solely on Tamriel. The prince's face was remarkably devoid of emotion, but she could read his anger in the tension in his body and the betrayal burning in his eyes.

"You helped Calum forge a false Guild contract on my life," he said, the words clipped. "You used your access to my father's documents to copy his signature. Later, when Calum tried to kill me, you framed Mercy for the attack. Do those sound like the actions of an innocent woman?"

"I did none of those things, Your Highness."

"You did, because you knew Calum was going to make a play for the throne after you two framed my father and had him deposed. You were planning to marry him after he ascended the throne."

"Your Highness, I have served your family faithfully for years. Your cousin and I are friends, yes, but that is all our relationship has ever been." At that, even Tamriel couldn't resist an eyeroll. "Even so, do you think me so foolish that I would expect the council to place a commoner on the throne? I assure you, I have a much greater grasp of the intricacies of politics than that."

"The girl has a point," someone behind Mercy muttered.

"Poor, sweet dear," another said.

"Considering that you committed treason, I haven't the slightest clue what you were thinking," Tamriel growled. "You used your skill with calligraphy to forge my father's signature on the contract."

Elise jerked her chin up, staring the prince dead in the eyes. "Claiming that I would use such privileges to undermine you is an insult to all the work I have done for this kingdom. My family has served yours for generations. We owe all we have to you; why would I risk throwing that all away?"

He opened his mouth to argue, but paused when murmurs of agreement rippled across the crowd. *Ghyslain was right,* Mercy realized, sudden panic gripping her chest like a vise. *They believe her.* She gaped at the people around her. A few nodded and pointed to Elise, sympathy on their powdered faces. Tamriel blinked at them, stunned, for a few moments before he remembered to hide his surprise.

"QUIET!" Master Adan shouted, but he may as well have whispered for all the good it did. The nobles had turned their attention from the girl before the throne to the man sitting atop it, and Mercy could feel their sympathy shift to suspicion. The king sat silently before it all. His face was quickly turning ashen.

She narrowed her eyes, struggling to keep her temper under control. All she wanted to do was jump up and shout, *She's lying! How can none of you see it?* But Elise had fooled Mercy once, too. She'd managed to trick an assassin into trusting her; it should have come as no surprise that the nobles would fall for her lies, as well.

Nynev leaned over and whispered, "I wish I'd brought my bow. One clean shot, and all this trial nonsense would be over."

"Next time, you have my permission to do just that."

Niamh shushed them as Seren Pierce pushed his way to the front of the room.

"It's remarkable that he managed to hold his tongue this long," Mercy murmured, but then she saw why: Nerida, Landers, and Leon were close behind him. They had likely counseled him against speaking up too soon, waiting for the tide to shift in their favor.

Pierce stepped forward and offered the king the barest imitation of a bow. "Your Majesty, it's clear these accusations have no substance. What is even more obvious, however, is that the arrest and mistreatment of my daughter—this entire trial, in fact—are nothing but a ploy to hide your own crimes." He ignored the king's scowl and turned to the crowd. "Do we all not suspect that His Majesty plotted his own son's death to keep himself in power? After the turmoil he caused with his affair with *Liselle*, do we really trust his ability to rule us? He turned his back on our beloved queen long ago. It's easy to imagine him turning his back on the boy who killed her," he spat, thrusting a finger in Tamriel's direction.

"The mad king finally cracked," someone whispered. "Just look what he's done to that poor girl."

"The grief that poisoned our dear king's mind has finally gotten the better of him," Pierce continued, smirking as the nobles began chattering to one another, no longer bothering to mask their whispers. "And our prince has fallen prey to the allure of the elves, just like his father."

"The Assassin is still here?"

"I saw her in the Plaza with a savage just the other day."

"Stop him," Tamriel barked at his father, seething. "Guards, get him out of here."

"Belay that order," Ghyslain snapped as two guards started toward the dais.

"Your Majesty?" Master Adan asked. "The evidence, perhaps?"

The king didn't respond.

"Father?" Tamriel said, uncertainty slipping into his voice. Ghyslain held himself still as a statue, his eyes trained on the girl kneeling before him. The throne room had gone completely silent.

Mercy clenched her fists. *Stand up to them, you coward!*

"We have evidence," the prince blurted, clearly grappling for control. "The contract—"

"The contract bearing your father's name, you mean?" Pierce replied smugly.

"We have letters—"

"Let her go."

Tamriel froze, then whirled on his father. "*What?*"

"You heard me. Guards, let her go. She's innocent."

Master Adan repeated the order, looking a little shocked himself, and the guards helped Elise to her feet and unlocked her shackles. They walked her to her father, who smiled and slung an arm around her shoulders.

"My baby," Nerida cried, stroking her daughter's tangled hair as tears slipped through her lashes. The three of them walked out of the room, every pair of eyes following them until they disappeared into the hall. Landers and Leon melted back into the crowd.

"He's giving *up?*" Mercy hissed, a red haze of fury filling her vision. "He's letting that weasel *win?*"

"Get out," Ghyslain ordered, and the nobles started to drift out after the LeClair family, murmuring to one another as they went. The king stood and brushed past his son, who gaped at him, on his way to the door at the side of the dais. Half of the guards followed him. Master Adan clapped

Tamriel on the shoulder, shaking his head, before trailing after the king.

"What the *hell* was that?" Tamriel bellowed to the quickly-emptying room. For the first time, his gaze found Mercy, Nynev, and Niamh, still standing at the foot of the dais, and he gestured for them to follow. "Come with me quickly, before my spineless excuse of a father shuts himself up in his room. I need to hear his excuse." He let out a sharp, humorless laugh. "He'd better have a damn good excuse."

11
MERCY

They caught up to Ghyslain just as he entered his study. He started to close the door, but Tamriel stuck his foot in the doorway before it could swing shut. "Don't think you're getting away so easily," he snarled, shoving the door open with his shoulder. "You have some explaining to do."

Ghyslain sighed and slumped down in his desk chair. He didn't look at any of them as they filed into the room. "Calm down, Tam."

"CALM DOWN?" he exploded. *"Calm down?* You presume to order me around after you let the smug son of a bitch walk all over you? What were you *thinking?*"

"Did I not tell you exactly what would happen in there?" Ghyslain snapped, anger winning out over his guilt. "Did Seren Pierce not do exactly what we expected?" When Tamriel opened his mouth to speak, Ghyslain held up a hand. "Listen to me. Who here has more experience with those snakes than I? Their loyalties were with the LeClair family, and I did what was necessary to keep the nobles appeased. If

I hadn't, both of our heads would have ended up on spikes on the castle walls before the week was over."

"Don't be dramatic," Mercy growled.

Tamriel stormed up to the desk. "Elise forged the contract. She tried to have me killed. She framed Mercy for attempted murder. *She must be punished*."

"Pierce is only a seren, but he's a talkative one. He knows how to persuade people to see his side and—like I said—the nobles will always choose one of their own over us."

"You're mad," Tamriel hissed. "Liselle's death has made you paranoid."

"And it has kept us alive for the past eighteen years."

Father and son glared at each other, neither looking at all inclined to back down.

"Why didn't you show the court the letters Tamriel found?" Mercy interrupted.

"It wouldn't have made a difference. Anyone can forge letters."

"But Cassius said... You said you would speak to..." Tamriel trailed off, his expression morphing from anger to sudden realization. "You lied to me, didn't you? You were always planning to release her."

"Not at first. We tried to come up with a plan to convince them, but the chances of them siding against the LeClairs were too slim. After what they did to Liselle, I couldn't bear to—"

Tamriel rolled his eyes. "It always comes back to Liselle. Did her death really traumatize you so much that you find yourself paralyzed in the face of court opposition? Do you not realize kings must sometimes make unpopular decisions?"

Ghyslain's eyes flashed. "When you are king, you will have the power to make those decisions yourself. Until then, you will obey my commands and never question me in front of the court again." He yanked open one of the drawers and shuffled through the papers. After a moment, he stood, a bundle of papers—the letters from Calum—crumpled in his fist.

Niamh and Nynev backed out of the king's way as he crossed the room and braced his hands on the fireplace's mantle. He hung his head, letting out a weary sigh. "I let the girl go to protect you, Tam. If they're not going to support us," he mumbled, "we must never give them an excuse to turn against us." He looked over his shoulder at his son, took a deep, shaky breath, and said, "*That's* what I learned from Liselle."

He tossed the letters into the fire.

The dry parchment ignited immediately, the edges curling in and turning black as the flames consumed them.

"*No!*" Mercy and Tamriel shouted in unison. Instinctively, the prince lunged forward and plunged his hands into the fire. He gasped and pulled the papers out, shaking them frantically. Mercy snatched them out of his hands and threw them to the ground as he gasped in pain. Heart pounding, Mercy stomped on the papers until the flames finally died.

Niamh rushed forward and took the prince's hands. "We must get you to the infirmary. Come."

"Tamriel—" Ghyslain began in a choked voice. "I didn't mean—"

"Can they be salvaged?" Tamriel interrupted, nodding to the papers. His hands were shaking, streaked with red burns and black soot.

Mercy bent down to pick them up, but the papers crumbled to ash at her touch. She shook her head.

The prince's shoulders slumped. "Are you happy now, you insufferable coward?" he snarled at his father. "Is that what Liselle would have done? Would she have told you to bow to the nobles' will? If that's all being a king is, I wish you a very long rule, because I don't want any of it." He yanked his hands away from Niamh and stormed out of the room, slamming the door behind him.

"Come," Nynev whispered, nudging her sister toward the door. "Those burns need to be treated. Mercy?"

She glared at the king, her hatred pouring out of her so intensely she was certain Ghyslain could feel it. He stared down at the burned, ruined letters, agony and regret plain on his face, but offered no apology, no explanation. She turned her back on the king. "Let's go."

Tamriel hissed in pain when Niamh applied a salve to his hands, gently massaging it into his tender skin in small, even circles. She wrapped each of them in bandages, biting her lip in concentration. "There," Niamh said softly. "You'll still be able to use your hands, just be careful. I'll make more of the salve so you can reapply it each morning and night."

"Thank you." He turned his attention to Mercy as Niamh moved to the desk and took up the mortar and pestle. "Will you please stop pacing? And perhaps move away from those surgical tools? They're awfully sharp, and I don't want the assassin in you to get any ideas."

"Not sharp enough." She tossed the scalpel she'd been examining onto a shelf. "We must do something about Elise. She cannot get off that easily."

"Unless we find new evidence, there's nothing we can do. She's had her trial."

"There is something *I* can do."

He frowned. "No killing her. The nobles believe she's innocent. Killing her would only give them a martyr and paint an even larger target on your back."

"I wasn't going to kill her," she snapped. Her lips parted into a cruel imitation of a smile. "Just pay her a visit."

"As long as you promise not to let your inner Assassin get the better of you."

"I'll play nice." Mercy slumped into the chair at the desk, eyeing the teetering stack of medical books they had yet to read. "Have you learned anything new about the plague from the healers? Any possible treatments?" she asked Niamh.

"Nothing more than we already knew. We're stuck doing trial and error, but we're afraid of using too much of the Cedikra."

"We'll find something soon." She plucked a bottle off the desk and tucked it into her pocket, the glass cool against her fingers. "First, though, I need to have a word with Elise. Nynev, would you accompany me?"

The huntress matched her wicked grin and grabbed her bow from the shelf where she'd left it the day before. "It would be my pleasure."

That night, Elise glided past the archway of the gallery in a whisper of ivory silk. She paused, turned back, and jumped when she saw Mercy standing in the middle of the room, wrapped in a hooded cloak the same color as the nighttime sky. Only Mercy's face and her hand, holding a lit oil lantern, were exposed.

"What are you doing here?" Elise asked. "How did you get in?"

"I have my ways."

"Out! Get out now!" She started forward, but someone reached out from behind her and grabbed a fistful of her hair, yanking her back.

"Don't make any sudden movements," Nynev warned as she pressed the blade of her hunting knife to Elise's neck, "or my hand might just slip."

"I'll scream. I'll scream as loudly as I can. My father will call the guards."

"Go ahead and scream." Nynev reached into her pocket and pulled out the bottle Mercy had swiped from the infirmary. She shook it in front of Elise's face. A few drops of shimmering Ienna Oil glinted in the light of the lantern. "Someone drugged your parents' drinks. I hope they don't blame your cook. She'll have such a headache when she wakes up, as it is."

"The neighbors—"

"You think you could get away in the time it takes them to call the guards? Are you willing to gamble your life on that?"

Elise swallowed, her voice wavering when she said, "You're going to kill me, then? Give me the execution I deserve?" She let out a shaky laugh. "That's exactly what I'd expect from an Assassin and a heathen."

"Confess your crimes," Mercy growled, her voice cool and sharp—the voice of an avenging Assassin. A voice promising death. The serenna's eyes widened a fraction in fear, then hardened.

"And give myself up to the hangman's noose? Not a chance."

Nynev pricked Elise. A small trail of blood wended its way down her slender, pale neck. "Listen to the Assassin's offer before you refuse her, girl. You might find her conditions quite agreeable."

Elise didn't say a word. She merely dipped her chin, as much of a nod as she dared with a knife at her throat.

"My offer is this, Serenna: confess your crimes before the court and accept the execution to which the king sentences you, or meet your end at my hand. It won't be the quick, painless death the executioner will give you," Mercy promised, a cruel gleam in her eyes. "I'll take my time doing it

—maybe a month. Maybe a year. I'll carve you up in little pieces, working in from your toes, then your fingers, all the way to your pretty, pretty face. I'll keep you in so much pain you'll forget your own name. You'll forget your beloved Calum. When I'm through with you, the Creator's punishment awaiting you in the Beyond will seem a blessed paradise."

The serenna's throat bobbed. "You can't do that. The nobles—"

"You're not stupid, Elise. You've heard the stories about the Guild. You know what I'll do to anyone who tries to keep me from giving you the reckoning you deserve."

"Calum—"

"Calum is dead," Mercy snarled, the lie falling easily from her lips. "He's not coming to save you, you lovesick fool. He died of an arrow to the heart in Xilor days ago. The guards found his body outside the city, left to rot."

She watched with cruel satisfaction as the last bit of resolve drained from Elise. Nynev released her as the serenna's knees went weak, and she crumpled to the floor. "Fine," Elise spat through the tears rolling down her cheeks.

"What was that?" Mercy purred.

"I said I'll confess. Don't make me say it again."

"Bring her over here."

Nynev grabbed Elise's arm and hauled her to her feet. The serenna's face paled as she was brought before Mercy. "I'm going to leave you with one more thing—one more reminder of what I'll do to you if you go back on your promise." Mercy paused, baring her teeth. "I learned a lot from the girls who tormented me in the Guild. Do you know the best way to crush someone's spirit? Destroy whatever she holds dearest in her heart." She stepped aside, revealing what she had been hiding behind the thick folds of her cloak.

Elise gasped, her eyes widening as she at last noticed the

bare patches of wall scattered about the room. A pile of canvases sat on the floor beside Mercy—every one of them a painting of Calum.

"Please don't—" she blurted when Mercy held the lantern over the pile. She flinched as the oil sloshed against the glass, her lower lip beginning to quiver. "P-Please don't ruin them. They're—They're all I have left of him. *Please*."

"You'll convince your father to stop working against the king?"

"Absolutely."

"You'll confess?"

She nodded.

"I knew we could come to an agreement." Mercy smiled and pulled the lantern back to her side. Elise breathed a sigh of relief. "But unfortunately, I'm still angry that you had me framed for Calum's attack on Tamriel, and I can't just let you go unpunished."

She stepped back and hurled the lantern at the stack of paintings. Elise screamed, "NO!" as the glass shattered and splattered burning oil everywhere. The paintings caught fire immediately, paint bubbling and cracking in the heat. Nynev sheathed her knife and shoved the trembling serenna onto the settee in the middle of the room.

Mercy tipped the girl's head back with a finger, forcing Elise to meet her eyes. "I look forward to hearing your confession."

12

CALUM

The morning after the attack in Fishers' Cross, an elven boy no older than thirteen—his face still pockmarked with breakouts under the twining thorns-and-roses tattoos of Lysander's clan—arrived from Fishers' Cross with news of the Cirisians' victory. Firesse immediately ordered the remaining elves to pull camp; they were to cross the channel to Beltharos later that day. Last Calum had heard, their numbers had swelled to approximately twelve hundred—not enough to outnumber the Beltharan army, but much larger than Ghyslain would be expecting.

Drake found the Strykers sitting around a large campfire, mending the elves' worn leather armor. "Pack your things—it's time to move."

Nerran frowned up at him. "They really took Fishers' Cross that easily?"

He shrugged. "It's a small town."

None of them said a word as they began gathering what few supplies they'd brought. Drake worked with Amir and Oren to disassemble the tent Firesse had given them. After a few minutes, he noticed Hewlin watching him. "What?"

The eldest Stryker scratched his scraggly beard, studying Drake with something like suspicion in his eyes. Perhaps it was only Calum's wishful thinking. "Nothing."

Firesse met them in the center of camp, trailed by the young elven boy. "Ivris will accompany you to Fishers' Cross on your ship," she announced. "I would like you to begin crafting as soon as you arrive."

After a few hours of trekking across the Islands, they emerged beside the bay where the Strykers had anchored their boat. They loaded their belongings, adjusted the sails and rigging, and cast off.

The Strykers seemed to breathe a little easier when the Cirisor Islands disappeared in the distance. It was oddly peaceful, Calum thought, to be off the Islands and sailing the open ocean. If he hadn't left the Strykers, he would have crossed these waters months ago on the way to Feyndara. The country had always intrigued him. Because of the animosity between Beltharos and Feyndara, few people from either country were allowed inside the other's borders. Calum would have been one of a handful of Beltharans to set foot on the forest-covered, elven-ruled land in generations.

Now, he'd likely never see it. He doubted Firesse would allow him to live past his usefulness—but if she did, where would he go? Tamriel was dead, struck down by one of Lylia's arrows in Xilor. Mercy had likely died with him. His mind drifted briefly to Elise, but he pushed thoughts of her away with a pang of sorrow and guilt.

Lost in his mind, it felt like only a few minutes passed before they spotted the rocky cliffs bordering Fishers' Cross. As they neared the docks, Calum watched the elven archers patrol the top of the bluffs, bows in hand. Below them, the town was nothing like Calum remembered.

It wasn't a large village—only eight buildings in all—but it had been bustling with people when he and Kaius had passed through a little over a week ago. A dozen ships had been docked in the harbor. Women and slaves had been hard at work in the fields, harvesting crops, and fishermen had stood casting their lines into the sea or the twining rivers that ran south of the town.

Now, though, the single street running through the village was devoid of humans. Firesse's fighters and hunters slunk across the dirt road, rummaging through houses for supplies. A column of black smoke rose from the top of the bluff, and the scent of burning meat—the bodies of the dead—wafted over on the breeze.

"Dear Creator," Hewlin muttered, followed by a string of curses from Nerran when something thumped against the side of the ship.

Drake and the others peered over the railing. A man in a sun-bleached tunic and loose-fitting trousers was floating faceup in the water, his face contorted in horror. The deep gash in his side leaked dark blood into the water.

"Poor soul," Oren whispered, his grip tightening on the railing. "I bet he didn't even have a chance to protect himself. I doubt any of these people even owned weapons to defend themselves."

On Drake's other side, the Cirisian boy kept his eyes locked on the docks ahead, steadfastly ignoring the body bobbing on the waves beside them. His face was pallid, and Calum wondered how many villagers he had killed in the fighting. *It's a stain on your soul,* he thought sadly, remembering the feeling of Odomyr's warm blood gushing over his hand, making the handle of Firesse's dagger slick in his palm. *It never leaves you.*

"We can't do anything about it now," Drake said. The sound of Calum's voice startled everyone out of their mourning silence. Hewlin looked at him sharply. "Let's just get to shore and do our jobs."

They tied up the sails and rowed into the harbor, where several empty boats bobbed in their berths, their captains and crews never to return. A few elves waiting nearby helped them unload their supplies. Ivris disembarked first and immediately turned his back on the sea, clearly eager to leave the villager's body far behind. He led them to a building at the end of the row, a stone chimney rising from its roof.

"Well, it's got a forge, at least," Amir said, pointing. "No more working over campfires."

Ivris ushered them into the workshop. A few tables were clustered around the forge, bits of scrap metal and half-mended sails cluttering the room. Tools of all different shapes and sizes hung from hooks on the back wall, and chests and crates of supplies were stacked in the corner. "Does this fit your needs?"

Hewlin peered into the dark, cold forge. "Well enough, for now. Have your people bring us whatever weapons they need repaired. In the meantime, we'll get started crafting some new stuff."

Ivris nodded and departed.

Nerran clapped. "All right, let's get to work. Oren and Amir, gather as much scrap metal as you can find and put it on that table over there. Calum, help me light the forge, won't you?" He searched the nearby crates until he found kindling, then arranged it in the center of the hearth. He pulled pieces of flint and steel out of his pack and set about lighting the fire. "How many people do you think died here?" he asked when Drake leaned down to work the bellows, softly enough only he could hear.

"A few dozen, I suspect."

He shook his head. "Firesse is intense, but I didn't think she would actually go through with the attack. She—*Damn it*," he hissed when the kindling caught, flared, and went out. He struck the flint and steel again, sending sparks flying in the dark forge. "She's got to be...what, fourteen?"

"Something like that." Drake didn't bother to mention the Cirisians' strange aging, or the fact that he had no idea how old she actually was behind that youthful face.

"Fourteen and the leader of her own army," Nerran mused. Then he glanced out one of the workshop's open windows at the elves prowling the streets, some still in their bloodied armor. "These people were innocent," he said in a low voice. "They didn't deserve to die."

"That's the price of war, isn't it? The rich get to sit in their mansions and drink wine while unlucky bastards do their fighting for them. People like that fisherman get caught in the middle. If everyone got what they deserved, my friend, the world would be a very different place." After the kindling finally caught and the flame grew into a healthy blaze, Drake straightened and turned to Nerran. "As for Firesse, she's only trying to reclaim what the people of Beltharos have taken from her and her people—what the *king* has taken from her."

"If there is any justice in the world, the king will get what's coming to him, mate. I just hope too many innocent people don't get caught in the middle."

FIRESSE AND THE REST OF HER ARMY ARRIVED AT FISHERS' Cross the next day, one long train of people carrying everything they owned on their backs. Drake and the Strykers stood outside the workshop as the elves spilled into town. They watched families reunite and friends chatter to one another in Cirisian. The language grated on Calum's nerves.

If I never hear Cirisian again in my life, he thought sullenly, *I'll die a happy man.*

In that, at least, we can agree, my son, Drake responded.

Firesse greeted the Strykers with a radiant smile, completely unaffected by the fact that so many people had died here on her orders. "I trust you found your way here without issue? How is the workshop?"

"We did, and it's fine," Hewlin responded, "although we don't have enough time or resources to make swords. If you have your people cut down some trees, we can craft spears and arrows for them to carry into the next battle."

"Consider it done. We'll find better resources when we move inland." She turned to Drake. "Did Myris assign you a place to sleep?"

"Right across the street." He nodded to the house behind her. "Next to yours."

"Come speak with me tonight after you've finished your work. We must discuss our next steps."

"You've given up on the Daughters, then?"

"No, I left scouts on the road to the Islands. If the Assassins show, they'll send them here."

"Firesse." Faye wove through the groups of elves milling in the street and stopped before the First. "What do you want to do with the slaves your people liberated?"

"Any who wish to fight may join our ranks. I will rely on you to train them. Those who are not capable or not willing will be granted safe passage to the Islands."

"Very well."

Calum watched the Daughter walk away, her raven-black hair swishing with every step. They'd been friendly back at the Keep, but the Daughter hadn't said a single word to him since the mess in Xilor. Did she blame him for Lylia's death? He doubted it. If he'd been the one who had shoved the knife into the girl's stomach, Faye probably would have hugged him for it. She'd loathed the Assassin almost as much as Mercy had.

When Firesse left to speak with Myris and Kaius, Calum realized that the street had already begun to empty. Most of the elves would be staying in their tents outside of town, while Firesse, the Strykers, and the other Firsts took houses in the village.

"This shit is so messed up," Nerran muttered to no one in particular. "Let's get this over with so we can collect our money and get the hell back to Rhys."

After Drake finished sharpening his last arrowhead, he stood and rolled his shoulders, grimacing at the knots between his shoulder blades. Hewlin and the others had left ten minutes ago to find dinner, leaving Drake to finish his work on his own. If anyone had noticed that Calum wasn't as proficient as he used to be at the forge and anvil, he'd had the grace not to point it out.

Drake splashed cool water onto his face from a bucket in the corner of the room, then stepped outside. The nighttime sky shone with countless stars. Calum recognized some of the constellations—the Maiden, the Imp, the Lost King, the Huntress—and it reminded him of all the times he'd lain beside Elise in the garden behind her home, competing to see who could count the most stars.

"Do you think there's life out there?" she had asked him once. They'd been stretched out side by side on the grass, almost touching, and the bare inch of space between them had been driving him crazy for the better part of an hour. It was the first time either of them had spoken for several minutes, and when he didn't immediately respond, she'd turned onto her side and propped her head on her hand so she could look at him. "Well?"

"What?" he'd choked out. He'd had to pinch himself to

keep his thoughts from returning to the way her chiffon gown clung to her soft curves, the way the moonlight turned her hair silver, the way her full lips spread into a grin. He was fourteen then, and he had been in love with her from the moment he'd laid eyes on her.

Her blue eyes had sparkled with mirth. "Do you think there's life out there?"

"No."

"Oh." She'd frowned, a little furrow between her brows, and lain back on the grass. He'd cursed himself for the disappointment in her voice. "*I* think there is."

"If there's life out there, then everything the church claims about the Creator is wrong. He never Created us. He doesn't have a plan for us all. Nothing we do means anything. We're just two out of a countless number of creatures wandering around the universe, thinking we know what we're doing."

"You'd prefer your wandering to have meaning?" she'd teased.

"The Creator put us here for a reason. A purpose. If we can't be certain of that, then what's the point of all this?" He'd gestured to himself, the grand mansions around them, the map of stars spread out over their heads. "Without that, we're like dust on the breeze or...or cork floating down a river. We're nothing."

"I would never think you're nothing." She'd met his gaze then, all traces of humor gone. He had never given voice to the worries that had plagued him since childhood, but she knew him well enough to sense the turn his thoughts had taken. For as long as he could remember, he'd had no place in the castle. He'd been searching for some purpose other than being the prince's common-blooded cousin, an afterthought, a footnote in the future king's story.

"You wouldn't?" he'd asked, suddenly breathless. He loved

Elise so much it hurt, but he had never allowed himself to dream she would one day look at him the way she was now—the way he had always looked at her.

She had shaken her head slowly, her gaze dropping to his mouth. "Not ever."

Then she kissed him.

When she pulled back, he had given her a slightly dazed, dreamy grin, and she'd burst out laughing. "You look like you're drunk."

"I feel like it, too. Kiss me again."

So she had.

Calum's heart fractured at the memory. It wasn't until the breeze snagged a stray piece of his hair and sent it dancing in front of his face, breaking the spell, that he realized Drake had not moved from the doorway of the workshop. His father had lived the memory right alongside him.

Drake started toward the home Firesse had claimed. He lifted his hand to knock on the front door, but he paused when he heard voices coming from inside.

"What have you done to him?"

The shutters on the windows were closed, but they did nothing to muffle Firesse's voice when she nonchalantly responded, "Who?"

"You know who." Hewlin's gravelly voice was colder than Calum had ever heard it. "Calum."

He noticed! Calum's heart stuttered. *He knows something isn't right!*

Drake rapped on the door, cutting off the First's response. "Firesse? You wished to speak with me?"

The lock clicked, then Firesse opened the door and waved him inside. Drake barely made it two feet past the threshold before Hewlin seized the front of his shirt and shoved him against the wall, pinning him in place. "What did she do to you, boy?" Then he glared at Firesse. "What did you do to him?"

"She's done nothing," Drake said.

Hewlin's eyes didn't stray from the First's face. "He's different. I could tell the moment he opened his mouth. You've done something to him, haven't you?"

"What is it you think I've done exactly? Cursed him? Put him under a spell? Do you still believe your wet-nurse's stories about the fearsome Cirisian savages?"

"Don't be insolent with me, girl." Hewlin scowled at Calum. "The man I knew would never condone the killing of so many innocent people, let alone help plan their slaughter. I don't know what she's done to you, but whatever it is, you'd better snap out of it *right the hell now*."

I'm trying! By the Creator, I'm trying!

Drake shot him an unnervingly calm smile. "Listen to Firesse, Hewlin. I'm fine. I'm me."

Hewlin shook him roughly. "I don't believe you. You didn't blink twice at that body we saw yesterday. You don't even care that the people of this town were massacred or that you led the elves straight to their doorstep."

I care! I care! Calum struggled against the bonds, against the ice-water in his veins, to no avail. *But I can't do anything to stop them.*

"You've changed, Calum."

"My circumstances have changed." Drake stared straight into Hewlin's eyes. Ever the actor. Ever the liar. "I told you my real surname. I told you how my father died. Should Ghyslain not pay for what he has done? He destroyed my family. I can't let that failure of a king go unpunished."

Hewlin studied him for a long time. He opened his mouth to argue, then released him and took a jerky step back. He shot a hateful look at Firesse. "You want to kill all humans?"

"All those who have wronged my people."

"I'll not be a party to genocide." He stomped toward the door. "The Strykers and I are leaving first thing in the morning. I want no part of this war."

"Hewlin—" Drake began.

"I'll pay you double what we agreed," Firesse blurted. "Triple."

"No." He pointed an accusatory finger at Drake. "You fix whatever's gone rotten in that head of yours, boy, and you'll be welcomed back to the Strykers with open arms. Until then, I'm keeping my men far from you and these murderers."

He turned to storm out, but Firesse darted forward and planted herself between him and the door. She unsheathed a dagger, and the blade glinted menacingly as she leveled the point at Hewlin's chest, right over his heart. "Back up."

He obeyed, backpedaling until he bumped into the corner of the kitchen table.

"Sit."

He slumped into the nearest chair. "If you think you can threaten me, girl—"

"Take off your shirt."

Hewlin paused, thrown off by her odd command. "My shirt?"

"You heard me."

Without taking his eyes off the knife, Hewlin pulled off his tunic and tossed it onto the floor. Firesse tucked the knife into the waistband of her pants. "Perhaps this will change your mind." She leaned forward and ran her fingers down the thick, ropy muscles of Hewlin's chest. He stared at her, confused and a little disgusted by a young girl touching him in such a manner. For a moment, Calum and Drake merely watched, puzzled.

What's she doing?

Hell if I know.

Firesse mumbled something under her breath, and Hewlin's face contorted in agony and horror. A moan escaped his lips as his skin broke out in a bright red rash. Boils the size of coins rippled across his chest, filled with a milky fluid. Everywhere Firesse's fingers touched suddenly inflamed. Before their eyes, the flesh across Hewlin's torso split and peeled like wet tissue paper.

The plague, Calum realized with a jolt of pure terror. *Firesse can control the plague.*

"Witch," Hewlin spat through clenched teeth. "Demon."

"Will you and your men help me?"

He took a tight, pained breath and nodded.

"Good." Firesse dropped her hands, and Hewlin's skin immediately knitted itself back together. He gasped as the rash disappeared. The First smirked and leaned forward until her face was inches from Hewlin's. "I trust you'll remember this little demonstration the next time you consider deserting."

Hewlin didn't say a word. He just gaped at her in horror.

"Get out," Firesse ordered. She picked up his shirt and flung it in his face. Then she moved to the door and held it wide open for him.

He tugged his tunic on, crossed the room, and paused in the doorway. He looked over his shoulder at Drake. "I pray you come back to your senses, kid. The Calum I knew would never have agreed to this, revenge or no."

13

TAMRIEL

"Father? You summoned me?" Tamriel called as he entered the throne room. He had debated not showing up at all, but the messenger had been adamant that he answer the summons. *It's about the serenna,* he'd said. "What do you—"

The words died on his tongue when he saw Elise kneeling before the dais.

Nerida and Pierce stood behind her, clutching each other's hands. All three of them were flanked by guards.

Elise's ivory dress was wrinkled and, inexplicably, soot-stained along the hem. Her long ice-blonde hair hung in limp snarls around her tear-streaked face. When she looked up at Tamriel, he noticed dark shadows under her eyes, as if she hadn't slept since her trial the day before. *By the Creator, Mercy, what did you do to her?* When Mercy returned to the castle after her visit to the seren's home late last night, she hadn't said a word. She'd merely grinned smugly at him and disappeared into her bedroom.

"What is this?" Tamriel asked.

Ghyslain glared at Elise, who ducked her head and shuddered under the weight of the king's gaze. He finally looked up at Tamriel when he climbed the steps and took his place beside the throne. "Serenna LeClair has had a change of heart, it seems. She wishes to confess."

"Confess?" He raised a brow. "Let's hear it."

"Elise—" her father began in a tight voice. Nerida placed a hand on his shoulder to silence him.

Elise's throat bobbed. "I-It's true. All of it. I helped Calum forge the contract on His Highness's life." Fresh tears streamed down her face at the admission. "When Mercy failed to kill the prince, Calum and I framed her for the attack in Her Majesty's house. Everything the prince said at the trial is true. I'm guilty."

For once, Seren Pierce said nothing. His shoulders were slumped, his eyes downcast. Every hint of his stubbornness, his superiority, had vanished.

Ghyslain leaned forward. "Will you admit to your crimes before the court?"

"Yes."

"And you are aware that the punishment for treason is death."

She sniffled again and nodded.

"Then you shall be executed at dawn in two days' time."

Elise let out a choked sob and flung herself into her mother's arms. Seren Pierce hugged them both tightly. After a minute, the guards forced them apart and secured Elise's hands behind her back. "I'm so sorry," she said as they tugged her toward the door.

"My daughter," Pierce choked out. "My baby girl—"

"Wait! Wait." She stopped and looked pleadingly at Tamriel. "I know I am in no position to ask anything of you, Your Highness, but if you ever held any affection for me in your heart, please hear me out." When Tamriel opened his mouth to order the guards to escort her out, she blurted, "It's my brother. He was locked in Beggars' End after the plague outbreak. You told me you'd find a way to get him out, but he's still trapped in there. I've been sending him letters and haven't received a response in over a week. It's not like him. I'm afraid he's fallen ill, or worse. Please, Your Highness—"

"Guards, take her to the dungeon," Ghyslain called.

"But my brother—"

"*Now.*"

She deflated, her face falling as the guards dragged her out of the room.

The second she disappeared from view, Seren Pierce let out a shaky breath. "Your Majesty—"

"Go home, Pierce."

"But—"

"I will not listen to any pleas for mercy," Ghyslain said, scowling. "Elise knew what she was risking when she forged my signature on the contract. You are lucky I am not revoking your title for speaking the way you did during the trial."

"I had no idea what she'd done, Your Majesty. I thought she was innocent—"

"I know. I do not hold you accountable for your daughter's crimes. Because you have served my family for so many years, I am offering you a choice: if you are ready to return to work in one week's time, you may—but I will brook no more complaints against me or my son. I expect your complete and utter loyalty. If you cannot abide by those terms, you may forfeit your title. Have I made myself clear?"

The seren's head bobbed up and down. "Yes, Your Majesty. Come, love." Pierce clutched Nerida's hand, and the couple shuffled out of the throne room. Once their footsteps had faded into the great hall, Ghyslain turned to the remaining guards.

"Gather my advisors in the council chamber."

"Yes, Your Majesty," they said in unison. They scattered—some to other parts of the castle, some out to the city—leaving Tamriel and his father alone for the first time since Elise's trial.

Ghyslain eyed the bandages on his son's hands. "Do they hurt?"

"It's certainly not pleasant." He flexed his fingers, grimacing when the tender skin pulled tight.

"And your back?"

"I try not to think about it." The stitches had been removed days ago, but he had not yet worked up the courage to look at the gruesome scar that spanned nearly the entire length of his back.

"Will you attend the council meeting?"

He shook his head, his stomach dropping at the thought of Atlas, trapped in the End. "I have to do something first."

Before he left, Tamriel changed out of his finery and into the simple tunic and pants Hessa had given him on their journey back from the Islands. He pulled the hood of his cloak over his head as he slipped through the castle gate and into the city. Rather than take one of the easily-recognizable carriages from the castle, he hired an unornamented one from a stop a few blocks down the street. None of these precautions would completely disguise him, of course, but he'd like to attract as little attention as possible.

"Where to, sir?" the driver called.

"Guinevere's Square." He climbed in and drew the curtains as the carriage lurched into motion. Normally, the roads leading toward the center of the city would be clogged with traffic, but the streets had grown emptier since the outbreak of the plague. They arrived in Guinevere's Square in half the time it would usually take. Tamriel called for the driver to stop in front of a quaint little bakery and clambered out, keeping his face turned away when he paid the fare.

After fifteen minutes of wandering between the narrow houses and old shops of the Square, Tamriel arrived at the northern gate of the wall surrounding Beggars' End. Three guards stood watch outside the solid iron gate. Thankfully, there hadn't been another mob outside the End while Tamriel and Mercy were gone, but Ghyslain had still taken every precaution to protect the slums. Every hole in the crumbling wall had been filled and a new padlock the size of Tamriel's fist held the gate shut.

The guards snapped to attention when they saw him approach. "Who goes there?" one called, reaching for his sword.

Tamriel pulled down his hood. "I have business in the End. Unlock the gate, please."

"Yes, Your Highness." The padlock rattled on its chain as the guard unlocked it. A high-pitched screech pierced the air as the guards pulled the heavy gate open. "Would you like one of us to accompany you?"

"No, thank you." He tugged the hood up and strode through the gate. Before they shut it behind him, he added, "I'll be back in an hour or so. Can you hire me a carriage?"

"It will be waiting here when you return."

The hinges screeched again as the guards closed the gate and fastened the padlock. He started down the road, scanning the dilapidated buildings warily. The insides were dark and quiet, but that didn't mean they were uninhabited. After becoming partners with Hero and Ketojan, he had never felt unsafe in the End—they had made sure the elves never taunted or threatened him like they did the other humans who entered the neighborhood—but he had no idea how much had changed, how desperate the people had become, since the plague took hold.

I should just turn around and go home. After everything Elise had done, he shouldn't be helping her. He shouldn't *want* to help her, but he'd given her his word all those weeks ago, and he wouldn't break it.

His stomach sank when he arrived at the warehouse and found Atlas's post empty. A man with one leg was sprawled outside one of the nearby houses, a ratty woolen blanket wrapped around his shoulders. He hacked and coughed as Tamriel approached.

"You know the guard who was stationed here?"

The man nodded and spat on the ground.

"When was the last time you saw him?"

"Few days ago. Went in an' didn't come back out."

"Was he sick?"

"Sure as everyone else is 'round here." The man offered him a toothless grin. "Unfortunate, isn't it?"

"It is. Thank you for the information." Tamriel pulled out his coin purse, but the man dismissed him with a wave.

"Don't want none a your coin, sir. Keep it to yourself, an' keep it outta sight."

"Are you sure there's nothing I can give you?"

"Nothin' the stronger, bigger bums won't take from me." He nodded to the warehouse. "Now scram. Someone's waitin' for you."

Tamriel turned and, after a moment of searching, spotted the silhouette of a person standing in one of the third-floor widows of the warehouse, watching him. He sucked in a breath. He couldn't make out anything more than the outline of her thin, angular body, but he'd recognize her anywhere.

Hero.

She's alive!

The putrid stench of disease hit him the second he pulled

the warehouse door open. A lone lantern hung from a hook across the room, illuminating the sick people lying in cots and huddling together on the floor. He glimpsed Ketojan's choppy white hair in the corner of the room. The elf noticed him a second later and straightened, wiping his hands on his pants as he crossed the room.

"What are you doing here?"

"Hello to you, too. I'm looking for the guard who was stationed outside. He's here, isn't he?"

"He is." Ketojan's eyes flitted to the floor above them. "Come on."

He led Tamriel up the stairs. When they reached the landing, Ketojan grabbed the lantern hanging from the bannister and picked his way around the cots and sick people slumbering on the floor, Tamriel close on his heels. He stopped beside a bed crammed in the corner of the room, a massive young man filling its rickety frame. His feet hung off the end, a stained beige blanket tangled around his legs.

"How much longer do you think he'll last?" Tamriel whispered, taking in the sores and boils marring Atlas's face and neck. The guard's eyelids fluttered at the sound of his voice.

"Not long now. Most don't last a week."

Atlas's chapped lips parted. His eyelids twitched again, then opened fully. "Your—" he croaked. "Your Hi—"

"Don't speak," Tamriel said softly. He glanced over his shoulder at Ketojan. "Can you fetch him some water?"

The elf padded silently across the room and returned a moment later with a dented tin cup full of water. Atlas's eyes widened when he saw it and he reached for it, but Tamriel pushed him back against the mattress and lifted the cup to the guard's lips. Atlas took a long, deep drink. Some of the water spilled over the lip of the cup and onto his soiled uniform, but he didn't seem to notice. Atlas's head dropped back onto the pillow.

"Your Highness," he groaned, grimacing. "What are... What are you doing here?"

"You didn't think I'd leave you here, did you?" Tamriel tried to smile, but he didn't quite manage it. He had known Atlas as long as he could remember. When they were children, Atlas had accompanied his sister to the castle every day, where they had helped their father with his work or played with Tamriel and Calum on the castle grounds. They'd spent entire days chasing each other through the hedge mazes. They'd raced across the manicured green lawn, swinging broken tree branches like swords as they reenacted legendary battles from the Year of One Night. "I'm going to take you back to the castle, my friend."

Atlas didn't seem to register his words. He peered over Tamriel's shoulder and frowned at Ketojan, his brows furrowing. "Am I dying?"

"No."

"Not yet," he corrected, his head dropping back onto the reeking mattress. His eyes drifted shut. "Soon."

Tamriel gripped his friend's hand tightly. "I won't let that happen. Do you hear me? As your friend and as your prince, I forbid you to die."

The boils on Atlas's cheeks pulled taut as his lips spread into a small smile. "Then I shall do my best to obey, Your Highness."

14

TAMRIEL

Ketojan disappeared up the stairs to fetch a change of clothes for Atlas and returned minutes later with Hero in tow. Together, the three of them helped the sluggish guard change into a too-short pair of pants and a worn shirt from Ketojan's wardrobe. They were much too small for Atlas, but they were clean, which more than made up for the size. Despite the waves of heat emanating from his fevered body, Atlas shivered so violently that Tamriel feared he would keel over before they even left the warehouse. He shrugged off his cloak and slipped it over the guard's shoulders.

"Thanks," Atlas mumbled. He took a step toward the stairs and stumbled, but Tamriel caught him before he could fall and slung the guard's arm over his shoulders.

"Lean on me."

"I'll squish you."

"I'm not the scrawny little boy I used to be," Tamriel said as they shuffled slowly through the maze of sickbeds. *Dear Creator, please don't let him fall,* he prayed when they reached the top of the rickety staircase. Despite his bravado, if Atlas tripped while they were descending, Tamriel wouldn't be strong enough to prevent them from tumbling all the way down.

"Neither am I," Atlas responded with a weak chuckle.

Tamriel snorted. "I doubt you've ever been called scrawny, you big oaf." Each step groaned under their weight. "What the hell do they feed you in the guard?"

By the time they reached the main floor, they were drenched in sweat, and Atlas's face had gone deathly pale. *Just a little farther,* Tamriel silently pleaded. With Hero and Ketojan's help, they picked their way through the warehouse and emerged outside. Tamriel and Atlas collapsed in the middle of the cobblestone road and sucked in lungfuls of clean air.

"Sweet Creator," Atlas mumbled. "I'd forgotten how much it stinks in there."

Tamriel swiped his sleeve across the perspiration on his forehead and forced himself to stand. "We're not done yet. Can you make it to the castle?"

"I'll try."

He turned to Hero and Ketojan. "Is there anything I can do to help you? Do you need food, clothes, money?"

Hero shook her head. "The cure," she said, the word slightly misshapen because of her missing tongue.

"We're doing everything we can."

She pressed a feather-light kiss to his cheek. Tamriel shot a stricken glance at Atlas, but the guard was too distracted by the sight of the one-legged man across the street to wonder how the prince had come to know two Beggars' End nobodies. "Go on."

TWENTY MINUTES LATER, TAMRIEL AND ATLAS SAT FACING each other in the carriage the guards had had waiting for them outside the End. The entire carriage jounced when they hit a rut. Atlas grimaced.

"We're working on a cure for the plague," Tamriel told him. His friend's wide shoulders were hunched, and he clutched the cloak tightly around himself, shivering. "We're going to heal you."

"Why? Why me? Why not the hundreds of helpless people in the End? You left them all behind. Don't you care about them?"

"Would I have risked my life in the Cirisor Islands if I did not care? Would I have risked the lives of my guards? The people of the End are my subjects, too, and I will do everything in my power to protect them."

The carriage turned a corner and the walls surrounding Myrellis Castle appeared before them. They rode through the gate, and Atlas peered out the windows at the gilded spires of the castle towers, the roofs flecked with chips of obsidian. "I was so certain I'd never see the outside of that warehouse again." He let the curtain fall back over the window, then said, "You never answered my question, though. Why me?"

Tamriel hesitated. He was not eager to tell Atlas about his sister's crimes. Learning of the death she would meet in a few short days would break Atlas's heart, and Tamriel wanted to spare his friend that pain as long as possible.

In the end, he merely said, "I made a promise to Elise."

He opened the door the second the carriage rolled to a stop before the castle steps. Atlas pulled the hood of his cloak over his head and clambered out of the carriage after him, trailing him up the steps and into the great hall.

A passing guard paused when he saw them, his brows furrowing. "Atlas, is that you? By the Creator, I thought you were dead. We all did."

"I may yet manage it," he rasped. "Don't tell anyone I'm here...or that I look like this."

"I won't, but—"

"On your way, Tanner," Tamriel said with a pointed look, and the guard hurried out of the room. He didn't need news spreading that a plague-infected guard was in the castle. He took Atlas's arm and escorted him toward the infirmary. They walked in silence for a while, until Atlas sighed softly as they descended the stairs to the castle's lower level.

"Were you ever told why Master Oliver assigned me to Beggars' End?" he asked in a quiet voice.

"I heard...rumors."

"Rumors. Right." Atlas let out a sharp, humorless laugh. "I've never dared to speak his name in the castle. I thought I was being so careful," he said. "Julien said it would never last."

"Julien," Tamriel repeated cautiously. Despite their many years of friendship, they'd never discussed the affliction that had haunted Atlas all his life. There had been whispers among the guard that Atlas was an Unnatural, as they called it, but there had never been any substance to the rumors—until Leitha Cain had stumbled upon the two young men holed up in one of the castle's many hidden alcoves a month and a half ago. "Have you seen him since...?"

"Since Leitha caught us? No, I was sent to Beggars' End immediately, and Julien was shipped off to guard the mines in Ospia that very day. The only reason Master Oliver kept me in the city was because my father is a seren. He tried to pretend it wasn't a punishment, but I know it was. He thought I could *change*." He spat the word, his voice trembling with pain and fatigue. "Everyone wants me to change."

"Even your family?"

He nodded. "My father especially. He pretends I was never born." They reached the bottom of the stairs and started toward the infirmary. When they passed a torch, Tamriel saw the hurt and bitterness in his old friend's eyes. "Don't you think if I could change, I would have? Do you think I enjoy being estranged from my family? Elise is the only one who still cares whether I live or die."

"She isn't the only one," Tamriel murmured, remembering the haggard look on Seren Pierce's face when he had learned his son was trapped inside Beggars' End.

When Atlas didn't respond, Tamriel allowed the topic to drop. *How could I not have seen it sooner?* he thought. *How could I not have done something to help?*

Although...he *had* known, hadn't he? When he was younger, he'd taken to watching the older boy at state functions, amused and bewildered by Atlas's complete lack of awareness of the pretty girls who vied for his attention. It hadn't taken him long to notice that Atlas's eyes always seemed to latch onto Leon and some of the other advisors' sons. He had thought Atlas's fascination was mere envy of the richer boys until one night about five years ago, when Leon had teased Atlas about never having been kissed. The young guard's face had flushed a bright crimson as he stammered out excuses. Calum, encouraged by the taunts of the other boys, had swaggered over, seized Atlas's face between his hands, and planted a fat, wet kiss on Atlas's mouth. Elise had shrieked and covered her eyes, while the other advisors' children had laughed so hard a few of them fell off their chairs.

"There," Calum had said after he'd pulled back, grinning smugly. "Now you've been kissed. I'm afraid no others will measure up."

Atlas had been so flustered he had burst into tears and bolted from the room. After that, he hadn't shown his face in the castle for a month.

Following the incident, Atlas had withdrawn from the other children. He still doted on Elise, still acknowledged Tamriel and Calum whenever they passed each other in the hall, but some invisible barrier had sprung up between them. Atlas began spending more time in the guards' barracks, throwing himself into his training with more resolve than ever. Tamriel had still occasionally caught Atlas watching some of the other recruits, but the boy had never acted on his desires.

That is, until Julien Bouchard enlisted six months ago.

Tamriel had heard the guards gossip about the new recruit when they thought no one was around. Julien Bouchard was the youngest son of a jeweler in Myrellis Plaza. Until he joined the guard, he'd made a habit of picking up odd jobs around the city, never managing to hold a position for more than a few months at a time. *I heard he fooled around with the cobbler's boy last spring,* one of the guards had whispered. *When the cobbler discovered them in his shop, he threw rubber soles at Julien and chased him into the street.* Tamriel hadn't cared about rumors—as long as it did not interfere with their jobs, he didn't care what the guards did in their personal time—but there were many in the country who still bore old prejudices.

When they reached the infirmary, Tamriel shoved open the door and they staggered through, startling Mercy and Nynev from their reading.

"Who is that?" Mercy asked as Tamriel helped Atlas to the nearest cot. The guard's hood fell off as he slumped onto the mattress, the wooden frame groaning under his weight. "Atlas?"

"Lady Marieve?" Atlas studied her through fevered eyes. "You're still here?"

"How much does he know?" she asked Tamriel. "About me. About us."

"Nothing."

"Why did you bring him here?"

"I thought Niamh could use someone to observe, to test treatments." After a pause, he added, "I couldn't leave him to die."

Mercy nodded and pressed a hand to Atlas's forehead,

being careful not to rub his raw, peeling skin. Her palm came away slick with sweat. "He's running a deadly fever. Nynev, mallowroot extract—top shelf." As the huntress searched for it, glass jars and bottles clinking, Mercy wetted a rag and placed it on Atlas's forehead. Then she filled a chipped ceramic mug with water and a few drops of mallowroot extract. "Drink," she commanded, holding it up to the guard's lips. He recoiled a bit from the concoction, but at a look from Mercy, he obliged.

"Thank you," he gasped.

"You're welcome." She offered him a fleeting smile. "Any friend of the prince is a friend of mine."

A bout of rattling coughs tore through Atlas's lungs. As Tamriel watched, Mercy plucked another vial from the shelf, uncorked it, and offered it to Atlas. "A tincture of starvay and evenberry. It'll ease your cough and help you sleep."

Again, he drank. Within a few minutes, his eyelids drooped. His labored breaths softened as he slipped into unconsciousness.

"Bringing him here could have killed him," Mercy said to Tamriel once Atlas finally fell asleep.

"Leaving him in that warehouse definitely would have," Tamriel responded, never taking his eyes off his friend. "Now, at least, we have a chance of saving him."

Nynev, who had been watching from the shelves, started toward the door. "I'll get Niamh. She and the healers can—"

"Your Highness?" someone called. A guardswoman stood in the open doorway, holding a rolled piece of paper in her gauntleted hand. "I've been searching everywhere for you. There's been an attack."

Tamriel stiffened. "Firesse?" Out of the corner of his eye, he saw Mercy's hands curl into fists.

She nodded. "They marched on Fishers' Cross. They slaughtered everyone."

"They *what?*" The news hit him like a blow to the gut. "What of the troops my father sent?"

"Still on the road to Cirisor, Your Highness. We did not anticipate that the elves would strike so quickly. We've sent word to our men, but the raven will not arrive for another day or two." She extended the note once more. "This arrived half an hour ago."

Mercy accepted the paper. Tamriel watched her brown-gold eyes skim the note and widen. She passed it to him without a word.

Three sentences were scrawled across the slip of paper:

Firesse has gathered twelve hundred soldiers. Fishers' Cross will fall first. Calum is alive.

—Dayna

Tamriel stared at the note, uncertain which revelation was most shocking: that Mercy's parents survived their return to *Ialathan*, that Firesse had managed to swell her ranks to thrice what they were before, or that Calum was alive. "How many people were killed in the attack?"

"Master Adan estimates about fifty in all. It may be more if slaves were caught in the crossfire."

Tamriel stilled, anger threatening to choke him. "I'll speak to my father in a moment," he said tightly. "You are dismissed."

The second the door to the infirmary closed behind the guard, Mercy murmured, "Tam—"

"Fifty people! Calum helped her murder fifty innocent people—*my* people." His fury, his helplessness, overtook him. He walked across the room and shoved every Creator-damned book in that useless, teetering pile off the desk. The covers flew open, pages fluttering as they fell and splayed open on the floor at his feet. He clenched his injured hands into fists, breathing hard.

"Firesse will burn in hell for all she's done," Nynev whispered, startling him. She'd been so quiet he'd forgotten she was there.

"She and all who follow her," Mercy agreed.

"Did the note say anything about Isolde?" the huntress asked.

"No." In the wake of everything, Tamriel had almost forgotten about Niamh's love, who they had left in the Islands after she'd sustained a nasty wound during their escape. "I'm sure Dayna would have mentioned if she hadn't survived."

He closed his eyes.

"Hey. Look at me," Mercy said. She grabbed his arm, and when he finally met her gaze, expecting her to be furious at him for undoing days' worth of work, her amber eyes—usually so sharp, so piercing—were full of sorrow. "Whatever we must do, we will see Firesse brought to justice for the crimes she has committed."

"Haven't you learned anything in your time here? Justice abandoned this city long ago."

Her grip on him tightened. Something darker than sorrow and infinitely more terrifying passed across her face: resolve—the promise of retribution. "Then we'll just have to mete it out ourselves."

Nynev stepped forward, picking her way through the mess of broken books littering the floor, and crouched to peer at a paper that had fallen from one of the tomes. "I'll be damned." She held it up for Tamriel and Mercy to see. When the light from the hearth illuminated the drawing in the middle of the page, Tamriel couldn't quite believe what he saw there.

Cedikra.

15

CALUM

When Drake arrived at the workshop the next morning, the rest of the Strykers were already hard at work crafting weapons for the Cirisians. True to her word, Firesse had provided the supplies they needed. The pile of spears beside the door grew steadily as Amir affixed long, barbed blades to the end of each shaft. Beside him, Oren hammered red-hot steel into daggers. The cool water hissed as he tempered each knife.

Nerran dumped a handful of arrows into a bucket, then wiped his forehead with a sleeve. He raised a brow at Drake. "Good morning, dear. Enjoy your beauty sleep?"

"Immensely."

"Have you seen Hewlin this morning? The man's been stomping around with a glower for hours."

"If you'd slept as poorly as he had, you'd be grumpy, too," Amir cut in. "Something kept him tossing and turning all night long."

Nerran rolled his eyes. "Please—you were dead to the world the minute you collapsed into bed."

"Exactly. His snoring usually keeps me up all night. *That's* how I know he didn't sleep."

"Maybe it was bedbugs," Oren suggested with a shudder. "I think one bit me last night."

"Those are just your fleas."

"I *don't* have fleas."

The door banged open and they fell silent as Hewlin strode through, scowling. The blacksmith ignored Drake completely and fixed the three other men with his stern, cold gaze. "I hope you were able to get some work done while you were standing around gossiping like a bunch of old crones." He pushed past Amir and Oren and examined one of the spears they'd crafted. "Good," he said, weighing it in his hands. "Make as many as you can with the supplies in this shop. Firesse's people need weapons, and I've vowed to provide them." At last, his dark eyes slid to Drake, and Calum could see the residual rage burning in their depths.

The Strykers wordlessly resumed their work. Calum hoped that none of the men had noticed the shadow flit across Hewlin's face when he had finally deigned to meet his eyes. He couldn't stop picturing the horror on his mentor's face as he had watched his skin split and peel at Firesse's touch. If she'd let the infection go any farther, she would have killed him, and the blood would be on Calum's hands. It was his fault the Strykers were here.

Firesse has power over the plague. For the millionth time, the revelation slipped unbidden through Calum's mind. *She can control it.*

But how? Why?

He remembered the day the guards had quarantined Beggars' End, and the panic and chaos that had ensued after news of the plague had spread. Hundreds of citizens had gathered outside the city gates, clamoring to purge the slums. If Firesse was truly behind the outbreak, why had she chosen to target the elves in Beggars' End first? What could she hope to gain by killing her own people?

Calum was so consumed by his worries that he didn't realize the sun had gone down until a loud, pounding drum beat pulsed from the center of the camp, startling him from his thoughts. Drake paused, his hammer caught mid-swing.

"What's happening?" Oren asked as, outside, several elves began shouting in Cirisian. He turned to Drake, eyes wide. "What are they doing? W-What are they yelling about?"

"I don't know." He crossed to the window and peered out at the dozens of Cirisians running from house to house, hastily donning their mismatched leather and plate mail. "But I think there's going to be a battle."

"A—battle? Creator save us."

There was a thump behind him, and Drake turned to see Oren slumped against one of the worktables, a cold sweat across his brow. The poor man was trembling so hard his knees looked like they'd give out at any moment.

He gets seizures, Calum whispered quickly, panic for his friend overriding his animosity toward Drake. *They come faster when he's stressed. Help him, please.*

"Nerran, grab that stool," Drake ordered. "Oren, sit." He schooled his features into an expression of concern, invisible tendrils prodding around Calum's memories until he found the one for which he'd been searching. "You haven't neglected your treatment, have you? Did you run out of Lusus blossoms?"

Oren shook his head. His eyes went unfocused for a moment as he nearly gave in to unconsciousness. Outside, the elves kept shouting to one another over the pounding of the drums.

"Hang on, friend," Hewlin murmured. He placed a hand on Oren's shoulder and pulled him upright when he began to slump off the stool. "Breathe deeply. Hang in there. Don't let it take hold."

"Has he been taking his medication?" Drake snapped to Amir, impatient now.

The blacksmith nodded. "We stocked up when we left Castle Rising."

Firesse arrived then, looking frazzled. Her hair was wild, half of her braids hanging free around her face, and the belt with her sheathed dagger hung low around her hips. She was clad in the fighting leathers Hewlin had repaired for her back in the Islands. "My scouts spotted a troop of Beltharan soldiers headed toward the Islands. We're going to intercept them before they reach the archipelago. Strykers, I need you to distribute the weapons you've made so far. Calum, join my ranks once you've finished helping them. I need you."

In the back of the shop, Oren let out a groan. Nerran and Hewlin stretched him out on one of the worktables as his eyes rolled back and tremors wracked his body. Amir forced a strip of leather into his mouth to keep him from biting his tongue.

Firesse's brows drew low. "What's wrong with him?"

"A seizure. He'll be fine in a few minutes."

"And you? You'll join the fight?" She wrung her hands, then leaned close, lowering her voice. "We were supposed to have more time. The Beltharans weren't supposed to mobilize so quickly." She bit her lip. "I don't know if my people are ready."

You should have considered that before you chose to invade, Calum thought darkly.

"They've been practicing their drills. Kaius, Myris, and I are fine teachers." Drake offered her a crooked, charming smile—the kind he must have flashed to all the pretty noblewomen in his youth—and Firesse seemed to calm. "I'll be at your side when we face my countrymen. How many?"

"Six hundred."

"Then you outnumber them two-to-one." He crossed the room and plucked two daggers from the chest of weapons Oren had made, tucking them into his belt. Then he grabbed a spear from the far wall. The shaft was longer than he was tall, and the spearhead had been crafted with a serrated edge to cause as much damage as possible to its target. The cold rush of Drake's anticipation danced down Calum's spine. *Let the slaughter begin,* Drake purred.

"And just what do you expect us to do while you're off fighting?" Hewlin asked, accusation thick in his voice. Calum inwardly flinched, recalling what Hewlin had said the night before: *The Calum I knew would never have agreed to this.* On the table between them, Oren had ceased shaking, but he was still unconscious, a thin trickle of saliva dribbling out of the corner of his mouth.

"Do as the First commanded! Distribute weapons, then get back to work. If we run out, everyone without a weapon will just have to be creative." When Firesse stiffened, Drake turned to her, smiling. "Don't worry. We'll teach those humans the cost of crossing you."

She took a deep breath, adjusted her armor one final time, then picked up a sword from the nearest table. She examined the razor-sharp blade as, in the distance, the drum beat grew faster and louder, pulsing like the beat of a heart. "Don your armor," she commanded, every hint of her fear trampled down, locked away. The scared little girl was gone, and the First of the most fearsome clan in the Islands stood in her place. "The battle begins in an hour."

What a sad, desperate bunch we must appear to the Beltharan soldiers, Calum thought as Drake marched onto the plain that was soon to become a killing field. The elves looked like children playing at war—their leather armor worn, their stolen steel ill-fitting and bearing the crests of the Beltharan and Feyndaran royal families. Before they left Fishers' Cross, Drake had helped the Strykers outfit the elves with the new Stryker-made weapons—a dozen daggers, two dozen spears, and nearly fifty arrows. It wasn't much, but it was more than they'd had before Hewlin and the others arrived. Firesse, Kaius, Myris, and the other Firsts were armed with the finest blades. The rest of the elves carried bows and arrows, swords they'd collected during the Cirisian Wars, or knives they'd pilfered from the village.

Across the plain, Ghyslain's soldiers stood in perfect rows, their armor shining under the light of the stars twinkling overhead. Each man and woman carried a sword and shield, and nearly one-quarter of the troops were cavalry, Drake noted with some concern. If not for Firesse's supernatural powers, the elves wouldn't stand a chance.

The Beltharan commander shouted something to his soldiers, and they responded with a rallying cry of their own. The elf beside Drake began to tremble.

"Stand still," he snapped, and the woman instantly stilled, her knuckles white around the grip of her sword.

Firesse, Kaius, and Myris wandered together down the rows of their newly-trained soldiers, shouting commands and encouragement. When she reached the front lines, Firesse paused and began speaking in Cirisian—something about redeeming their ancestors, if what little Cirisian Calum had picked up over the past few weeks was to be trusted. Although, in truth, she could be describing how to make a ham sandwich in painstaking detail and he'd be none the wiser.

Drake glanced to the side, and Calum used the opportunity to study the elves around him. He noticed the woman with jet-black hair almost immediately; she stood a few rows in front of him, her unmistakable wild curls like a mane around her head.

Dayna—his mother.

The man beside her, tall and stoic, was undoubtedly Mercy's father. They had been Drake's slaves for years, yet it seemed their former owner failed to recognize them, for his eyes glided past without a pause.

After Firesse finished her speech and started down the line to where Faye and the Firsts waited, Calum whispered, *Please tell me you'll endeavor to not get me killed.*

Have some faith in your father, my dear boy, his father crooned.

"*Ajo!*" Kaius shouted, and the archers nocked their arrows, arrowheads glinting in the moonlight as they took aim at the Beltharans. Across the plain, the human soldiers followed suit. The woman beside Drake lowered her head and murmured a prayer under her breath.

"*Retalla!*" Kaius commanded, and the archers loosed their arrows. They soared through the air, whistling, as the archers scrambled to nock the next round. The Beltharans fired a moment later.

An elven man screamed when an arrow pierced his chest. He fell, blood bubbling over his lips. The woman beside him shrieked and jumped back, straight into the path of another arrow. It tore through her throat, and she crumpled.

All around Drake, the Cirisians were falling out of line, panicking amid the arrows that fell upon them like rain. Without the natural cover of the Islands' wilderness, they were open targets, easy pickings, and they knew it. Calum could hear Firesse yelling, but her words were lost in the cacophony of terrified voices.

"Fall back!" Lysander shouted from somewhere to his

right. The elves of his clan surged toward him, crying out when arrows pierced flesh.

Drake shoved his way through the chaos and grabbed the First by the arm, yanking him close. With his other hand, he pressed the point of his dagger to Lysander's side through a gap in the elf's armor. The First's eyes widened. "Order your men to hold their position," he growled, pricking the man with the dagger.

Chin wobbling, the elf obeyed.

"*Retalla!*" Kaius shouted again, and the archers fired another volley. Across the field, most of the Beltharans deflected the arrows with their shields, but a few stumbled and fell when bolts hit their marks.

"Go!" Firesse screamed. "Advance!"

"Go, go, go!" Drake cried. He lifted his spear and rushed forward with the surge of elves. Their faces blurred as they ran, their intricate tattoos blending into one another in the darkness. Calum caught glimpses of Firesse's leather armor, Kaius's bronze skin, Faye's dark locks, but they vanished a second later.

"Release!" the Beltharan commander ordered. Another wave of arrows rained down upon Drake and the elves. When the elf in front of him collapsed, an arrow sticking out of his chest, Drake merely leapt over the body, pushing himself faster.

The Beltharans rushed forward. The two sides met in a crash of steel, swords clanging, blades scraping against armor. Cries of pain filled the air. Drake thrusted his spear upward and caught a Beltharan in the throat. The man swayed and slashed weakly with his sword as blood painted his armor crimson. He fell.

Dead.

One by one, Calum's countrymen fell to his father's blood-coated spear, dead before they hit the ground. Drake hissed when a sword grazed his arm. He turned and shoved his spearhead through the offending soldier's eye. The man wailed, and a quick jab of one of Drake's daggers through a gap in his mail sent him to his knees. Drake yanked the spearhead out of the soldier's eye, hot blood spraying across his face.

Another soldier dead.

Someone bumped Drake's shoulder. He whirled around, trading his spear for daggers, only to see an elven kid staggering toward him, one hand on the hilt of the knife protruding from his stomach. *Ivris,* Calum realized—the boy who had sailed with them from the Islands. His leather armor was coated with blood.

"*Help,*" he croaked, reaching a trembling, bloodied hand toward Drake. His eyes were wide, bright with fear. "*Help me.*"

He crumpled and did not stand up again.

He couldn't have been a day over fourteen.

Faye appeared beside him, speckled with blood. "The elves are losing," she shouted over the sounds of steel meeting steel. She ducked under the arc of a Beltharan's sword and dispatched him with a flick of her wrist, a throwing knife embedded in his jugular. "You could run, Calum."

"If only it were that simple," Drake yelled back.

The Cirisians were slowing, tiring and dying quickly. They weren't used to battles. Despite many being adept fighters—lashing out and dancing back so quickly Calum could hardly keep track of them—they were better suited to Island skirmishes than fights in an open, unprotected field. When Drake paused, searching for another target, he realized that Faye was right—the Cirisian troops were dwindling. They still outnumbered the humans, but Firesse was rapidly losing more soldiers than she could afford. The once-green field was now littered with bodies, blood and gore leaking out and turning the earth slick under Drake's feet.

The rebellion could die right here, right now, Calum realized with a burst of hope. *This could be the end.*

Then a cry rang out over the chaos and Calum recognized the sound of one of Firesse's guttural, ancient incantations.

For a moment, nothing happened.

Then, slowly, the corpses around him began to rise. Calum watched in horror as they clambered to their feet, their eyes empty, and attacked the nearest Beltharan soldiers.

"What the hell?" one of the humans gasped a second before his reanimated comrade shoved a sword through his stomach. A few yards away, an elf with a gaping wound in his stomach slashed at a soldier's arm, cutting through the bone just below the elbow. The human screamed and slipped in the blood-slick grass in his attempt to retreat. He clutched the stump of his arm to his chest, his cries of pain swiftly cut off when the elf dragged his blade across the man's throat.

The slaughter was happening all around him. The Cirisians and the dead worked together to dispatch the horrified, terrified Beltharans, who could do nothing but gape as their fallen friends turned their blades on men they had fought beside not five minutes before.

Before Calum could fully comprehend what had happened, the battle was won.

The Beltharans were dead.

Across the field, surrounded by her horde of living and undead soldiers, Firesse lowered her sword and wiped the blood from her face. Her hair was matted with it, but her eyes were bright with victory.

"*T'veja*," she said, her voice carrying over the unearthly silence that had settled on the battlefield. *Leave us.*

One by one, the undead soldiers dropped to the ground. They made no sound except for the soft *whump* of their bodies hitting the earth.

Slowly, the Cirisian survivors gathered in the center of the field, studying their leader with a mixture of terror and reverence on their gore-coated faces. "*Blessed*," they murmured to one another. "*Myrbellanar's Chosen*."

Firesse smiled at them. "We... We did it," she said, her trembling voice raw and full of amazement.

Then her eyes rolled back in her head, and she collapsed.

16

CALUM

Kaius scooped her up in his arms, cradling her gently. "Archers, gather every weapon you can find. Gods know we need them. Fighters, search for survivors among our fallen. Slit the throats of any humans who are still alive. The rest of you, return to Fishers' Cross and tend to the wounded." His expression was cool, collected, but Calum could see the effort it took to maintain his calm façade. Firesse's breathing was shallow. Her face, tucked against his chest, was pale under the layers of blood and grime. "You," he said as he brushed past Drake, "are coming with me."

"Yes, sir." He helped Kaius pull Firesse onto his horse—one of the few they'd found in Fishers' Cross after the attack—then mounted his own. They rode as quickly as Kaius dared, and soon burst through the doorway of Firesse's house.

"Clear the table."

Drake did as he said, shoving bowls and papers to the ground, then the archer gingerly lay Firesse down on the kitchen table. Kaius hardly seemed to breathe as he began removing her armor, searching for a wound. Calum did not fail to notice that the elf's hands were trembling.

Kaius swore under his breath, fumbling with one of the straps. "I can't tell how much of this blood is hers." When he finally loosened the strap, he tossed the chestpiece aside and ran his fingers across her ribcage, her stomach, her sides. "She's unharmed," he sighed a moment later. "Not so much as a scratch on her."

"The magic made her weak, then?" A shudder went through Calum. Summoning Drake and Liselle from the Beyond had been intimidating enough. Now that she could turn the fallen soldiers against the Beltharans, now that she could raise an army who couldn't fall to blades or arrows, how could the Cirisians possibly lose?

"She wasn't supposed to risk it yet. The ritual she uses to wield Myrbellanar's abilities draws her closer to the other Old Gods, but she's still mortal. Our bodies were not intended to contain the power of deities." He let out another string of curses. "She may die."

And, hopefully, her rebellion with her. Without her magic, they would never stand a chance against the Beltharans.

Someone knocked on the door.

"*Na t'enja,*" Kaius snapped, stepping in front of Firesse.

"I don't speak Cirisian," Nerran called as he opened the door, "so I'm going to assume that means 'enter.'" He froze the second his eyes landed on Firesse's still form. He took in the blood coating her, the table, and Drake and Kaius, his nose wrinkling at the coppery tang in the air. "Is she dead?"

"No."

He nodded, his gaze never straying from the girl. "I came to tell you we've run out of iron. We can't craft anything new unless we find more in another town."

Kaius dismissed him with a wave. "We'll find some."

"Okay. And..." Nerran turned to Drake then, studying him as if he was not quite sure he recognized the man standing before him. "May I have a word in private?"

Drake followed him out into the street. As soon as they were out of Kaius's earshot, Nerran whirled on him. "Care to explain this?"

"I explained everything when you arrived in the Islands. You know why I have to help her."

"You're willing to do all this to avenge your father? Look at you, mate!" He gestured to the blood and dirt caked on Drake's boots, the scratches in his armor, the shallow gash in his arm. "Who *are* you?"

Drake rolled his eyes, a lazy grin playing across his lips. "Don't play that game. You know me."

"I know Calum Vanos, a smug, charming, promising young smith. He's my friend. I don't see him when I look at you." He ran a hand down his haggard face. "I understand that you hate the king. What he did to your father was despicable—unforgivable. But leading an army to his doorstep? You would really shed so much innocent blood for revenge?"

No! Calum cried, desperate to make his friend see the truth, but his traitorous lips did not obey.

"I do what must be done," his father said instead.

"Don't do that, mate. Not with me. Don't pretend you're blameless in this." Nerran pointed an angry finger down the road, where Firesse's soldiers had begun to trickle into the village. "Is killing Ghyslain worth risking all these people's lives? Is it worth all the people who have already died?"

Drake narrowed his eyes, and Calum could feel his father's patience reaching the end of its rope. "It is worth these people's lives and more."

Nerran staggered back as though struck. "Hewlin was right. You've changed."

"Maybe I've been like this all along. Maybe I was only pretending before. Maybe I missed my calling as an actor."

He shook his head. "I'm sorry, mate. I'm sorry I didn't see it sooner." He started back toward the house the Strykers share, then stopped. "I didn't just come to tell Kaius about the iron," he said without turning back. "I saw you ride back and thought you might want to know that Oren's okay. He's resting now. I guess the stress of traveling with the Cirisians is really getting to him." Without waiting for a response, he crossed the street and slammed the door to the Strykers' house behind him.

Drake watched him leave, then turned toward the cliff overlooking the village. Beyond the lip of the bluff, a spot of orange light shone faintly in the distance—the fire Myris's fighters had built to burn their dead. Black smoke rose into the night sky, blotting out some of the stars.

Two elves shuffled past him, their heads bowed as they whispered in Cirisian. Dayna clutched the bandages wrapped around her chest, the white linen stained red from a wound near her ribs. Despite the fatigue on Mercy's father's face, he supported Dayna's weight as she hobbled along beside him, trembling violently. *Do you recognize them?* Calum whispered to his father. *They were your slaves once. After you helped murder Liselle, after you died, they fled to Cirisor. They survived. They're not yours to torment anymore.* When Dayna looked up and met his eyes, he could swear she saw past Drake and looked straight at him.

Firesse awoke early the next morning and sent Kaius to gather her generals—Drake, Myris, and the other Firsts—in her house. They arrived to find the window shutters latched, a lone candle burning on the kitchen table. Its flame cast long, shifting shadows on the floor as Lysander paced.

"Stop fidgeting," Firesse said, but she was too exhausted to put any bite behind the words. She was slumped in the chair at the head of the table, the light from the candle sharpening her features, deepening the hollows of her cheeks. Kaius and Myris flanked her on either side, wearing identical worried expressions.

"That was a slaughter. That *should* have been a slaughter. What you did with those—those *things*..." The First shuddered and dropped into a chair. "That was unnatural."

"I know. It nearly killed me."

"You cannot try it again," Kaius blurted. "Not until you regain your strength. It was foolish enough to attempt it last night—"

"I did it to save my men," she interrupted with a sharp glare at the archer. "I would do it again if the situation demanded it."

Kaius frowned but remained silent.

"How many dead?" Drake asked.

"A third of our forces," Myris replied, her mouth set in a grim line. "No Beltharan survivors. We've bought ourselves a little time, but the king will soon send more soldiers. We must be better prepared for the next battle."

"The next battle will end us!" Amyris argued. "I'll not allow some girl to bring about the decimation of all our clans. We should return to the Islands and pray the king does not purge our land when he learns of the massacre of his men."

"Some girl?" Firesse echoed. "Some girl who raised the dead to save your hide?" She pinned each of the Firsts with a glare. "I should think you'd be grateful, yet here you sit, suggesting a retreat. What will you do when the king sends his soldiers to our Islands? Will you cower before his men while they slaughter your families? Will you stand aside while they rape and enslave your women?

"Turning back is not an option. We fight and win, or we retreat and forget the crimes they have committed against our kind for generations." She pushed to her feet with a grimace.

"But you are correct. No matter how much my soldiers train, they will never be able to match the Beltharans' prowess on the battlefield. We don't have the numbers or the time. Fortunately, I did not come here to conquer the king's land. I have no need for battles or sieges. I came here to avenge our ancestors and to free those who still bear the bonds of slavery.

"When the Daughters arrive, we are going to divide our forces. Each of you shall lead a troop of soldiers and Assassins." Her lips curled into a smirk, a hint of that mischievous sparkle returning to her bloodshot eyes. "We're going to deal the king a blow he won't soon forget."

TWO DAYS LATER, FLECKS OF ASH STILL FELL LIKE snowflakes from the sky—remnants of the bodies the fighters burned after the battle—and covered the village's dirt road in a light dusting. When Drake left the house he shared with the Strykers, he caught a glimpse of the shore, the sand and shallows tinged black with soot. He was halfway to the workshop when a shout rang out from somewhere beyond the bluff. A cheer followed. Moments later, hoofbeats thundered down the road.

"*Donahe-jva!*" the rider yelled. "The Daughters have arrived!"

The soldiers who had been training beside the docks wandered over, craning their necks for a glimpse of the infamous Assassins. Curious elves began to line the lip of the cliff and gather along the road. Hewlin and the Strykers filed out of the workroom, blinking against the bright sunlight. Oren spotted Drake and waved him over.

"I never thought they'd actually come," he whispered once Drake had reached him. "Between our weapons, Firesse's powers, and the Daughters' skill, they might actually stand a chance of making it to the capital."

That what I'm afraid of.

"Is what they said about the battle true?" He swallowed and lowered his voice. "She can raise the dead?"

"That's not all she can do," Hewlin murmured.

Across the street, Firesse stepped out of her house, Kaius trailing behind her. She'd regained most of her strength, but Calum doubted she'd risk using her powers anytime soon for fear of losing more than just consciousness. As she went to speak with the scout, the Cirisians and liberated slaves she passed bowed their heads in respect. Since the battle, they'd begun calling her '*Lo Benii*'—the Blessed One.

A few minutes later, fifteen Daughters rode into the village, led by a cloaked figure who could be none other than Mother Illynor. Half of the Assassins were disguised in rough-spun tunics and patched linen pants, like the poor workers who tilled the fields of the agricultural sector. The other half were dressed as merchants, driving wagons laden with fruits and vegetables, dried meats, bolts of fabric, and brightly painted wooden toys. A disguise—and a clever way to make coin along the road.

Illynor dismounted her horse with a grace uncharacteristic of the Qadar. When she lowered the hood of her cloak, her green, brown, and gold scales glimmered in the sunlight. At a flick of her wrist, the Daughters dismounted and gathered behind her.

"Firesse really thinks fifteen Assassins will turn the tide of the war?" Nerran asked, then hissed when Amir elbowed him sharply.

"Keep your voice down, lest you find yourself on the pointy end of one of their swords. You've seen the way they fight."

"Mother Illynor," Firesse said loudly, grinning. "I am

honored you have decided to join our war against the mad king."

"As you should be." The headmistress of the Guild cast an appraising eye over the girl before her, then the elves watching from the sides of the road and the top of the cliff. A few straightened their shoulders and stared right back at her, while others withered under her heavy gaze. "Let us speak in private."

Drake leaned against the counter in Firesse's kitchen, watching Firesse and Illynor study each other from opposite ends of the table. Kaius, Myris, and the other Firsts milled about in silence, waiting for one of the women to speak.

"Now that you've joined us—" Firesse began.

"How old are you?" Illynor interrupted. Her slitted eyes flicked to Drake. "Calum did not mention in his letter that we'd be following a child into battle."

"Old enough to know what must be done to protect my people."

"Just ensure that your ambition does not make you rash." She leaned forward, propping her elbows on the table, and turned her attention to Drake. "You visited my Keep at spring's-end, did you not? You brought me a contract from the king you now seek to destroy."

"Yes," he responded curtly. "Long ago, he hired your Assassins to kill my father, and I want revenge."

"So long as you keep your sights set on Ghyslain, and not on my Daughters. Business is business—we were paid to complete a contract, so that's what we did. Speaking of business," she said, glancing back at Firesse, "my girls are not your soldiers. They shall remain under my command. You and I are partners—equals. When we reach the capital and deliver you your mad king, you'll pay us the rate you promised in your letter and we'll go our separate ways."

"I thought only royals were allowed to buy a contract on another royal," Ivani said, piping up for the first time. "Cirisor has no ruling house."

"Under normal circumstances, that is true. But these are hardly normal circumstances, wouldn't you say? This is war," she said. "This brings me to my next condition. When we arrive in Sandori, I want Mercy. She is not to be harmed in the fighting. After we kill the prince, I'll deal with her myself."

Kill the—? Calum's world tilted on its axis. *Tamriel is alive? H-He wasn't killed by Lylia? But Firesse said—*

She lied to you, Drake responded coolly.

Why? Dangerous, dangerous hope bloomed within him. If he could somehow break free of his father's grasp, warn Tamriel what was going to happen...

It's easier to gain control of someone whose spirit is broken, along with his body. You'll always belong to me, my dear son.

I used to think so, but you've just given me someone to fight for.

Firesse's voice cut through their silent conversation. "Agreed."

Drake shot upright. "You promised me the prince." Images flickered through Calum's mind—his father's memories from before he'd been summoned from the Beyond. Tamriel had been Drake's price for helping her in the war; what better way to take his revenge on Ghyslain than by forcing him to watch his only child's life slowly bleed out?

"As long as Tamriel Myrellis is dead before we leave the capital, I don't care who deals the killing blow," Illynor conceded. She raised a brow to Firesse. "What is the plan?"

Drake stepped forward and spread a map of Beltharos on the table. "The king's highway is the only direct route from the capital to the Islands, and Ghyslain's soldiers will have to follow it if they don't want to risk crossing the flooded rivers and losing half their supplies. That means we'll have a rough idea where they are most of the time, and scouts can confirm their location. Luckily, since we don't have cavalry, we can move much more stealthily about the sector. We don't have the numbers to attack in force, so we're going to do what the Daughters do best—strike from the shadows."

"We're going to divide the army," Firesse continued. "You and the Daughters will lead a few groups, and Kaius, Myris, and the other Firsts will command the rest until we meet up outside the capital. It'll be easier to evade the Beltharan troops and city guards if we're separated. Plus, smaller groups will allow us to use the natural features of the land for cover. That's *my* people's specialty."

Illynor pursed her lips in thought. "How will you ensure everyone arrives in Sandori at the same time?"

"We're going to plan the routes before we split up. If an attack goes sour, that group will get out and move to the next position as quickly as possible. We'll have to select a meeting point outside the city."

Illynor pointed to a spot on the map. "I have a contact outside Knia Valley—that's the last village between here and Sandori. Look for our emblem on the sign of the locksmith's shop and leave a note with the man inside. We'll find you."

"You really think this will work?" Firesse asked, practically bouncing in her chair. Her mask slipped, and Calum could see the young girl she should have been—uncertain and hungry for approval. Then she remembered where she was, that she was supposed to be their confident leader, and she stilled. "I mean, of course it will work."

"As long as you honor our deal, you have our aid," Mother Illynor vowed.

After discussing a few more details, Firesse dismissed

them so she could speak with the Guildmother in private. Drake was the last to leave, and he was halfway to the house he shared with the Strykers when a bird squawked loudly overhead.

A raven soared through the sky and perched on the post of the nearest dock. It cocked its head as Drake approached, its beady eyes following his every move. Drake spotted the small metal canister affixed to one of the bird's legs and grinned. "Do you have a message for me, friend?"

It squawked again.

He flipped open the lid of the canister and pulled out the rolled piece of parchment. The bird took off immediately. His lips curled into a smirk as he scanned the short, hastily-written note.

Do not engage the Cirisians under any circumstance. Reinforcements are on their way. Do. Not. Engage. Await further instructions.
—Master Adan

Drake laughed and crumpled up the paper. If he squinted, he can just barely see the raven in the distance, a perfect little spot of darkness against the blue sky. "If only you'd flown a little faster." He dropped the note and ground it into the dirt with the toe of his shoe. "Maybe the king's men would still be alive."

17
MERCY

"Have we done it? Is this all we needed for the cure?" Nynev breathed, staring down at the drawing of Cedikra in her hands.

"No, but it's a very, *very* good start." Mercy stepped carefully over the broken glass littering the floor and read over the huntress's shoulder: "'Cedikra. Found in the Cirisor archipelago and the southern rim of Gyr'malr. Poisonous, but may be used to cleanse infections and reduce inflammation with the addition of starvay blossoms to neutralize the toxins.'" She paused and looked up at Nynev. "Starvay blossoms? But they're useless. They're no better than weeds. You could go out to the plains and pick hundreds of them without making a dent. If this works..."

For a moment, they simply stared at each other in disbelief, Atlas's soft snores rumbling in the background.

Then, Tamriel grinned. "You always said we'd find something. I should have believed you."

"Is this the part where I get to say 'I told you so?'"

He laughed. "I suppose it is."

"I told you so."

"Well, what are you waiting for?" Nynev gestured to the door. "Niamh's working with the healers as we speak. Go. I'll stay here with the guard." She moved to the desk and pulled out the box of potential cures Mercy and Niamh had made days before, the vials clinking as she lifted it out of the drawer. "Take these, too." Nynev shoved them out the door, practically slamming it on their heels.

Tamriel glanced helplessly at the box she'd shoved into his arms, then down the hallway. "I still have to meet with my father about Fishers' Cross."

"Go on. I'll speak with the healers."

After he left, Mercy wandered the first floor of the castle until she found a guard who could direct her to the room where the healers were working. It had once been a grand dining hall, but now the massive table was covered in papers, vials, jars, bundles of dried herbs, and bright, colorful pills and powders. All of the red-and-gold brocade chairs had been shoved against the far wall, half of them bearing stacks of ancient-looking medical books like those in the infirmary. Tabris and three other healers were huddled at the end of the table. They muttered amongst themselves and pointed to passages in the books spread out before them.

Niamh stood beside them, a foot of space between her and Tabris. Even with the makeup hiding her Cirisian tattoos, she looked unbearably uncomfortable in the presence of the healers. She straightened the second she saw Mercy. "Oh, thank the gods," she sighed, startling the healers out of their argument. "Please tell me you have good news."

Mercy held up the paper with the drawing of Cedikra, and Niamh's jaw dropped.

"Is that...?"

Mercy nodded. "One step closer to the cure. We even have a sick guard downstairs for you to study. We can test the treatments on him once he's rested."

Niamh let out a sharp breath, relief softening her features. "Then let's get to work."

OVER THE NEXT FEW HOURS, THEY HAULED CRATES AND chests of Cedikra from the infirmary with the help of some off-duty guards and began preparing more possible cures. They started with recipes from Alyss's notes—what little they could decipher from the scribbles—and moved on to poultices and tonics from books of medical treatments. By the time they took a break for dinner, their hands aching from peeling, slicing, and mashing the strange fruit, Mercy felt truly hopeful for the first time in weeks.

"I can't believe we may soon have a cure," Niamh said as they dined on plates of roasted rabbit swimming in sweet plum sauce. She nibbled on a leg, then licked the thick sauce off her fingers. "I cannot wait to be home...although I must say I will miss the food."

"It is magnificent, isn't it?" Mercy said, then frowned, unable to keep her worries at bay for long. "We still don't know how much Cedikra is needed to cure the plague, though. I doubt we have enough to cure all the sick in Sandori, let alone Beltharos."

"Still, a limited supply is better than no cure at all. The king can send ships to Gyr'malr to collect more, can't he?"

"He can," she conceded, "but the trip may take more time than we can afford."

Niamh dropped the piece of rabbit she'd been eating onto her plate, half of the meat still hanging from the bone. "I don't have much of an appetite anymore."

"Sorry."

"Don't be. I haven't been eating much since we left the Islands."

"Do you want to talk about it?"

"It's... It's Isolde," she sighed. "I miss her so much, it physically hurts. She was my first friend after Mama brought Nynev and me to the Islands. She was my first...everything." She blushed and lowered her voice, glancing sheepishly at the healers seated at the opposite end of the table. None of them seemed to be the slightest bit aware of the girls' presence, each of their noses stuck in a book while they ate. "I just... I just left her behind. She was in shock; she didn't even know what was happening. If something went wrong... I would never forgive myself for leaving her like that."

"I'm sure she's fine. Dayna didn't mention anything about her in the note she sent. No news is good news, right?"

"I suppose," she muttered, but she looked so heartbroken Mercy ached for the poor girl.

She nodded to the plate of half-eaten food, desperate to take Niamh's mind off Isolde. "Tell me more about that. If you can't die, do you still need to eat every day?"

"I can still starve, I just don't die from it. Two years ago, after Firesse changed me, I tried to starve myself. That was... before Isolde came to stay with me." Niamh looked away, her eyes haunted. "I was certain I wasn't meant to stay in this world. I could...I could feel that something was wrong, so I stopped eating. The hunger, it—it consumed me. It was all I could think about. I was like a wild animal." She shuddered. "That's how Isolde found me. She nursed me back to health—back to myself—and hasn't left my side until now."

When Niamh looked back at her, absently tracing the line of her grotesque wound through her sleeve, Mercy wrapped an arm around the girl's shoulders and gave her a tight squeeze. "You'll see her soon enough," she promised.

18
TAMRIEL

When Tamriel rose the day of Elise's execution, the sky outside his bedroom windows still glittered with stars. His body was heavy with exhaustion—his father's emergency council meeting the day before had run late into the night—but there would be no rest for him until the plague was cured, Firesse's army defeated.

Elise jolted awake when Tamriel walked into the dungeon, accompanied by two of his personal guards. The chains binding her wrists and ankles jangled as she rose and moved toward the door of her cell. When she stepped into the light of Akiva's torch, Tamriel remembered how painful it had been to see Mercy locked in the very same cell, how her fingers had curled around the iron bars, his blood still caked in her fingernails. He had thought it would be less painful to see Elise in this place, but he'd been wrong. They'd grown apart over the years, but she'd been one of his few true friends during his painful childhood.

"Your Highness," Elise said. Her soot-covered dress was wrinkled from lying in the dank stone cell, her bare arms studded with goosebumps. "Have you come to take me away?"

"I have."

He tried to quash the pity that rose within him when Elise flinched, shame and resignation flitting across her face. Criminals were not allowed to be given final rites upon their deaths—leaving their souls doomed to wander the In-Between for eternity—but the sorrow in Elise's eyes was so profound Tamriel couldn't stop himself from asking, "Shall I send for a priestess?"

Although the guards did not say a word, he sensed their surprise. Elise's eyes widened a fraction.

"How can it be that you still find it within yourself to show me kindness?" She shook her head, knotted tendrils of long blonde hair dancing with the movement. "I damned myself when I wrote that cursed signature on the contract. Today I pay the price, even if it costs me the reunion with my love in the Beyond. What of Atlas?"

"He's resting in the infirmary."

She offered him a shaky smile, tears welling in her red-rimmed eyes. "Thank you."

At a nod from Tamriel, Akiva passed the torch to the other guard and unlocked Elise's cell. Her chains rattled against the floor as the guards led her out of the dungeon.

"There is one more mercy I must ask of you before we depart, Your Highness," she blurted as they stepped into the hallway. "May I say goodbye to my brother?"

Elise burst into tears the moment she saw Atlas lying in the infirmary bed, the sheets tangled around his long legs. His forehead still glimmered with sweat and his eyes were bright with fever, but he was conscious. Mercy, Niamh, and Nynev were working on possible cures at the desk, while the healers attended the three infected guards who currently occupied the other cots; Mercy had had them brought in to serve as test patients. Elise ran across the room and fell to her knees at her brother's side, a strangled sound escaping her. Mercy's expression darkened.

"She does not deserve your kindness," she muttered to Tamriel as she walked past to tend another guard.

I know, Tamriel thought, but something within him knew this was the right thing to do. Mercy wouldn't understand—she'd only met Elise a matter of weeks ago, only knew her as a villain. Although Tamriel had grown apart from Atlas and Elise over the years, they'd been some of his only true friends in a time when he'd sorely needed them. Elise had committed terrible, unforgivable crimes, but Tamriel would not sink to her level. In honor of the bond they'd once shared, he would extend to her this one final kindness.

"Elise?" Atlas croaked. He blinked up at Elise, brows furrowed, uncertain whether his sister was real or a creation dreamt up by his plague-addled mind. When he lifted a blistered hand to her face and found that it was real, a smile spread across his lips.

"I'm here," she breathed, her voice tight.

"I thought I'd never see you again. Why are you crying?"

Elise looked at Tamriel sharply, clutching her brother's hand. "You did not tell him?"

He shook his head, and Elise let out a soft sigh of relief.

"Elise?" Atlas rasped again. A bout of painful-sounding coughs crackled through his lungs. "You're not sick, are you? Why are you here? And wh—why are you crying?"

"Because I'm leaving, Atlas. I have to go away." Her lower lip began to tremble. "I've made some terrible, terrible mistakes, and I'm trying to set them right."

His face contorted in confusion. Tamriel could see him

fighting the haze of disease to make sense of what he was hearing. "When will I see you again? Soon?"

"Not for a very long time, I hope. But I need you to promise me something before I go."

"Anything."

"Speak to Mother and Father. Fix everything broken between you. Take care of them for me, won't you?"

"But—" he began, the meaning behind her words finally dawning on him.

"Just promise me, Atlas. Please."

"...I promise."

Someone knocked on the door—Akiva, telling them it was almost dawn. Tamriel extended a hand to Elise and she rose, gently kissing Atlas's cheek before stepping away from his cot.

"Goodbye, brother," she whispered.

"No, not yet. Elise? Elise!" Panic flashed across Atlas's face. "Don't go—not yet." He began thrashing, trying to rise, to chase after her. Niamh and Nynev darted forward and held him down.

"I'm sorry," Elise murmured when they reached the door. Behind them, Atlas let out a grunt, and Tamriel turned back in time to see Mercy pulling a syringe from his arm. The sedative quickly took hold, and he slumped back onto the pillow. Elise hung her head, silent tears rolling down her cheeks, and followed Tamriel out of the room.

19
MERCY

Despite the plague sweeping the city, a huge crowd had gathered in Myrellis Plaza to witness Elise's execution. Mercy, Niamh, and Nynev stood among the sea of bodies a short distance from the platform atop which Ghyslain, Tamriel, and their dozen guards were positioned. Ghyslain was dressed in finery, his diadem sparkling in the early-morning sun. Beside him, Tamriel's face was impassive as he stared at the stage that had been erected before the fountain in the middle of the square. A lone wooden block sat atop it, stained with blood from countless deaths. The prince's expression did not change as two guards led Elise up the steps and onto the stage. Whispers rose from the crowd at the sight of her chains.

"Serenna Elise LeClair has confessed to conspiring to kill the prince," one of the guards boomed, cutting through the voices. "The sentence for treason is death."

"Pawn of the king!" someone shouted.

Mercy turned, eyes narrowed as she scanned the crowd, searching for the source of the outburst. Guards disguised in roughspun tunics and pants were scattered in a loose circle around her and the sisters, keeping an eye out for danger without drawing undue attention to the prince's *elven plaything*, as the courtiers liked to call her. They frowned at one another, hands moving toward the blades hidden in their sleeves and the waistbands of their pants.

Her gaze landed on two finely-dressed nobles in the middle of the square: Elise's parents. Seren Pierce's face was pale and full of anguish as he gaped up at his daughter, studying her as if he did not recognize the woman standing before him. Beside him, Nerida swayed and clutched his arm, her eyes glassy with tears.

A ray of sunlight broke through the rooftops lining the Plaza, and the guard dragged Elise into the light. "The Creator will see you pay penance for your crimes. Have you any last words?"

She swallowed tightly and shook her head, her gaze fixed resolutely on a distant point. Mercy could see how much she was fighting not to look to her parents for comfort, and the Assassin within her rejoiced at the sight. *Let her see how much her crimes have cost her.*

The guard blindfolded Elise, then forced her to kneel before the execution block and lean forward, exposing her long, graceful neck. The crowd began to buzz with anticipation as Master Adan climbed the steps, a massive axe in his hands. The blade glinted in the sunlight, reflecting Elise's terrified face. When Adan lifted the axe high overhead, the crowd sucked in a collective breath.

For a moment, time seemed to stop.

Then the blade dropped in a whistling arc.

Mercy watched Tamriel as the axe fell, cleaving flesh and bone. The prince's expression was still hard, unreadable, but his hands clenched into fists when someone in the crowd let out a bloodcurdling shriek, the sound so raw and grief-filled that it was nearly inhuman. Nerida had fallen to her knees on the dirty stone street, her hands over her mouth as she let out wave after wave of wracking, wailing sobs. Pierce knelt and embraced her.

Behind them, Landers Nadra and his wife glared at Ghyslain in equal parts fear and outrage. Their daughter Maisie was clutching her brother, sobbing. Leon stared at the body of his betrothed, numb with shock and pain.

The crowd began to dissipate as the guards lifted Elise's body and carried it off the platform. On the other side of the fountain, a carriage was waiting to take her to the cemetery for burial in an unmarked grave.

Niamh let out a tight breath as the square began to empty around them. "Well, that was—"

Pain exploded in Mercy's chest.

She gasped and staggered back, every thought flying from her mind when she looked down and saw the arrow impaled in her chest, just above her heart. Before she could so much as shout, another one punched through her shoulder.

"No! *Nononononono!*" Niamh screamed. Mercy stumbled, and Niamh caught her, lowering her gently to the ground. Nynev leapt over them, her bow already in hand, and disappeared somewhere amidst the throngs of people running for cover from the unseen archer. "She's been hit! Someone get help! Find a healer!"

"Mercy!" Tamriel shouted, his voice tight with terror. She couldn't see him, but she could hear him fighting the guards on the platform, trying to reach her. "Mercy!" he screamed again.

I've... I've been hit. Through a wave of pain, Mercy dimly registered something warm and sticky and wet spreading across the front of her tunic. Blood—far too much blood. Niamh's tears dripped onto her face as she cried for help.

"I should know what to do! I-I—I don't know what to do!" When Niamh pressed her hands to the wounds, trying to stanch the bleeding, agony flooded every fiber of Mercy's being. She'd been struck by arrows in the Guild before, but never more than a graze. Clouds of black crept into the edges of her vision. "Mercy, stay with me. Tell me what to do!"

"I-I can't... Keep pressure—" she gasped. She tried to sit up, all her years of Guild training screaming at her to *Get up, get up, eliminate the threat*, but Niamh grabbed her shoulders and forced her back down.

"Don't you dare move."

Her eyelids fluttered shut.

"Mercy, stay with me," Niamh pleaded. "Open your eyes."

She obeyed, although the spots in her vision made it nearly impossible to see. She turned her head toward the main part of the square, trying to catch a glimpse of her attacker.

Chaos ran rampant in Myrellis Plaza. The people who had lingered after the execution were sprinting every which way, shouting to one another, their faces pale with fear. Some were huddled in the doorways of shops. Others ducked into narrow alleyways. She could hear guards running and yelling commands, but she could no longer hear Tamriel calling her name.

"Where's... Where's Tamriel?"

"He was trying to get to you, but the guards forced him and his father into a carriage bound for the castle. You'll see them soon."

Nynev appeared over her sister's shoulder. "She's alive?"

"Yes, but she's bleeding a lot. Too much."

"We have to get her to the healers in the castle. I'll find a carriage."

A laugh bubbled from Mercy's lips as the huntress departed. "They did it."

"Who?"

"The Daughters. They found me at last."

Over Niamh's shoulder, she saw the silhouette of someone standing in the third-floor window of a plague-marked house, bow still in hand. Her would-be killer was much too large to be a Daughter. He was reaching back to pluck another arrow from his quiver when something silver flashed across his throat.

He staggered, clutching his neck, and crashed through the remains of the broken window. Through the ringing in her ears, Mercy heard the crunch of his body hitting the stone. A stranger—her savior—had taken her attacker's spot in the window. He stared at her for a long moment, then turned and disappeared into the depths of the dark house. In the square below, a handful of royal guards broke down the door of the house and rushed inside. More examined her attacker's broken body.

"Stay with me," Niamh pleaded.

"I'll do my best," she said with a grimace, but the simple act of speaking caused even more blood to leak out of her wounds. Niamh shouted her name again as Mercy's eyes drifted shut, and the blackness swept in and swallowed her whole.

20

MERCY

Mercy awoke with a start, the golden light from the chandelier above her bed thrusting daggers of pain through her head. Her body felt heavy, the backs of her eyelids coated in sandpaper. Medicine—the healers had drugged her, but not enough. She tried to sit up and groaned when the wounds in her chest sent waves of agony through her.

"Mercy!" Tamriel cried. The corner of her mattress dipped when the prince launched himself onto it, taking hold of her shoulders and easing her back onto the downy pillows. "You're all right. You're all right. Try to rest, love," he said soothingly. He leaned back and stared at her as if reassuring himself she was really there, really alive. "I feared you might never wake up. You lost a lot of blood."

"They'll have to try harder to kill me next time," she croaked.

Nynev and Niamh appeared beside her bed, their faces pinched with concern. The huntress held a glass of water to Mercy's lips and she drank eagerly, not realizing until then how dry her throat had become.

Niamh shook her head. "Don't joke about that."

"I wasn't." Mercy looked down at the thick bandages wrapped from her left shoulder to halfway down her ribcage. Another two inches, and the first arrow would have struck her heart. "Who shot me?"

Tamriel's face twisted in rage. "Drayce Hamell," he spat. "The third son of a minor noble family and a member of the royal guard. He'd been stationed in that house to keep an eye on the crowd during the execution."

"Then why didn't he shoot me earlier?"

"The bastard must not have had a clear shot until everyone started leaving," Nynev said, her fingers tightening around the glass. "Whoever killed him did a nasty job of it. Slashed his throat from ear to ear."

"My father immediately ordered Hamell's family to be brought in for questioning. They maintain that they had no idea what he was planning, but there is no doubt in my mind that they conspired to murder you. Drayce was the youngest son and never would've inherited the family estate. They lost nothing when he died." A shadow passed through Tamriel's eyes. "This is only the beginning, I'm afraid. The nobles are hunting you the same way they did Liselle, but this time, they aren't bothering to hide it. I've already posted guards outside your door—men and women I know we can trust, unlike that son of a bitch Hamell—and you're not to go anywhere without them."

"Or me," Nynev added, her mouth set in a grim line. "Anyone tries to touch you, I'll fill them with so many arrows they'll look like a human pincushion."

Mercy closed her eyes, the pain making it hard to focus on what they were saying. She wished again for unconsciousness to drag her under, to wash away her agony. "Do you know who saved me?"

Tamriel shook his head. "Akiva and a few others are out

looking for him now. I'd like to give him a reward for saving your life."

Sensing her discomfort, Niamh stepped forward and nudged the prince aside. "Open your mouth."

Mercy obeyed, and Niamh dropped two small capsules onto her tongue. She swallowed them dry before Nynev had a chance to raise the glass of water to her lips. "Thank you."

"Leave us, please," Tamriel said to the sisters. When they hesitated, he added, "If her condition changes, I'll alert you. For now, you should check on Atlas and the others."

When Mercy forced her eyelids open again, they were alone. Tamriel snuffed out the candles and stretched out beside her on the bed. Through the window behind him, the sky was dark and dotted with stars.

"Come closer," Mercy mumbled, the drugs making her tongue thick and clumsy.

"I don't want to hurt you, love."

"You won't."

He inched closer until they were sharing the same pillow, their noses nearly touching. "Is this better?" he whispered, his warm breath tickling her face.

"Much."

He smiled, but the gesture was tinged with sorrow. "I'm so sorry, Mercy. I'm so, so sorry." He inhaled sharply, and it took all of Mercy's concentration to focus on his voice, to not let the medicine drag her under just yet. "I swore that I'd never let anyone hurt you. I promised myself I'd never let another scar mar your skin, but I've failed you. I've been too distracted, too focused on the plague and the war. I'm so, so sorry, my love."

"...Tamriel?"

"Hm?"

"When I get out of this bed, you and I are going to kick their asses."

His deep chuckle rushed over her, and she smiled. "That we will."

Agony jolted through Mercy's chest. She awoke with a hiss, biting her lip to keep from crying out. The pain medication must have worn off long ago; she felt as if she'd been trampled by a horse.

A dozen horses.

All at once.

She lay on her back, staring up at the blue and gold swirls of paint across the vaulted ceiling. Through one eye, she could see the bright summer sun beyond the open window, already high over the city. It must be almost noon, but no one had come to wake her or Tamriel.

The prince was curled against her side, his face tucked in the space between her neck and her shoulder, his breathing slow and even. He was still clad in the clothes he'd worn to Elise's execution. Briefly, Mercy considered asking him to call for a healer, but he looked so peaceful she couldn't bring herself to wake him. Instead, she simply watched him. Even in sleep, there was something about him that entranced her. It wasn't merely his beauty, it was that he had chosen *her*—chosen an *Assassin*, of all people—to love; to cherish; to protect. She marveled at her luck...then let out a quiet chuckle. *How strange,* she thought, *to be arrested, hunted by assassins, struck by arrows, and still count myself lucky to know him.*

But she did.

By the Creator, she did.

Out of the corner of her eye, she saw the shadow beside her wardrobe shift. She stiffened as a lithe figure silently approached her bed. It was the man who had saved her life. She was certain of it. Between the hood of his cloak and the scarf wrapped around his face, all she could see were his brown eyes, framed by dark lashes. He lifted a finger to his lips, his gaze flitting to Tamriel.

Don't wake him, the gesture said.

Mercy nodded.

He pressed a folded piece of paper into her hand, then reached into his pocket and pulled out a vial of clear liquid. "Trust me?" he whispered in a gruff voice.

Mercy nodded again. She had no idea how he sneaked into the castle without alerting the guards, but he'd saved her life. If he had wanted to hurt her or Tamriel, he would have done it while she was unconscious.

He broke the vial's wax seal and tipped the contents into her mouth. A sweet tonic dribbled down the back of her throat. He tucked the vial back into his pocket and stalked across the room. When he reached the door, he tugged off his hood and scarf and slipped a white slave sash across his shoulders.

"Who are you?" she whispered.

He stiffened. Without turning back, he murmured, "When you wake up again, you may not remember me. That's strong stuff." The door of her bedroom creaked softly as he stepped into the hallway.

Within minutes, the medication began to work its magic. It was so unlike whatever the healers had given her; their medicine had made her body heavy, cumbersome, her mind slow. This one turned her leaden limbs to feathers. It reminded her of the hundreds of times she'd swum in the Alynthi River as a child. She'd loved to float on her back and stare up at the fat white clouds, imagining the foreign cities she'd one day travel and the adventures she would experience.

Gone was the headache pounding behind her eyes. Gone was the agony, and the relief was so sudden and strong that

Mercy—heartless, ruthless Mercy—began to cry tears of happiness.

"What's wrong?" Tamriel jerked upright, immediately alert. His hair stuck up on one side, the lines of the pillowcase imprinted in his cheek.

"Nothing," she giggled, the potency of the drug making her mind spin in the best possible way. "Absolutely nothing at all."

THREE DAYS LATER, MERCY WAS STILL CONFINED TO bedrest—a fact which simultaneously delighted Tamriel and infuriated her. *I should be helping with the cure,* she'd argued, but Tamriel had shot her down immediately. *You can't fight,* he'd said, nodding to her sling, *and we have no idea when the nobles will strike again.* He'd said that often over the past few days: *When,* not *if* the nobles would strike. *You're safest here, where the guards can watch over you. Leave the work of the cure to the healers.*

She'd been readying an argument, but when she saw the desperate plea in his eyes, she'd relented. *When I saw those arrows hit you,* he'd confessed, his voice wobbling, *I thought I'd lost you forever, and it nearly destroyed me. So, please, indulge me and rest for a few more days.*

Mercy had not been left alone for one minute since Elise's execution. Nynev sat at her bedside constantly, sometimes telling stories of her childhood in Ospia or her family's journey to Cirisor, sometimes saying nothing for hours at a time. True to her word, Nynev did not leave until Tamriel returned late at night from his various meetings and duties, and she reappeared first thing every dawn.

During her few breaks from the infirmary, Niamh visited Mercy and filled her in on their progress. Atlas was still sick, but the rash and boils on his arms had begun to heal. They'd tested multiple recipes on Atlas and the other guards, and the starvay blossoms were *working*. That common, useless weed may very well be one of the keys to saving them all from the plague. All they needed now was to figure out the optimal quantities of each ingredient.

"Atlas asks after his sister constantly," Niamh had admitted after giving Mercy the good news. "None of us have had the heart to tell him the truth."

Even Ghyslain—*Ghyslain*—had come to visit her, offering his sympathy and wishes for a speedy recovery. Despite the awkwardness of their short conversation, the king was not the visitor Mercy was most surprised to see.

It was Lethandris.

The knock at her bedroom door came in the middle of lunch, startling Mercy and Nynev out of their silence. The huntress rose and cautiously opened the door, then waved the priestess inside.

"Mercy!" Lethandris gasped. She gaped at the sling binding Mercy's arm to her chest. The wounds in her chest had been stitched shut, but the arrowheads did enough damage to her muscle and bone that her left arm was still useless—and would remain so for a while. "I heard from the other priestesses that you'd been hurt, but I had no idea it was this serious. By the Creator, you could have *died!*"

"Luckily for me, Drayce Hamell was not a great marksman."

"How do you feel?"

"I've been better."

"I should have visited you sooner, but I didn't want to come without the information you requested." She dropped into the chair Nynev had vacated and pulled a few leather-bound books from her bag, the covers worn and faded with age. "The High Priestess will kill me if she finds out I've taken these from the vaults, but you need to see what I've found." The top book's spine crackled as she opened it.

"What language is that?" Mercy asked when she caught a glimpse of one of the weathered, yellow pages. The cramped script was unlike anything she'd ever seen.

Nynev frowned, peering over the priestess's shoulder. "It looks like an ancient form of Cirisian. I can't read it, though. How old is this book?"

"Three hundred years, give or take a few decades."

"And you understand it?"

"Some of it," the priestess said. "I used commonly repeated words and phrases to translate as many of the passages as I could. Most of them are nothing more than legends about the Old Gods, but this one caught my attention." She pointed to the middle of the page. "The details are fuzzy, but it discusses the *Aitherialnik*, the thread which tethered all of the *Aitheriali*—the Old Gods—to one another. If an *Aitherial* exhausted too much of his magic, he could draw on the others' strength to bolster his own. I think... I think he could even borrow another's power."

"So if that's true..." Nynev began, a note of fear slipping into her voice, "Firesse not only has claim to Myrbellanar's power over the realms of the living and the dead, but perhaps *all* the Old Gods' powers, as well?"

"How is any of this possible?" Mercy asked, dread settling in the pit of her stomach.

"Blood magic."

"You must be joking."

"I wish I were. You know the legend that a piece of Myrbellanar's soul lives in every elf. If Firesse managed to strengthen that connection by murdering human soldiers as Calum claimed, she'll only grow more powerful the bloodier her war becomes."

Nynev leaned back, rubbing her temples. "Shit."

"I could be wrong," Lethandris added. "Frankly, I have no clue how all this works. The *Aitherialnik* could be nothing more than myth."

"After seeing what Firesse did to Calum at *Ialathan*, I don't want to wager my life on that possibility," Mercy responded dryly.

"You should show this to Niamh," Nynev said. "She's the one who is fated to cure the plague. Maybe she'll think of some way to turn this to our advantage. She's working in the infirmary now."

Lethandris nodded and bent down to place her books in her bag. "What's this?" She reached under Mercy's bed, then straightened, a small slip of paper pinched between her fingers.

"Let me see that."

The priestess dropped it into her hand. Mercy stared at it, wisps of a memory floating back...brown eyes...a sickeningly sweet tonic...her savior pressing the note into her palm. Mercy must have dropped it after she'd fallen asleep. She unfolded the note. An address had been scrawled across the paper in a hurried hand—some house near Guinevere's Square—and below it was a single word:

Bareea.

21

TAMRIEL

"I think we've done it," Niamh said, a hopeful smile on her lips. She leaned back in the infirmary's desk chair and handed Tamriel a piece of paper, on which she'd scrawled a recipe. "One cup mashed Cedikra, two spoonfuls extract of tulsi, and a half cup dried starvay blossoms," she recited, beaming. She led him over to the bed where Atlas was sleeping and gently rolled back one of his sleeves. The flesh of his forearm was pink and raw, covered in dozens of little scabs, but blister-free. "Tabris and I applied the mixture topically after using Pryyam salt to remove the layer of infected skin, and it seems to be doing the trick."

Tamriel set a hand on her shoulder and smiled, hope igniting within him. "I told you you'd figure it out. You shouldn't have doubted yourself."

Her grin faltered. "I shouldn't get the credit. I still hardly know anything about healing; I'm more likely to accidentally poison someone than I am to save his life. Alyss had the idea of using tulsi and Pryyam salt, and the other healers figured out the proper ratio of ingredients. I did nothing except peel and mash Cedikra for a few hours."

"You've been working on the cure harder than anyone. When was the last time you slept more than a few hours?"

"I could ask you the same question, prince," she retorted, pinning him with a knowing look. Indeed, in the six days since Mercy was struck by those arrows, he'd hardly taken the time to eat or sleep, instead devoting every waking moment to learning who else had been involved in the plot to assassinate Mercy. Drayce had been well paid—that much was obvious by the new fine clothes he'd packed in the rucksack he'd stashed in the house. The wicked barbed arrows Tabris had pulled out of Mercy's chest were expensive, too—above the pay grade of a common guard. The question of which noble was behind the crime remained to be answered; Adan's interrogation of the Hamell family had turned up no leads. "How is Mercy recovering?"

"Pretty well. After being confined to her room for nearly a week, I'm sure she'll be skipping through the halls now that Tabris is about to clear her from bedrest." Tamriel grinned at the mental image. Yesterday, she'd been so desperate to leave her room that she'd tried to bolt when a slave brought lunch. When Nynev caught her not two feet past the threshold, she had struggled so much the wounds in her chest and shoulder had begun to bleed again. It had taken the huntress threatening to tie her to the bedposts to make her agree to stay in bed.

"Niamh?"

They jumped at the sound of Atlas's voice. Niamh gripped the guard's hand tightly, her eyes again sweeping over the scabbed, raw flesh on his forearm. "How do you feel?"

"Better."

"I can make something to soothe the inflamed skin, to keep it from itching—"

"Leave it."

She paused, frowning. "But—"

"Leave it," he growled, his gaze sliding to Tamriel. His expression hardened. "The pain keeps me from—from thinking of her."

"I'm sorry for your loss," was all Tamriel could bring himself to say, his stomach clenching at the anger and grief in his old friend's eyes. Two days ago, Niamh had finally given in to his incessant questioning and told him the truth about Elise's crimes and execution. Atlas had hardly said a word since.

Now, the guard merely turned his face toward the hearth.

Niamh laid a cool cloth over his forehead, then gestured for Tamriel to follow her to the next bed, where a guard he didn't know was slumbering. "Give him time. Gods be good, he'll soon be well enough to return to work, and it'll take his mind off her long enough for that wound to begin to heal."

The door creaked open. "Tamriel, are you in here?" Ghyslain called. Niamh whirled around and dropped into a bow as the king appeared at the end of the row of shelves. "No need to be so formal, Niamh. I've been informed that we have a viable cure thanks to you."

She straightened, fidgeting with the hem of her shirt. "It's not certain yet, Your Majesty, but our initial tests have yielded positive results." She nodded to the guard behind them, whose face was dotted with thick scabs everywhere the blisters had once been. "To be honest, I really didn't do that much—"

"Tabris told me quite the opposite," the king responded, raising a brow. "Including that you've taken to sleeping here." He nodded to the curtained-off alcove in the back of the room, where Alyss had once slept.

"Yes, well, I wanted to stay close in case one of them took a turn for the worst."

"I'm grateful for your help—for everything you've done here." Niamh's cheeks turned bright pink as Ghyslain offered her a small bow. When he straightened, his expression turned grim. "Tam, speak with me outside."

As soon as they turned the corner and were out of earshot of the guards, Ghyslain said, "Firesse and her people have attacked again. We received the news from Sapphira's guard-commander ten minutes ago. A dozen of Sapphira's most wealthy citizens were slaughtered in their beds two nights ago, cut open from their necks to their bellies and left to bleed out. The Cirisians shredded their bedsheets, tied their victims to their beds, and carved their ears into points. Then they freed all the slaves and snuck them out of the city. A patrol rode out after them, but none of them have been seen since."

Tamriel's hands began to tremble with fury. "Firesse is evil —evil and cruel and rash. She just wants us to watch our country bleed. She doesn't care who she hurts in the process."

"With luck, her army won't last the week. Soldiers are on their way to Fishers' Cross as we speak, and Master Adan has written to the guard-commanders in all of the eastern cities with orders to increase patrols until further notice."

"What about Feyndara? You could petition the queen to send ships, trap the Cirisians between us and the sea—"

"And indebt my kingdom to a country with whom we have been enemies for generations?" Ghyslain asked sharply, the words almost a snarl. "Never."

"But—"

"No." His father started to walk away, then paused and added, "Mercy's mother has sent another note. The Strykers and the Daughters have pledged their aid to Firesse's cause. It seems Calum has been working with the smiths to outfit them with arms and armor, as well as fighting beside them on the battlefield."

"As a hostage or a soldier?" To whom had Calum given his loyalty now?

"We'll find out soon enough. Our soldiers have orders to arrest him on sight so he may face trial. I swear to you, Tam, I will see him given the justice he deserves."

Tamriel nodded, too furious to speak. He listened to his father's footsteps fade down the hall, then slumped against the cold stone wall of the corridor, burying his face in his bandaged hands. Five seconds—he allowed himself only five seconds to mourn his people's deaths, before he straightened and started after the king. He willed that mask of cool indifference to slide over his face. Grieving wouldn't save his people's lives. Grieving wouldn't undo the damaged Firesse had already inflicted on his country.

"Your Highness? Your Highness!" Seren Pierce called to him as he passed through the great hall. Tamriel almost didn't recognize him; he was dressed in a drab black tunic, so different from his usual pomp and flash, and he didn't stop wringing his hands as he stammered, "I know I'm not supposed to be here, but I wish to beg your forgiveness for...for everything. For threatening Mercy. For speaking out against your father. For taunting you." He dropped into a low bow. "For my insolence, I offer you my sincerest apologies, Your Highness."

"Why the sudden change of heart, Pierce?" He couldn't keep the venom out of his voice as he glared at the seren. "I thought you hate my family and everything we represent."

Pierce shook his head, still staring down at the toes of his boots. "The rift between your father and me has been there for longer than you've been alive. It was destined to reach a breaking point sooner or later. It's hard to believe His Majesty once considered me a friend, is it not?" He dared a glance up, his watery brown eyes full of sorrow. "I *am* sorry, Your Highness, more than you can imagine. I just keep thinking...it's my fault she's gone. My Elise. If—If I'd just said yes when Calum asked for her hand, if I hadn't pushed the betrothal with the Nadras, perhaps she would not have gone to such lengths to get Calum on the throne. Maybe neither of them would have gone through with the contract on your life. Maybe she'd... Maybe she'd still be here.

"Cassius found me after the trial and told me about the letters. I-I didn't know she was guilty. Even after she confessed, I didn't want to believe it. All I have ever wanted was to protect her, and now that she's gone..." Pierce's voice broke on the last word. He sniffled. "If your father will take me back, I would proudly renew my oath of fealty to the crown."

Tamriel didn't say anything for a long time. The seren continued to bow, sniffling every few seconds, until at last Tamriel commanded, "Rise."

Pierce obeyed.

"Swear your oath to the crown and I'll forgive your past indiscretions." The seren let out a breath of relief. Tamriel loathed offering him this mercy, trusting him after all he'd said and done, but they were in need of allies now more than ever.

"Thank you, Your Highness. It will be an honor—"

"I'm not finished," he snapped. "Before you seek out my father, you will go down to the infirmary, fall to your knees before your son, and beg his forgiveness."

"He's—He's in the infirmary? Not the End?" A spark of hope returned to the seren's eyes. "You got him out?"

"I made your daughter a promise."

"Thank you, Your Highness. I'll go see him now." He turned on his heel and started toward the infirmary, then paused. "If I may leave you with one thought, though, Your Highness? I warned you what would happen if you kept Mercy in the capital. That bastard Drayce Hamell put two arrows in her in front of half the city, and soon the rest of her enemies will try to do the same. You should send her away before the next arrow finds its mark."

22

MERCY

Mercy practically leapt out of bed when Healer Tabris finally cleared her from bedrest. "About time," she groaned, her knees wobbling a bit as she pushed herself upright.

"Careful," Tabris warned, reaching out to steady her. "Your wounds are still healing, and the medication has made you weak. Take it easy for a while. Maybe enjoy a leisurely walk around the castle gardens before you dare to venture into the city. Build your strength back up."

Behind the healer's back, Nynev smirked. "Of course. Our Mercy is always one to take it slow."

Mercy ignored her. She rolled her neck, grimacing when the strap of the sling binding her left arm chafed against the already raw skin. After a week of doing nothing, she was desperate to go outside, to *move*, but she didn't dare admit it to the healer. He wasn't above having her locked in her room, and if she had to spend another day in this gilded prison, she'd go mad.

"Thank you, Tabris. I'll do exactly as you instruct."

He snorted at her saccharine smile. "I've patched up

enough guards to know that gleam in your eye means you'll do whatever the hell you please. There's no time to rest—there are rounds to do and training to attend. What would an old man like me know about that?" He packed up his medical kit and shuffled to the door. "Send for me tonight. I do love getting to say 'I told you so' after my patients tear their stitches."

Nynev rolled her eyes as he ambled into the hall, shutting the door behind him. "Nutty old bat."

"He's not wrong."

"I didn't say he was."

With Nynev's help, Mercy changed into clean clothes, and together they wandered toward the great hall, accompanied by the guards Tamriel had assigned her. Every day since Elise's execution, Mercy waited for the return of the stranger who had saved her life, but he never appeared. She reached into her pocket, her fingers brushing the note he'd left her.

Bareea.

Only a handful of people knew her true name: Liselle, who had not appeared since they left the Islands; her parents, in Fishers' Cross alongside Firesse's hundreds of soldiers; and her siblings—Ino, Cassia, and Matthias. When Liselle had told her about their siblings, she'd confessed she didn't know where they'd gone after her death or if they were even still alive.

Apparently, one of her brothers was in the city. She could only hope the rest of her siblings were with him.

Did he work in the castle? How many times had she passed him in the hall, completely oblivious to his existence? And why had he never approached her before?

Consumed by her thoughts, she didn't realize they'd wandered into the great hall until Seren Pierce's voice floated to them from the throne room. She stopped dead in her tracks, bristling. "What is *he* doing here?" she hissed to Nynev.

"Hell if I know."

They peered into the throne room to see the seren kneeling before the dais, clad in his black mourning clothes. Ghyslain was lounging on the throne, Tamriel behind his shoulder, as Pierce said, "I swear I will perform my duties as your seren to the best of my ability, Your Majesty. Never will I raise a sword against you or knowingly allow harm to befall you or your family. I vow, on my honor and that of my forefathers, to serve you faithfully until I am no longer fit to do so."

"An oath of fealty?" Mercy called, unable to hold her tongue. She stormed up to him, Nynev and the guards on her heels. "What good is the word of a man who tried to make a fool of his king before his own court?"

"On my daughter's grave, my vow is sincere."

"Your daughter was a traitor and a liar."

Without standing, he looked at her over a shoulder. "My daughter was one of the few people in this world I cherish. Now she's gone, and my son clings to life in the infirmary as we speak. I stand nothing to gain and everything to lose by opposing His Majesty."

"Do you not recall threatening my life, Seren?" She turned on Ghyslain. "Is this the type of man you wish to appoint to your council? A liar and a would-be murderer?"

"Pierce is not the only would-be murderer in this room," the king responded, fixing her with a stern look. "Or am I misremembering the events leading up to your arrival in Sandori, Mercy?"

"No, Your Majesty," she forced through clenched teeth.

"Then if we can trust an Assassin to behave civilly, why not him?" The king's gaze slid to the seren. "Rise, Pierce. I accept your apology and your oath of fealty. If you are ready to return to work, you may reclaim your place on my council."

"Thank you, Your Majesty. Your Highness. My...lady." He stood and bowed. "If I may be so bold, Your Majesty, I believe my time would be better spent investigating the Hamell attack than serving on your council. The courtiers trust me; I may be able to glean more information about the plot against Mercy's life than your guards."

"Very well. Speak to Master Adan and Evelynn Cain. They're the ones who questioned Drayce's family."

The seren bowed once more, then hurried out of the room.

"If you are to remain here at court, Mercy," Ghyslain said, a warning in his voice, "I suggest learning when to keep your remarks to yourself. A tongue as barbed as yours will earn you few friends among the nobles."

"I don't want them to be my friends."

"One would think your position on that would have changed after nearly being killed by one."

"Funny how being stuck full of arrows would fail to endear them to me."

"At the very least, try not to make enemies of every person you meet."

"Oh, but she's so very good at it," Tamriel interjected. "How else would we know she's feeling better?" His eyes sparkled when they met hers, devoid of the contempt with which he had regarded Pierce. "It's good to see you up and about."

"Good to *be* up and about. You trust the seren?"

"We've made amends. I think he'll stick to his vow."

"And how do we know he didn't help Hamell plan the attack?"

"He knows many of the guards through Atlas. If he were behind it, he'd have chosen a better marksman. Besides, now that Elise is dead, he has finally realized how much he still stands to lose by turning against us."

"So, all we have to do to earn the nobles' loyalties is kill off some of their family?" she asked, a wicked gleam in her eyes. "That could be arranged."

Ghyslain shook his head. "Mercy..."

Behind her, some of the guards shifted uncomfortably.

Tamriel shook his head. "If only it were that easy." He paused, his gaze drifting down to her sling for the first time, and his face paled. He nodded to the door set into the wall a few yards away. "Speak with me in private a moment, won't you?"

He led her into the corridor—a rarely-used one, by the looks of it, leading past the great hall and into some part of the castle where Mercy had never ventured—and shut the door behind them. The walls were so narrow they stood nearly chest-to-chest. Mercy stared up at him, his warm breath tickling her face, as he grabbed the hand of her uninjured arm and laced his fingers through hers.

"I can't stop thinking about the moment you were struck by those arrows," he began, his voice a hoarse whisper. "I saw you fall. I heard Niamh scream. I thought... I thought you were dead, and it nearly killed me." Agony passed across his face, and he clutched her hand tighter. "I should have seen it coming. I should have done more to keep you safe. More guards—"

"It's not your fault, Tamriel. I'm here. I'm alive." She nodded toward her sling. "Only a little worse for wear."

He looked down, a strand of dark hair falling into his face. "You should leave, go somewhere safe. Ospia, maybe, or Blackhills. You'd be away from the nobles, away from Firesse and the Daughters if they march on the capital—"

"No."

He fixed her with an imploring look. "Consider it."

She waited a beat, then said, "There, I've considered it, and my answer is no. I'll stay right where I am—with you.

We'll stand against the nobles together. If Firesse and the Daughters make it to the city gates, we'll stand against them *together*."

"My father thought he could protect Liselle by keeping her close, and look at what the courtiers did to her. I'm not losing you the same way."

"You won't. Liselle was brave, but she wasn't trained in the Guild."

"She also wasn't being hunted by Assassins."

Mercy rose onto her toes and kissed him. "You worry too much," she murmured as she pulled back. "I'll be fine. I have my daggers, my guards, and a no-nonsense Cirisian huntress to protect me."

He sighed and released her hand, reaching past her to open the door. "You may have a point," he conceded. She followed him into the throne room, where Nynev and the guards were still waiting. He studied the swords sheathed at the guards' hips, then Nynev's hunting knives, bow, and quiver of arrows, and raised a brow. "Creator help the next man who wrongs you."

They arrived at the armory not five minutes later. Already, the short walk from the throne room had left a dull throb in Mercy's shoulder. Perhaps she *should* wait to train. She braced a hand against the doorframe as she surveyed the racks of weapons.

"Are you sure you're up for this?" Kova—the youngest of the three guards, a pretty girl with a port-wine stain down one cheek—asked, her brows furrowing.

Nynev scoffed. She shouldered past Mercy and plucked a broadsword off the wall, examining its razor-sharp edge. "I bet she could best any one of you with an injured arm and a blindfold over her eyes."

"We train hard to become members of the royal guard," Tobias objected.

The huntress grinned at Mercy as she said, "Compliment to the Guild, not a slight to you. Although, if you truly wish to protect your prince, maybe the Assassin could teach you a thing or two about hand-to-hand combat." She nodded toward the dagger on Mercy's belt. Since her left arm was out of commission, she'd left the other tucked away in her room.

"That's right." Mercy drew the dagger, the red and orange gemstones of the handguard twinkling in the light of the lanterns hanging overhead. Between the sling and the weight of the weapon, her balance was off, but that wouldn't stop her from training; quite the contrary. If her left arm was going to be useless for as long as Healer Tabris feared, she'd better get used to fighting one-handed. "So, who's first?"

SHE AND KOVA FACED OFF IN THE TRAINING ROOM adjacent to the armory, inside a circle Nynev had drawn in the sawdust coating the floor. The guard wielded a broadsword in her right hand, a dagger in her left, and she was clad in the light leather armor the guards favored when patrolling the castle. Mercy had chosen not to don armor; it would have been too much hassle with the sling and bandages, and her blood was already thrumming in anticipation of a fight.

"I don't want to hurt you," Kova said. "The prince will kill me if something happens to you."

"That's why you're in the ring, and we're not," Bas, one of the other guards, called from where he, Tobias, and Nynev were watching across the room.

"Enough talk," the huntress called. "Let's see some action."

"But—"

While Kova was distracted, Mercy lunged and swung her dagger low. The guard knocked her blade aside and slashed at her half-heartedly, uncertainty in her green eyes. Mercy parried the strike and rolled her eyes.

"Don't insult my skills by taking it easy on me." She nodded at the girl's dagger. "Show me you know how to use that thing."

Kova leapt forward, and the real onslaught began. Slash. Parry. Lunge. With every whistling arc of her sword, her dagger flew out a second later, ready to rend Mercy's flesh. It was all she could do to block each blow as it came. Kova flipped her dagger and swung it low. Mercy jumped back a second too late and the blade sliced through the ruby crepe of her tunic.

"So you *do* know how to use it."

Mercy feinted to the right, then lunged left, knocking the dagger out of the guard's hand. It clattered to the ground. Before Kova could retrieve it, Mercy pressed the advantage, slashing again and again, forcing the guard to give up precious ground with every near-strike.

"You fight like a damn hurricane," Kova panted. She swiped at the perspiration beading on her brow with a sleeve, lifting the sword in her other hand to block Mercy's next swing.

Mercy grinned, ignoring the bone-deep fatigue, the waves of pain radiating down her left side. She'd been injured in the Guild before, but she'd never had the luxury of resting in bed while the others trained. So many weeks without constant sparring had left her rusty and weak.

Kova jumped forward. At the last moment, she turned to the side and slammed her shoulder into Mercy, knocking her even more off-balance. They landed on the ground in a heap, Kova kicking up sawdust as she scrambled up and crawled toward the dagger lying a few feet away. Mercy groaned, shards of pain shooting through her ribcage, and pushed to her feet. She touched the fabric over the wound in her chest and her fingers came away wet. At some point—she wasn't sure when—it had begun to bleed.

Kova straightened and turned, her dagger clenched in her fist, just as the flat of Mercy's blade hit her in the back of the head. Kova stumbled and fell to her knees, blinking dazedly. Mercy had been careful to only hit her hard enough to stun her. She sheathed her weapon and extended her good hand to Kova.

"Good fight," she said as she pulled the guard to her feet. Out of the corner of her eye, she saw Bas hand Tobias a small coin purse. "You almost stood a chance." She turned to the other guards. "Who's next?"

Bas's brows shot up. "You're bleeding."

"It's just a flesh wound."

"He's next," Kova said, pointing her dagger at Bas. "The bastard bet against me."

He shrugged. "Because I'm not a fool."

She pushed him into the ring, taking his place against the wall beside Tobias. "Let's see if you fare any better than I did."

"Great," Nynev purred, grinning at Tobias as she ran her fingers over the hunting knives sheathed on her belt. "Save the biggest one for me. Ever fought a Cirisian heathen, boy?"

"No."

She beamed. "Then today's your lucky day. We're going to have some fun."

By the time Nynev knocked Tobias onto his ass the second time, Mercy's muscles had turned to gelatin, the blood on her tunic now dried and crusted to her wound. She peeled it back gently, grateful to see that although the skin around the wound was red and swollen, she'd only torn a few of the stitches.

They returned to Mercy's room in silence—the guards sullen, their pride smarting—to find their dinner already prepared for them. The guards waited outside while Mercy and Nynev quickly ate and dressed. Less than an hour later, they set out for the address Mercy's savior had left in his note.

Kova hailed a carriage from a stop down the block—both to protect them from any would-be assassins lurking on the rooftops and to give them all a chance to rest their muscles after sparring. When they were all seated inside, clattering along toward Guinevere's Square, she asked, "Are you sure it's wise to be venturing so far from the castle?"

"If I let the nobles scare me into hiding behind those stone walls, then I let them win. Two measly arrows don't change anything."

Nynev frowned. "You nearly died. That's not something to be taken lightly. I was on board with sparring, but I don't know about this."

"My brother—a brother I didn't even know was alive until a week ago—saved my life. I'm not waiting any longer to meet him."

Nynev grumbled, but fell silent. Mercy parted the curtain over the window as they passed under the arch into Guinevere's Square. The houses were nice—nothing like the grand mansions of the Sapphire Quarter, but a far cry from the leaning, creaking buildings in Myrellis Plaza and the shipping district. Some of the shutters over the windows hung crookedly or were missing slats, but the window-boxes were well tended, colorful flowers bobbing merrily in the breeze. Like the rest of Sandori, the streets were nearly empty, the citizens either working or languishing in the makeshift infirmary tents outside the city limits.

The street where Mercy's brother had told her to meet him was too narrow for the carriage, so the driver let them off outside a private college a block away. Students floated from the school to the nearby bookseller or tavern, whispering to one another as they caught sight of Mercy and her strange company.

One of the passing students spat at Mercy's feet. "Whore."

Nynev drew her hunting knife, lunging forward with a feral snarl, but Kova grabbed her arm and hauled her back before she could strike. "What did you say, asshole?"

"Haven't you heard what the people have taken to calling you?" he asked Mercy, basking in the attention of the little crowd rapidly forming around them. "His Highness's Whore? The next Liselle? You've managed to trick the prince into giving you free rein of the castle. How long until you revive her failed rebellion? You and the other knife-ears are an infestation in this city. You should have been chased out long ago."

"Or put down like lame donkeys," someone muttered.

"The only asses I see here are you," Tobias snapped. He crossed his arms and stared down his nose at the man. "Keep going. Make one wrong move and you'll spend the night in a cell."

"Let's go before this gets ugly," Kova said, tugging at her uninjured arm, but Mercy didn't budge. She wasn't afraid of some insolent prick.

The student lifted his hands in surrender, offering Tobias a grin that must have charmed many tutors over the years, but the guard's scowl didn't waver. "Woah, big fella. I'm not picking a fight with you." He grinned at Mercy. "Hiding behind the castle's muscle, now, are we?"

"Oh, no. He's only here to make sure I don't turn your innards into sidewalk art."

Before he could respond, she turned on her heel and walked away, Nynev and the guards falling into step behind her.

"You handled him well," Bas murmured as they turned onto the next street.

"Don't tell Ghyslain that I've failed to make a friend again."

Behind them, someone laughed. "You don't want a racist piece of shit like him to be your friend, anyway."

They whirled around to find a woman walking several paces behind them—and judging by her grin, she'd witnessed the whole spectacle. Her heart-shaped face was pretty, finely-boned, and her hair was hidden under a scarf that matched the deep plum of her dress. She cocked her head, her brown eyes twinkling. "Wouldn't you agree?"

"Do I know you?" Mercy asked. Something about the woman was familiar, but she couldn't place what.

"You don't recognize me? I'm hurt. But I suppose it was to be expected. Last time we met, you were a mere babe." She beamed and extended a hand for Mercy to shake. "Pleasure to make your reacquaintance, sis. I'm Cassia."

23

CALUM

A few days after the attack in Sapphira, Drake found Kaius standing in the middle of the road, watching Faye and the other Daughters spar beside the docks. Their slashes and parries were so quick even a Cirisian warrior would be jealous, and Calum could tell by the furrow between the archer's brows that he was.

Kaius pursed his lips. "A place for orphans and runaways to learn to kill for money. What must it be like?"

"From what I've heard, rather bleak," Drake said. "The girls are strong, though. It's rumored that no man is a match for them."

"We'll see in the coming weeks. Did you see the magnificent weapons they brought? Those alone could be enough to give us an edge in the war."

Drake nodded. The wagons the Daughters had driven from the Guild were rigged with false bottoms; the trapdoors hidden under the crates of fruit and boxes of fabric opened to reveal a rolling armory, complete with bows, crossbows, spears, maces, and enough blades to render the Strykers practically useless.

Calum's gaze found Faye in the midst of the slashing blades. It hadn't escaped his notice that she'd been quieter than usual since the Daughters' arrival. According to Amir, who had wandered too close to the Daughters' house the night they arrived, Mother Illynor had raged at her for allowing Lylia to die and Mercy to slip through her grasp. *And then,* Amir had said, shuddering at the memory, *she just went deathly quiet. Just like that. I think that terrified the poor girl more than the shouting. Illynor really, really wants Mercy back.*

How could she not? The weapon Illynor had spent seventeen years crafting had betrayed the Guild and caused the deaths of two Assassins. Calum shuddered to imagine what terrible punishment Mother Illynor would inflict once she got her hands on Mercy. If the cool rage simmering in those flat, slitted eyes was any indicator, she certainly wouldn't do Mercy the favor of killing her quickly.

Kaius's gaze lifted to the bluff guarding the town. "Scouts report Beltharan troops a half-day's ride away. It seems the king has decided to send reinforcements. Firesse wants everyone packed and ready to move in an hour."

"I'll let the Strykers know."

Hewlin and the others were sitting around the kitchen table playing cards when Drake entered the house they shared. "Want to play?" Nerran asked. "Since we've finished all the repairs, there's nothing to do around here. I'm taking these chumps for everything they've got."

"No, we need to start packing. We're leaving in an hour."

"Off to kill more innocents?" Hewlin snarled. The rest of the Strykers fell quiet. Oren glanced sidelong at Amir, then buried his face in his cards as the tension grew thick.

Images flashed through Calum's mind—guards lying dead outside Sapphira's city gates, Faye's throwing knives embedded in their throats; men and women dying in their beds; a young elven woman cowering behind velvet curtains as she watched her master choke on his last bloody breath. Calum had screamed and raged and fought with everything he had against his father's control, but nothing had happened. No—one thing had happened. One minute, he'd been yanking at the bonds of his mental prison, trying to free himself of the shackles holding him hostage within his own mind, and then a thick wave of blackness had swept over him. The next thing he knew, Drake and the others were back on their horses, riding to Fishers' Cross. Several hours had passed without his knowledge. The realization had terrified him to his core. Until then, he'd been there with Drake every minute, forced to watch the atrocities his father committed. But the darkness that swept over him had been so complete even the pained cries of the nobles Drake murdered hadn't penetrated it.

Drake offered Hewlin a smile, chilling in its delight. "Do you consider slaveowners innocent? Do they not deserve it?"

Hewlin's expression didn't soften, but he turned back and shuffled the pile of cards before him. "No one deserves to be butchered like that."

Nerran cleared his throat. "Well, uh, I suppose we'll finish this hand, then start packing. I'd offer to share some of the winnings with you like we did in that gambling hall in Ospia, but you're rich, mate."

He grinned as he clambered up the narrow staircase. "There isn't enough in that little pile to share, anyway. You're not that good at cards, my friend—you're just better than they are."

Firesse was standing atop the bluff when Drake and the Strykers exited the house an hour later, her commanders —Kaius, Myris, the other Firsts, Mother Illynor, and a handful of Assassins—flanking her as she stared down at the army gathered before her. As much as he hoped she'd fail, Calum had to admit she'd managed to pull together quite a fearsome little force—over eight hundred Cirisians; Mother Illynor and her fifteen Daughters; the Strykers; and the slaves they'd liberated in Sapphira. With her unearthly powers and Calum's knowledge of the country, she might just eke out a victory.

"We're going to divide the army into twenty groups," Firesse was shouting, first in the common tongue, then in Cirisian. "Each commander will lead about three dozen soldiers, and they each have a specific route to the capital to follow. Harkness, Graystone, and Briar Glen will fall by the week's end, and the cities of Cyrna and Xilor will soon follow. Strike hard, strike fast, and strike true. Remember the horrors their soldiers have subjected our people to for generations, and make them pay for every man, woman, and child we've lost."

A cheer rose from the troops, and she beamed down at them. Beside Drake, Oren began to tremble. "By the Creator, she's insane. Really, truly insane. She's going to get them all killed, and us along with them."

Drake shushed him. "Don't be a coward."

Last night, when he and Firesse had finalized the routes each group would take to Sandori, Calum had begged him to convince the First to let the Strykers leave. *Ask Firesse to dismiss them,* he'd pleaded. *They've done their jobs, now let them go on their way. Send them their payment after you arrive in the capital. Oren won't make it through the war. He was fine traveling Beltharos with Hewlin and the others, but we slept in taverns and inns, not on the cold ground—not when we could help it. He's been losing weight again, growing sicker. He won't survive much longer like this.*

His pleas had fallen on deaf ears.

Firesse gave a few more orders, then the crowd dispersed

to finish packing the last of their belongings. Because they'd need to set up and disassemble their camps quickly, they were leaving behind over half of the tents they'd brought from the Islands, carrying only enough to shelter the members of each party. They'd be forced to sleep like sardines, but it would enable them to flee at a moment's notice.

The Daughters clustered around their fake merchants' wagons at the end of the dirt road, arming themselves so thoroughly they appeared more weapon than human: throwing knives on belts, daggers strapped to thighs and forearms, bows and crossbows slung across backs. Faye even tucked a tiny oyster-shucking knife into the collar of her lightweight leather armor, the handle concealed at the nape of her neck by the thick braid that fell to the small of her back.

While Drake helped the Strykers load their supplies onto the wagon Mother Illynor had given them, Firesse gave each of the group leaders their orders and helped them locate the soldiers under their command. The newly-liberated slaves would be scattered among the troops, as well, but kept out of intense fighting until they were comfortable wielding a sword.

Faye rapped on the side of the Strykers' wagon, peering up at Drake as he loaded the last crate of tools. It wouldn't be easy to maneuver across the sector, but it would be better than carrying their supplies on their backs. "You ready?"

"To watch the annihilation of my king and the murders of every human we run across? Always."

The Assassin looked over her shoulder at Hewlin and the others, standing beside the docks and staring out at the sea, likely wishing they were in Rhys. "Drake," she murmured. Her large, deceptively innocent-looking eyes met his. "That's you in there, isn't it?"

Yes! Calum wanted to shout. *Yes! Help me!*

"What are you talking about?" Drake closed the trapdoor

of the wagon's false bottom and shoved the crates of fabric back into place. He hopped out and started toward the Strykers. The Assassin fell into step beside him.

"You're Calum's father. I heard the Strykers talking about your death while you were finishing up in the workshop the other night. Between the elves' whispers about their Blessed One's gifts and that...that *thing* she did during the battle—raising those corpses—I figured out what she did to you. I should have realized it sooner. Why else would Firesse trust you so completely if you weren't under her command? Why would she keep you so close?"

"Maybe she just enjoys my company."

She huffed in irritation. "Like father like son. Never a straight answer. Does anyone else know?" She grabbed his arm to stop him, and before he could blink, the oyster-shucking knife was out of its sheath and pressed to his stomach. "I want a real answer, you silver-tongued snake."

"You couldn't kill me with that. Even if you could, Firesse would only bring me back again."

"I don't have to kill you to make you suffer."

He smirked and leaned close, their noses almost touching. "I'll give you one answer for free. No one knows except Firesse and Kaius."

Fear flashed through her eyes, so fast Calum wasn't certain if he'd imagined it. "Calum is still in there, isn't he?"

"A piece of him. What do you care? You hardly spoke to him before."

"I have a weakness for creatures forced to wear shackles."

"Or perhaps you want to know what it's like in case Firesse decides to make you play host, too. Don't worry. Play your part in the war to come and you'll remain yourself." He swatted the knife away and gripped Faye's chin tightly enough that she winced. "It's nice to see how concerned you are for my son...Faye, is it?"

"You know my name," she spat.

"You remind me of an elven bitch I used to own. She was pretty, too. Bore me a son."

She slapped his hand away. "Don't touch me, you ass."

"But she didn't ever have the guts to say *that* to me." He laughed and caught her wrists in one hand. "I'd enjoy breaking your spirit, Faye."

She jerked back, anger flashing across her face. "You're disgusting." She broke his hold on her wrists and snarled, "I'll gut you like a fish if you ever lay a hand on me again."

Faye softened her expression as Firesse breezed past. "Your orders," the First said as she handed Faye a slip of paper and continued walking. The Assassin took the opportunity to shoot Drake one last hateful look before striding away to find the soldiers she'd be commanding.

JUST LIKE THAT, THEY WERE WANDERING AGAIN. They started off trailing out of Fishers' Cross as one big caravan, the clomping of the horses' hooves and the groaning of the wagon wheels punctuating their progress. One by one, Lysander's, Ivani's, Faye's, and Mother Illynor's groups broke away from the main force. Then Aoife's, Tanni's, Kaius's, and Myris's followed. Drake ignored the dark looks Dayna and Adriel shot him as they hurried after Myris and the rest of their company. Calum's spirit sank. Two more potential allies lost.

Finally, the last few groups branched off, leaving Firesse and her forces alone in the middle of a vast plain. Drake, the Strykers, and the three dozen Cirisians whose names he had not bothered to learn trailed her. They'd follow the Bluejet River inland to Graystone and Rockinver, then join up with Faye and some of the others outside Cyrna.

"We never should have opened your damn letters," Hewlin murmured to Drake as he passed. He gazed back at the wagon slowly rolling behind them and the blacksmiths sitting atop its bench seat, his expression hard. "We should have continued on to Rhys like we were supposed to, not joined up with this wicked little rebellion of yours."

"Yes," Drake intoned, "if only you'd known."

24

MERCY

Mercy gaped at the stranger's—her *sister's*—outstretched hand. Cassia was *alive?* And not just alive, but standing right in front of her, grinning like she'd just performed the world's greatest magic trick. Before leaving the Keep, Mercy had thought she was completely alone in the world. Over the past few weeks, she'd met her half-brother, the ghost of her sister, her mother, her father, and now, another sister. A *living* one. She appeared to be in her late twenties, only a few years younger than Liselle would have been if she were still alive.

"Cassia," Mercy said.

She nodded, dropping her hand to her side. "Bareea."

"That's not my name. The Guildmother changed it when I was taken to the Keep. I'm Mercy."

Cassia burst out laughing. "Of course that's your name. Oh, the Creator has a wicked sense of humor, doesn't he?"

"Family reunion aside," Nynev interrupted, "who the hell are you?"

"One of the few allies our smartass former Assassin has in this city. Come with me and I'll explain everything." She marched straight through the middle of their small group and took the lead, pointing to a tailor's shop halfway down the block. What little they could see of the interior was dark; the door and windows bore red slashes of paint, marking the building as one tainted by the plague. "Don't worry," she added, catching Kova's doubtful expression. "Any traces of the plague are long gone. Now let's go—the others will be home soon."

"The others?" Mercy asked. "Ino and Matthias? They're alive?"

"Yes. You already know their names? Frankly, I'm surprised the Guildmother told you about us."

"She didn't, actually. It's...a long story."

When they reached the shop, Cassia unlocked the door and ushered them inside, a little bell tinkling overhead as they filed in.

"I worked here before you were born. I was lousy with a needle—pricked myself more times than I did the fabric—but the tailor kept me on because she knew the alternative was selling myself into slavery." Her fingers trailed along the bolts of silk and lace as she led Mercy and the others toward the back of the building. They passed through a narrow doorway, climbed a spiral staircase, and emerged in the apartment above the shop. It was a quaint little place—a kitchen to their right, a sitting area with a big bay window overlooking the street, and two small bedrooms tucked against the left wall. "I haven't seen her since we fled the city after Liselle's death. When we returned not two weeks ago, I didn't know where else to go for help but here, but she'd already been taken away. I have no idea if she's dead or alive."

Cassia moved into the sitting area and kicked aside the blanket someone had left crumpled on the floor. "Damn it, Matthias," she muttered. "Pig." She sank onto the couch and gestured for Mercy to do the same.

"It seems I owe you some answers. First, to your Cirisian friend's question of who the hell I am," Cassia said, nodding to Nynev. The huntress still stood in the doorway with the guards, surveying the room as if expecting an attacker to leap out of the shadows. "Cassia Mari. Third child of Dayna and Adriel Mari. Would you like to ask me anything, or should I simply monologue?"

"Go ahead." Mercy waved a hand, then reached up and shifted the strap of her sling. The damn thing had begun rubbing her neck raw again. "If I ask all the questions I have, we'll be here for days."

"Okay, but—does she always look like that? So angry?" Cassia asked, eyeing Nynev.

The huntress crossed her arms. "This is my normal expression. You don't want to be around when I'm angry."

"I'm beginning to see that. Won't you sit?"

"Not while there's a threat to Mercy's life."

"I see." She turned her attention back to Mercy. "Quite a friend you've found. Anyway...I don't know where to begin. You know about Liselle's death, don't you? And why you were sent to the Guild?" When Mercy nodded, she continued, "Our parents saw you out of the city first. Once you were safe, we were supposed to accompany them to Cirisor, but they trusted the wrong people along the way. There used to be a system for identifying those who were committed to aiding runaway slaves on their escape to the Islands—you know, a symbol painted above a doorway, a pattern in a blanket hung from a clothesline. A few days after leaving Sandori, we stayed with a farmer and his wife. They fed us at their table and gave us clothes and shoes from their children's closets. One night, Ino, Matthias, and I fell asleep under a pile of horse blankets in their cellar while the farmer supposedly helped Mother and Papa plan the rest of our journey.

"Instead," she said, her voice turning bitter, "one minute,

we were sleeping peacefully, our stomachs full for the first time in days, and the next, we were tied up, blindfolded, and shoved into the back of a wagon. His wife and their three brutish sons drove us to the next town over and sold us to a slaver."

"They really did that?" Kova asked, her face slack with shock and disgust.

"Don't pretend you don't know the sorts of things people like you do to people like us. They saw three healthy kids and they knew they'd be able to make a fat lot of coin off us. I bet we were locked in the slaver's cages before our parents even realized something was amiss." She scowled and flapped a hand in dismissal. "Doesn't matter—can't change it now, anyway. The only one who ever bothered to try and make things better for elves was our sister, and those rich bastards killed her for it. Liselle was a fool for becoming the king's mistress. She had wanted to help the people of Beggars' End, and she loved the king—she truly did—but she took too many risks. She lost her life for it, and she destroyed ours in the process."

"I'm sorry," Mercy said softly.

Downstairs, a bell chimed, and Cassia straightened as footsteps tapped up the stairs. "Our brothers are back."

A few moments later, two young men appeared behind Nynev and the guards, who stepped aside to let them through. One was tall, a few years older than Cassia, with jet-black hair and a faded scar on one side of his jaw. The other was a few inches shorter—still surprisingly tall for an elf—with a muscular build and a hint of Calum's handsome, angular face. They froze mid-step when they saw her.

"You found her?" the one with the scar asked.

She nodded, first to the elder brother, then the younger. "Ino, Matthias, meet Mercy."

Matthias's lips twitched, fighting a smile, when he heard

her name. Without saying a word, he pushed past Ino and crushed Mercy in a hug. "I'm glad to see you're safe, sister. I've missed you."

Despite her aching wounds, she hugged him back just as tightly. They were strangers, but she had spent so many years thinking she was alone in the world. She'd never imagined she had parents or siblings who remembered her—who *missed* her.

"We didn't know you were still alive until we heard about the arrest of an elven Assassin," Matthias told her. "I thought the nobles would have killed you for sure."

"They tried their best." When she stepped out of his embrace, she found that she and her siblings were alone.

"The others went downstairs to give us some privacy," Cassia said to her unspoken question. "Let's sit. You look like you've seen a ghost." She guided Mercy back to the couch and pulled her onto the cushion beside her. Ino and Matthias settled in the armchairs across from them.

"How—how did you find me?" Mercy asked. "How did you know I was here?"

"We were working as hired swords in Blackhills when news of the attempt on the prince's life swept through town. When we heard that an Assassin matching your description had been arrested, we sold what we could afford to lose and bought passage here in a merchants' caravan. By the time we arrived, you'd already left for Cirisor."

"We had no idea if you were coming back," Ino added, "but because of the plague, transportation out of the city is hard to find. We were hoping to lie low until we could manage to scrape enough coin together to get out of this shithole of a city, but then you came back. Imagine our surprise when we learned you had fallen for the prince you once sought to kill."

"Why didn't you approach me sooner?"

"*We* wanted to," Matthias said, gesturing to himself and Ino. "But *she* had other plans."

Cassia fidgeted with her skirt, shame flashing across her face. "I didn't think we should. To be honest, I…I resented you. You never knew Liselle. You didn't have to watch the nobles turn on her, to see our parents' master defile our mother—"

"I know what Drake did to her and I know Calum Zendais is her son. I've met him."

"But you didn't have to watch it happen. I remember the way Drake tormented and tortured her. I was nine when she fell pregnant with Calum; after that, Drake didn't lay a hand on her. He didn't have to. The memory of what he'd done drove her into a depression for months."

"I wanted to kill him," Ino whispered, gripping the arms of his chair so tightly his knuckles turned white. Mercy could hear the barely-restrained rage in his voice. "The bastard deserved a much more painful death than the one that Assassin gave him."

"I resented you," Cassia continued, "because even though you'd been raised by the Guild—a harsh life for any child, I'm sure—you were sheltered. Protected. You weren't constantly looking over your shoulder, fearing the day that slavers clapped you in irons once more. You'd made a life there, a home—"

"It wasn't my home," Mercy said sharply.

"—and I was jealous of you. I've spent most of my life wishing I could forget all the pain we've gone through. You were so blissfully ignorant, and I envied you for it."

"What changed?"

"The first time I saw you, you and your Cirisian friend were walking through Myrellis Plaza. I'd been trying to find work, but no one's hiring elves on account of the plague—they think we're no better than rats, spreading disease wherever we go. I was sitting by the fountain and you passed me. I recognized you immediately. Something about the way you move...it's just like our father. And, of course, there's the hair." She reached out and gently tugged on one of Mercy's curls. "Just like Mother's." Her hand strayed to the scarf wrapped around her own head before she let it drop back into her lap.

"Cassia and I took turns keeping an eye on you whenever you left the castle," Matthias said. "Ino got a job in the castle kitchens, which is how he was able to sneak into your room that night. The castle is one of the few places still hiring elves, and did you know nearly all the elves who work there aren't slaves at all? They're free—paid modest salaries in secret. Ghyslain just makes them wear the sashes to keep up appearances for the nobles. It seems our Liselle did change one thing for the better."

Cassia nodded. "There are still quite a few humans who would like to see us dead for Liselle's little revolution. The fewer people who know we're here, the better. I didn't want to approach you until I was sure I could trust you. Unfortunately, you went and got yourself stuck full of arrows before I could decide, so I had to make do with the time we had. I was in the crowd that day—that's how I was able to find the guard who tried to kill you you so quickly. Do you know his name?"

"Drayce Hamell."

"Drayce Hamell," she repeated, her lip curling. "Even with him dead, you're not safe here."

"I know. Tamriel suggested sending me away so the nobles wouldn't be able to hurt me."

"Did you accept?"

"Of course not."

Matthias nudged Ino with an elbow, grinning. "Hear that? 'Tamriel.' Not 'His Highness.'"

"You should have heard him screaming after she'd been struck by that arrow," Cassia told them. "As if someone had reached in and ripped his heart out of his chest."

Mercy's stomach clenched as she remembered the look in his eyes earlier that afternoon—not fear, but pure, unadulterated terror.

"We need to get you away from the capital and the Guild. The Daughters must be looking for you, are they not?" Before Mercy had a chance to answer, Cassia barreled on: "It doesn't matter. We'll head to the Islands, find our parents—"

"There's a war brewing," Ino interrupted. "I overheard the council members discussing it. The Islands aren't safe for anyone right now."

"Then we'll go to Rivosa or Feyndara. Hell, we could make a home in the swamps of Gyr'malr for all I care. It doesn't matter as long as we're safe."

"Yes, it damn well does matter," Mercy snapped, standing. "I've told Tamriel and I'll tell you the same: I'm not tucking tail and running. I'm not a coward, and I'm not leaving him here to face a council of snakes and a war on his own."

Cassia rose, and Ino and Matthias followed suit. It struck Mercy then how much larger they were than she: Ino and Matthias were each a head and a half taller, their muscles pronounced from their work as hired swords, and, although Cassia was built like an acrobat—all long limbs and sharp angles—there was something dangerous about her.

Cassia narrowed her eyes, her voice hard as granite. "This is not about what you want, Bareea. This is about our family. Those damned nobles murdered our sister and would have killed the rest of us if we hadn't run. We have spent every day of the last seventeen years constantly looking over our shoulders, praying that the slavers and the men who wish us dead won't find us. We haven't felt *safe* for seventeen years," she said. "I was thirteen when we were ripped away from our parents. Ino was sixteen and Matthias was only six. None of us remembers what they look like. The nobles stole that from us—it's one of a long list of things they've stolen from us. Now that we've found you, I'm not going to let them take you, too."

"Come with us," Matthias implored her. "We'll sail somewhere far away and make a fresh start. When the war is over, we'll send for Mother and Father. We could start a farm or find work in a village somewhere. No more death. No more cutthroat nobles. We'd all be together for the first time in decades. We'd be a family again."

She shook her head, hating herself for the way Matthias's face fell. When she had chosen Tamriel, she'd made him a vow, and she would not break it. They'd cure the plague. They'd bring the nobles to heel. And if Firesse's troops reached the capital, they'd stand against her together.

Mercy turned to her eldest brother. Ino had been silently examining her the whole time, a faint frown on his lips. Of her three siblings, he seemed the least likely to let go of his grudge against the nobles. She could see that barely-restrained rage simmering in his eyes. "Did you agree to this? Running away and letting Liselle's murderers run free?"

"Our family and our safety are more important to me than revenge," he said, but she caught a flicker of pain and anger flash across his face.

Mercy threw her uninjured arm up in frustration. "Does no one in this Creator-forsaken city possess a spine? Liselle is little more than a stranger to me, but I won't allow her murderers to go unpunished." She jabbed Ino's chest with a finger. "You say you care about our safety, but you'd rather scurry about in the shadows like rats than avenge your own sister's death. You could help me find the people who want me dead! Instead, you'd have me leave everything behind to run away with you and pretend everything's fine."

"'Leave everything behind?'" Ino echoed, batting her hand away. "What about your life is so great that you would turn your back on your own blood? You're an Assassin on the run from the Guild and you have no place in the court. If you stay here, you'll die. What could you possibly cherish so much that you'd risk your life to keep it?"

"Tamriel."

It was the truth, but she hated the way it made her sound like a naïve, lovesick girl. All her life, she'd been taught that her own survival was more important than anything. She'd fought tooth and nail to earn her spot among the best apprentices in the Guild, and then she had *become* the best apprentice in the Guild. She'd become hard, cold, violent. Falling in love had never been part of the plan. "I told you, I'm *not* leaving him."

"And what will you do when he leaves you? Tamriel is a *prince*. Princes marry princesses. Tamriel is eighteen and unmarried—he's not even betrothed. He belongs to some Rivosi or Feyndaran bride, not to you."

"Who said anything about me being his bride? I've known him all of a month and a half."

Ino shot her a look. "Don't insult my intelligence. Even if it were possible without your head ending up on a spike outside the castle gate, you're not a queen."

Mercy lifted her chin, willing them not to see how much her eldest brother's words hurt. "I fared well enough playing Marieve. *If* it came to that, I could learn to rule."

"An actor can play a healer well enough, but I wouldn't trust him with my health. You'd be of more use in the guard than anywhere else in the castle. You don't belong anywhere else."

"I certainly couldn't do worse than Ghyslain. He's done more harm to the country than good."

"Ghyslain has managed to rule for twenty years without

anyone sticking him with an arrow. You didn't even last a week."

"I'll buy the best armor I can find."

"Won't stop the poison in your dinner."

"I'll hire a taster."

They glared at each other, neither willing to back down.

"There's no doubt we're related. You have our father's stubbornness." Cassia elbowed Ino out of the way. "He's being pushy because we've been part of this conversation before. Our parents tried every day to convince Liselle to break it off with the king, but she always refused. She loved him, and he felt the same about her, but he wasn't enough to protect her from the nobles.

"Every day for nearly eighteen years, I've wondered if this all could have ended differently, if we could have saved her somehow. Now that we've found you, we can't let you start down the same path she walked."

Mercy looked at Ino, Cassia, and Matthias in turn, then started for the stairs. Her body was heavy with fatigue, and Nynev and the guards had waited long enough.

"If you don't want the nobles to kill me, stay and help me find those who wish me harm. Help me bring Liselle's murderers to justice." As she passed the kitchen, she pulled out the coin purse Mistress Sorin had left for her at Blackbriar, which she'd retrieved upon their return from the Islands. She tossed the purse onto the counter, the coins jangling when they hit the wood. "If not, I wish you luck on your journey. Use this to buy your passage. If there's any left over, write me once you've arrived. Maybe I'll visit you someday."

When Mercy reached the bottom of the spiral staircase, Nynev jumped up from where she'd been sitting on one of the worktables, tying a series of knots in a scrap of silk. Her expression morphed into sympathy and understanding when she saw the dark look on Mercy's face. "Didn't go as you'd hoped?"

"The nobles want me dead. The Assassins want me dead. My family wants me to forget everything I've done and everything I've risked to be here so I can run off and hide with them in some Creator-forsaken corner of the world."

Nynev fell into step beside her. Together, they wandered through the dusty bolts of fabric toward where the guards were waiting at the front of the shop. "Family isn't worth shit," Nynev muttered.

"You don't believe that."

"No, but I thought it'd make you feel better to hear it."

Mercy stopped. "Did you just try to spare my feelings?" She opened her eyes wide and pressed a hand to her chest, just over her heart. "Nynev, you *do* care!"

"No, I don't." The huntress crossed her arms. "I told you Niamh and I are leaving the second this plague is cured. We're going back to whatever mess Firesse has made of the Islands and we're going to try and make things right. You and I might never see each other again."

"You consider me a friend," Mercy insisted, grinning. "Admit it."

Nynev let her arms drop to her sides, not bothering to fight a smile of her own. "Don't tell anyone."

"So, the violent Cirisian huntress has a heart after all. Your secret is safe with me."

After one last glance at the staircase to make sure Cassia or her brothers hadn't come to try and change her mind, Mercy followed the guards out of the tailor's shop and onto the street. Overhead, the once clear blue sky was blotted with dark storm clouds. Bas hired a carriage from a stop down the street and they all clambered inside just as it began to pour. Rain drummed against the top of the carriage, the wind whipping the curtains hanging over the narrow windows, as the driver started the horses toward the castle. Just before they turned the corner, Mercy reached past Nynev and shoved the curtain back, ignoring the huntress's protestations as she took one last look at the building her siblings had made their home.

She may never see them again. *Good,* whispered the coldhearted Assassin within her. *They're just like Ghyslain—too weak and afraid to stand up for themselves, for justice.*

Or maybe I'm the one who is the fool. Ino had a point—Ghyslain had lived this long without losing his throne or his head. If Mercy were still the Assassin the Guild had trained her to be, she'd have said yes to her siblings in a heartbeat. She wouldn't have cared about the plague, the war, or Tamriel. She'd have boarded a boat and watched the shore of her country fade into a speck on the horizon, then into nothing, without a second thought. She would have been free.

Thank the Creator, she was no longer that woman. If staying with Tamriel would cost Mercy her siblings, she would pay that price. She would mourn the loss of her family, of course, but she wouldn't let everything they'd fought for mean nothing.

25
TAMRIEL

Fat droplets of rain lashed the council chamber windows as Tamriel stared out at the city, drumming his fingertips along the sill while his father and the council members argued about something unimportant behind him. Every few seconds, lightning flashed, throwing the rain-slick peaks of the nearby roofs into sharp relief against the blue-black sky. Beyond the city walls, small cottages spilled out over the land, and beyond them, dozens upon dozens of white infirmary tents dotted the fields. When they'd realized a storm was brewing, Adan had sent guards to move the sick into some of the plague-marked houses outside the city limits for shelter. They had quickly run out of room and time. Over half of the people lying in the fields had nothing more than the wax-coated canvas tents to protect them from the storm.

Master Adan had lost count of the death toll. It was well into the thousands; likely tens of thousands across the country. When they first discovered the plague, the deaths had been sporadic—two in one day, none the next, three the day after. Now, corpses were very nearly piling up in the streets.

The guards had done their best to move anyone suffering from Fieldings' Plague to the infirmary tents, but every day they found a handful of bodies huddled in an alley or curled up on the steps of the Church. Wary of burning any more bodies and contaminating the lake, they'd begun burying the dead in mass graves.

Niamh and the healers were still tending Atlas and the other sick guards with the newly developed cure. Their main problems now were twofold: their limited quantity of Cedikra, and the difficulties of sending thousands of doses across the country in time to save all of the sick. In addition to her duties in the infirmary, Niamh had begun meeting with Lethandris late in the evenings. They spent hours poring over the ancient Cirisian texts the priestess had managed to smuggle out of the Church, trying to translate the words and predict what other tricks Firesse may have planned. Right now, they could only guess where and when she would strike.

"The damn savages killed a dozen men in the middle of one of the oldest fortress cities in the country!" Porter Anders shouted, drawing Tamriel's attention back to the conversation. He turned to find the courtier standing at the opposite end of the table from Ghyslain, staring down the king. This had become a familiar sight over the past few days—the nobles blatantly ignoring court etiquette and speaking to Ghyslain as an equal, not as a subject to his monarch. Elise's confession and execution had scared them into obedience for only a short time; the day the news of the attack in Sapphira had reached them, the tension between the council and the king had nearly reached a breaking point. No one had said it explicitly, but Tamriel knew they blamed his father for allowing Firesse's rebellion to go on for so long. "How the hell did Firesse and her forces survive the six hundred men you sent to Fishers' Cross?"

"The girl is resourceful," Cassius Bacha said. "She's doing what she thinks is right for the people she's lost."

"Are you excusing her crimes, Bacha?"

"Quite the opposite," he retorted, stung by the accusation. "I fear that you are vastly underestimating to what lengths she'll go to avenge her people. Let's not forget that she orchestrated the murder of one of her own—a First of a clan, for the Creator's sake—to incite war."

Ghyslain stood and pointed to the map of Beltharos spread across the table, tracing the line of the king's road from Sandori to the Islands. "Fifteen hundred men are marching for Fishers' Cross as we speak. They'll arrive tomorrow night at the latest, and they'll stamp out any hopes of war among the Cirisians. If Firesse and her commanders do not fall in battle, they will be brought here to face trial and execution. They *will* answer for the deaths of our people." His finger stopped on the squiggly line that represented the bluff protecting Fishers' Cross. The village was so small, the cartographer had not even bothered to mark it on the map. "By the Creator, I swear they will be punished."

Lightning crackled outside the window, so close that the glass panes rattled in their frames. A second later, a clap of thunder filled the air, the sound reverberating through the stone tiles beneath Tamriel's feet.

Every pair of eyes swung his way when he joined his father at the table. "Last we heard, Firesse has twelve hundred soldiers at her disposal. We assume she lost a good portion of her troops in the battle, but we cannot be sure how many. She also has the help of the Daughters of the Guild, the Strykers, and Calum." *And her otherworldly powers*, he didn't say. They had yet to allow any word of her blood magic to escape their inner circle. They'd had no rational explanation to offer the council when informing them of the deaths of the soldiers Ghyslain had sent to Fishers' Cross a week ago. Tamriel wouldn't have believed in Firesse's magic if he hadn't witnessed it, and he was certain the nobles did not have enough faith in him or his father to take them at their word. "We cannot underestimate the value of their aid."

"What about Mercy?" Landers Nadra piped up. Surprisingly, his son was not at his side. Good. For a while, Tamriel had thought the man had two shadows. "She was a Daughter of the Guild. What is to keep her from sharing information about our plans with the Cirisians?"

"Need I remind you she betrayed the Guild weeks ago? They want her dead as much as they do me."

"What if she traded information for her life?" he pressed. "She helps the knife-ears in the war, and the Guildmother overlooks her slights against the Assassins. It's not a bad trade. I'd bet my estate the headmistress is dying to bring her wayward Daughter back into the fold."

A few of the council members nodded. Ghyslain said smoothly, "Mercy is not on trial here, and my son does not owe you any explanations, *Nadra*." He leaned heavily into the title, a warning in his tone. The Rivosi noble merely shrugged, clasped his hands over his bulging stomach, and leaned back in his chair.

"My apologies, Your Majesty."

Cassius snorted.

"Have something to say, Bacha?"

"Only that your appointment to this council never ceases to amaze me. If you thought half as much about what comes out of your mouth as what goes in it, you'd know better than to paint yourself as such a monumental ass."

"Gentlemen—" Ghyslain began, but another lightning strike cut off his words.

"My job is to ensure the security of our country," Landers shouted over the rumble of thunder. "I'll not overlook an

Assassin living in the castle in order to protect my position. She cannot be trusted."

"Neither can you," Tamriel snapped. "Someone helped Drayce Hamell plan the attack on her life."

"Drayce Hamell was a moron and a mediocre guard at best. Give me a little credit, Your Highness. If I'd helped him plan it, he wouldn't have failed. In fact, he wouldn't have been involved in the first place."

"You—"

"ENOUGH!" Ghyslain roared. "One more snide comment and I'm stationing the lot of you on the front lines against the Cirisians. I called you here to plan in the event Firesse's troops somehow manage to reach the capital. If you cannot suppress your hatred of one another long enough to complete this simple task, perhaps you're not worth saving."

A heavy silence settled across the room, broken only by the patter of raindrops against the window and the occasional clap of thunder. Half of the council members shuffled the papers before them sheepishly, their eyes downcast. The other half gaped at Ghyslain, certain their king had truly lost it.

That's it, Tamriel thought as he gazed at his father, pride filling his chest. *Stand up to them.*

"Now," Ghyslain said, his voice as sharp as a knife's edge, "what are your thoughts on the war?"

Cassius scanned one of the papers in front of him, eyes squinting behind his crooked spectacles. "Firesse is angry. She ordered the attack on Sapphira to prove a point. What she fails to realize, however, is that the havoc she wreaked caused more harm to the elves of that city than good." He handed the report to Ghyslain. "Since the attack, violence against elves in Sapphira has tripled. Just two days ago, a guard patrol found two female slaves huddled in an alley, each suffering from a broken nose and multiple broken ribs. The people of

Sapphira are angry, and they're taking it out on the most convenient enemy."

Bile rose in Tamriel's throat. "We should station additional troops there until the war is over."

"Master Adan already ordered the city guards to be on high alert, but I'll have him send backup tonight," his father said.

Porter Anders jumped up from his seat. "They should be protecting the people. Firesse is going after the humans, not the elves. *That's* the most immediate threat. With the Daughters on her side, the people need as much protection as we can afford to give them."

Ghyslain shot him a look. "They are *all* my people. One race is no more worthy of survival than another. We're sending troops to keep the peace, not to pick sides."

"Back to the discussion at hand," Tamriel said, gesturing to the map. "Hypothetically, if Firesse were to reach the capital, what is our plan to stop her?"

Cassius's lips pursed as if he'd bitten into a lemon. He was the only council member who knew the truth about Firesse's powers—and about the very real possibility she might reach Sandori. "We'd have to move the sick from the infirmary tents to a quarantine facility somewhere else in the city. Possibly some of the abandoned warehouses along the Alynthi. It would take a lot of time and effort—some of those people can hardly stand, and others are barely lucid. The citizens outside the city walls would have to be brought inside, as well. After that, who knows? With the lake and the river, the city can stand a siege for years. Firesse doesn't have that much time or patience. The walls are impregnable, but there is a tunnel near the infirmary which leads outside the city. It was built centuries ago to allow the royal family to escape in the event of a war. Does Calum know about it?"

"I don't know. I never told him, but it's possible he found

it on his own." Tamriel himself hadn't known about the hidden escape until Master Oliver had shown it to him when he was sixteen. *Just in case*, he'd said as he led Tamriel down the dim hallway, searching for the carving of the Myrellis family crest in the ancient stone bricks. *Sometimes it's better to run from a fight. You know that, don't you?*

I don't run, he'd shot back, crossing his arms. *I'm not a coward like my father.*

You're not a fool, either. You'll know when you're facing an enemy you can't defeat, when you're staring death in the eyes, and you'll make the wise decision. Only a fool faces Death believing in his own immortality.

Later, Tamriel had used the tunnel to help Hero smuggle elven slaves out of the city. He'd stolen food from the kitchen, bound it in small pouches with enough coin to pay the elves' way to Cirisor, and sent them to their freedom. He hadn't risked it often—too many slaves go missing, too many nights stealing "snacks" from the kitchen, and someone would have caught on—but he'd managed to help several elves over the two years since Master Oliver showed him the passage.

"We'll operate on the assumption that Calum knows every possible advantage we have," Ghyslain said. "We'll be prepared for anything coming our way. Adan will station guards at regular intervals through the tunnel. It's only wide enough for a few men to stand abreast, so the guards won't be facing the entirety of Firesse's army at any one time."

"Meanwhile, the rest of the men and women will meet the Cirisians in the field," Cassius added, nodding.

"It's a solid plan." Landers leaned forward, grinning as if *he* were the mastermind behind their strategy. "Fortunately, we will never have cause to use it."

For once, Tamriel hoped he was right.

Ghyslain nodded, somewhat mollified. "Then that's what

we'll do. Fioni and Anders, I want you to find suitable warehouses and prepare them for quarantine. I'd rather them be ready and unused than be caught unprepared if the Cirisian army manages to reach the city. You're all dismissed."

After the council members shuffled out of the hall, Tamriel turned to his father, whose gaze was trained on the map and the papers surrounding it. "We *will* win."

"I hope so, Tam." The king moved to the window and peered through the glass, frowning at the smattering of white tents just visible through the raging storm. "For all our sakes, I really, truly hope so."

THE HALLS BELOW THE CASTLE WERE COLDER AND DANKER than usual, the walls slick from the water leaking through the cracks in the ancient bricks. The thick, earthy scents of dirt and rain hung so heavily in the stagnant air that Tamriel could taste them. He turned the corner just in time to see a guard step out of the infirmary, closing the door softly behind him. The second the young man saw him, he shot Tamriel a dazzling smile. "I made it in from Ospia right before for the storm," he called as Tamriel approached. "I was told I have you to thank for that, Your Highness. Julien Bouchard, at your service." He dropped into a theatrical bow, the golden royal crest on his uniform shining in the torchlight.

Tamriel raised a brow. "I've heard a lot about you."

"Only half the stories the guards whisper about me are true. The fun is in figuring out which are, and which are not." He straightened. "They call me an Unnatural—a claim to which our dear Leitha Cain could testify, but I've heard she's rather busy in the afterlife and unable to make social calls. A pity, really. I liked her until she discovered my relationship with Atlas and convinced Master Oliver to station me in the mines. I assume the rumors don't bother you, since you were the one who had Master Adan bring me back."

"If you do your job well, I don't care what you do on your own time...or *who* you do."

Julien laughed. "I'll be honest, Your Highness, I never thought you had much of a sense of humor before this very conversation."

"I'm full of surprises." He nodded to the infirmary door. "How's Atlas faring?"

"Better. Still feverish, but the healer seems to think he has a good chance of recovery." Julien bowed again. "I should return to my rounds. Spend too much time alone with me and soon *you'll* be the subject of the guards' whispers."

As the guard's footsteps faded, Tamriel let himself inside the infirmary. The warmth from the hearth offered a welcome respite from the damp chill of the hall. When he emerged on the other side of the supply shelves, he found Niamh and Lethandris murmuring to one another in Cirisian, bent over a thick tome lying open on the desk.

"Any progress?"

"Not much, I'm afraid," the priestess responded, lightly tracing a line of text across the aged yellow parchment. The nib of her pen scratched against a piece of paper as she transcribed the phrase, her brows furrowed in concentration. "Ancient Cirisian is difficult to translate because it originated as a spoken language. Eventually, with the influence of Beltharan and Feyndaran explorers, they developed a written alphabet, but the symbols varied wildly between the various clans."

"We've managed to decipher a bit more about the *Aitherialnik*, though," Niamh added. "It seems each Old God was part of a gens—a family, of a sort. Each *Aitherial* could draw on the *Aitherialnik* to bolster his own magic, but he could only borrow and wield the power of a member of his gens."

"So Firesse doesn't have unlimited powers," Tamriel said, some of the tension in his chest lessening. "Which Old Gods were in Myrbellanar's gens?"

"That's the problem. Their names and stories are lost to time, just like the true names of the Creator and Myrbellanar. All we know for certain is that the magic she can control through the *Aitherialnik* is related to Myrbellanar's powers over death and the realms of the living and the Beyond."

"Could she summon more spirits, like she did Drake and Liselle?"

Lethandris paused, pursing her lips in thought. "Probably, but she can't wield blood magic without depleting her own health. With the Daughters fighting on the front lines, I doubt she'll risk it unless she absolutely needs to."

Niamh stood and examined the guards while the priestess spoke. Tamriel watched her roll back Atlas's sleeve and slather more ointment onto his forearm. Atlas gritted his teeth when her fingers brushed the tender skin. The scabs where the blisters had been were still healing, but the rash appeared to have lessened. As Niamh continued tending her patients, Lethandris gathered her books, bowed, and excused herself.

"They've been eating better and sleeping more peacefully," Niamh told Tamriel when she returned to the desk, wiping the medicine off her hands with a rag. "The healers and I will observe them for a few more days, and if their recovery continues going smoothly, I'd venture to guess we can start distributing the cure by the week's end."

His shoulders slumped in relief. "That's the best news I've heard all week."

"Tamriel?" Atlas croaked, his voice still hoarse from the plague. Tamriel knelt on the floor beside his friend's cot, bracing himself for the hatred he knew he would find in the guard's eyes. Instead, Atlas swallowed painfully and said, "Julien's here. That was your doing, wasn't it?"

He smiled. "I thought you might like to see him again. I actually met him in the hall. He's an unusual one. I'm sure he'll serve my father well...until he inevitably gets into trouble and winds up shipped halfway across the country again."

"You're telling me," Atlas chuckled. He glanced at Niamh and the other guards, then lowered his voice. "You knew about my...affliction...before I told you about Julien, didn't you?"

"Your pining wasn't exactly subtle, my friend."

"I never *pined* for anyone."

"You most certainly did. But if it makes you feel any better, I won't tell a soul."

"And I suppose you were the reason my father visited me earlier and begged my forgiveness?"

Tamriel nodded. "I hope I didn't overstep my bounds. I just couldn't stand by and watch him treat you like shit any longer."

Atlas waved away his concerns. "My relationship with my parents has been strained for a long time. I can't forgive them completely—not yet, at least—but I've agreed to sit down with them and talk. I owe it to Elise to try. Even after they kicked me out, she did everything she could to fix things between us."

Grief filled Atlas's eyes. He and Elise had been closer than most other siblings in the court. For a long time, one would never go anywhere without the other. Elise had made some terrible decisions, but she would have died for her brother if necessary.

"After you recover," Tamriel said, desperate to distract his old friend, "I'd like you to join my personal guard. No more Beggars' End for you."

For the first time since leaving the End, his friend smiled. "It would be an honor, Your Highness."

AFTER VISITING WITH THE REST OF THE SICK GUARDS, Tamriel bade farewell to Niamh and trudged up the stairs to the guest wing, where he found Mercy's room dark, the pot of tea on the desk cold and untouched. A pile of discarded clothes lay on the floor before the wardrobe, the left shoulder of the tunic crusted with dried blood. He rolled his eyes at the sight. He'd have been more surprised if Mercy *had* listened to Tabris's orders to rest; he'd have feared Drayce's arrows had knocked something loose in her head.

The doors to the library were ajar when he stepped onto the second-floor landing, a sliver of light escaping through the gap. They didn't make a sound as he pushed them open and walked inside.

It took his eyes a moment to adjust to the darkness; built into the center of the castle, the library had no windows, and the only light came from the low, crackling flames in the fireplace at the far end of the room. Eventually, he spotted Mercy sitting with her back to him before the fire, exactly where they'd first kissed so many weeks ago. Neither Nynev nor the guards were in sight.

"They're in the hall outside," Mercy said without turning back, somehow reading his thoughts. That she'd known it was he who had found her surprised him; he'd been all but silent walking in, not wanting to disturb her but aching for her company. Was her Guild training really so good that she was able to identify someone without them even speaking? She gestured toward the door set into the left wall of the library. "I needed a moment to think."

"About what?" he asked as he started down the long center aisle.

"About my siblings. Liselle told me about them when we first left for the Islands, but she didn't know if they'd survived the aftermath of her murder. Apparently, they did, and they came here to find me." When he sank onto the couch beside her, she explained everything—their flight from Sandori, their enslavement, their search for her—and finished by describing how Cassia had saved her life the day of Elise's execution. "They want me to run away with them."

He didn't say anything for a few long moments. "Is that what you want?" he finally forced himself to ask, his chest tightening. He'd wanted to send her away to keep her safe from the nobles, but that would have been temporary; the thought of her leaving forever nearly cleaved his heart in two.

She reached up and cupped his cheek with her good hand. His gaze traveled once more to the sling—that Creator-damned reminder of exactly how ruthless the nobles could be. "What would you do if I said yes?"

"I don't know if I'd be able to bear seeing you leave," he confessed. He tucked her curls behind her ear, the point cast in gold by the light of the fire. "But if that's what you decide, I won't stand in your way. I'd secure you and your siblings safe passage wherever you wish to go."

"You'd forget about me? You'd marry some princess and make lots of little heirs?"

He shook his head. "I could never forget about you, but if you really want to leave, you are free to do so. You don't belong to the Guild anymore. You have a family waiting for you. If I have to choose between watching the nobles destroy you and letting you walk away—knowing you're alive out there, somewhere, even if I can never see you again—I'll pick the latter every time."

Mercy didn't respond for a long time. She searched his gaze, the darkness turning her brown eyes into chips of onyx.

Then she shoved him and pushed to her feet, storming down the aisle.

"*What?*" he sputtered, jumping up and jogging after her. "What the hell was that for?"

She whirled around, trembling with anger. "I don't *want* you to let me go! Have you gone mad? I want you to stand with me against the nobles! Why does no one in this Creator-forsaken city stand up to them?"

"They'll *kill you*, Mercy," he snapped, his own temper flaring. "Maybe I *will* have you sent away for your own good. You may be a great fighter, but eventually your defenses are going to slip. I'm not going to watch them torture and slaughter you like they did Liselle. One day, we'll stand against them, but it *won't* be when we're facing a deadly plague and an army of elves hell-bent on drowning my country in blood."

"There will always be another enemy, another excuse," she snarled. "You sound as paranoid as the king."

Tamriel stilled, cool fury filling him. His voice came out terrifyingly calm when he said, "Take that back."

"No."

"I am *not* my father."

Mercy lifted her chin. "The nobles have already tried to kill me once. Now I get to show them what a terrible, terrible mistake they've made in pissing me off." She turned on her heel and stomped toward the library doors. "I'm going for a walk. Don't follow me."

26
MERCY

She could hear Nynev and the guards running after her as she stormed down the stairs. She didn't slow as she continued down the long corridors toward the great hall, shoving past guards and servants before they had a chance to jump out of her way, and stepped through the front doors of the castle. The sky was still dark from the storm, blue-black clouds hanging low over the city. Strong gusts of wind snagged on her hair and clothes.

"Mercy," Kova said, trailing down the stairs behind her. "Stop."

"No." Her dagger was in her hand before she even thought to reach for it. *Guild training*. She whirled and lifted the blade, pressing the point into the unprotected flesh of Kova's underarm. The guard's eyes widened in fear. Behind her, Bas, Tobias, and Nynev halted at the top of the stairs. "I meant what I said to Tamriel. I know you were listening. I need to think, and if any of you follow me, I'll have you bleeding out at my feet before you can even draw your swords." To emphasize her point, she pressed the tip of her dagger a little farther into Kova's flesh. "Even injured, you know I'm good for my word."

"You're being rash, Mercy," Nynev called, looking about two seconds from drawing knives of her own. "What if someone's watching you? What if the nobles decide to strike?"

"Let them try," Mercy said coolly, ignoring the ache in her wounds, the pain radiating through her entire left side. She was exhausted, but she couldn't spend one more minute in the castle. "Creator's ass, just give me some time to clear my head."

Mercy sheathed her dagger and continued down the stairs, ignoring the huntress completely when she called, "Twenty-four hours, then I'm dragging your ass back here whether you like it or not."

The gate creaked when she pushed it open, emerging in the small square outside the castle walls. The flush of her anger began to fade, leaving her cold and shivering as she wandered the narrow streets with no particular destination in mind. She should find shelter, she knew, but where would she go? Blackbriar was the obvious choice, but Tamriel and the guards would know to find her there, and she was in no mood to argue anymore. All she wanted right now was space and a warm bed. And a tonic to ease her pain. She shifted her arm in her sling, grimacing. A tonic would be good, but she wouldn't find one tonight. All the healers were either in the castle or tending the sick in the infirmary tents.

She wouldn't go crawling back to Cassia and her brothers, either. They were no better than Tamriel, slinking around in the shadows, trying to keep out of the nobles' attention, telling her that she should be grateful the courtiers haven't managed to kill her yet. No, that wasn't right. They had warned her about the nobles, but they'd do nothing to stop them.

So.

She was on her own.

Again.

She found herself drawn toward Myrellis Plaza. She ducked under colorful awnings and dodged the large puddles on the sidewalk until she arrived in the middle of the square, near the fountain where she'd almost died a week ago. The statue standing on top, one of Tamriel's ancestors, frowned down at her, his glower made all the more fearsome by the fat, angry storm clouds hanging overhead. Behind her was the well where she'd stood the morning after Tamriel kissed her for the first time.

She looked up at the plague-marked house where Drayce had hidden, half expecting to see him standing in the third-floor window, another arrow trained on her heart. After Elise's execution, someone had placed a padlock on the door. It was a flimsy thing, meant to keep out the few people desperate enough to risk breaking into a plague-marked house, and the lock gave way with a sharp *snap!* after a few shoves on the door with her good shoulder. She stumbled inside, off-balance, then shut it behind her and clambered up the stairs to the third-floor bedroom. There was a small pool of dried blood on the floor by the window, which no one had bothered to board up. A cool, storm-scented breeze swept in, whistling around the shards of broken glass hanging from the window frame.

Mercy looked out the window, scanning the nearby rooftops, buildings, and alleys for eyes. Nynev and the guards had followed her—she was certain of it—but they wouldn't dare to approach her until her twenty-four hours were up. From the looks on their faces, they'd known her threat was sincere.

She sprawled out on the bed and tossed her sling on the floor, gingerly feeling along her stitches to ensure her wounds had not become infected. Aside from the bit of blood that had leaked out during her sparring match that morning, they were fine. Two more scars to add to her collection.

Mercy ran her fingers over her dagger's smooth leather grip. She wasn't an Assassin of the Guild any longer, but that life would always be a part of her. That girl—that cruel, vengeful, merciless killer—would never leave her.

The nobles think I'm such a danger to their precious city? That I'm going to ruin their lives one pathetic, back-stabbing courtier at a time? A smile tugged at her lips and she closed her eyes as, outside, the storm began to rage anew.

Well, it would be a pity to disappoint them.

FOOTSTEPS ON THE STAIRS WOKE MERCY FROM A FITFUL sleep a few hours later. She jumped to her feet, instantly alert, and pressed her back to the wall beside the door, waiting for the intruder to appear. Her grip on her dagger tightened as she listened to the person step onto the landing.

"Bareea?"

"Cassia?" She hadn't expected to hear her sister's voice again so soon—not after their argument earlier that day. She backed away from the door and sheathed her dagger. "What are you doing here?"

"Nynev sent a note telling us what happened." Her sister nudged the door open and pulled a letter bearing Nynev's familiar scrawl from her pocket, the ink slightly smudged from her rain-soaked clothes. "She thought I might be able to talk some sense into you."

"I'm not leaving the capital."

"I know." Cassia grabbed her hand and led her to the bed, the sheets rumpled from her thrashing. Her sleep had been plagued by nightmares of nobles chasing her through the darkened halls of the castle, some armed with knives and swords, others holding chains to string her body across the gates, right next to her sister's corpse. She shuddered at the memory. Her friends' paranoia was getting to her.

"After you left," Cassia began, "Ino, Matthias, and I agreed you need to know what our lives were like after Liselle's death. It's a long story, and a painful one, but you need to understand what standing against the nobles means, how cruel they can be to people like us." She took a steadying breath and continued, "The only good thing that came of our kidnapping was that we were bought from the slaver together. Our master had a share in one of the mines in Ospia, and we were to live with him on his estate—me as a housemaid, servant, and plaything for his young daughter, and Ino and Matthias as workers in the factories he owned for smelting ore.

"Honestly, I don't know how we made it through that first year of slavery. We were still children, torn away from our parents, from our home, from our eldest sister. Liselle had been...she'd been my everything. Until those last few months of her life, when we'd begged her to leave court life behind and accept her place as Elisora's slave, she could do no wrong in my eyes. I'd wanted to be just like her when I grew up. When I saw what those bastards did to her, I died inside. Ino and Matthias were no better off.

"One night, when I was seventeen and Leopold—our master's son—was almost twenty, he and some of his school friends got obnoxiously drunk while our master and his wife were on holiday in Rivosa. They liked toying with the female slaves, so they—they called me in and held me down on the table while they took turns kissing and...touching me. They said they wanted to see what about elven women had captivated the king so completely." She shuddered, her voice breaking when she said, "Ino heard me crying. He beat the boys bloody for what they did to me and broke Leopold's arm in the process. After they ran away, Ino promised he'd find a way to free us. The next day, after the humans had sobered up and Leopold's arm had been set, they'd taken turns...they'd taken turns beating him with a switch while they forced me to watch."

Bile rose in Mercy's throat. "How did you escape?"

"*That* took another year. I was washing the dishes after supper when I heard the door to the kitchen swing open behind me. I assumed it was Ino or Matthias and kept working—they'd done their best to make sure one of them was always in the house when Leo was home from school—but I didn't learn until later that they'd gone back to the smelting factory to retrieve something for our master.

"When I finally turned around, Leo was standing there, watching me. He... He grabbed me and pushed me against the wall, kissing me over and over and over." She closed her eyes and sucked in a shuddering breath, her face waxy and bloodless.

"Stop." Mercy grabbed Cassia's hand and squeezed, trying to spare her sister the terrible memories. "You don't have to tell me the rest. I'll just assume that bastard got what he deserved for doing that to you. *Slowly*."

Cassia let out a shaky laugh. "Not quite. When he tried to force himself on me, I panicked and bit his lip so hard my teeth cut right through. He hit me. Before I knew what was happening, he had a knife in one hand and my hair caught in the other. He pushed me facedown onto the table and did this..."

She hesitated, then unwrapped the scarf on her head. Her hair had been shorn so short Mercy could hardly tell it was black, and below it, one of her ears was a mangled mess of flesh.

"He told me that I was worth less than shit, and that I wasn't even worthy of being a knife-eared savage. He was going to cut off my ears. He had only managed part of one when Ino and Matthias returned and heard me screaming. Matthias ran straight for us, and when Leopold turned the knife on him, Ino grabbed an iron skillet off the stove and swung. He nearly shattered the boy's skull. We left him lying in a pool of his own blood and ran before our master could call the guards. We had no money, no weapons except for Leo's knife and that damned skillet, and no clothes except what was on our backs. We vowed that night that we'd take our own lives before we ever let anyone enslave us again."

Anger rushed over Mercy like a tide. "He didn't die slowly enough," she said through clenched teeth. "Or painfully enough."

"He didn't die at all. We left for Blackhills that night, but I heard a rumor a few months later that he'd dropped out of school. He'd gone soft in the head, people said, and he suffered from terrible migraines that left him sickly and shaking for days on end." Her knuckles turned white as she bunched the silk scarf in her fists. "Sometimes it's enough to know that he's suffering, that he's no longer the man who attacked me and that he'll spend the rest of his life paying for what he did. Other times...I spend entire days imagining what it would be like to wander through the gardens of that beautiful estate again, to stride through those halls as a free woman, and how satisfying it would be to see the look on Leo's face when I kill him in his sickbed. Some days, it's all I can do to not pack up my few belongings and march back there."

"Once the plague is cured, I'll go with you," Mercy promised. The vow felt feeble in light of the horrors her sister had recounted, but she meant it with every fiber of her being. "If you'll have me."

"Liselle would have said the same thing, but no, I won't kill him."

She jerked back, surprised. "Why the hell not?"

"He's too sickly to leave his house, he cannot use a chamber pot without aid, and he'll never be more than a husk of the person he was before. He'll spend the rest of his miserable existence wallowing in his own filth. His head will feel like it's splitting open from the force of the migraines Ino gave him, and even though he likely does not remember why they ail him, *I* remember. The Creator remembers and will give him a fitting punishment in the Beyond. I have too much hatred in my heart to cut his suffering in this world short." Cassia lifted her chin, her eyes hard and her soft-spoken words underscored by a quiet, lethal strength. She'd seen her beloved sister tortured and strung up on the castle gates. She had been the victim of unspeakable violence. She had quietly endured living in the same house as that *monster* for an entire year before she and her brothers escaped their gilded prison. The torture and torment she'd suffered would have broken anyone, yet somehow—*somehow*—here she was.

Mercy scooted forward and surprised them both by pulling her sister into a hug with her uninjured arm. Cassia buried her face in Mercy's neck, clutching her as tightly as she dared around the arrow wounds. "No matter what you say," Mercy murmured, "the offer will always stand, should you change your mind."

"If I ever do, you'll be the first person I tell."

"You'd better." She pulled back, smiling. "What good is all my Guild training if I cannot use what I've learned to wipe evil bastards like Leopold off the face of the earth?"

"What good, indeed? I'll admit, I'm surprised you didn't end up in an all-out brawl with Guildford this morning."

"Who?"

"Guildford Hastings Hayes, Jr.," Cassia said, smirking at the ridiculousness of the name. "That prick who spat at you outside the college. His father is some well-to-do portrait artist in the Rivosi courts, and because of that, he feels entitled to piss on everyone unlucky enough to cross his path."

"Then I'm glad I got the spit and not the piss. These are new shoes."

Cassia grinned. "And exquisite ones, at that. Life in the castle has been good to you." She nudged the toe of Mercy's boot with her own. "Speaking of which, when are you going back to Tamriel?"

"When I no longer have the irresistible urge to punch him in the face." She flopped back onto the bed, wincing at the sliver of pain that shot down her left arm, and said to the ceiling, "I love him, but Ghyslain's court is infested with liars and traitors and murderers, and neither of them will do anything about it. He'd rather ship me off to some far-off corner of the world than stand up to the nobles." She rolled onto her side and frowned at her sister. "I suppose now you'll tell me you agree with him."

Cassia shook her head. "That's what the boys and I were discussing when Nynev's letter arrived. As much as we want to keep you from harm, your life is your own. If you choose to brave the dangers of the court to stay with your prince, we will support you in any way we can."

"Really?" Mercy breathed, scarcely believing what she was hearing. "You're going to stay?"

"You were right about Liselle—about her murderers. We may never find everyone who plotted to kill her, but we sure as hell won't let them hurt you again. At this very moment, Ino and Matthias are out there with your guards, watching the street for signs of danger." Cassia pointed to the broken window and smiled sadly. "If I believed in fate, I'd think Liselle has been watching over us all these years, waiting for the right moment to guide us to you."

You'll never know how accurate that statement is, Mercy thought. She wandered down to the kitchen and returned a moment later with a bottle of cheap wine and two chipped ceramic mugs. Cassia smirked as Mercy set them down on the mattress and began to pour.

"Stop grinning. I couldn't find any wine glasses."

Cassia merely shook her head and accepted the cup Mercy handed her. She lifted it up in a toast and murmured, "To Liselle."

"To our sister," Mercy echoed with a wistful smile. They clinked mugs and drank in silence, the only sound the gentle pattering of rain against the broken shards of the window.

After a few minutes, Cassia reached into her pocket and tossed Mercy's coin purse onto her lap. "Since we're not leaving, we won't be needing this."

She pushed it back. "Keep it. I'm willing to bet it's more than the three of you have combined." Mercy hid her grin at Cassia's affronted expression behind the lip of her cup. "Besides, I've seen the inside of your apartment. You need it more than I do."

27
CALUM

With Drake's help, Firesse and her soldiers committed countless atrocities as they marched inland. Every farm and fishers' hut they stumbled upon were swiftly broken into, robbed, and then set ablaze, the helpless owners left to watch from a distance as their entire world was reduced to ash. Every garden and field was destroyed. Every horse was taken by a Cirisian soldier and every flock of livestock was slaughtered, the corpses picked clean of meat and left to rot under the hot sun.

Each night, they made camp in a thick copse of trees or along a secluded riverbank. The scouts had reported Beltharan troops moving east along the king's highway, but they'd managed to stay well away from the road. The Cirisians were so used to their nomadic life that it took them less than an hour to set up the half-dozen tents and build a low-burning fire for roasting meat. It took them even less time to pack up in the mornings. Through it all, the Strykers didn't say more than a dozen words to Drake. They had resigned themselves to their roles, working silently and sullenly late into the night, and made it clear that there was no place among them for the man they believed Calum had become. Calum knew Hewlin hadn't dared to tell them about Firesse's power over the plague—he valued their safety too much to risk Firesse's wrath—but Nerran and the others hadn't missed the distrustful looks Hewlin often shot Drake.

The days began to blur together. While traveling with the Strykers, Calum had loved seeing his county in such an intimate way—meeting the people of the small towns, walking along the twisting, twining rivers, riding through the long-grass prairies and plains. Now, he spent every second fighting his father's presence. He raged against the shackles holding him hostage in his own mind, the ice-water tentacles peering into his memories, until he was exhausted. He didn't know where he always went when the last of his energy faded and that blackness once again swept over him. He simply...disappeared. One minute he was there, screaming as he watched his father and the elves murder a merchant family who stumbled too close to their camp, and the next he was staring at the glowing embers of a fire with no memory of what had happened in between. Even so, he didn't stop fighting. Once, he thought he felt a flicker—the kiss of the sun on his skin, the weight of the dagger in his palm—but the sensation faded so quickly he feared he'd imagined it.

THEY ARRIVED AT THE OUTSKIRTS OF GRAYSTONE IN THE dead of night. Unlike Sapphira, there were no ancient fortress walls to be seen as they followed the swell of the Bluejet toward the town; instead, its people relied on the two rivers surrounding the narrow strip of land on which the village sat for protection. Nestled on the island were several dozen houses, shipping compounds, shops, and taverns, the gray-black buildings packed so tightly together Calum began to feel claustrophobic just looking at them. *One strong gust, and the entire town might tip over like a row of dominoes.*

Firesse lifted a hand, and they halted. "Dismount here. Hewlin, have your men watch over the horses while we're gone. The rest of you, come with me."

Drake ignored the frowns of disapproval on the Strykers' faces and moved to the First's side. The rest of the elves followed suit, crouching behind them in the long grasses lining the riverbank. Two village guards were walking along the water's edge on the opposite side. Two arrows sent them to the ground, dead before they could so much as shout.

"Where do we strike first?" Firesse asked, looking over at Drake in the darkness.

"The docks, the warehouses, the citizens—take your pick," he responded, studying the ships docked on the opposite bank. A hundred years ago, Tamriel's great-grandfather had overseen the construction of this town, yet another checkpoint for the trade ships on their way from Sandori to Fishers' Cross and Feyndara. There were a dozen villages like it all across the fishing sector, turning the web of rivers and waterways into a lucrative form of transportation for travelers, traders, and merchants. Taking down one would be a minor inconvenience for Ghyslain and the shipping companies whose taxes filled the royal coffers, but decimating Graystone and the seven other shipping villages along their route to Sandori would be crippling. That was exactly what Firesse and her commanders intended to do.

Tonight, Graystone and three of its sister villages would fall. Drake and Firesse had planned each of the Cirisian troops' routes meticulously, ensuring that their coordinated attacks would strike a blow from which the country wouldn't recover for a long time. Calum knew, as they crouched there in the cover of the swaying grass, that Myris and her elves were gathering on the northern end of the town, preparing their own assault. Kaius and Ivani were doing the same outside Harkness; Lysander and Aoife outside Briar Glen; Tanni and Faye outside Fairwater. Mother Illynor and the rest of the Daughters rode west, where they'd soon fell the remaining four villages.

So many dead. So many—because I was too damn stupid to see who Firesse really was, Calum thought miserably.

His father's voice slid over him: *You're not the first to make the lethal mistake of underestimating her, my son, and you will not be the last.*

"People first," Firesse finally decided, turning toward the soldiers waiting behind them. "Archers, remain on this side of the river and kill anyone who tries to flee."

The soldiers murmured their assent, and then they were off, moving as silently as shadows as they waded into the Bluejet. Drake followed Firesse, and Calum could tell by his sharp intake of breath that the water was cold, and moving faster than they'd expected. The river had swollen from the summer rains. The current was strong, bits of leaves and broken branches swirling around them. They had to fight for every step.

By the time Drake and the Cirisians emerged, soaked and shivering, on the opposite bank, Firesse had already wrung out her hair and slipped two daggers from their sheaths. The blades in her hands gleamed under the warm light of the oil lanterns hanging from the posts lining the docks. "Just like Sapphira," she whispered. None of them needed ask the meaning of her command: small groups, in and out of each house before the people of this village realized what had hit them—only this time, they were not leaving any humans alive.

The First slipped into an alley, two elves flanking her, and disappeared.

Drake surveyed the remaining elves and jerked his chin

toward two sisters he'd helped train back in the Islands. They were twins—long and lean, a few years older than Calum, and fearsome with weapons. "You two. What are your names?"

"Kenna," one said.

"Farren," said the other.

"Want to help me make some humans bleed?"

Kenna's lips spread into a cruel, delighted grin. "More than anything."

FARREN GROWLED AS SHE SHOVED HER DAGGER THROUGH the gut of her first victim. The man groaned as she yanked the blade out, dark blood immediately pouring out of the gaping hole in his stomach, and fell back against the wall, his eyes glazed with pain. "That was for my mother, you despicable piece of shit," she snarled, wiping the blood on her dagger on the back of the man's shirt.

"Mother was worth a hundred of his kind," Kenna said from the hall.

"Luckily for you, there's a whole town out there for you to massacre," Drake drawled as he crossed to the bathing chamber and dunked his hands into the bucket of water beside the bath, scrubbing at the blood on his sleeves and under his nails. It was a useless act—they'd be drowning in blood and gore by dawn—but Calum could sense his father's revulsion underneath his hunger for revenge. As horrible as he was, Drake was a nobleman's son, perfumed and pampered all his life. He'd probably never gone a day without bathing. He'd been many terrible things in his life, but he hadn't become a killer until Liselle.

Drake exited the bathing chamber and leaned against the doorway, crossing his arms as he cast a lazy glance from the dying man on the floor to the woman's body sprawled across the mattress. He'd driven a dagger into her heart mere minutes ago. She hadn't even had time to cry out.

He gestured to the door. "Shall we?"

The house was eerily quiet as they crept down the staircase and out the front door. They'd done as Firesse had asked and freed the two household slaves before they'd gone upstairs to kill the masters. They would continue like this, freeing and killing, freeing and killing, alongside Firesse and her soldiers until they met Myris and the others in the town square. They hadn't seen any guards save for the two by the docks, but in a town so small and so isolated from foot traffic, whatever forces they'd meet would be easy enough to defeat. Until now, the largest threats to Graystone had been smugglers and rowdy sailors.

Across the street, another group of elves emerged from a house, weapons in hand and fighting leathers coated in dark, sticky blood. They shot Drake and the sisters smug grins and continued down the street.

"Come on," Kenna whispered, waving them toward the next building. With a flick of her wrist, her lockpicks slipped out of her sleeve and danced between her slender fingers as she worked the lock. A heartbeat later, the door opened with a soft *click*. She didn't say a word as she sauntered down the hall in search of slaves to liberate.

This time, their victim woke before Drake had a chance to end his life, thanks to Farren stumbling over an ottoman and muttering a curse. The man jerked upright in bed, his mouth opening to let out a scream. Drake shoved his dagger through the man's throat, and all that escaped was a wet, bloody gurgle.

Drake glared at Farren over his shoulder. "I thought you people can see well in the dark. Isn't that the point of a midnight attack?"

Her gray eyes, glimmering like a cat's, narrowed. "I'm

doing my best, asshole. I've lived most of my life in a tent. I'm not used to maneuvering around all these pointless furnishings."

"Your best isn't good enough if our targets hear you coming down the hall. Let's go."

They found Kenna and a young slave waiting for them in the foyer. The girl fingered her white slave sash nervously, her eyes red-rimmed and full of terror as she took in the myriad daggers tucked into the sheaths on Kenna's arms, legs, and waist.

"An elf by the name of Quirin is waiting for you at the docks," Kenna was saying when they arrived. "Keep your sash on until you've crossed the river and found our people, otherwise our archers might mistake you for a fleeing human and shoot. Make it to the opposite bank, and you're a free woman."

The slave's head bobbed up and down, and she ran out of the house without a word.

"You're welcome," Farren hissed as the girl disappeared around the corner. Her sister jabbed her with an elbow and hissed something in Cirisian, but Farren cut her off. "I don't care if she's scared. She should be grateful."

"Tell her that after we've won the war and returned back home. Don't forget that if she fights with us, she'll be turning her back on her country and signing her own death warrant. Either way, she won't be safe until she gets to the Islands."

"As long as that broken fool sits on the throne, she's not safe anywhere."

"Can we table this discussion for a later time?" Drake snapped, picking at the blood drying on the cuff of his sleeve. Farren snarled something in Cirisian, but she didn't argue as Drake led them onto the street and down the block, hitting each house along the way. Calum tried in vain to escape to wherever he went when the blackness came for him. He couldn't bear to watch the slaughter any longer.

After hitting their sixth house, the bells of the village's Church began to clang.

Their peals shattered the nighttime calm, ricocheting off the stone façades of the buildings and echoing down the narrow streets. Drake crossed the bedchamber and pushed the shutters open. All down the road, the sleepy, curious faces of the people they had yet to kill peered out at the commotion.

"Myris made it to the bell tower," Drake said to Farren, who had come to look out over his shoulder. "The guards will be coming soon, so be careful."

They descended the stairs and found Kenna already waiting for them. "Altaïr, Kassian, and Vanya are across the street, ready to join us."

"Then let's not keep Firesse waiting." He left the house, and they fell into step behind him. Overhead, confused whispers fluttered from house to house as the villagers caught sight of the strangers below. The three elves Drake had seen before were waiting for them in the shadow of a home they'd invaded. Altaïr waved them along, leading them toward the center of town where they were to meet Firesse and the others. Distantly, Calum could hear the shouts of the village guards as they scrambled to organize, but their voices were almost completely drowned out by the ringing of the bells.

They wended their way through the narrow alleys and along the winding streets, sometimes catching glimpses of other groups of elves as they answered the call of the bells, until the clusters of buildings gave way to the square. Considering Graystone's size, it wasn't much to see: a few stores and artisans' workshops lined each side, and the Church—nothing more than a drab two-story building with a spire and a bell tower—sitting at the far end. Firesse stood before the

Church's open doors, flanked by Myris and a dozen other armed Cirisians. Every one of them was splattered with blood.

So many innocent lives lost.

Drake and the others joined Firesse outside the Church. Within moments, two dozen guards in leather armor poured into the square. The First smirked at the sight. "It appears your information was correct, Calum." The guards in the smaller villages had no need for steel or plate armor. It was heavy, expensive, and hard to maintain. Leather armor was more than enough protection against any thieves or smugglers they might encounter in their small town. They'd never expected to be caught in the middle of a war.

The commander stepped forward and shouted, "Lay down your weapons! We have you surrounded!"

Drake turned, and Calum saw guards approaching from every side of the square, cutting off any chance of escape…or so they thought.

"You're holding the priestesses hostage, aren't you?" the commander continued. "That's why they set off the alarm? Release them, unharmed, and we can come to some agreement. Food, money, clothing—any supplies your people need, we can provide it."

A sliver of moonlight broke through the heavy clouds, and Firesse stepped into the light. One of the guards sucked in a breath when he saw the blood soaking Firesse's armor and the daggers in her hands. Her eyes were bright with bloodlust. "Food, money, and clothing won't bring the people I loved back from the dead, now, will it?"

"I offer you one last chance," he growled. "*Surrender*."

She flashed a wicked smile. "*Never*."

The commander unsheathed his sword and opened his mouth to shout the order when a spearhead punched through the leather covering his chest. The guards watched in shock as he staggered and slumped to the ground, blood pooling on the stone.

Firesse cocked her head. "What was he saying about being surrounded?"

In groups of twos and threes, the remainder of Firesse's troops—over five dozen elves—melted from the shadows and filled the square, trapping the guards between them and Firesse.

"Stand your ground, men," one of the guards shouted. He raised his sword. "You'll pay for your crimes, knife-eared bitch. Attack!"

They launched themselves at the Cirisians, blades clashing, roars of rage filling the square. Even in the dead of night, Calum could see the humans didn't stand a chance. They were fighting back-to-back, covering each other's weak points, but they were vastly outnumbered. One broke away from the main group and charged at Firesse, but Drake leapt in front of her and parried the slash of the man's sword, ducking and driving his dagger into the back of the guard's leg. The man toppled, howling, and Firesse buried one of her wicked little knives in the man's eye, all the way to the hilt.

Screams spilled out from somewhere in the town, ringing out over the clanging of the Church bells and the chaos filling the square. The guards paused, their grips on their swords going slack when they saw the bright flames licking the night sky. Half of the shipping warehouses were ablaze, and the inferno was quickly spreading to the houses the Cirisians had yet to invade. The columns of black smoke nearly blotted out the stars. Drake grinned. The signal had worked. Myris's men had been scattered across the village, standing by with torches, oil lanterns, and barrels of pitch until they heard the Church bells.

Firesse's smile grew. Only six guards still stood, bleeding and panting. "I'll give you a choice," she said to the one who had ordered the attack. "Die here right now, or run. Maybe you'll make it past the archers I've posted outside your village. Maybe not. We'll make a game of it. My archers could certainly use the target practice."

He glared at her. "The king will hear of this."

"Oh, I'm planning on it."

"He'll send more troops—"

A loud splintering interrupted him. They all watched as the roof of one of the warehouses crumbled and collapsed, sending a column of bright sparks into the air. Firesse called, "What is your decision?"

The guards shot her hateful looks, but, at a nod from their leader, they sheathed their swords. "You'll pay for this," he shouted as he and his men retreated. Firesse gave a command in Cirisian, and her men stepped aside to allow the guards to pass. They obeyed, sending icy glares at the humans as they filed out of the square. The second they were gone, Myris whirled on Firesse.

"Why in the gods' names did you allow them to live?"

She sheathed her daggers and started across the square, toward a narrow road they'd been careful to leave free of flames. Myris, Drake, and the others fell into step behind her. "The archers deserve some fun of their own."

They fell silent as they made their way toward the southern tip of the island, ignoring the cries of the terrified citizens. Sure enough, when they reached the docks where they'd first crossed the Bluejet, they found the guards floating facedown in the water, stuck through with arrows. Firesse watched her people slip into the cold, rushing water and wade to the opposite bank. At last, only Drake, Myris, and Firesse were left standing by the water's edge. Without a word, Firesse walked to each of the three posts lining the bank and picked up the oil lantern hanging from the hook. She handed one to Myris and one to Drake.

Calum could see the elves' glowing, glimmering eyes peering out at them from the cover of the grass across the river. They chittered quietly in Cirisian as they watched Firesse, Drake, and Myris throw the lanterns at the ships docked there. The glass shattered when the lanterns hit the decks, splattering burning oil everywhere and igniting the sails. Drake and the others dove into the water as the shrieks of the people trapped in the burning village swelled. The sounds of collapsing buildings and the tolling of the bells echoed across the plain as they crossed the river and stumbled onto the opposite bank, their clothes heavy with water and blood.

The Cirisians whooped and cheered when Firesse beckoned them forward, their shouts of '*Lo Benii!*' full of victory and pride. The First strode to her horse, not sparing a glance at the Strykers as she passed, her soldiers trailing her step like a pack of wild dogs. Hewlin grabbed Drake's arm when he made to mount his horse.

"You led them into this battle," he hissed, his eyes full of rage. The sight made Calum flinch. "You helped massacre all these people. Do you count this a victory?"

"This is war, Hewlin. Do you think I enjoy watching my countrymen burn?" As his father spoke, Calum heard the quiet *thunk, thunk, thunk*, of the archers' arrows striking flesh. Some of the villagers were swimming across the river in an attempt to flee the flames.

He shook his head. "I don't know anything about you anymore, lad. There's a darkness in your heart I've never seen before." His gaze shifted to Firesse, already well out of earshot, and the elves following her. "You should turn your blade on that she-demon before she leads us all to our deaths. She's a blight, Calum. Villains like her are not meant to survive long in this world."

"She's trying to achieve peace for her people."

"Don't feed me that bullshit. You think spilling all this blood is going to achieve peace? Ghyslain's forces will crush her little rebellion like a bug. I hope to the Creator that you come to your senses and flee long before that happens," he said, scowling. "I once loved you like a son, Calum. I don't agree with anything you're doing, but at least I have the courage to tell you to your face when you're making a mistake. Give me the respect I deserve and treat me the same way. You know how this war will end."

Drake lowered his voice, watching the rest of the Strykers climb atop their supply cart and snap the horses' reins, begrudgingly leaving the burning village behind them. "You're forgetting about her powers."

"I will never forget watching my own skin split at the touch of her fingers. She's unpredictable, and she's going to get you killed." He stepped back, starting toward the horse he'd left by the riverside. "I've said my piece before, and I'm getting tired of repeating myself."

28

TAMRIEL

"How quickly can you make it?"

The castle's armorer glanced up from the sketch Tamriel had given him, his thick, calloused fingers curling around the edge of the parchment. "A week or so, Your Highness. It's...not like the guards' armor."

"I'll pay for whatever materials and aid you need. Just let Akiva know how much it'll cost and he'll secure you the funds." He nodded to the guard, who was leaning against the post in the center of the room, watching the armorer's assistants hammer away at pieces of glowing metal.

The armorer bowed. "Yes, Your Highness."

Akiva fell into step behind Tamriel as he exited the room, the scent of leather and smoke clinging to his fine tunic. The guard's limp was more pronounced than usual, Tamriel noticed as they walked through the labyrinthine halls.

"Have you taken a day off since we returned from the Islands?"

"No, Your Highness."

"It would do you well to rest."

"That's what Healer Tabris said, but I won't sit on my ass doing nothing while there are people here who would see you harmed." He grimaced. "It's just that damned storm making it sore."

"Please, take a day off already, Akiva," Master Adan called from the next hall. A moment later, he turned the corner, flipping through various letters and reports. He bowed to Tamriel, then raised a brow at Akiva. "If I didn't know any better, I'd think you were trying to steal my job."

Despite the teasing in the Master of the Guard's voice, Akiva stiffened. "No, sir."

"Do you have news of Firesse and her troops?" Tamriel asked.

"Our soldiers arrived in Fishers' Cross only to find the entire town deserted. They said the elves had built pyres across the top of the bluff to burn the men they killed, and that there was so much ash along the shore that the water was more akin to sludge."

Tamriel suppressed a shudder at the words. How many of his people had died? How many of hers? "Where did the army go?"

"We're...not entirely sure. It appears the Cirisians have scattered across the fishing sector to wreak as much havoc as possible—burning houses and razing fields of crops. Our soldiers are on their trail, though."

"Find them. Let me know when you have more information."

Adan bowed, and Tamriel and Akiva continued to the great hall. When they arrived, Tamriel stopped in the doorway, automatically searching for Mercy. He found only disappointment. He shouldn't be surprised—her temper was not likely to have cooled in the few hours she'd been gone—but blind, sharp panic swept over him at the thought of her roaming the city streets where her would-be killers still lurked. Nynev and the others were watching over her, he knew, but they'd been caught unprepared before. It could happen again.

I will not lose her to the nobles. I will not *let them take her away from me.*

His earliest memories were of his father's wailing cries echoing down the castle corridors, raw and ragged with grief. As a child, he had often tiptoed to Calum's room and slipped between the silken sheets, burying his face in his cousin's chest to muffle his terrified sobs as priceless porcelain shattered against the stone walls. Love was a weakness. That was what his father's fits had taught him all those long, sleepless years. Love was that strange, foreign thing that had left Ghyslain so broken. Long ago, Tamriel had sworn he would not fare the same. He would not become his father.

As he grew, those words had become his mantra. They were the reason why in his adolescence, even as he charmed and danced with some of the noblemen's pretty daughters at state functions and celebrations, he had never let the walls around his heart falter. When he turned fifteen and the noblemen began suggesting that they find him a fiancée, he'd shot down every princess and noblewoman they'd recommended. For years, he had kept everyone at arm's length, everyone except Calum and the few friends he'd made among the council members' children.

Until Mercy.

She'd been different—so refreshingly, unabashedly, stunningly different from everyone else that the armor around his heart began to fracture, to crumble, whenever she was around. He'd finally found someone who shared his contempt of the nobles' games. He'd found someone around whom he hadn't needed to pretend to be the stoic, brooding son of the mad king, and he hadn't realized until it was too late that he'd fallen for her. Those words, that mantra, all those years of pushing people away...they'd all failed him.

And in return, he'd failed Mercy. He'd given in to all the fears, all the paranoia his father had instilled in him, and he'd let the courtiers' threats blind him to what needed to be done to the snakes who called his city home.

The realization had struck him the moment the library's doors slammed shut behind Mercy. As Nynev and the guards chased her down the hall, he'd grabbed a piece of parchment from one of the side tables and begun designing a suit of armor for his beloved—something strong enough and beautiful enough that anyone who beheld her would see it for what it truly was: a love letter to Mercy, a thank-you for all she'd done and an apology for all the ways he had wronged her, and a warning to the courtiers. He was finished masking his hatred of them behind a smile. He was finished watching them walk all over his father. He was finished letting them hurt the woman he loved.

29

TAMRIEL

Someone roughly shook him awake. His eyes fluttered open to a pitch-black room, and he bolted upright immediately, her name on his lips. "Mercy—?"

"No, it's me," Nynev whispered, her grip tightening on his shoulder. He blinked up at her, trying to make out the details of her face in the darkness. "It's late. Or early. I don't know. It's my sister—I don't know where she is."

He frowned, fighting against the grogginess still clouding his mind. "She's not in the infirmary?"

"Oh, is that where she would be? I should have thought to look there before I woke you." She smacked his arm, hard. He hissed in pain and recoiled, bumping his shoulder against the headboard. *Damn her Cirisian eyes,* he thought, scowling as he rubbed his shoulder. "I already checked there, Your Royal Daftness. She's not in the castle, and Atlas and the others were asleep whenever she left. I went to visit her around midnight, and she said she'd come to our room when she finished working with Lethandris on the translations. I haven't seen her since."

"Maybe they went to the Church." Tamriel pushed off his

blankets and reached blindly for the boots he'd left beside his bed. When he found them, he slipped his feet inside. Before he could even stand, Nynev pushed a cloak into his hands.

"The guards in the great hall never saw them leave, which means they used the servants' entrance. They wouldn't have sneaked out unless they didn't want anyone knowing where they've gone or what they're doing."

"Take a deep breath, Nynev. We'll find her. Just give me a moment to dress, then we'll go."

She stalked into the hall, and he quickly changed into the pants and tunic he'd tossed aside when he'd crawled into bed late that night. He had tried to wait up, hoping Mercy would return, but his eyes had fallen shut mere moments after his head hit the pillow. When he stepped into the hall, he found Nynev pacing outside his door. She stopped when she saw him. "Took you long enough."

"Do you want my help or don't you?" Without waiting for a response, he tossed her a cloak he'd taken from his wardrobe and pulled his own around himself. "Come on."

As they passed Mercy's bedroom door, he couldn't keep himself from asking, "Did she come back?"

The huntress shook her head. "Cassia and the guards promised to keep an eye on her so I could check on Niamh. Since we learned about the attack in Sapphira, she's been keeping to herself too much. She feels the nobles' hatred of our people more acutely now than ever. I hope to the gods that they're not somehow involved with her absence."

"She's immortal, though. If someone *did* take her, he can't hurt her, right?" he asked as they strode down the carriageway and through the castle gates, gravel crunching underfoot. He could see fairly well by the light of the moon and the few lampposts they passed, but he still allowed Nynev, with her quick pace and strange Cirisian night-vision, to take the lead as they started toward the Church.

"The nobles can hurt her; they just can't kill her." Her irises shone gold when she looked at him. "And I'm not sure she'd do anything to stop them if they tried."

"What do you mean?"

"She tried to kill herself more times than I care to remember after she realized what Firesse had done to her—what *I* let Firesse do to her the night she nearly died." Nynev's voice tightened, turning raw with guilt and fear, and Tamriel instantly regretted the question. "I'm terrified that if someone tries to hurt her for Firesse's crimes, she'll just sit there and take it. Her soul straddles the line between the realms of the living and the dead, and sometimes I think she wishes someone would find a way to tip her over the edge. That's why I've been so protective of her. That's why I agreed to come here with her. I love her too damn much to let her destroy herself."

When the groggy-faced High Priestess closed the door of the Church in their faces half an hour later—having informed them that Lethandris had not returned since she left that evening to work in the castle—Nynev kicked the door over and over and over again, spitting curses in Cirisian and the common tongue. After a few moments, her shoulders slumped and she sank to the ground, wrapping her arms around her knees. "I don't know where she is," she whispered, looking up at Tamriel with pure panic in her eyes. "I don't know where they could have gone."

He sat on the ground beside her. "Tell me what she said when you went to see her. Was she acting strangely at all?"

"She and Lethandris were going to work on translations for a while longer, so she told me not to wait up for her. Still, I went back to our room and tried to stay up to speak with her, but I fell asleep the moment my head hit the pillow."

He frowned. "I...I tried to do the same for Mercy, but I couldn't stay awake, either. You don't think she—?"

"What, that she drugged us?" she scoffed. Then she jerked upright, her hands dropping to her sides in shock. "She offered me a cup of tea when I visited her and Lethandris. How—How did she get you?"

"She poured both our drinks at dinner. She must have smuggled something out of the infirmary. Where would she go that she couldn't tell us? Where would you refuse to let her go?"

Understanding dawned on Nynev's face. "Gods damn her tender heart," she spat. "The infirmary—that warehouse in Beggars' End. Lethandris told me yesterday that when Atlas described how horrible the conditions are there, how many sick people are suffering there, my sister began to sob, saying she should have figured out the cure sooner—that she should have gone to help them sooner."

"She wouldn't be able to get past the guards at the gate."

"She's the most important healer in the city right now. By the king's order, the guards are required to give her whatever aid she requests. If she went to the End, they'd have let her through." As she spoke, Nynev's face drained of blood, turning a ghostly white under the light of the moon. She stood and brushed the dirt off her cloak. "Let's go find my sister."

THE SECOND THE GUARDS LET THEM THROUGH THE GATE, Nynev broke into a run, her cloak flapping behind her. Tamriel struggled to keep his footing on the weathered, uneven cobblestones as they careened around corners and raced down the narrow streets. He nearly plowed straight into her back when she stopped short before the warehouse-turned-infirmary. A soft orange light seeped through the shuttered and boarded-up windows. He followed Nynev to the warehouse door, peering over her shoulder as she turned the handle and pushed it open. Before he could catch more than a glimpse of cots and slumbering bodies, outlined in gold by the pale glow of the lantern on the far wall, the huntress paused.

He touched her shoulder. "Is she there?"

She shushed him, quietly closed the door, and waved him over to the window. "I didn't want to interrupt them," she whispered, pointing at a gap between the boards. "They're praying."

Two women were kneeling beside a cot in the middle of the room, their heads bowed and faces shrouded in shadow, but Tamriel recognized Niamh by way her shoulders hunched when someone let out a dry, rasping cough. She pulled something out of her pocket as Lethandris rose and moved to the head of the bed, murmuring something in Cirisian as she brushed sweat-slick hair from their patient's brow.

"What are they saying?" he asked as Lethandris looked to Niamh and nodded encouragingly.

"A prayer for—" She frowned, brows furrowing as Niamh unfolded a piece of paper and began to read aloud in ancient Cirisian, the words guttural and savage. "A prayer for passing."

Her sister pulled a slender knife from her sleeve and, in a flash of silver, drove it into the sick man's heart.

They watched in stunned silence as Niamh dipped a finger into the blood pooling on the man's soiled tunic and began drawing strange, swirling symbols along the man's blistered face, neck, and arms. Lethandris continued whispering to him as he let out a soft groan and went still. Out of the corner of his eye, Tamriel saw Nynev lift a trembling hand to her mouth.

A heartbeat later, the blood began to—

Tamriel went completely, utterly still.

The blood began to *glow*.

The glyphs Niamh had traced with her delicate, shaking finger bathed her solemn face in a warm red light, like sunshine filtering through a stained-glass window. She continued her work down to the tips of the man's fingers, then sat back, loosing a shuddering breath. When the light flared and faded, Lethandris grabbed her hand and led her to the next cot.

"No one else." Tamriel could hardly hear himself over the pounding in his ears as he stormed into the warehouse and snarled, his voice nearly unrecognizable, "Put down the knife, Niamh, or I swear to the Creator I will personally find a way to send you to the Beyond. Just what the *hell* do you think you're doing murdering my people?"

Lethandris stepped forward, hands up in surrender. "We can explain, Your Highness—"

"I didn't ask you," he snapped. "I asked *her*."

Niamh clutched the bloody knife in her hands, her wide eyes flitting from her sister—standing in the doorway, gaping as if she didn't recognize the woman standing before her—to him. "I-I-It's an ancient Cirisian ritual," she stammered. "A similar magic to the one Firesse uses to manipulate the *Aitherialnik*—blood magic. We wouldn't have risked it if it weren't absolutely necessary."

"The cure is working," the priestess cut in, "but too slowly. On its own, you'll need massive amounts of Cedikra to cure all the sick in Sandori, let alone the entire country. If you want to save as many people as you can, we need help. The Old Gods' magic can enhance the body's natural healing abilities enough to fight the disease with a smaller dose of medicine."

"You learned that from the Church's books?"

She nodded.

"And you didn't see fit to tell me before you took the life of one of my citizens?" He looked pointedly at Niamh's blood-coated hands, still wrapped around the handle of the knife, then to the body lying on the bed beside them.

Niamh bit her lip. "He was already dying. He only had another day or two left in this world, and his mind was gone already. This way, his death means something. It'll save lives. The stronger my connection to the Old Gods, the more people I can heal. Killing a few for the sake of the many is a sacrifice we have to make if you wish to see your people survive this outbreak."

"Be careful walking that line, *mo dhija*," Nynev warned. "Firesse is using that same logic to justify her attacks on this country."

Niamh opened her mouth to retort when footsteps clomped down the rickety steps. They all turned to see Hero standing halfway down the staircase, surveying the four of them and the dead man lying on the bloody cot. Ketojan hovered behind her.

"Did you know what they were planning?" Tamriel asked, frowning.

"We did," Hero said, the words garbled.

"And you do not object to them killing the people you've treated for so long?"

"If a few mercy killings will save thousands from long, painful deaths," Ketojan responded, "we will gladly see their suffering ended."

Every set of eyes swung to him, waiting to see what he would say.

He took a deep breath, swallowing his residual anger, and

turned to Niamh and the priestess. "No one else dies. You will test your theory on Atlas and the other guards first—two with magic, and two with only medicine. We will discuss how the rest of the sick in the country will be treated *after* we know the Old Gods' magic works. The next time you make a discovery like this, you will tell me first. Have I made myself clear?"

Niamh let out a relieved sigh and bowed, her body visibly relaxing. "Yes, Your Highness."

Lethandris nodded. "As you wish, Your Highness."

"Good. Clean up this mess and report back to the castle when you are finished. Nynev, let's go." Tamriel walked out into the street, the cool, storm-scented breeze sweeping over him. He closed his eyes and turned his face up to the sky, where patches of twinkling stars were visible through the thick clouds, as Nynev softly closed the door behind them. He couldn't keep the memory of the man's glowing blood out of his mind.

Creator, let them be right.

30

MERCY

The next morning, Cassia hired a carriage to take them back to the tailor's shop and led Mercy up the narrow stairs to the apartment, then back to the bedchamber. She didn't say a word as she helped Mercy remove her sling and tunic, although anger flashed across her face when she saw the bandage over the arrow wounds in Mercy's chest and shoulder.

Mercy shifted, the wounds already throbbing. She'd never sustained such severe injuries. Even once the scars healed, she'd never be able to move her arm with the ease she had before; the muscle had been too damaged. She'd have to adjust the way she fought—favor the right side. Use that arm for blocking heavy blows, use the left for quick slashes and easy jabs. She would adapt. Her Guild training wouldn't allow it to remain a weakness for long.

With Cassia's assistance, she changed into a set of borrowed clothes—soft, well-worn black pants and an embroidered white top from her sister's wardrobe. They returned to the common room to find Matthias slumped on the couch with a mug of tea in his hand, his hair still mussed from sleep. He eyed Mercy's outfit and chuckled. "She got you to play dress-up, did she?"

"What?"

"Cassia made that." He gestured toward her shirt. Embroidered roses swept across the fitted bodice and coiled down the sleeves, the red blooms as bright as blood against the white cotton. At a glance, the pattern was delicate and feminine, but a closer look revealed the long, sharp thorns poking out from the vines wrapping around her arms. The workmanship was exquisite. "She could have been working with Ino and me, escorting a merchants' caravan to Bluegrass Valley—but no, she had to spend a week sewing that."

"In case you've forgotten, brother dearest, if not for me and my sewing needles, you wouldn't have had any clothes to wear for the first few years after our escape," Cassia responded, crossing her arms.

"Like that would have been a shame," Matthias retorted. He winked at Mercy. "I look wonderful without clothes on, for your information."

"I'll take your word for it."

He grinned at Cassia. "I like her."

"I should hope so. You'll be seeing a lot of each other in the days to come." Cassia turned to Mercy and smiled, excitement brightening her hazel eyes. "Now," she said, "to turn you into a queen."

Tamriel's jaw dropped when Mercy walked into the castle a little over an hour later, flanked by her siblings. The king and Master Adan did the same. Mercy beamed when the guards and courtiers who had been passing through the great hall stopped and stared.

"You— You look—" Tamriel shook his head, his throat

bobbing when he swallowed. "You look...different."

She raised a brow. "That's it? Just different?"

Beautiful, he didn't need to say. She could read it on his face.

Cassia had braided Mercy's hair into a crown and pinned small, silken roses into every few stitches, her deft fingers making quick work of Mercy's wild curls. The blood red roses on her shirt appeared to tumble out over the top of the leather breastplate she wore, and the gemstones encrusted on the hand guard of her dagger caught the red of the blossoms, sending flecks of light throughout the room as she moved. She looked like a warrior queen from the legends of the Year of One Night, and Tamriel couldn't stop gawking. Cassia and Matthias flanked her on either side, armed and clad in leather armor. Ino, rendered nearly invisible to the nobles by his white slave sash, was already somewhere in the castle, eavesdropping and gathering information.

Mercy stopped before the king and bowed. When she straightened, she looked straight at Tamriel. "What did I miss?"

He blinked at her a few times, clearly at a loss for words. When he swallowed again, she grinned at the hint of desire she glimpsed through his shock and bewilderment. "There's been an attack," he finally said. "Multiple attacks."

Every hint of levity vanished at the pain in his voice. "What? Where?"

"Harkness. Briar Glen. Fairwater. Graystone," Master Adan answered for him.

Mercy felt the blood drain from her face. Beside her, Cassia and Matthias stiffened.

"Our Cirisian friends have coordinated their attacks well," Ghyslain said grimly. "Each town was hit in the dead of night in the exact same manner. Come. Let us speak of this in private."

He turned on his heel and gestured for them to follow. When they reached the council chambers, Cassia and Matthias took up positions on either side of the double doors, hands on the hilts of the swords sheathed at their sides. Mercy trailed Tamriel and Master Adan into the room, and the king slumped into his seat at the head of the table. "Through some blend of magic, strategy, and our own Creator-damned bad luck, Firesse and most of her soldiers have managed to evade the troops I sent and incapacitate four more towns. How the hell did they make it past our men, Adan?"

The Master of the Guard hesitated, then said, "I'm...not entirely sure, Your Majesty. Her powers—"

"She's a girl with a thousand scarcely-trained elves at her back and my bitter fool of a nephew at her side. I expect my Master of the Guard to be able to keep our enemies from marching straight into the heart of our country unimpeded, but I may have grossly overestimated your skill in that regard, Adan. I suggest you come up with a new strategy before you find yourself out of a job."

Master Adan's face paled. As they began to discuss troop movements, possible future attacks, and guess at what sensitive information Calum might have given Firesse, Mercy turned to Tamriel. The prince was still standing by the closed double doors, watching her. When their eyes met, he started toward her and she stiffened, expecting another round of the fight they'd had the night before.

"I'm sorry," he said, surprising her. "You were right about the courtiers, about fleeing—about everything. After Drayce hurt you, all I wanted was to protect you, but I ended up making everything worse. He got inside my head," he murmured, nodding to his father. "When I should have had your back, I let fear paralyze me. It won't happen again."

She wrapped her arms around his waist. "I'm sorry, too. It wasn't fair for me to lash out like that. Can you forgive me?"

He nodded. His lips brushed the point of her ear when he leaned down and whispered, "I love you so much, Mercy. No one will ever take you away from me." As he spoke, his fingers slid down to the bottom of her breastplate and slipped under the hem of her shirt, tracing light circles across her bare skin.

"I love you more."

"Not possible. And I assume the strangers waiting outside are your siblings?"

"I'll introduce you. They've promised to help us fight the nobles."

He grinned. "The more the merrier."

Someone cleared his throat, and they jumped apart. Ghyslain frowned as Adan hurried out of the room. "Has Seren Pierce found any more information about the people involved in Drayce's plot to kill Mercy, Tam?"

"The Kelaya and Ehren families may have been the ones who bribed him. The heads of each estate have had a long-standing rivalry, but a few guards reported seeing them speaking outside Kelaya Zavian's art gallery in the Plaza several times since we returned from the Islands. Pierce did a little digging into the gallery's finances and noticed a large withdrawal from its account at the bank, ostensibly to purchase a painting from a private collector, but there hasn't been a delivery to the gallery in months. He's looking into Ehren as we speak. We think the money was used to pay Drayce for the attack."

"How do you know Ehren wasn't just looking to buy a painting?" Mercy asked.

"Ehren Tallis has been blind for the past ten years, and his only relatives live in Bluegrass Valley. He's not in the market for home furnishings." Tamriel's expression darkened. "They were involved. I'm sure of it. Once Pierce finishes his investigation into Ehren, we'll root out the snakes in the court, starting with those two."

"Good." Ghyslain nodded and rose. "Send for me when the guards bring them in. For now, I have to go make sure my Master of the Guard doesn't unwittingly hand over my kingdom to that Cirisian witch." He grumbled to himself as he left the room, mumbling something about wishing Master Oliver were here to guide the troops. Cassia and Matthias entered the council chamber before the doors could swing shut behind the king. They immediately dropped into low bows before the prince.

"Your Highness."

"Stand, please, and call me Tamriel," he said, extending a hand for them to shake. Cassia raised her brows, clearly surprised and impressed that he would greet her as an equal, and smiled as she clasped his hand. He turned to Matthias next. "I've been told you'll stand with us against the nobles."

"We'll do anything for Mercy," Cassia vowed.

"And for Liselle," Matthias added as he shook the prince's hand.

Tamriel gestured to the long table in the center of the room, and they sat, Tamriel at the head, Mercy to his right, and her siblings opposite her. When the prince leaned forward and propped his chin on his hand, his dark eyes roving over Cassia and Matthias, she caught a glimpse of the king he would one day become—honest, courageous, regal. He would always fear for her safety, she knew, but he would risk the nobles' anger to do what was right for her and the rest of his people, human and elven alike. The light of the candelabrum in the center of the table gilded his black hair, and she had no trouble at all picturing the sparkling diadem that would one day sit atop his head.

"Well," Tamriel said, his voice even and sure, "where should we strike first?"

31

CALUM

Four days after the attack in Graystone, Drake and Myris were working on training drills with some of the elves they had liberated when a shout rose from somewhere across camp. Drake paused in the middle of demonstrating a move and tossed aside the blunted practice sword. The Cirisians in the surrounding tents peered out at the commotion.

One of Firesse's scouts appeared at the opposite end of the valley, a small company of elves trailing his horse down the rocky slope of the hill. Calum recognized the bronze-skinned warrior at the front a second before Drake's surprise flashed through him. *Kaius.* His group, alongside Faye's, were supposed to meet them outside Rockinver tonight for another attack. From the haunted looks on the faces of the soldiers shuffling along behind him—one of them holding a bloodied rag to her arm—something had gone terribly wrong along the way.

Firesse stepped out of her tent, the beads in her braids flashing in the sun as she whirled around, searching for the source of the disturbance. "What's going—*Kaius*!" She barreled through the camp and seized Kaius by his shoulders. Her eyes were wide, her face bloodless, as she scanned him for injuries.

"Take a break," Drake called to the slaves he'd been training, and they scattered as he started across camp toward Firesse and the hunter.

"They found us in the middle of the night," Kaius was saying when he approached, shaking his head. "The Beltharans took out the men on watch, then found our camp and killed half my people in their tents. It was chaos. The soldiers were everywhere. We only managed to take down a few before I had to call a retreat." He glanced at the five elves that remained of the group he'd been leading, pain and guilt in his green eyes. "We barely made it out with our lives."

Firesse threw her arms around him. "I'm so glad you're alive."

"No one is more glad of that than I," he responded, and stepped out of her embrace. "We need to discuss how this will affect our attack tonight."

"You're right," Drake cut in. "We'll need a new strategy now that ninety percent of your troops are missing."

The archer's expression didn't change, but Calum could see the hatred smoldering in his eyes as Firesse agreed and led them into her tent. The archer had never liked Calum, and it was obvious he only put up with Drake for the sake of winning the war.

After an hour, they emerged with a plan.

LIKE GRAYSTONE, THE FISHING VILLAGE OF ROCKINVER was not protected by walls or gates, spilling over the land in a cluster of stone and wood houses just off the highway to the capital. Unlike Graystone, however, the people of Rockinver were awake, the village alive and thrumming with energy, when Drake and the elves approached from the eastern woods just shy of midnight. They were celebrating the Bounty Fest—the fishing sector's version of a harvest festival.

Myris's group split from Firesse's to take up a defensive position along the southern rim of the town, each soldier wielding a razor-sharp dagger or arrows steeped in a poisonous concoction one of the elves had created. Faye's group was doing the same in the north. Together, they'd maintain a perimeter and press inward, forcing the city guards and any soldiers stationed within to fight in the cramped streets, among the civilians they were sworn to protect.

As they neared the village, Calum could hear the laughter and joyous music drifting over from the feast outside the town hall. He and Tamriel had attended one Fest when they were children—back when Ghyslain still bothered to tour the country over which he ruled—and Drake had had no qualms with digging through Calum's happy memories of that night to learn about the town's defenses.

A dozen men in plate mail stood guard at the edge of the town's main road, blades in hand as they stared out into the darkness. Firesse let out a low whistle, and six of the guards—Cirisians in disguise—immediately shoved their swords through the backs of the men in front of them. Without a word, the elves lifted the visors of their helmets and dragged the Beltharans' bodies into the cover of the woods.

Faye stalked out of the shadows, her ink-black hair and dark leather armor rendering her nearly invisible. "It was a lucky thing encountering those soldiers on the way here," she said to Firesse, nodding to the armored elves now sheathing their swords and resuming their post, looking to the world like Beltharan soldiers on watch. "The king's soldiers have set up checkpoints around the town square. I sent the few archers I could spare into the town already. Creator willing, they're already in position on the rooftops with Kaius's men, ready to provide cover. Just give the signal"—she raised a hand and closed it into a fist—"and they'll fire."

"Thank you, Faye."

The Assassin dipped her head and glanced once at Drake, no doubt remembering their last conversation. "I'll see you at the feast," she said as she melted back into the night.

Firesse surveyed her soldiers one last time, their blades and leather armor hidden under the cloaks and peasant clothes they'd pilfered on the trek from Graystone. With the colorful face paint hiding their tattoos, the only hint of their elven blood—their pointed ears—were tucked away behind artfully pinned braids or low-brimmed hats. She nodded, smiling faintly, and gestured for them to advance.

Drake and the rest of the soldiers emerged from the forest and began making their way in twos and threes into the village, stopping every so often to watch the revelers dancing in the streets or to sample a piece of fried fish from one of the merchants' tables. Like the humans, they *ooh*ed and *aah*ed at the paper lanterns strung from building to building, the soft orbs of light guiding them toward the heart of the village.

Three Beltharan soldiers in commoners' clothes wandered toward Drake. They had opted for ease of access rather than true disguises; the bulk of their swords was visible through the folds of their lightweight cloaks. Drake averted his gaze as they neared, pretending to watch a young girl with pieces of tinsel braided into her hair dance as her father played the fiddle. In his periphery, Calum saw Kenna surreptitiously touch her hair to ensure her elven ears were hidden as another group of soldiers—these ones in mail—cast a wary gaze over the crowd.

Someone bumped Drake's shoulder.

"There are more soldiers in the streets than I thought," Firesse whispered as she passed. "I sent messengers to the others to advance their lines sooner than we'd planned. Be at the square in ten minutes."

Drake watched her out of the corner of his eye, and only when she had reached the end of the block did he risk another glance around. As far as Calum could tell, the houses on either side of him were empty, but it was likely the guard-commander had posted men cloaked in black in the windows or on the rooftops. The paper lanterns didn't penetrate the darkness enough for him to get a clear view. Below, however, the winding roads and shadowed alleys crawled with guards and soldiers. Calum could tell by the way they moved, the way their eyes lingered too long on the faces of the people around them and not on the spectacles of the holiday, that they had been sent to defend the town. Unfortunately, Drake and Firesse had planned for it. Soon, Faye's and Myris's troops would sweep through the city, cutting down citizen and guard alike to distract them from the chaos Firesse would unleash at the feast.

Drake trailed behind Firesse as she continued toward the square. She grinned at everyone she passed, bouncing on her toes with excitement and swaying her hips to the music, the picture of delight. Calum could tell the display wasn't entirely feigned; growing up in the Islands, she'd never seen a celebration save for *Ialathan,* and the joy of the revelers they passed was infectious. Her hair was free of its braids and swept up into the high bun favored by the young women of the fishing district, her locks glowing like a crown of flames under the lantern light. She slipped around a blind corner, and Drake nearly slammed into her when he followed.

A huge crowd had gathered in the street. The people were shouting over one another, pushing and shoving in an effort to get closer to the town center. They'd arrived at one of the checkpoints. Drake craned his neck, and over the sea of heads he spied four soldiers standing in a line in the middle of the block, carefully inspecting every person who stepped forward. "They're turning away all the elves," he told her as he watched a slave disappear into the crowd.

A half-dozen Cirisians were clustered among the waiting villagers, glancing nervously at the soldiers and whispering to one another. They'd been ordered to resort to violence if necessary, but they were outnumbered and trapped in the middle of a human city.

"Get ready to push forward," Firesse murmured. She whispered something under her breath—an incantation.

At the checkpoint, two of the soldiers stumbled, clutching their stomachs. Their faces turned an almost comical shade of green a heartbeat before they doubled over and vomited onto the cobblestone, eliciting cries of disgust and surprise from their brothers-at-arms. The second their line broke, the revelers—annoyed and impatient after being kept out of the festivities—surged forward. Drake and Firesse let the current of bodies carry them through the broken checkpoint. Calum glimpsed similar chaos on the streets they passed. Firesse's magic had affected the guards at the other checkpoints, as well.

"Clever girl," Drake murmured, and she grinned up at him, her skin wan from drawing on so much magic.

"Hold on." Someone snagged Firesse's arm and yanked her backward. Drake whirled in time to see a soldier hauling her back, fighting against the sea of people running past. With his free hand, he smeared Firesse's colorful face paint, revealing her Cirisian tattoos. "I thought you looked familiar, girl. You're to face trial in the capital."

"Unhand her," Drake growled, his voice so low and vicious that the man actually paused. Recognition lit up his eyes.

"You're the traitor Calum Zend—"

Firesse twisted, shoving a dagger into the man's stomach, and jerked out of his grip, allowing the crowd to carry her back to Drake's side. Someone shrieked at the sight of the dying soldier, but Drake and Firesse were already turning the corner into the town square when the soldiers began shouting, searching for the culprit.

Tables laden with platters of fish, roasted vegetables, colorful fruits, and pastries were scattered throughout the town square. There was a fountain in the center, covered withs strands of silver tinsel that fluttered in the breeze, reflecting the stars and the torchlight. Music spilled over the square, light and flowing and—

Blackness swept over Calum, drowning him, dragging him away from that busy town square, away from the terrified faces of the revelers.

CALUM JOLTED OUT OF DARKNESS, PANIC CONSUMING HIS every thought as he struggled to orient himself. Drake and Firesse had just arrived in the town square when that strange blackness had come for him, swift and unforgiving as an icy wind. It had been happening more and more often lately— falling into that strange, featureless void—but it had never happened so suddenly, so completely. Worse, he'd done nothing to provoke it. Most of the time, it happened after he tried to fight Drake's hold on his body, his mind. This time, he had merely watched through eyes he could not control as Drake and Firesse marched into the square.

One second there, the next gone—to where, he still didn't know. The only think he knew for sure was that the gaps in his consciousness were growing longer. One day, he realized with a jolt of panic, he might not return at all.

"Look at that," Firesse breathed to Drake, oblivious to the change within him. They were standing on the rim of the fountain, the eye of the storm.

Most of the feast tables had been overturned, their porcelain platters in shards on the ground. The stench of rotten food hung in the air. The baked roasts that had sat in pools of rich gravy now buzzed with flies. The skin of the once-ripe fruit was wrinkled and pitted with spots of green and white mold. A silver-blue fish seemed to writhe on the cobblestone as if alive—although after studying it more closely, Calum realized the fish wasn't moving at all; its body was crawling with fat, wriggling maggots. Every person who had partaken of the feast doubled over and retched, their half-digested food crawling with bugs.

Firesse's magic.

The First had turned the food putrid inside their stomachs, a power Calum hadn't known she possessed. All he'd heard during their planning of the attack was that she would somehow disrupt the celebration. He had never expected *this*.

A few of the villagers stumbled and collapsed, looking so sickly and pale that Calum doubted they'd survive the night. A few yards from him, a little girl hugged her knees close to her chest and rocked back and forth, a waxy pallor to her sun-kissed skin. The sight sent Calum into a rage.

How can you let her do this to your countrymen? he snarled at his father. *To this child?*

I'll let her do as she pleases, if it means I get my revenge on the king, Drake responded coolly.

Soldiers rushed into the square, swords drawn and armor splattered with fresh blood—Cirisian blood. Firesse went still at the sight. Faye, Myris, and their people had made it into the city, then, and taken heavy losses.

The soldiers gawked at the scene before them—rotting food, ill townspeople huddled behind the overturned tables, and Firesse and Drake watching over it all, smiling. They were still gaping when a hail of arrows rained down upon them, burying themselves in eye sockets, throats, in the gaps in the soldiers' armor. One tried to stagger away, a hand gripping the arrow protruding from his thigh, but a Cirisian stepped into his path and slashed out with his sword. Blood sprayed, and the soldier crumpled, his head thumping to the ground and rolling away from his body.

"Thank you, Kaius," Firesse crooned, looking up at the archers on the rooftops. Her skin was pale, her eyes slightly unfocused. Drake stepped down from the wall of the fountain and extended a hand to her, ready to catch her should she fall unconscious, as she had at Fishers' Cross. She waved him away. "Go find—"

But Calum didn't hear the rest. On the other side of the square, concealed in the mouth of an alley, stood Mercy's father with a bow in his hands, a poison-tipped arrow aimed straight at Firesse's heart. Neither Firesse nor Drake seemed to have spotted him.

Strike true, Calum silently prayed as the elf loosed his arrow. *End this now.*

Drake caught the flash of movement in his periphery and tackled Firesse. They landed in a sodden heap in the fountain, a tangle of limbs. Calum could do nothing but watch as Drake pushed to his knees, being careful to stay below the rim of the fountain, and grasped the First's shoulders. "Stay down! Stay down. Were you struck?"

She winced and reached for her left arm. When her fingers came away, they were wet with blood. A shudder passed through her body, and realization dawned in her eyes. Calum could feel his father's panic, even as his own heart sang with joy; if Firesse died, her magic might die with her. He would be free, and this nightmare would finally be over.

"You'll be alright," Drake said quickly, already reaching for his dagger. "I'll kill that son of a bitch—" He started to rise, but she grabbed the hem of his shirt and pulled him back down.

"Wait," she gasped. She grimaced, then said something in ancient Cirisian.

He watched incredulously as a dark green cloud seeped out of the wound and hovered in the air an inch from her skin. The poison—she was leeching it from her body.

Firesse breathed another guttural incantation, and the green cloud shot past Drake and over the lip of the fountain. He looked up just in time to see the poisonous gas envelop Mercy's father and slither into his mouth and nose. He clawed at his throat, his eyes widening in horror. Somewhere behind Drake, a woman screamed. *Dayna*.

They weren't supposed to be here. They must have snuck away from Myris's group to murder Firesse.

"Adriel!" she cried as Mercy's father collapsed, his eyes rolling up into his head. "*Adriel!*"

NO!

Dayna threw down her bow and ran toward her husband, tears streaming down her face. Another Cirisian stepped into her path, but she didn't hesitate—she whipped out a dagger and plunged it into his heart, straight through his leather armor. Drake jumped out of the fountain as she fell to her knees beside Adriel. Her shoulders shook with sobs.

"Help Firesse," Drake ordered a passing elf. As the boy leapt into the fountain to aid his First, Drake stalked toward Dayna. Amidst the chaos and her own ragged sobs, she didn't hear him approach until it was too late—until he had one hand knotted in her hair, dragging her up and away from Adriel. Her hands flew up to protect herself, but she was unarmed; she'd left her dagger in the chest of the elf she'd killed. She landed a few good kicks to Drake's legs before he threw her to the ground, her knees cracking hard against the stone. When she tried to rise again, he gave her a swift, sharp kick to the ribs.

NO! STOP IT! STOP! The leash on Calum's temper

snapped; everything within him railed against the bonds holding him captive in his mind. Damn the consequences. Damn the blackness lurking at the edge of his consciousness, waiting to drag him under. Drake had tormented his mother for years. Calum would not allow him to do it again.

"Do you know who I am?" Drake snarled as Dayna gasped, one hand clutching her side. Caught up in the height of the attack and his own cruel nature, he didn't bother to masquerade as Calum.

"Drake." She spat the name like a curse. "I could see the evil in your eyes."

"I should have killed you the moment I recognized you," he growled as he flipped her onto her back, straddling her hips so she couldn't kick out, "for bearing me a bastard without a spine."

She pummeled his chest with her fists, thrashing and bucking. He caught her hands and pinned her wrists to the ground above her head. When he leaned down and ran his tongue up her neck and along the line of her jaw, she stilled, terror pouring off her in waves. "Do you remember the last time we were in this position, my darling?" he whispered into her ear. "Do you remember how I made you scream?"

She spat in his face.

When he reared back in disgust, wiping his face with a sleeve, she blurted, "I know you're in there, Calum. I know you're watching, that he's making you do these things. Stop him. Fight back. *Fight back*, my son."

I'M TRYING!

Drake backhanded Dayna across the face. He grabbed the dagger sheathed at his hip and raised it high, preparing to drive it into her chest.

"FIGHT HIM, CALUM!" Dayna screamed.

As the blade began its downward arc, Calum shoved everything within him against the walls of his mental prison, letting his rage and guilt and fury boil over. *You will* not *kill my mother, you heartless bastard!*

Something within him cracked.

Then he was gasping, panting, stopping himself short right before the blade in his hand—*his hand*, not Drake's—would have lodged in Dayna's heart. He froze. The ice-water in his veins was gone. He could smell the stench of vomit and the coppery tang of blood hanging in the air, could feel the cold of the sopping wet clothes hanging from his body.

"I-I-I'm free," he choked out. He met his mother's wide-eyed gaze and let out a hysterical sound somewhere between a sob and a laugh. "He's gone. You did it."

She shook her head, breathing hard. "*You* did it."

Calum tossed the dagger aside and helped Dayna to her feet. She rose slowly, clutching her ribs. "You need to run," he urged, pushing her toward the nearest alley, where the archers stationed high above wouldn't be able to strike her. They hadn't loosed any arrows yet, although he knew they were watching. They still thought he was Drake. "Warn Mercy and Tamriel what's to come."

She looked over her shoulder at Adriel, sprawled on the ground, and began to tremble.

Within his mind, a presence stirred—one with a vengeance.

"He's coming back," Calum said. He picked up a sword from a fallen soldier and pushed it into her hands. "Stick to the alleys. Run as fast and as far as you can. Firesse will kill you if she finds you."

Dayna seized his hand. "Come with me. Keep fighting him. We'll find some way to free you."

"I-I can't." He could already feel Drake drawing nearer, a predator circling its prey. He could only hold his father back long enough for her to escape. "You need to leave now. Tell Tamriel—" Calum choked on the name, on the shame that accompanied it. "Tell him I'm sorry. Tell him it wasn't me." The words were flimsy—how could he possibly hope for forgiveness now, after all he had done, after all the destruction he'd wrought?—but he needed Tamriel to know. He needed Tamriel to know he would not have traded his country's secrets and spilled his countrymen's blood if he could have avoided it. He suspected he would never get a chance to tell him face-to-face.

She nodded, fresh tears shining in her eyes, and kissed his cheek. "Thank you, my son," she whispered. "I pray we meet again one day. Stay strong."

With that, she turned and ran as fast as her injuries allowed. He watched her leave, funneling every bit of his quickly-fading strength into holding his father back.

Just a little while longer. Just a little while longer. Just a little—

He gasped and crumpled to his knees as agony nearly cleaved his head in two. His hands flew to his temples. He couldn't stop the scream that ripped free of his mouth, the waves of pain that made his stomach roil. Every nerve felt like it was on fire.

Oh, I'll make you pay for that, my insolent, spineless excuse for a son, Drake hissed in a voice laced with violence. Calum almost couldn't hear his father over the ringing in his ears. Bursts of light flared in his vision. Drake's presence slammed fully into his mind, those prison bars sliding shut on him once more, the ice-water filling his veins with such acute agony that Calum's heart stuttered. It was almost a relief when the darkness, thick and absolute, dragged him under once more.

But—before everything went silent, before the pain finally abated, his father picked up the dagger he'd tossed aside and murmured, "Let the hunt begin."

32

CALUM

When Calum came to, he found Drake standing in the middle of a tent, gazing down at a bound and gagged Dayna. Adriel was slumped beside her. His skin was pale and waxen, but he was breathing. He was *alive*.

"See what happens when you try to play savior, Calum?" Drake said.

Let them go.

Not a chance. They tried to kill Firesse, and now they'll face their punishment. Besides, he said as someone entered the tent behind him, *it's not up to me.*

"I gave you a chance to fight for our people," Firesse snarled as she joined Drake in the center of the tent. She was still dressed in the colorful clothes she had worn to the Bounty Fest, a slender strip of linen wrapped around her arm where Adriel's arrow had grazed her. She gripped Dayna's chin roughly, her eyes burning like molten metal. "I gave you a *chance*," she hissed again, yanking down Dayna's gag, "to take your revenge on the people who murdered your daughter and chased you out of your home. And you repay that kindness by trying to *kill me*. What do you have to say for yourself?"

"I still have family in the capital. My daughter stands beside the prince you so desperately wish to slay," Dayna growled. "You must be a bigger fool than I thought if you assumed I would choose the Cirisians over her—and over my son." Her eyes slid to Drake's, slitted with hatred. "I know the truth about who attacked whom at *Ialathan*. Calum was nothing but your puppet."

"I did what was necessary to save my people."

"If you cared about your people, you wouldn't have burned Graystone to the ground with dozens of elven slaves still trapped inside. I will never follow a leader who ends innocent lives without batting an eye. The Creator looks down on you and weeps, child."

Firesse reared back as though struck. "You would let that villain's name poison your tongue? Have you forgotten our gods?"

"The only villain here, Firesse, is you."

A shadow passed across the First's face. She looked at Adriel, still slumped and half-conscious beside Dayna. "Be careful how you speak to me. My magic is the only thing keeping the poison from reaching your husband's heart. Without me, he's dead." She dug her fingernails into Dayna's cheeks, her eyes narrowing. "You vastly underestimate how easy it would be for me to destroy everything and everyone you hold dear."

"You're going to kill us shortly, anyway. Why shouldn't I use what little time I have left to tell you exactly what I think of you?"

Firesse bared her teeth in a grin so chilling it made Calum's stomach drop. She shoved Dayna back and straightened, her flame-red hair falling like a curtain around her deceptively pretty face. "You're not going to lose your life just yet. You're so desperate to see your daughter again, and it wouldn't be fair if I didn't let you see her one last time." She strode out of the tent. Just before slipping through the flap, she told Drake, "Have Kenna and Farren keep an eye on them while one of Myris's men scrounges up some rope."

As Drake wandered through the camp, Calum's thoughts returned to those brief minutes of freedom in the town square. For the first time in what felt like an eternity, he'd been able to *move*, to *speak*, to feel the breeze against his face. By the Creator, he'd been *himself* again.

Then the darkness had swept in and claimed him.

He wasn't sure exactly how long he'd been lost in that strange, featureless void, but it had been long enough for the Cirisians to set up camp in the bottom of a valley, the wide expanse of the Bluejet River cleaving a jagged line through the land. The gaps in his consciousness were growing longer, his tenuous connection to his body and mind slipping. His attempts to fight Drake's control only exacerbated it. The next time he disappeared, Calum feared it would be permanent.

A small, instinctual voice within him urged him to stop fighting his father, to wait and pray he lasted long enough to survive Firesse's war. However small the chance, however remote the possibility, Firesse might release him once she'd claimed her revenge. The Calum he'd been only a few weeks ago would have done it. Now, though, he would not hesitate to resign himself to oblivion it it meant ending this senseless war. If he could find one more opportunity to break through, to end Firesse's life and save those of his countrymen, he would do it. He would save everyone he loved, even if it cost his life.

Tamriel—his cousin by blood, his brother by choice.

Dayna—the mother he'd always needed.

Elise—the girl who loved him.

Even Mercy—cunning, ruthless, infuriating Mercy, with her sharp eyes and barbed tongue.

They were his family, not Drake. Not this monster wearing his face.

He tested the shackles around his mind, poking and prodding as gently as he could without drawing Drake's attention. *There*—a crack. Calum wasn't sure how he knew it, only that he could feel its existence. He had broken something when he slipped through, left a hole in the walls of his prison. If he could direct enough willpower toward the fault, perhaps he would be able to break through one last time—if only long enough to free Dayna and Adriel or shove a blade through Firesse's black heart.

For Dayna, for Tamriel, for Mercy, for Elise, for Adriel, for every innocent person Drake helped Firesse slaughter, he would risk it.

Dayna and Adriel were being held under heavy watch in a tent across camp, far enough from Firesse's that Calum would have to choose between saving them and killing the First—he wouldn't have time to do both. He could find a way past the guards and release Mercy's parents, but they'd still have an entire camp full of Cirisians between them and freedom, and Calum wasn't sure he'd be able to hold on long enough to help them fight their way out. They'd likely be killed before they could even set foot outside the valley.

Targeting Firesse wouldn't be any easier. Calum didn't doubt that Drake had told her about his betrayal during the attack, which meant she would be careful not to lower her guard around him. Earlier, he'd noticed two heavily armed elves standing watch outside her tent, and another trailing the First through the camp. Between that and Kaius's watchful, distrusting gaze, the window of opportunity was slim. Calum would have to bide his time, waiting and watching.

Quiet laughter drew him out of his thoughts. He watched through eyes he couldn't control as Drake crested one of the hills surrounding the valley, and Faye and Nerran came into view. They were sitting side by side in the waist-high grass, shoulders nearly touching, and staring out at the swirling pinks and purples of dawn. They spoke in low tones, not wishing to break the quiet calm that lay over the valley.

Nerran glanced up first, his smile fading. "Come to join us? Or to drink your troubles away?" He took a swig from a half-empty bottle of wine, then offered it to Drake. "I've drunk enough to be able to stand your presence for a little while."

"How gracious of you to offer. Isn't it a bit early to be drinking?"

"It's not morning yet," Faye said, pointing to the eastern horizon. "I'm choosing to consider it very, very late last night."

Drake settled down on Nerran's other side, stretching his legs out before him. "It's not Cirisian wine, is it?"

By the Creator, I hope not. Calum remembered with a flush of embarrassment the night he'd gotten drunk off that Creator-damned Cirisian wine. Just his luck that Drake had seen *that* memory.

"Beltharan through and through. One of Kaius's men swiped it from the fest, and he gave it to us as a thank-you for aiding them in the war." Nerran's face was carefully composed, but Calum heard the note of disgust slip into his friend's voice. When Drake didn't reach for the bottle, Nerran took another sip and handed it to Faye. "We'll reach Xilor in a few days. I thought you should know—we're leaving when you reach Sandori."

"Leaving?"

"Hewlin already cleared it with Firesse. She was not happy, to say the least, but he convinced her to see reason. We're not soldiers, and we're not trained killing machines," he said with a nod toward Faye. "Our place is not in a war. We'll stay with you and provide weapons and repairs until the final battle, but duty calls. We've been away from Feyndara for too long."

Sadness washed over Calum. Over the year they'd traveled and worked together, Hewlin and the others had become his family. They were loud and argumentative and, frankly, obnoxious at times, but they cared for one another. They'd taught Calum almost all he knew about smithing. They were the first friends he'd ever had who had not known him as Calum Zendais, who had not judged him for the infamy of his father. Despite his better judgment, despite his own selfish reasons for accompanying them to the Keep, they had become special to him.

Under the sorrow, however, he felt a rush of relief. *He* had dragged them into the middle of this war. His hope that they could somehow free him from Drake's grasp was nothing but the dream of a fool. There would be no freedom for him—not after taking down Firesse. Watching the Strykers leave would be bittersweet, but it was necessary. They never should have been here in the first place.

"I'm grateful for your help," Drake responded. "I'll pay you for services rendered when we reach the city."

"Keep your money."

He looked at the smith sharply, surprised. "What?"

"Keep your money."

"I heard you the first time, but I've never seen you refuse payment for anything. You'd face down a Rennox if it owed you two aurums."

Nerran shook his head. "We discussed it yesterday while you were in Rockinver. We want to walk away with no memory of this wretched job, and we can't do that if our pockets are filled with blood money. We can bear the loss."

"You're telling me you don't wish to be paid because you don't want to be reminded that things you made killed people?" Drake asked, incredulous. "You're armor and weapon smiths, for the Creator's sake. You think someone who pays a thousand aurums for a sword uses it to trim his hedges?"

"Of course not, smartass. But there's a difference between a man trying to protect his family and a coward who slaughters innocents in their own damn beds."

"What about assassins?" Drake asked, jerking his head toward Faye. "Where do they fall on your morality scale?"

"Leave me out of your quarrels," she responded. "I just came to enjoy the sunrise."

It was only then that Drake and Nerran realized the sun had half-risen above the horizon, its rays turning the expanse of long, swaying grass and rolling hills before them into a gilded sea. Save for the distant silhouette of Rockinver and the snaking ribbon of the king's highway, the wild landscape was uninterrupted, untouched by human hands. Deep blue rivers and slender streams wended across wildflower-dotted meadows. If Calum were not trapped within his mental prison, the sight would have taken his breath away.

"It really is a magnificent dawn, isn't it?" Nerran breathed, his anger melting away. He tilted his head back and watched the fat clouds drift languidly across the sky. Then he murmured, so quietly Calum almost couldn't hear him over the rustling of the long grass, "What horrors will today bring, do you think?"

The question hung in the air. Neither Faye nor Drake ventured a response.

They sat there for several long minutes, watching the sun continue its slow ascent. No one spoke, yet the hillside was far from silent; crickets chirped, the stalks of grass whispered against one another, and the Bluejet gurgled in the valley behind them.

"I hope I never see another war," Faye whispered, her voice thick with emotion. "I don't think I'll ever forget the sounds of the attack last night—the way the people gagged and retched when Firesse turned the food in their stomachs rotten. I wasn't even in the square, but I could hear it from blocks away." Her hazel eyes fell from the scene before them to the rough calluses across her palms and fingers, memories of a life spent in the Guild's service. She swallowed. "I can't stop thinking about all the people I've killed. Forty-four. Forty-four people in the span of a few weeks, all because Firesse offered Mother Illynor a payday she couldn't refuse."

"You're an Assassin—getting paid to kill people is part of the job description," Drake replied. "It's the *entire* job description."

"Delicately put, mate," Nerran mumbled. "Don't forget that she's armed."

Faye glared at Drake. "I know that, *Calum*," she snarled, her tone making it clear she knew exactly to whom she was speaking. "But we're not soldiers. Our business is in killing courtiers who shirk their duties or overstep their bounds; in staging *accidents* for corrupt businessmen or slavers—that's what Mother Illynor always says. Just because we're assassins doesn't mean we can't have morals and standards. If we didn't, we'd be just like those Feyndaran bastards who butchered Emmalyn."

"Who?" Drake asked, and Calum silently wondered the same. Mercy had never mentioned an Assassin named Emmalyn—not to him, at least.

"Mercy didn't tell you about her?"

"No."

"Then count yourself lucky." She tore up handfuls of grass as she spoke, a shadow passing across her delicate features.

"All my life, Mother Illynor has claimed that we're better than those Feyndaran dogs who like to call themselves our equals. They'll kill anyone, so long as the pay is good. But Mother Illynor... She's more selective when accepting a contract—a corrupt politician here, a dishonest businessman there." She paused and glanced sidelong at Calum. "The brooding son of a mad king, perhaps. No one really knows what goes on in that mind of hers, but it's like she has some sort of tally, a code of right and wrong to which only she is privy. Step too far over the line and you're fair game. That's what she always claimed, anyway. It's the reason I sought out a Daughter of the Guild when I was seven, why I wanted to learn to be strong and tough and fearless like the assassins in the stories. I thought—" She stopped abruptly, scowling, and took another sip of wine.

Drake and Nerran exchanged a glance, debating whether to press her further. This was the most Calum had ever heard her speak. He realized with a flicker of surprise that he wanted desperately to hear how Mercy's sole childhood friend had found her way into the Guild. How could someone—how could a *child*—make that sort of decision? Mercy had never had a choice, but Faye and the other girls had sought out this life.

When the Daughter did not continue, Nerran gently placed a hand atop hers and asked, "Thought what?"

"I thought I was going to be ridding the world of assholes like the man who tried to buy my hand in marriage when I was only seven years old. Who sent men into my childhood home to beat and cripple my father when he tried to break the betrothal. Not slaughtering fishermen and farmers in their beds."

Nerran opened his mouth, closed it, and blinked, clearly at a loss for words.

"It'll be over soon," Drake said. He glanced over his

shoulder at the camp. While they'd been sitting there, drinking and watching the dawn, the soldiers had begun to stir. A few Cirisians were sitting in little clusters along the banks of the Bluejet, working with the rest of the Strykers to repair armor and sharpen weapons. In a few days, they would arrive in Xilor, then Cyrna, and stage the largest attacks yet. After that, Sandori. To Tamriel. To Mercy. To watch Firesse and Drake destroy Calum's home.

"It'll be over soon," Drake repeated, pushing to his feet. Faye and Nerran rose, as well. He sneered, "You can get back to your righteous killing after we make it through this war."

She shot him a hateful look and leaned in close, lowering her voice so only he could hear. "Make no mistake, Drake," she whispered as Nerran picked up the now-empty wine bottle and began strolling back toward the camp, "if you were still alive, you'd be first on my list, you despicable prick."

33
TAMRIEL

Tamriel walked into the great hall early that morning only to stop dead in his tracks, his mouth falling open at the sight before him. "Atlas?"

The guard turned. His uniform pooled around his frame, slim and sickly where he'd once been toned, but he was really there, standing before him. *Alive*. Atlas bowed. At his side, Niamh did the same, joy and pride in her eyes. "At your service, Your Highness," his old friend said with a grin.

A matching smile grew on Tamriel's face. "I'm glad to see you on your feet again." He clasped his old friend's hand warmly, noting the smooth, unblemished flesh where there had once been blisters. "You're completely healed?"

"I am."

Niamh stepped close and whispered, "The magic worked. The fever broke two days ago, and the physical symptoms disappeared sometime during the night. He's in no danger of infecting anyone, and the other guards are faring almost as well as he is. Lethandris's gamble on the ritual was correct. I ask only your leave to continue my work."

His smile faltered at the request. Niamh could cure the

outbreak, but how many of his citizens would she have to sacrifice? How many was he willing to let her kill to save the rest?

Niamh seemed to sense his troubled thoughts. She murmured something to Atlas and, after he nodded, gestured for Tamriel to follow her. She led him to the far corner of the room and ducked behind one of the tall pillars lining the hall, out of sight and earshot of any passersby.

"I know you have doubts, Your Highness," she said softly. "By the gods, I wish there were another solution. Lethandris and I searched for days, but this magic is the only way we can be certain we'll save as many of your people as possible. I would give anything for more time. Anything. But if we wait any longer to start healing those sick people in the tents outside the city, we risk losing them all. The Cedikra will only help them so much."

"...Are you sure you want to do this?"

Her fingers drifted to the sleeve covering her left arm, tracing the line of that jagged, gaping wound. She shuddered. "Do you know what it feels like to wield the same dark powers that Firesse used to manipulate Calum? Do you know how...how *wrong* I feel manipulating the blood magic she used to kill Odomyr, to destroy so many of your people?"

"Niamh, I—" Tamriel began, reaching out a comforting hand.

Niamh jerked back before he could touch her, pain and guilt on her face. "When I woke up in Firesse's tent the night I nearly died, I vowed that I would never kill another person. No one—human or elf—would meet his death at my hand. Helping you has forced me to break that vow. That is the price of curing this plague. I wish there were another way," she said again, "but this is why Cassius saw me in his vision of the cure. It must be. I was meant to save your people, Tamriel. I promised you that I would do everything in my power to save them. I may have broken my vow to myself, but I will not break the one I made you."

"Does my father know what you wish to do?"

"I spoke with him this morning, after I discovered that Atlas was healed, and he gave me permission to continue with the rituals. Even so, I have not disobeyed your orders. You're my—friend," she said hesitantly, color creeping up her cheeks, "and I would do anything to keep it that way."

"As would I." Tamriel took a deep breath and nodded. "Continue working with Lethandris and Hero to heal the people in the End. The guards have been limiting travel in and out of the city since the outbreak, but I'll speak to Master Adan to secure you transport to the infirmary tents."

Relief transformed her face. "Thank you, Tamriel."

He wasn't certain, but he could have sworn that was the first time she had ever addressed him by his name. He smiled, trying to ignore the weight on his chest. "Anything for a friend."

She excused herself to escort Atlas to the guard quarters, and Tamriel continued toward the throne room, his initial destination. As he walked down the short corridor that connected the great hall to the throne room, he caught the eye of one of the guards standing at attention beside the throne room doors. Julien bowed, one corner of his mouth rising into a crooked grin, and murmured, "Thank you for helping him," as Tamriel passed.

Ghyslain was already seated on his throne, his council gathered before him, when Tamriel entered. Master Adan and a dozen royal guards surrounded them. The council members swept into low bows as Tamriel climbed the steps of the dais and took his place beside his father.

"You're late," the king murmured.

"My apologies. I was speaking to Niamh."

"And where is Mercy? I would have thought she'd like to be here."

A smile played across his lips. He simply said, "On her way."

Ghyslain shot him a curious look, but finally bid the council members to rise. As they straightened, he said, "It's time you learned the latest developments of this war. We've lost Graystone and its sister cities."

A ripple of shock passed through the nobles. None of them—Tamriel included—had ever expected Firesse and her band of untrained soldiers would manage to make it so far beyond the border and wreak so much destruction within their country. Countless lives had been lost. Shipping in the fishing sector had ground to a complete halt. Buildings in a half-dozen cities and villages had been razed to the ground.

"Additionally," Ghyslain continued, his voice carrying easily through the near-empty room, "Firesse and part of her army attacked Rockinver during their Bounty Fest celebration. A raven arrived a few hours ago with the news."

At this, the nobles' expressions shifted from surprise to anger. Before they could question Adan about the troops he'd sent to guard the fishing sector cities, Ghyslain added, "She has more than Assassins and a few gifted smiths at her disposal. She has also found a way to wield blood magic against us."

"Blood magic?" Landers scoffed. His son, standing behind him, looked equally disbelieving.

"That's right." Ghyslain straightened, leveled Landers with a hard stare for interrupting, and said, "That's why she's been two steps ahead of us this whole time."

Then he began to explain.

THE KING TOLD THEM EVERYTHING—CASSIUS'S VISION OF the cure; how Firesse manipulated Calum into inciting war; the dark magic she had wielded in battle. He also explained why Nynev and Niamh had accompanied Tamriel from the Islands, and the plague treatment Niamh and the other healers had discovered. By the time he finished, half of the councilmembers were staring at him in horror, their faces bloodless, their eyes wide. The other half gaped at the king as if he had just suggested they invite the Cirisians into their own homes for dinner, drinks, and dancing.

"It—It can't be true," Landers finally stammered. "*Blood* magic?"

"I implore you to suspend your disbelief, Nadra," Ghyslain said. "You've read the reports. You've seen my soldiers train. It would be impossible for a force as small as Firesse's to claim so many victories without it. *That* is why she can so easily destroy our towns. *That* is why she can face down a host twice the size of hers and walk away without a scratch."

"How can we possibly hope to defeat someone who can wield the powers of the Old Gods against us?" someone asked.

Master Adan stepped forward. "Firesse may wield unnatural powers, but her soldiers are flesh and blood. They die just as easily as any other. Kill enough of them, and she'll be forced to surrender. All we need is one devastating blow," he said. "I've sent orders to my men in the fishing sector. Every soldier will be reporting to Cyrna, Xilor, and the other major cities along the road to the capital—every location I believe the Cirisians will target next. When the elves finally show their faces, we'll be ready."

"But—"

The doors at the back of the throne room swung open, and Tamriel grinned when he saw Mercy stride through, a confident smirk on her lips. She had given up the sling, although he could tell by the way she held herself that her wounds still pained her. "Sorry we're late," she called as the nobles turned to gawk. She winked at Tamriel, the heels of her boots clicking against the stone floor with each step. "I simply couldn't resist a dramatic entrance."

Mercy was clad in a sapphire-blue top, the sleeves embroidered from shoulder to wrist with whorls of thread-of-gold, and tight leather pants, her fearsome curved daggers sheathed at her hips. The gemstones in the hand guards reflected flecks of red and orange light on the faces of the outraged council members as she pushed straight through the crowd and continued toward the dais. She wasn't the only one they stared at, though. Their anger shifted to confusion as Nynev, Cassia, Matthias, and Ino trailed behind her, each armed and wearing a suit of pristine leather armor that Tamriel had commissioned for them.

"What the hell is that on their chests?" Edwin Fioni demanded.

Mercy bared her teeth in a grin. "My crest."

A simple design had been pressed into the leather over their hearts; they had adopted the symbol of slaves—two upside-down V's meant to represent elf ears—and bracketed them with two half circles: on top, a chain to symbolize Liselle's murder at the hands of the courtiers, and on the bottom, Mercy's curved daggers, back-to-back. The idea for a crest, for something to distinguish them from everyone else in the capital, had been Ino's. The idea to turn their weaknesses into a source of strength had been Cassia's.

Mercy stopped before the dais and bowed to the king. Then she turned toward the council members and spread her hands to encompass the elves flanking her. "Meet my personal guard," she announced, nodding to each of them in turn. "Nynev and my siblings—Ino, Cassia, and Matthias Mari. You may recognize the surname from a certain courtier who was murdered here seventeen years ago. Liselle Mari was my sister. That makes two of us you nobles have tried to kill."

Some of the nobles turned pale at the statement. Most of the men gaped at her, but a few protested outright when Mercy climbed the steps and positioned herself at Tamriel's side—claiming her place among the court hierarchy. Her arrogant grin dared the council members to challenge her. Nynev, Cassia, Ino, and Matthias spread out before the dais, their hands resting on their daggers in a clear warning to the courtiers.

"Your Majesty," Landers forced out, "this...display...is highly improper. The girl's a commoner—and an *Assassin*. She should not be privy to sensitive information about the state of this kingdom."

Ghyslain glanced at Mercy, then Tamriel. Although the king's expression did not change, Tamriel could read the warning in his gaze. They were making a dangerous move, standing against the nobles when so much was at stake with Firesse, but Tamriel was willing to risk it for Mercy.

The king turned back to Landers and raised a brow. "Improper as it may be, she protected your prince from Assassins, Rennox, and Cirisians, and journeyed to the Islands to find a cure for the plague which is currently ravaging our country. Need I list more ways in which she has proven that she is trustworthy?"

"But the guards," someone interjected. "They're *elves*."

And you're an asshole, Tamriel thought. "They are citizens of this country and members of the royal guard. You will treat them with the respect they are due."

Mercy reached over and grabbed his hand. He wasn't entirely sure whether it was out of gratitude or simply to make the nobles' blood boil, but he'd bet on the latter.

Unsurprisingly, every pair of eyes latched onto their joined hands.

"In addition to the news about the war," Ghyslain said, peering over at her, "I believe Seren Pierce has made some progress in his investigation into the attempt on your life."

"So I've heard." Mercy nodded to Nynev, and the huntress waded through the crowd—the council members recoiling as if she were diseased—and stepped into the hall. A few moments later, she returned, Seren Pierce, Kelaya Zavian, Ehren Tallis, and several guards in tow. Shackles bound Zavian's and Tallis's wrists and ankles, the chains clanging as they shuffled toward the throne.

"My hunch was right, Your Majesty," Pierce called as they approached. When they reached the front of the room, the guards forced Zavian and Tallis to their knees before Ghyslain. "These are the men who conspired with Drayce Hamell to kill Mercy. Tallis put up half the bribe, and Zavian tried to disguise his withdrawal from the bank as a gallery expenditure. Fortunately for us, he was either too stupid or too lazy to hide it better in the accounting records."

"I wasn't—" Zavian objected, but one of the guards shushed him.

"You have definitive proof of their guilt?"

Pierce nodded and pulled a bundle of papers from his pocket. "The bank records from the gallery, and Tallis's and Hamell's accounts. The numbers match. Not to mention," he added, grinning when the council members begin to murmur, "they've confessed."

Tamriel's brows shot up. "Really?" The question slipped out before he thought to stop it.

Mercy squeezed his hand, glaring down at the men before them. "After a little interrogation, they gave us all the information we desired." The ice in her tone—the implication behind it—sent a shudder through him. From the looks on the faces of the council members, they felt it too. Whatever she had done to convince Zavian and Tallis to confess, she had left no visible marks on the men's flesh.

"Very well. Adan, take these would-be murderers to the dungeons. They'll be transferred to the prison in Oldony after this mess with Firesse is over." Ghyslain dismissed the council with a wave of his hand, and Tamriel felt a little tremor go through Mercy as the nobles began to clear out of the room. A few shot her hateful looks, but the majority did not acknowledge her presence at all. He'd take that over them trying to kill her any day.

"We did it," she breathed as Ghyslain left to speak with Master Adan. Nynev and the others turned to her with matching grins. "*We did it.*"

34
MERCY

After the last of the nobles and guards filed out of the throne room, Tamriel barely had time to release Mercy's hand before Matthias let out a whoop, bounded up the steps to the dais, and swept her into a bone-crushing hug. "You are so *badass*," he said. She laughed, ignoring the pain in her still-healing wounds, and hugged him tightly.

Tamriel chuckled. Mercy backed out of her brother's embrace, and Tamriel leaned in and whispered, "I'll leave you to celebrate your first successful day in court with your siblings." He brushed a kiss against her cheek and added, "*We* can celebrate later—in private."

A shiver danced down her spine at his husky tone. Matthias, Cassia, and Nynev pretended not to overhear, but Ino couldn't resist shooting her a knowing look as Tamriel left the room. Her face flushed, and she smacked Ino's shoulder as she descended the steps. "Jerk."

"What's the point of being your brother if I can't tease you every once in a while?"

She rolled her eyes. "I should have left you scrubbing pots in the kitchen."

"We all would have preferred that," Matthias said. "He never does the dishes at home."

"Neither do you," Cassia shot back.

As they began to good-naturedly bicker, Nynev sat on the top step of the dais, a wistful look on her face. Mercy sat beside her. "What's on your mind?"

"I... I don't want to leave when the war is over," the huntress admitted, looking surprised by her own words. "I could do without the courtiers and the secrecy, but the city's beautiful, and I don't want to leave all of you. My...friends."

"You don't have to go back to the Islands if you don't want to. Stay here. Stay on as my personal guard. Niamh could work as a healer's apprentice. Just stay. Help us change things."

Nynev shook her head. "I wish I could, but before my mother died, I swore to her that I would look after Niamh. Our place is in the Islands."

Mercy nodded, burying her sadness at the thought of saying goodbye to Nynev and her sister. "Well, you'll always have a place to stay, should you decide you're sick of having to hunt your own meals."

"And you can stay with us anytime the nobles begin to grate on your nerves."

"So, tomorrow?"

They laughed, distracting Matthias and the others from their conversation. Mercy's siblings walked over and settled on the steps around them. Cassia fidgeted with the end of the scarf wrapped around her hair and asked, "Do—Do you know our parents?"

The huntress nodded, a faint smile tugging at her tattooed lips. "I met them at *Ialathan* when I first arrived in the Islands. They were so kind to Niamh and me. We didn't speak the language, of course, so your father translated for us when it came time for the storyteller to recite the tale of Myrbellanar and the Creator. Your mother even held my hand while they gave me my tattoos."

"Really?" Cassia's eyes widened, and she leaned forward, hungry for more information about the parents they had lost so many years ago. Nynev graciously indulged her. As she spun story after story about Dayna and Adriel and life in the Islands, Mercy studied each person in the circle—in the family she and Tamriel had found over the past few weeks.

Cassia, with her quiet strength and easy smile, beautiful even with the scars Leopold had given her. Ino, stoic and protective, a boy forced to grow up and provide for his family far too early. Matthias, only a few years her senior, with the same angular face and teasing glint to his eyes as Calum. Even Niamh and Nynev had become more than mere allies since their arrival in the capital.

Mercy's heart swelled with pride and affection as she listened to them converse and laugh. Before leaving the Guild, she never could have imagined her life becoming anything like this. For seventeen years, she had only been concerned with her own survival, her own training. Nearly two months ago, she had betrayed her best and only friend for a chance to fight in the Trial.

But now—

Now, she would give anything for the people sitting around her. She would give anything for Tamriel, to see him take the throne his father had so terribly abused, and that was why she interrupted Nynev in the middle of a story, her expression turning grim. "I need you all to promise me something."

After she bade goodnight to Nynev and Niamh, then to her siblings—who had been given quarters in the guest wing—she entered her room to find Tamriel already waiting for her, seated in a plush velvet armchair. A pile of reports lay on the floor at his feet, and another sat on his lap. His eyes lit up as she closed the door behind her and slung her belt with her sheathed daggers onto the vanity table. "Enjoy your celebration?"

"Only briefly. It seems that when you're facing a deadly plague and an impending attack from a blood-magic-wielding Cirisian, the work is never done."

He snorted softly. Mercy watched in the mirror as he placed the unread reports with the others on the floor and rose, his smile turning into a smirk when her gaze drifted to the undone buttons at the top of his shirt, offering a glimpse of his lean, muscular chest and flawless olive skin. "I hope you haven't forgotten about *our* celebration."

She turned as Tamriel stalked closer, grinning in that private way of his. His hands cupped the curve of her waist and drew her close. "I've missed you," he murmured, ducking his head to kiss her jaw, right below her ear. "We've had so much to do lately, I feel like I've hardly spent any time with you since we returned. It's killing me."

"Well, we can't have that, now, can we?" she whispered. "Not after all the work I've put in trying to keep you alive."

He laughed. "No, that wouldn't do at all."

When his hands slipped under the hem of her shirt, she arched against him and pulled his mouth to hers. Her heart began to pound in her chest. Even after today, even now, she could hardly believe he was *hers*—that he had looked at that cruel, cold Assassin she'd been so many weeks ago and found someone worth loving. She deepened the kiss, teasing his tongue with hers. Tamriel let out a little moan of desire and guided her backward until she bumped the edge of the vanity table.

"Ow."

"Sorry." Then, without warning, he shoved everything off the top of the vanity—her daggers, various combs and brushes, jewelry she'd never bothered to wear, hair pins, all clattering to the floor—lifted her up, and set her on the vanity table. "I've always wanted to do that."

She cocked her head. "And how old are you, again?"

"Come on—I'm always cleaning up after my father's messes. Let me make one of my own for once. It'll give the servants something to gossip about."

Mercy brushed a stray strand of hair from his face, tucking the dark curl behind his ear. "You're horrible."

"And you love me for it."

"Are you so sure about that?" She looked pointedly at her precious daggers, lying in a heap among everything else he'd knocked off the table. "Regardless of my feelings for you, the guards won't be enough to protect you from my wrath if you damage them."

His lips twitched, fighting a smile. "Cruel, beautiful woman," he murmured, a teasing glint in his eyes. "You wound me."

Then he kissed her again.

Mercy was certain he could feel her heart hammering against her ribcage when he pushed the neckline of her shirt down and pressed a feather-light kiss to one of the arrow wounds in her chest. Tamriel shuddered when his lips brushed the ugly black stitches.

"Did we make the right choice today? With the council?"

"I don't know," she admitted. "I hope so."

"I hope so, too. I don't know what I'd do if I lost you, Mercy," he breathed, his voice a hoarse whisper.

His hands trailed down her thighs and nudged her knees

apart. When she wrapped her legs around his hips, pinning him in place, he merely scooped her up and carried her to the bed, gently laying her down on her back atop the silken sheets. He knelt over her, his gaze full of love and desire and hunger. "I've been terrified of falling in love my whole life. I saw how it destroyed my father, and I was determined not to let myself fall into the same trap." He chuckled softly. "What a fool I was. Meeting you, Mercy, is the best thing that has ever happened to me."

She bit her lip, then said, "I feel the same about you. Until I came here, I never cared about anyone but myself. I didn't think I *could*. But you—you changed everything. Growing up in the Guild stripped me of every bit of kindness and compassion I once had, but knowing you..." Mercy swallowed, trying to force the words past the sudden lump in her throat. She had never been so honest, so vulnerable, in front of anyone before. Every instinct within her screamed to shut up, to hide any weakness her enemies could exploit. Mother Illynor did that to her. Mother Illynor turned her into that unfeeling killer. *Not anymore,* Mercy thought. *She does* not *control me anymore.* "You taught me how to be a *good* person, Tamriel."

She barely managed to finish her sentence before he kissed her again, passionate and insistent and desperate. She fumbled with the buttons on his shirt, and only made it halfway down the row before Tamriel let out a growl of impatience and ripped it the rest of the way off, tossing it aside. His skin was flushed, his muscles tensing under her touch when she ran her fingers down the hard planes of his stomach. He caught her hands before she could reach for the waistband of his pants. "Your turn."

He helped her slip her top off, then that, too, went sailing over the side of the bed. He propped himself up on an elbow and stared down at her, drinking her in. "You're so beautiful, Mercy. You have no idea how beautiful you are."

She shivered at the raw emotion in his tone. "Then I suppose you'll have to keep telling me until I believe you."

He did. He said it over and over and over again as he unlaced her leather pants and tugged them down, until she lay there in nothing but her underclothes. When he reached for his own, reality crashed back down, and she blurted, "Tamriel, stop."

He froze instantly. "Is it too fast? Do you want me to leave?"

Mercy nodded, then shook her head. "I don't know. I just —" Mortification filled her, and she couldn't meet his eyes when she whispered, "I don't know what I'm doing."

"Neither do I. We can figure it out together, whether it's tonight or tomorrow or a month from now. Whenever you're ready."

"Really?" Mercy couldn't help the note of surprise that slipped into her voice. "You've never slept with *anyone*? The noblemen's daughters have been throwing themselves at you your entire life."

"You're surprised? I told you I was afraid to fall in love."

She shot him a look. "You and I both know two people don't need to be in love to have sex."

"I never wanted to risk it. Fortunately for us, whenever it happens, that won't be an issue. You already adore me."

Mercy laughed, and Tamriel eased her back onto the monstrous pile of down pillows at the head of the bed. "Is that a yes?" he asked between kisses, his fingers trailing the waistband of her underwear. Every touch sent heat flaring under her skin.

She sucked in a breath and nodded. "Yes," she breathed. "*Yes*."

35
MERCY

The next four days passed in a blur of reports and paperwork. Since Ghyslain revealed the truth of Firesse's powers, the council thinned considerably. Seemingly overnight, Edwin Fioni and several other prominent noblemen packed up their most prized belongings and hired carriages to carry them out west, where they would stay with family and watch from afar as Cirisian invaders marched toward their homes.

Cowards, Mercy had snarled the night Tamriel told her the news, but the council members' sudden flight had had an unintended benefit: in their absence, the council's work had started to pile up, leaving Mercy an opportunity to insert herself into the heart of the city's inner workings. Seventeen years ago, the nobles had killed Liselle for doing the exact same thing. Now, they seemed willing to endure the presence of an elf—if only because the plague and war were much more immediate threats than a former Assassin who had (according to the rumors) taken to warming the prince's bed. Mercy didn't care that they were merely biding their time until they could rid themselves of her. The Cirisians were marching toward Sandori, and she wouldn't let some prejudiced old men keep her from protecting her city.

Firesse had been smart to divide her troops into groups; just as the Beltharan soldiers seemed to catch up with one, they were called upon to defend a village miles away. By the time they returned, the elves were long gone. Luckily—or *unluckily*, given the circumstances—Firesse appeared to be saving her power for the siege on Sandori. Two days ago, the king received word that Firesse, Calum, and their soldiers had managed to set fire to a dozen buildings across Xilor and liberate nearly fifty elves before the city guards and Adan's soldiers forced them to retreat. The commander had confirmed in his report that as far as he could tell, the First had not used any magic during the attack, despite losing almost half of the hundred-odd soldiers she'd led. As the days dragged on, it became apparent that if the Cirisians continued advancing, they could arrive at the city gates in less than a week.

Tamriel was waiting for her outside the council chambers when they broke for lunch. "So," he said, falling into step beside her, Nynev and her siblings trailing behind, "how is life on the king's council? Is it as exciting as you hoped it would be?"

"Well, no one has tried to kill me, so it's falling somewhat short of my expectations. Landers enjoys finding new ways to insult me during the meetings, and it's amusing to watch the little vein in his forehead throb when your father brushes him off completely. We've even started to keep count of the number of times he insults me. How many was it today, Matthias?"

"Thirteen. Seven of those were within half an hour of us arriving—a new personal best."

Ino's deep chuckle rumbled behind her as they began

descending the stairs to the first floor. "He lost me three aurums. My money was on eight."

Tamriel shot the three of them a strange look. For a moment, Mercy thought he might chastise them for making light of something so cruel, but then he grinned. "I'll bet on five insults within ten minutes of returning from lunch." He pointed at Mercy. "I'm counting on you to keep them honest."

"Deal."

When they reached the bottom of the steps, Mercy looked sidelong at Tamriel. "Your father informed me this morning that he'll be paying me a salary for my services. Was that your doing?"

"No. You deserve it."

"You know the first thing I'm going to buy when I get my first paycheck?" Matthias asked no one in particular. "Some proper bedsheets."

"Proper bedsheets?" Tamriel turned to him, incredulous. "You were living on the run for months and you're complaining about the bedsheets?"

"They're *silk*. The pillowcase is silk. I'm afraid if I roll over too quickly, I'll slide right out onto the floor." Mercy glanced back just in time to see Cassia jab Matthias in the side with her elbow. Ino merely shook his head and muttered, "Idiot."

"No offense, Your Highness," Matthias muttered, glowering at Cassia.

Tamriel laughed. "None taken." While her siblings began talking amongst themselves, he leaned down and whispered in Mercy's ear, "I quite like the bedsheets. Especially the way they look tangled around you."

Mercy's cheeks flushed, and she forced her expression to remain neutral as a group of guards—Atlas and Julien among them—passed them in the hall. Julien raised a brow and shot her a sly, knowing grin.

When they reached the dining room, Tamriel kissed her and excused himself to attend his duties. She caught his arm before he could step out of reach. "Stay. Eat with us."

"As much as I want to, my love, I can't. There's too much to do." He gently extricated himself from her grasp. "Who is going to help the people of the End if I don't?"

"Cassius will."

Since Niamh began treating the people of the End, Tamriel and Cassius had been working around the clock to ensure that the sick had enough food, blankets, and clothing to go around. In addition to helping Hero, Tamriel had been dividing his time between preparing for the attack and overseeing work on the cure. He was running himself ragged—anyone could see it.

"Take a break," she begged.

"I'll rest when I'm dead. Until then, there's work to do." He walked away before she could stop him again, his hands in his pockets. "I'll see you tonight," he called over his shoulder.

Late that night, Mercy was almost asleep when Tamriel eased the door open and crept into her bedroom. Instead of crawling into bed beside her and passing out—as he had done the past several days—he knelt on the floor beside her and brushed a strand of hair from her cheek. She cracked an eye open and frowned. "What time is it?"

"Almost three."

Mercy groaned and rolled over. She'd tried to wait up for him, but after days of him arriving in the late hours of the night and leaving before she woke up, she hadn't known when he'd show up. "Great. Maybe you'll be lucky enough to get two hours of sleep tonight."

He chuckled and joined her under the covers, too exhausted to even change out of his tunic and pants. He wrapped his arms around her and pulled her close. "I have a surprise to show you in the morning."

Seventeen years of being tormented by the Guild apprentices had not left her a great fondness for surprises. "What sort of surprise?"

He swept her hair aside and nuzzled her neck, pressing a kiss to her sleep-warmed skin. "A gift. You'll see soon enough. How was the rest of your meeting with the council?"

"Long. Excruciating, especially where Landers is involved —but he does bring up some good points in discussion when he isn't trying to come up with clever insults to undermine me. Which reminds me, you owe Ino four aurums. Apparently, Landers spent all of lunch thinking up new insults; he managed six within the first ten minutes of our afternoon meeting."

She waited a few long moments for Tamriel to respond. When he did not, she rolled back over only to find him fast asleep, the moonlight turning his dark hair a deep, shining silver. Even in sleep, his brows were furrowed, as if whatever problems he and Cassius had been pouring over had chased him into his dreams. She kissed the tip of his nose, and his arms tightened around her waist reflexively.

"Goodnight, my sweet prince," she murmured, resting her head in the little hollow where his shoulder met his neck and closing her eyes.

ONLY A FEW HOURS LATER, TAMRIEL PRACTICALLY DRAGGED her out of bed in his excitement. He paced before the foot of the bed as she quickly dressed and attempted to run a comb through her sleep-knotted hair. He didn't even wait thirty seconds before snatching up a fan-shaped pin from her vanity and sweeping her hair up into a messy knot. Then he grabbed her wrist and dragged her out of the room, startling Nynev and the others, who were already waiting outside.

"Where—?" Matthias began. He let out a huff of frustration when Tamriel started down the hall at a clipped pace. "It's not even seven in the morning!"

"Your sister will be returned to you momentarily," he called back. "In the meantime, swipe breakfast from the kitchens or find some noble to annoy."

"Is the rush really necessary?" Mercy asked as Tamriel pulled her around the corner.

He grinned at her over his shoulder. "Wait until you see the surprise, then you can tell me."

She rolled her eyes, but did not fight the smile tugging at her lips. "I suppose now would be a good time to tell you that you do not have a promising career as a hairdresser ahead of you, Your Highness," she said, trying to keep her hair from falling out of the knot as he led her through the labyrinthine corridors. Finally, they arrived at the door to the armorers' workroom. Tamriel swung the heavy redwood door open. When her eyes landed on the mannequin standing in the middle of the room, Mercy's jaw dropped.

The armor was breathtaking. Glittering silver and black rings interlocked to form the fitted chainmail breastplate, shimmering like an oil slick under the dancing flames from the hearth. A cowl of blue-black raven feathers sat on the mannequin's head, bleeding into the lightweight cloak that tumbled to the floor from a silver clasp at each epaulet. The arms and legs were covered in dark plate armor, daggers in smooth leather sheaths strapped to the inside of each forearm and tucked into the tops of the leather boots sitting on the floor. It was nothing like the heavy and cumbersome suits of armor the Strykers had made for the Trial. This one was...her. Lightweight but protective; beautiful but intimidating. The material was such a deep black it was like a shadow given form, a starless sky woven into fabric and metal.

"Tamriel, this is..." she breathed, unable to come up with a word that encapsulated how wonderful a gift this was, how much it meant to her. "Where did you *find* this?"

He beamed at her, and there was no small amount of pride in his voice when he said, "I designed it for you." Then his smile faded, and he rubbed the back of his neck, grimacing. "I had the head armorer start working on it the day you left. I should have given you something like this from the start. I don't want there to be any misconceptions among the nobles about your place in the court." He reached for her hand and squeezed once. "Or your place with *me*."

When she didn't respond—too dumbfounded and awestruck to bother coming up with some semblance of a reply—he led her further into the room and began showing her the intricacies of the armor. The chainmail was so tightly interlocked and so well reinforced that it would stop all but the strongest and sharpest of arrows, he told her. The cloak and cowl were lightweight enough to be bearable in Sandori's intense summer heat. There were four razor-sharp, skinny little blades hidden in the seams of the cuisse—one on either side of each thigh.

As he walked in a slow circle around the mannequin, pointing out details here and there, Mercy simply stepped back and watched him, letting his rich voice sweep over her. He had designed this for *her*. He had made mistakes, true, but unlike his father with Liselle, he had chosen to stand up against the nobles, knowing full well the consequences.

When Tamriel moved to straighten the cloak, the firelight from the hearth illuminated the shadows under his eyes. Even before they learned about Fieldings' Plague, he had been working tirelessly to help his people. He had been helping Hero and Ketojan free slaves in secret—an offense which, had the wrong people learned of his actions, would have ended with his head spiked on the castle walls—for *two years* before she had met him.

He was a better son than his father deserved.

He was a better prince than this Creator-forsaken country deserved.

He was a better person than she deserved.

Tamriel stepped back and caught her eye. "What are you thinking about?" he asked, holding out a hand.

"Miracles," she said as she approached. The moment their fingers touched, Tamriel spun her around and held her close, her back against his chest so they were staring at the beautiful armor together, his arms wrapped around her waist.

He rested his chin on her shoulder. "There's one last thing I want to show you."

She raised a brow. "Another surprise?"

"Are you warming up to them yet?"

"I'd say I've discovered a newfound appreciation for them. Also, I think I need to get a lot better at gift-giving. You're spoiling me."

"That look on your face alone was a gift. I don't think I've ever seen you rendered speechless before," he said, chuckling.

"I hope you enjoyed it while it lasted. It doesn't happen often."

"I'm taking that as a challenge." He released her and pointed to a sigil imprinted in the leather of the sheaths on the mannequin's hips—the crest she and her siblings had designed to represent their family. She'd been so overwhelmed by the thoughtfulness of his gift that she hadn't noticed it before.

"It's perfect." She reached out and traced the elf ears,

Liselle's chain, and her daggers with a light finger. Then she turned on him. "Now I'm going to have to find *you* an absolutely amazing gift, you charming, thoughtful, selfless jerk."

He laughed and wrapped his arms around her again. "Just stay right here with me, and we'll call it even."

36

CALUM

The blackouts were growing longer. Every day, the darkness ebbed and eddied, leaving him with only glimpses of the Cirisians' march:

Elves packing up their tents, preparing to leave the valley in which they'd made camp; mud splattering underfoot as they trudged through a summer storm; the Strykers huddled around a campfire, soaked and shivering, a blanket of stars twinkling beyond the treetops; a company of Beltharan soldiers trembling in their suits of armor as Drake and the Cirisians barreled toward them, swords and spears and daggers raised; blood spraying across his face.

Then...Xilor.

Drake led a dozen elves—Cirisians and liberated slaves alike—through the winding streets, some carrying torches and blades, others a barrel or pitch or a cask of ale. When a drunk patron stumbled out of a tavern and spotted them, Kenna pinned him to the wall and shoved a rag down his throat to muffle his screams, then plunged her dagger through his gut.

The next thing Calum knew, they were standing outside a

large warehouse, watching fire consume the walls, flames leaping through the broken windows. The building groaned. Something inside let out a loud *crack!* and a heartbeat later, the roof collapsed, sending glowing embers into the night sky.

Then they were burning a factory—no, a makeshift infirmary, just like the one Calum had visited with Tamriel and the others in Cyrna. Agonized wails filled the air as the walls splintered and gave out, as the flames devoured the floorboards Drake and the elves had soaked in alcohol and pitch. The wails rose to bloodcurdling shrieks. Then they stopped. All at once, the sick fell silent.

Dead.

Alarms clanged across the city, soot falling from the sky and collecting in the cracked cobblestone streets. Drake and the elves under his command emerged from a narrow alleyway to find Firesse and her elves sprinting toward them, tripping over one another. Firesse was screaming something, her eyes wide and armor soaked in blood, but her voice was hoarse from the smoke in the air. Calum couldn't make out the words. It was only when countless Beltharan soldiers in gleaming plate mail appeared on the street behind them, when archers emerged on the rooftops and began picking off Cirisians, that he realized what she was yelling:

"*RETREAT!*"

The next thing Calum knew, it was daytime. The Cirisians were trudging along a narrow forest trail in complete silence, an anxious energy thrumming in the air.

Their eyes scanned the woods, their hands never straying far from their blades. The Strykers' wagon bounced and groaned each time it hit an exposed rock or root. When Drake looked back at Firesse and the host trailing her, Calum realized that the loss in Xilor had cost the First a large chunk of her force. Before, they were nearly a hundred strong. Now, they were lucky if they had half that.

Kaius and his hunters were guarding the rear of the group, Dayna and Adriel stumbling along between them, their wrists bound with thick rope. Calum's stomach clenched at the sight of them. They were alive, but barely—Adriel's face was gaunt and pale, his skin sallow from the poison flowing through his veins. Dayna looked like she hadn't been given food or water in days.

Just a little while longer, Calum silently pleaded as he watched them struggle to keep up. *Stay strong.* He hadn't dared fight his father's control since the attack in Rockinver. He needed more time to gather his strength, to plan how he was going to free Dayna and Adriel or kill Firesse.

Just before Drake turned forward, Calum saw Dayna reach over and clasp Adriel's bound hands in her own. Something fierce and defiant shone in her eyes, something that reminded Calum so much of Mercy, it made him ache. He'd seen that same fire within Mercy the day they'd met. *I have taken so much from you. If it's the last thing I do,* he vowed to her, *I will see them safely home to you.*

OVER THE NEXT SEVERAL DAYS, FIRESSE PUSHED THEM TO march long and hard, stopping for only a few hours each night to eat and rest. The devastating loss at Xilor had shaken her, and she and Kaius had decided to forgo their plans of attacking Cyrna; they'd lost too many elves to risk another ambush. Sandori wasn't far. It was there they would now focus the brunt of their force. With every mile they closed between them and the capital, the wicked gleam in Firesse's eyes grew brighter. If her plan worked, Tamriel's and Ghyslain's heads would be staked upon the city walls by the week's end, and Mercy's would join them.

As they approached the heart of the country, two Cirisian scouts rode ahead to meet one of Mother Illynor's contacts in Knia Valley. They returned half an hour later with directions to a meeting place outside the little village—a farmhouse a half-day's ride from the town limits, whose owner the Daughters had slaughtered the moment they'd arrived.

It was just before nightfall when Firesse and her force reached the farm. Mother Illynor and one of her Daughters met them at the edge of the property, Illynor's eyes narrowing as they swept over Firesse, Drake, and their bedraggled troops and horses. "Where are the rest of your soldiers?"

"We suffered heavy losses in Xilor," Firesse responded. "Kaius's troops were ambushed on their way from Harkness, but we'll still have more than enough once we regroup with the others."

The Guildmother nodded to Dayna and Adriel, still limping along behind Kaius. "And those two?"

"Traitors. Alive only because I have a special use for them in Sandori."

Fear shot through Calum at the ice in Firesse's voice, the arrogant smirk on her lips.

"Some of the other groups suffered similar losses. That does not bode well for the coming attack." Illynor raised a brow, her green and gold scales shimmering. "Perhaps I was too hasty in allying with as ill-prepared a force as your own."

Firesse's hands clenched around her horse's reins. "I'm

paying you to fight for me, Guildmother, not to patronize me. What of your numbers?"

"My Daughters are unscathed, as expected."

"Then your concern is misplaced. Between your Assassins, the Strykers' weapons, and my magic, we'll breach the castle by midday tomorrow." She turned to Drake and smiled. "Calum has a plan."

He nodded and said, "We'll discuss it once we've had a chance to rest. For now, take solace in this: When this war is over, Guildmother, people far and wide will tell stories of the beautiful, fearsome Assassins who toppled a kingdom. You'll have your riches, and your rivals across the sea will quake when they whisper your name. You'll be drowning in contracts from the Feyndaran and Rivosi courts once word of your Daughters' prowess spreads."

Behind Illynor, the Daughter's eyes widened, a dreamy, almost greedy look coming over her face. It was the same expression Mercy had worn when Calum showed her the Trial armor and pledged to help her win. It was the hunger all the Assassins shared—for battle, for bloodshed, for renown, for perfection. Deep down, below that flat, level gaze, Calum knew Illynor hungered for it, too. She wouldn't be here if she didn't.

Slowly, Illynor nodded. "Later, then." She turned on her heel and started toward the farmhouse, the Daughter trailing her like a pup after its master. "Come," she called over her shoulder. "Eat and rest. We march at dawn."

Firesse, Drake, and the others followed them past a field bursting with colorful fruits and dark green herbs, backed by a stable, a hen house, and a barn. A windbreak shielded the house from view, with a single opening in the trees just wide enough for the Strykers' wagon to pass through.

As they rode through the entrance, Calum heard Faye murmur a soft, "Wow."

The farmhouse was huge, rambling, with a wraparound porch and tall pillars supporting a second-floor balcony. The land around it was packed with tents. As Firesse led her small host toward the house, the Cirisians wandering the makeshift camp stopped and cheered when they saw the First.

Mother Illynor led them up the groaning, sagging steps and into the house. It was easily hundreds of years old; the wooden planks of the walls were faded and weathered around the entryway, peeling paint and pockmarked with termite holes. They passed a dining room and a sitting room, a study, a kitchen, a wide staircase, and about a dozen bedrooms.

"The bedrooms are for us—you, me, my Daughters, and your commanders," Mother Illynor said to Firesse. "The rest can pitch their tents outside or join the others in the stables and the barn. With your protective wards, we'll be out of sight of any Beltharan patrols who might wander past."

"Has anyone taken a count of the troops?" Myris asked.

"Ivris's group has yet to arrive. We're not sure if they're alive. As we've nearly run out of room, Sienna, Tanni, Aoife, and Giovanna have taken their soldiers to another farm a few miles from here. They'll meet us here in the morning to go over the plan of attack. All in all, we have just over eight hundred soldiers, including the slaves we liberated along the way."

They spent the next hour unpacking and settling into their rooms. When the last of the soldiers were situated and the Strykers busy repairing armor and weapons, Mother Illynor gathered Firesse, Drake, Kaius, and the rest of the commanders in the cool, dark cellar—the only place free of the stifling midsummer heat. Under the light of an oil lantern hanging from the rafter, they examined a crude map of Sandori Drake had sketched on a piece of weathered parchment. He gave them information about the guards, their schedules, their patrol routes, their training, their arms and armor—every minute detail plucked from Calum's memory like a fruit ripe for the picking. He answered their questions about each of the neighborhoods and the city gates, the weakest points of the city walls, the layout of the castle, and where the guards might set up blockades. Calum tried to pay attention, to keep track of every sensitive piece of information Drake provided, but it wasn't long before the blackness swept over him and dragged him under.

WHEN HE SURFACED, DRAKE WAS SITTING BESIDE THE Strykers on the porch steps, listening to Amir tell some story about their travels in Feyndara. The stars glimmered brightly overhead, and the camp was almost completely silent; everyone was trying to get as much rest as possible before the battle. Drake chuckled softly when Oren leaned forward and picked up the rest of the tale, too excited to wait for Amir to get to the punchline.

Back already? Drake whispered, his cool voice tinged with faint amusement. *I thought you might be gone for good this time.*

Sorry to disappoint, Calum retorted.

Don't be. Disappointing me seems to be your only talent—you might as well excel at it, his father sneered. *I was hoping you'd come back so I can show you all the cruel little ways I'm going to torture your cousin before I slaughter him. I do hope Firesse lets the king live long enough to watch his son draw his last breath.*

White-hot rage rushed over Calum, temporarily replacing the ice-water in his veins. For the briefest second, he could feel the rough wood of the stair under him, the breeze on his face, the fatigue tugging at his body—and he knew what he needed to do.

Then Drake slammed fully into his mind, his fury palpable. *Nice try, son of mine.*

I'm not finished yet. This was the opportunity for which he'd been waiting. It wasn't perfect, but he was nearly out of time. They were a half-day's march from Sandori. If he wanted to free Dayna and Adriel, it had to be now. He had no idea how long Firesse's magic would prevent the poison in Adriel's system from killing him, but he prayed that it would be long enough for them to make it to Sandori and find an antidote.

Calum summoned his willpower again and struck at the bonds holding him captive, but Drake was ready for it. Calum only managed to let out a small gasp before the shackles of his mental prison clamped down on his mind.

Oren paused mid-sentence, sensing something was amiss. "Are you okay, Calum?"

Drake shot him a cocky grin. "Perfect, as always."

Amir snorted. Oren returned to his story, but Nerran and Hewlin continued to watch him with matching doubtful frowns.

So you do *have a spine,* Drake whispered. *Defying your dear father. You're much too old to be going through a rebellious phase, don't you think?*

You will not hurt the people I love, Calum snarled. He could feel the darkness creeping in at the edges of his consciousness. It called to him, sang to him, and it took every ounce of his strength not to give in. One last push—that was all he'd be able to manage. One last push—and then oblivion. He gathered every ounce of hatred, loathing, rage, and guilt within him and slammed against the bonds of his prison. *I WILL NOT BE YOUR PUPPET ANY LONGER!*

Calum gasped as the barriers around his mind shattered. His body was his own, at least for a little while. He jumped to his feet, startling the Strykers, and clapped a hand over his mouth to hold in a hysterical laugh of shock and relief.

"What's going on, mate?" Nerran asked, rising. "What's wrong?"

"I did it." A stupid, dazed grin spread across Calum's face. "I really did it."

"I think he's finally gone soft," Amir whispered.

"He's cracked," Oren agreed.

Calum whirled around and slapped a hand over their mouths, scanning the camp for movement. Firesse had posted guards, but they were somewhere outside the windbreak, and no one on the inside emerged from his or her tent. He turned back to the Strykers, keeping his voice low. "Dayna and Adriel. Where are they?"

"Perhaps you should sit down, lad." Hewlin made to grab Calum's arm, but he jerked out of reach, nearly tumbling down the steps in the process. He wasn't used to his body or the way it moved anymore. His heart pounded so quickly it was no longer distinct beats, just a constant thrum in his ears.

"I don't have much time. Dayna and Adriel—the elves Kaius was leading. Where are they?" As he said it, he felt Drake begin to stir with a vengeance. He didn't have long before his father would seize control. A headache began pulsing behind his eyes. "*Where are they?*" he growled when none of the men responded.

"The hen house, but they're under guard."

Nerran hadn't even finished his sentence before Calum was shoving past him and charging toward the windbreak, being careful not to trip on the tents he passed. He didn't have a weapon on him, he realized belatedly—Drake must have left his daggers in his room—so he stopped and picked up the first heavy rock he saw.

Someone grabbed his arm just as he neared the opening, and he whirled around, lifting the rock on instinct. Hewlin flinched and released him, genuine fear flashing through his eyes. The rest of the Strykers hovered a few steps behind him. "Put the rock down, Calum, and tell us what's happening."

"I can't—I don't have much time. I'm sorry for everything I've done, more sorry than you can possibly know. It won't make sense to you, but it wasn't me. Not really. Sort of. It's my fault, but—" Calum squeezed his eyes shut, the pounding in his head making it nearly impossible to form coherent sentences. "You need to leave now. You never should have come to the Islands."

"We're not leaving you like this, mate," Nerran hissed. "You're hysterical."

"He's having some sort of episode." Oren wrapped his arms around himself. "I know what it feels like."

Drake struggled for control again, and Calum gave him a huge mental shove. That pounding. That damned *pounding*. He crept to the edge of the windbreak and glanced toward the hen house across the field. Two guards stood at the entrance, but in the darkness, he couldn't make out anything more than their silhouettes.

He pointed to the hen house. "Mercy's parents are in there. They're going to die if I don't get them out right now, so I need you to go back and pretend you never saw me."

The Strykers exchanged glances, then Hewlin announced, "We'll help you."

"What? No, you can't. If Firesse finds out you helped free them, she'll kill you. I won't let you risk it."

"Shut up and let us help," Nerran said. "I don't know what the hell is happening to you, but you're clearly in no position to go after them on your own. So, either we all help you, or we drag you back to the house and tie you down until you explain. Your choice."

Drake surged again, and Calum winced. "All right, all right. The plan is—take down the guards, free Dayna and Adriel. Improvise. Sorry, it's— He's fighting again. Come on. Quickly." He emerged from the tree line and started across the field, the Strykers trailing behind him, each picking up a rock of their own. One of the guards called something in Cirisian—a question, based on the inflection, but Calum didn't understand a word. He cringed. Hopefully, the elves in the barn and the stables were too deeply asleep to be awakened by the guard's shout.

Creator, I could use some luck right now.

When they reached the middle of the field, he broke into a sprint. Every stride sent waves of pain through his skull. The Cirisians cried out again—a warning this time—and lifted something in their hands.

Bows.

Calum ducked, and the Strykers followed suit right before an arrow whizzed over their heads. Then they were running again. The elves dropped their bows and unsheathed their daggers just as Calum and the Strykers crashed through the last row of bushes. While Hewlin and Oren took on one of the guards, Nerran and Amir the other, Calum yanked the door of the hen house open and hissed, "Dayna? Adriel?"

"We're here." The voice floated from the back of the hen house, so soft he almost couldn't make out the words.

"We're a half-day's march from Sandori." He stumbled blindly through the darkness, his hands out to keep him from colliding with anything. "Are you strong enough to run?"

"Do we have any other choice?"

One of the Strykers let out a grunt of pain, and Calum gritted his teeth, worry consuming him. *They're master weaponsmiths,* he reminded himself. *They can hold their own in a fight.* It didn't make listening any easier, though.

Something thudded, and there was a soft *whump* as a body hit the ground.

"We're okay," Nerran called, his voice tight, "but you might want to hurry it up a bit, Calum."

By then, his eyes had adjusted enough that he could just make out his mother and Adriel slumped against the back wall. He knelt before Adriel and pressed a hand to the man's brow. His skin was still clammy, but he might be able to survive long enough to reach Sandori.

"Try to stand," Calum whispered.

He pulled them to their feet none too gently, his nerves running too high to care much when Adriel let out a groan of pain. There was a sledgehammer battering his skull now—Drake raging in whatever corner of Calum's mind he'd been imprisoned—and the tremors rocked him from head to toe, threatening to split his skull in two.

Outside, the fight had gone quiet. Through the walls, he could hear the elves in the neighboring barn and stable speaking to one another in groggy, sleep-thick voices. It wouldn't be long before they sent someone outside to investigate the commotion.

Calum led Dayna and Adriel out of the hen house. Hewlin tossed him a dagger, and he frantically sawed through the ropes binding Dayna's and Adriel's wrists while Oren and Amir dragged the guards' bodies into the hen house. He tried not to notice how gaunt Mercy's parents' faces were when they turned around and followed him to the rear of the building, the Strykers trailing behind.

"Run to Sandori. Mercy is there," he told them.

"They'll never make it to the capital on their own," Nerran cut in. "Look at them—they can hardly stand. We should go with them, make sure they reach Sandori safely."

"If one of us goes, we all go," Hewlin said, nodding. "Firesse will punish anyone who stays behind."

In the distance, the barn door slid open, and they all tensed. "*Whej?*" someone called. "*Mai? Olyver? Whej-a-to?*" A few others muttered to one another, their voices ranging from confused to alarmed.

Calum turned to Hewlin. "Go quickly. I'll try to hold them off as long as I can. It won't buy you much time, so make every second count. I won't be able to fight Drake much longer." The more distance the Strykers could put between them and the Cirisians, the better.

"Who's Drake?" Oren asked, but Adriel shushed him.

"Thank you," Dayna sighed. She embraced Calum, then took Adriel's hand and started a lurching, pained run through the grove behind the farm. The Strykers followed close behind, and they all melted into the darkness within a matter of seconds.

The elves had begun wandering out of the barn and stable. Calum took a deep, steadying breath, bracing himself against the migraine pulsing behind his eyes, and peered around the side of the hen house, being careful to keep out of sight. A group of six elves pulled the door open, and several gasped when they saw the bodies. One began to sob. The rest whirled around, searching for the culprit. Calum waited until one started toward the grove, then stepped out into the open, his shoulders hunched as he started at a brisk walk toward the farmhouse.

"*Iv!*" one of the Cirisians yelled. "Stop!"

He broke into a sprint. *Keep chasing me. Keep chasing me. Don't look for the others. Creator, I really, really need that good luck.* He leapt over the first row of bushes and crashed through the next as quickly as he could. All six elves gave chase, shouting and spitting curses as, behind them, more sleepy Cirisians wandered out of the barn and stable.

One of the elves tackled him, sending him sprawling face first into the dirt. Inside his skull, Drake was a swirling, raging tempest. *Have fun explaining to Firesse how you let this happen, you evil bastard,* Calum snarled as his hold on his body snapped, ice-water rushing through his veins once more.

37

CALUM

"*'irja.*"

The word floated to Calum from somewhere in the depths of the black sea, its power an ancient, glittering tether between the darkness and the world he'd left behind. He snapped back to consciousness with a start—somehow returned to his mental prison, to the hell of having to watch his father play him like a marionette.

For a moment, he couldn't remember where he was. He didn't recognize the dark wooden walls or the colorful quilt under his legs—under *Drake's* legs, now that his father again had control of his body. Then Firesse, kneeling on the floor beside him with her eyes closed, muttered something in guttural ancient Cirisian, and the ice-water in his veins surged forth, along with the memories. He'd freed Dayna and Adriel. The Strykers had fled, promising to protect them on their journey to Sandori. Then Calum had blacked out, expecting never to emerge from the darkness again.

But, impossibly, here he was.

Firesse opened one eye and peered at Drake, lying atop the bed in his small farmhouse bedroom. "He's back?"

He nodded. A cruel, mocking laugh echoed through Calum's mind, still aching from the effort it had taken to overpower his father. *I can't let you slip away just yet,* Drake purred. *We have unfinished business.*

She pulled me back? Calum asked, unable to contain his curiosity. *With magic?*

Apparently, pulling one out of wherever it is you go when you fade is not terribly different from summoning a spirit from the Beyond. Our Firesse was happy to oblige my request to bring you back, with a few added safeguards, of course, should you get any ideas.

Calum fought against the shackles binding him to his mental prison. They were stronger, and the ice-water in his veins was so frigid he wouldn't be surprised if ice crystals had formed below his skin. He wouldn't make it out again no matter how hard he struggled; Drake wouldn't underestimate his strength a second time. Calum had played the only hand he'd been dealt, and now he was nothing more than a witness to whatever destruction Firesse and the elves were planning to rain down upon the capital tomorrow.

Firesse staggered to her feet and squeezed Drake's shoulder once. "Sleep now. We'll march for Sandori in three—three hours," she said through a yawn.

"You stay—I'll go out with the search parties."

Dayna and Adriel were still out there, Calum realized with a rush of relief. The Cirisians hadn't found them yet.

Drake began to rise, but she dismissed him with a wave. "You'll be on the front lines tomorrow. You need all the rest you can get." She left the room without waiting for a response.

As Drake stretched out on the mattress and closed his eyes, Calum cast his thoughts to Mercy and Tamriel, probably sleeping soundly in their beds in the castle at this very moment, unaware that the army marching toward their doorstep was so close. *I've done everything I can to help you,* he thought. *I know it wasn't enough, but I tried. I really, truly did. The rest is up to you.*

THREE AND A HALF HOURS LATER, THEY GATHERED THEIR belongings and began the march toward Sandori. Firesse, the Daughters, and the commanders rode the few horses they'd taken from Fishers' Cross, and the Strykers' wagon, driven by one of the Daughters, clattered along behind them. The remainder of the forces trailed behind them in clusters of four or five, all quiet and solemn in the face of the impending attack. How many would perish? How many would return to the families they had left in the Islands?

Kaius and the other commanders wore the silver armor they'd pilfered from the Beltharan troops, the metal shining under the early-morning sun, and the rest were clad in an amalgam of plate mail and their own leather armor. Overhead, the sky was a pale, cloudless blue, and a warm breeze swept across the plain from the west, sending the long grasses dancing around them. The day was much too beautiful for the horrors they'd unleash in a few short hours.

By the Creator, Calum hoped Dayna and Adriel had made it to the capital.

For the first few hours of the ride, time seemed to stretch out into an eternity. The elves gradually began to grumble and complain as their skin grew slick with sweat beneath their armor and their sore feet blistered inside their worn boots. Thankfully, they caught no sign of Mercy's parents or the Strykers. Relief washed over Calum, but it was quickly replaced with dread when Sandori appeared on the horizon.

The city was nothing more than a smudge of darkness in

the distance; the only discernible features were the tall spires of the Church and Myrellis Castle, the latter sitting high on its hill overlooking the city.

The sight caused shame to rise within him. He would give anything to undo the mistakes he had made, but no amount of wishing and praying would erase the terrible crimes he had committed. He had dug his own grave the moment he and Elise forged that damned Guild contract, and now it was time to lie in it.

Firesse lifted a hand to halt their march. She turned to Drake, anticipation and a hint of madness sparkling in her eyes. A wicked, cruel grin spread across her lips. "Let's pay a visit to the king, shall we?"

38

TAMRIEL

Shortly after lunch, Tamriel found Mercy standing alone outside the door to his old chambers, staring at the wrought iron handle as if gathering her courage to enter. Neither of them had set foot inside since they left for the Islands over a month ago. The memory of his guards' bodies lying there, gushing dark blood over the stone floors, had been too fresh when they returned, and they'd each fallen into the routine of avoiding his former chambers when walking through the halls. For whatever reason, he'd been drawn to it today. Apparently, she had, too. Perhaps the threat of the plague and Firesse's impending attack had sent them here, to the place where so much had changed.

Mercy reached for the handle, but paused before her fingers could make contact. "I thought Liselle might speak to me if I go inside," she said, again surprising him with her ability to sense him before he even made a sound. "I haven't heard her voice since we left the Islands, and I thought that since she first appeared to us here, it might be easier to reestablish a connection to wherever she is. The In-Between. The Beyond." She turned around then, fear and grief in her eyes. "But I'm afraid that I'll go inside and she won't be there. It's foolish, I know. She could have spoken to me hundreds of times since we returned from the Islands. There's nothing special about this room. I just—I just thought I had more time to get to know her. I don't want to find out I was wrong."

The sorrow in her voice broke Tamriel's heart. After so many years of being alone, Mercy had gained a sister only to have her ripped away. In a way, it was as if Liselle had died a second time. He tried to imagine what it would be like to see his mother's ghost, to speak with her and laugh with her, and to lose her all over again—but imagining it paled in comparison to reality.

"Well, I'm glad I found you," he said, being careful to mask his own sadness. Liselle had only appeared to him a few times, but she had saved their lives time and time again. He smiled at Mercy and held out a hand. "I think we could use some closure."

She offered him a small, unsteady smile and slipped her hand into his own. Then she reached forward, turned the handle, and let the door swing open.

The room was empty, of course. The guards' bodies had been moved long ago, the blood cleaned and the floor mopped, the ruined furniture and ornate rug replaced with new décor. The wardrobe doors stood open, every rack and drawer empty since the day the servants had taken his clothes down to the room he'd chosen in the guest wing. It both was and was not his room. The furnishings were new, nearly identical to the previous ones, but the memories of the deaths he'd witnessed here had tainted everything.

Mercy released his hand and took a few steps into the room, until she was standing in the exact place her sister had first appeared to them. "Liselle?" She turned in a slow circle, then tried again, raising her voice. "Liselle, are you here? Can you hear me?"

No answer.

Her shoulders slumped, and she sank onto the edge of the bed. "I should have known better than to hope."

Tamriel sat beside her and squeezed her hand. "Liselle was a great woman," he said softly. "I wish you'd had more time to get to know her, and I wish I could tell you that you'll see her again. What I *can* tell you is that you have three siblings here who will do anything for you. They're not going anywhere, and neither am I. We won't forget those we've lost, but we'll make new memories." He wrapped an arm around her shoulders, and she looked up at him, her eyes overflowing with emotion: fear, sadness, grief, pain, and a tiny flicker of hope. "We'll make happy memories, my love."

Her expression softened at the endearment. Mercy rose and walked to the desk, where the servants had left a tray with a bottle of wine and a couple goblets. She uncorked the bottle, poured them each a glass, and carried them over to the bed. "To closure," she said, lifting her goblet in a toast.

"And to our future," Tamriel responded.

They drank, and before Mercy could lower the goblet from her lips, Tamriel asked, "So when do you want to get married?"

She choked on her wine. "Who said anything about getting married? I love you, Tamriel, but we've barely known each other for two months."

"I did. Remember the day I took you and Leon down to my mother's tomb? I asked you to marry me, and you said yes." His smile turned smug. He'd been planning to ask her for a while, and what better time was there than in the midst of a war? "We'd known each other a lot less than two months when you agreed."

"I didn't think it was binding, considering I was planning

to kill you at the time." Mercy walked to the double doors that led to the balcony. A warm breeze sent the curtains dancing when she pushed the doors open. "Not to mention," she said over her shoulder as she stepped outside, "you asked Lady Marieve to marry you, not me."

Tamriel feigned confusion as he followed her to the railing of the balcony, trying to pretend his heart wasn't pounding with nerves. "I haven't proposed to you yet?"

"Not that I can recall, no."

"Well, that simply cannot do," he said. She watched in stunned silence as he reached into his pocket and pulled out a silver ring. A deep blue sapphire sat in the center of the slender band, surrounded by a dozen shimmering diamonds. She bit her lip and grinned like a fool when he dropped down to one knee. "Mercy—my love, my savior—will you marry me? Will you do me the honor of one day becoming my queen?"

"You aren't worried about the nobles?"

"I'll always worry about the nobles, but I'm not going to bow to them any longer. They can accept you as their future queen, or they can forfeit their titles and leave." Together—he'd vowed that they would stand against the nobles together, and this was the final step, the line even his father would never have dared cross. He'd unintentionally and irrevocably given his heart to her over those few weeks before they left for the Islands, and now he was offering her his most prized possession—his kingdom, the land and the people he'd do anything to protect.

Mercy beamed. "Then I accept. Yes, Tamriel, I'll marry you."

He jumped to his feet with a laugh and swept her into his arms, spinning her around and around and around again. The moment he set her on the ground, she grabbed his face and kissed him.

When she pulled back, he slipped the sapphire ring onto her finger. It fit perfectly.

"It's beautiful," she murmured in awe.

"Like it was made for you, princess."

Mercy tilted her head, grinning. "You know, I used to hate it when Calum called me that. Now I don't mind it at all. In fact, I think I like it."

She looked down to admire the ring again, and Tamriel said, "It was my mother's. With my father's blessing, I went down to her tomb the day we returned from the Islands, and I've been carrying it ever since. I think she would be glad to know you'll be wearing it now." His smile slipped, just a fraction. "I wish she were here to meet you."

She cupped his cheek with a hand, and he leaned into the touch, drawing strength from it. "If she was anything like her son," she whispered, "I would have loved her. It would have been my honor to know her."

THEY STOOD THERE FOR NEARLY AN HOUR, RELIVING memories of those they'd lost, reveling in their joy and the possibilities for their future. When Tamriel followed Mercy out of his former chambers, he was so caught up in his own bliss that he didn't think his feet touched the ground once as they made their way through the halls. That was, until they reached the bottom of the stairs and saw the guards and slaves running back and forth, nearly bumping into one another in their haste. Tamriel stopped mid-stride, his throat tightening. The flurry of activity could only mean one thing. *Not today.* He'd thought—he'd prayed—they had more time.

Seren Pierce stopped before them, his face pinched with worry. "I've been looking for you everywhere, Your Highness," he said between puffs of breath. "The Cirisians will be here soon. The Creator has seen fit to bless us with a warning. They're waiting downstairs, in the infirmary. We've sent for Healer Niamh, but I don't know if she'll make it in time."

"In time for what?" Mercy asked.

Pierce's eyes slid to her. "It's your father. I'm afraid he's dying."

"He's..." Mercy went still as a statue, the blood draining from her face. Without another word, she turned and bolted down the hall, snarling at anyone in her way.

Pierce grabbed Tamriel's arm before he could follow. "Your Highness, we must get you and your father to safety. Creator only knows what destruction that Cirisian girl can bring about with her powers, and we must plan for the worst."

"How long until they arrive?"

"An hour, if we're lucky. Mercy's parents were in bad shape when the guards found them. They wouldn't have managed to outrace the elven army if they had not had the Strykers' help." His grip on Tamriel's arm tightened. "Master Adan prepared for this, Your Highness. There is a carriage waiting at the other end of the tunnel leading out of the castle. Adan and your father will meet you there to take you to safety in Ospia. Once the Cirisian army is within sight, we'll send a decoy carriage with your family crest and a contingent of guards through the eastern gate and hope they give chase."

Tamriel shook his head. "Firesse and her people will come after us as soon as they realize we've tricked them, and I won't put Ospia's people in harm's way just to secure my own safety. The city walls haven't been breached in hundreds of years. Should Firesse find her way in, we'll make our stand here. I'm not leaving the people of my city to fend for themselves." He jerked out of Pierce's grip and started running down the hall toward the infirmary, toward Mercy. Slaves and guards jumped out of his way as he passed. "See my father out of the castle, then get somewhere safe!"

"You're being reckless!" Seren Pierce shouted. "You're going to get yourself killed! Let the guards—"

The rest of his words were lost when Tamriel veered around the corner and plunged into the stairwell.

❧ 39 ☙
MERCY

"Oh, thank the Creator," Dayna gasped when Mercy burst into the infirmary, breathing hard. Her stomach sank. The cots had been empty since Atlas and the other guards were healed, but now Adriel lay atop the bed nearest the hearth, his face so pallid she could see the veins in his temples. Dayna had been sitting on the edge of Adriel's bed, but she rose and started toward Mercy, her arms held open for an embrace. "I thought we'd never see you ag—"

"Sickness or poison?" Mercy sidestepped her mother and moved to her father's bedside, ignoring the hurt look on Dayna's face. There was no time to exchange greetings. Sorin had taught her to be a healer, and that was who her father needed her to be right now.

"Poison," a male voice answered from the corner of the room. Mercy started—she'd been so preoccupied with her father, she hadn't noticed the Strykers sitting on the far bed. "We don't know what kind, though," Nerran continued. "One of Firesse's soldiers made it from a plant in the woods. It had bright purple flowers with white spots in the center."

She leaned down and looked into her father's eyes. The pupils were huge, dilated so large she could hardly see the gold-brown of his irises. His breaths came out in ragged pants, and a sickly-sweet scent emanated from his skin. "Does your tongue feel thick and heavy? Do you have a pounding headache at the base of your skull?"

Adriel nodded weakly. The collar of his tunic was damp with sweat.

"It's Widowsbane," Mercy said. She moved to the shelves and began searching for a vial of willowroot and blossoms of Claudia's Song.

"How can you be sure?" Dayna asked, moving back to her husband's side.

Mercy spared her mother the briefest glance. "Because that's exactly how I felt when my tutors forced us to ingest poisons and identify their antidotes. Willowroot and Claudia's Song blossoms will neutralize the poison." She'd never forget that day. They'd lost Amber, an apprentice of only nine years, because she had not been able to identify the proper antidote before the toxins reached her heart. Trytain had not let Sorin or any of the other apprentices treat Amber as the little girl fell to the ground, clutching her chest. *If she is not smart enough to know how to save her own life, why should I do it for her?* Trytain had sneered as Faye began to cry and beg her to help. *The world has no mercy for orphans and runaways like you. The sooner you learn that lesson, the longer you'll survive its cruelties.*

Dayna made a strangled noise at the reminder of the Guild and let the subject drop. Mercy poured some of the willowroot oil into the mortar Niamh had left on the desk, and mashed the little white blossoms to form a paste.

Tamriel stepped through the door. "Your father, is he—" His eyes landed on Adriel, and he let out a relieved sigh. "I had feared we'd be too late. Do you know what ails him?"

"Widowsbane," Dayna answered for her. "Firesse poisoned him during the attack in Xilor."

Mercy paused. "In Xilor? That was four days ago. He should've been dead in two hours. That's how long—" she stopped herself and focused on mashing the blossoms. That was how long Amber had lasted. The girl's whimpers of pain had haunted Mercy's sleep for months afterward.

"Firesse used her magic to keep the poison from killing him. He's grown weaker ever since we left. I was so sure we weren't going to make it."

"I'm beyond grateful you did. Here." Mercy perched on the bed beside her mother and lifted a spoonful of the concoction to Adriel's lips. He drank it eagerly, one swallow after another, until only the dregs remained in the bottom of the bowl. His eyes fluttered shut, the pain on his face finally abating.

"Why didn't she let the poison take him?" Tamriel asked quietly, giving voice to the question they'd all been thinking. "Why keep him alive if he betrayed her?"

"She said— She said she had a use for us. I don't know what she was planning, but if Calum hadn't helped us escape..." Dayna shuddered. "I don't want to think about it."

All the air seemed to leave the room at the mention of the traitor. Mercy's hands clenched into fists. "And will Calum be joining Firesse in the attack, or is the bastard going to shift loyalties again?"

"You don't understand," Oren piped up from the corner, his voice thin and reedy. "He was different. Something was wrong. When we last saw him, he was acting insane. Said everything he did wasn't really him."

"He let the elves catch him to buy us time to escape," Amir added. Hewlin hadn't yet said a word; he was merely sitting there, his expression hollow and pained.

"It's Drake," Adriel croaked, the words nearly unintelligible. "That's why he was different. Firesse let his father possess him again—for good, this time."

"She... She did what, mate?" Nerran gawked at Adriel, then looked to Mercy. "Is the poison messing with his brain?"

"Calum broke through somehow. He fought back. That's why he was able to free us, and why he had seemed so eager to help Firesse," her father continued. "We'd suspected it for a while, but we didn't know for sure until Calum tried to help Dayna escape in Xilor."

"So Calum didn't help Firesse willingly?" Tamriel asked. When Mercy looked up at him, she couldn't decipher his expression. Relief? Anger? "He was her prisoner this whole time?"

Adriel nodded.

Mercy frowned at the prince. "That doesn't change what he has done. He's still a traitor."

Tamriel nodded slowly. "Of course not. But it does... complicate matters." He turned to the Strykers. "As for you, and the fact that you helped arm her troops—"

"We agreed to help her before we knew what she was capable of," Hewlin finally interjected. "When I realized how far she was willing to go to hurt you and your people, I told her we were going to leave, but she threatened to unleash the plague on us if we fled."

Every pair of eyes snapped to him.

"What do you mean, unleash the plague?" Mercy asked, hardly breathing.

"It's one of her...powers. She can control it." He shuddered, ignoring the Strykers' looks of absolute disbelief. He ran a hand down his face, then looked up at Tamriel. "We'll gladly pledge our swords to your cause, Your Highness. We may not be soldiers, but we know our way around a blade."

Tamriel nodded, the blood draining from his face. "Very well. Report to—"

JACQUELINE PAWL

Cassia's cry cut him off. She ran into the room, Ino and Matthias close on her heels, and let out a heart-wrenching sob when she saw her parents. Mercy leapt out of the way as her siblings flung themselves into their mother's arms. Cassia and Dayna burst into happy tears.

"Master Adan is likely in the great hall. Report to him," Tamriel said over their cries.

The Strykers nodded and quietly shuffled out of the room to give Mercy's family privacy.

"Momma," Cassia sobbed, her voice muffled. "I've missed you so much."

"I've missed you, too, my babies," Dayna said between sniffles.

Matthias reached over and brushed a sweaty tendril of hair from his father's forehead. Adriel opened his eyes and reached up to grasp his youngest son's hand. Already, some of the color had returned to his cheeks.

Standing beside Tamriel, watching them, something fractured inside Mercy's chest. Family—they were her family. For the first time in eighteen years, they were all together...all except one. Liselle should have been here. When Cassia reluctantly stepped out of her mother's embrace, her smile not quite hiding her sorrow, Mercy could tell she was thinking the same thing.

Tamriel touched Mercy's elbow. "Go on," he whispered, nodding to Dayna and the others. His eyes were shining and slightly red-rimmed, and it struck her then how much it must pain him to witness this reunion. Like her, he had never had a family. Not a real one, at least. Even so, he smiled at her. "Spend some time with your family before the attack."

Some of them might not survive it, he didn't need to remind her.

Her chest tightened, but Mercy shook her head and started toward the door. "Let them have their reunion.

They deserve it." They'd endured so much together, it seemed only fitting. She couldn't help but feel like an outsider, watching them hug and cry and talk over one another.

Tamriel frowned, but he didn't argue.

Mercy was halfway to the door when her sister called, "Where are you going?"

She turned to find Adriel and the others staring at her. Cassia raised a brow. "You didn't think you could just sneak out of here, did you?"

"I just thought—"

"You thought wrong, little sis." Matthias walked over to her, grabbed her hand, and guided her back to Dayna and the others. The second they reached Adriel's bedside, Matthias pulled them all into another group hug, with Mercy squished in the center. She squirmed, and her brothers' deep chuckles rumbled through her. "Don't try to fight it," Ino whispered. "You're one of us—you're going to have to put up with being hugged every once in a while."

"I can't breathe." Somewhere behind them, Tamriel laughed. *Melodramatic as always,* she imagined him saying.

"You should go now. Prepare for the battle," Adriel said before Ino could respond. They broke apart, and he looked each of them in the eyes. "Stay together. Protect each other."

Ino and Matthias nodded grimly. Cassia touched the elf-ear crest pressed into her leather armor and dipped her head. "We will, Papa," she vowed. Mercy merely nodded, still in awe that her family was finally reunited.

"I love you, my children. If I could, I would be fighting right alongside you." His gaze shifted to Mercy and Tamriel. "This will be a bloody, horrific, destructive battle. The other attacks were simply to get the king's attention, to show off. Firesse has more tricks up her sleeve. Mercy, if the tide of the battle turns, you must promise me that you'll do whatever it takes to survive. Flee the city. Lie low until the war is over. Let the guards and the soldiers do their jobs."

"But—"

"Promise me." His eyes flashed, his tone making it obvious he would brook no argument. "We did not come this far only to lose a daughter we just met. Survive, all of you. Promise me that."

"I'll do my best," Mercy said with a tight nod. That was all she could offer him.

Dayna kissed her cheek. "I'll see you after the battle, Bareea," she whispered. For the first time, Mercy didn't feel like correcting her. Mercy was the name Illynor had given her, one more way for her Guild to tighten its hold on her. Bareea was a little baby girl who had her whole life ripped from her. Bareea had had a home, and a family who loved her. Perhaps one day, she could be Bareea again.

"I'll see you then."

Tamriel bowed to her parents, grabbed her hand, and led her out of the infirmary. Cassia and her brothers trailed behind them. Mercy tried to ignore her mother's quiet sobbing as Ino pulled the door closed, but the aged wood only partially muffled the sound of her cries.

Fear and foreboding filled Mercy. She was the greatest apprentice the Guild had ever trained. She had spent almost every day of the last seventeen years perfecting the art of killing, and today would test everything she had ever learned.

Today, she could die.

A SHARP KNOCK SOUNDED ON THE DOOR OF MERCY'S bedroom just as she finished pulling on her chainmail breastplate. The silver and black links jangled softly as she crossed to the door and opened it. She had expected to find her siblings standing there—they'd gone to the armory to arm themselves—but instead, Nynev was waiting outside, her expression hard as granite.

"The attack has begun," Nynev said without preamble. She was dressed in leather armor, a quiver of arrows on her back and her bow in hand, and there were three hunting knives strapped to her hips. She gestured for Mercy to follow her down the hall. "There's something you need to see."

"What is it?"

"It... Just come and see for yourself."

Tamriel was waiting for them in the great hall. He had donned fine silver armor emblazoned with his family's crest, and a longsword was sheathed at his side. His expression was grave. Dread filled Mercy, and she twisted the sapphire ring on her finger, praying that the Creator would not claim his life today.

"Ready to go to war?" Tamriel asked. He reached out and grabbed Mercy's hands, gripping them like a lifeline. "We *will* make it through this."

She nodded, her throat tightening when a distant boom rumbled through the castle.

"Come on." Nynev led them through the massive castle doors and out to the top of the stairs. From there, they could see over the city walls to the cramped, crooked houses and the large infirmary tents beyond.

Or—the place where the infirmary tents had once stood.

Mercy sucked in a breath when she saw the inferno blazing across the fields, great plumes of black smoke rising into the cloudless sky. As they watched, the white tents turned black and collapsed as the flames consumed them. Several death carriages had been abandoned on the sides of the road, their wooden frames aflame. Others careened toward the safety of the city gates, streaked with soot and burn marks.

Tamriel started toward the stairs, but Nynev caught his arm. "Don't be an idiot," she hissed. "There's nothing you can do for them now."

His face filled with anguish. "The sick—"

"The death carriages have spent the last several days relocating everyone the healers deemed healthy enough to survive transport to Beggars' End. Many of the tents were empty." The huntress paused, pain flashing through her eyes. They had all caught her choice of words. *Many*—not all. "They saved as many as they could, Tamriel," she said in an uncharacteristically gentle voice.

He closed his eyes, his chest rising and falling rapidly. Mercy could see him fighting the urge to charge down there, to risk his life to save his people. She exchanged glances with Nynev. The huntress offered her a solemn nod, remembering the promise Mercy had made her and her siblings swear, and tightened her grip on her bow.

Already, ash had begun falling from the sky, and the air was thick with the acrid scent of smoke. Distant booms echoed across the city. Cannons. When she squinted, Mercy could just make out the guards standing atop the city walls, firing cannonballs through the black clouds of smoke.

"That's not what I wanted you to see, though," Nynev choked out. Mercy had never heard her sound that way—strained and high-pitched. The huntress pointed to a gap between the columns of smoke, where several hundred elves marched toward a line of Beltharan soldiers across the field. "Watch."

Just before the two sides met, a cannonball crashed into the middle of the Cirisian ranks. Blood and dirt and bodies went flying. The sight made Mercy sick. For a few long moments, nothing of note happened. The Cirisians skirted the hole in the earth the cannonball had made, stepping carefully over the bodies of their brethren, lying limp in the dirt.

Then the dead rose.

Mercy's blood ran cold. The Cirisians who had undoubtedly been dead—their bodies torn and shredded, their limbs bent at awkward angles or missing entirely—stood, retrieved their fallen weapons, and continued marching. They clashed with the Beltharan soldiers, swords and armor flashing in the sunlight.

"Th-That's impossible," Mercy stammered, her heart thundering in her chest. Beside her, Tamriel didn't even seem to be breathing. "Firesse can't be that powerful. She can't just *raise the dead*." If she had learned anything in the Guild, it was that dead was dead was dead. It was the only certainty in life; *death claims every man, prince and beggar alike*, Kaius had once said. Not even the gods could change that, her tutors had claimed.

They'd been wrong.

A geyser of dark earth shot into the air when another cannonball slammed into the battling soldiers, killing Beltharans and Cirisians alike. Sure enough, the broken bodies rose and resumed fighting only a few seconds later.

"Firesse was outnumbered, and she knew it," Tamriel murmured, gaping at the chaos on the battlefield, "so she found a way to change the odds."

Nynev nodded. "She must have strengthened her blood magic from the lives they claimed on their march here. That's why she refrained from using her magic for so many of the attacks in the fishing sector—why she sounded the retreat in Xilor instead of wiping them off the map. She was saving her strength to deal your city a blow from which it will never recover. Every death today will swell her ranks until you and your father have no choice but to surrender."

How long until the scales tipped in her favor?

"Firesse is going to be well protected," she continued, nodding toward the battlefield. Firesse was out there somewhere, marching toward the gates. "Mother Illynor and the Daughters are likely protecting her. Forget about the rest of the city—all of our strength must be directed at finding the First and putting a blade through her heart." Nynev flinched as another distant boom echoed across the city. "I ran into Niamh on her way to the infirmary to check on your father. She thinks we might be able to end her magic by killing her, but we won't know for sure until the moment her heart stops beating."

"And we have no idea what other powers she's hiding," Tamriel added in a shaky voice. He wrapped his hand around the grip of his sword until his knuckles turned white. "Going after her is a death sentence."

"Then it's obvious who has to do it," Mercy said. When he turned to her, already opening his mouth to object, she rose onto her toes and kissed him—kissed him to silence him, just as she had so many weeks ago in Hessa's farmhouse. She was an Assassin, trained practically from birth to be a better fighter than any soldier or guard. If anyone could kill Firesse, it was her.

Tamriel caught her wrist when she pulled back, agony on his face. "No. You won't survive."

"I'm the best Assassin the Guild has ever trained." She peeled Tamriel's fingers off and stepped out of his reach. She shot him a cocky grin, the gesture more confident and steady than she felt. Out of the corner of her eye, she saw Nynev slip through the castle's doors and disappear into the great hall. "Firesse doesn't stand a chance."

"Especially not with us helping you," someone said.

Cassia, Ino, Matthias, and Dayna were standing in the doorway, grim determination in their dark eyes. In unison, her siblings touched the crest pressed into the leather over their hearts in a salute. Her mother watched her with warring pride and sorrow, taking in Mercy's priceless black armor, her

Guild daggers, her fingers laced through Tamriel's. Then her gaze turned to the prince. "It would be an honor to fight for you against that monster, Your Highness."

"I'll be right there at your side."

"No, you won't," Nynev called.

Cassia and the others moved aside as Nynev and a half-dozen guards strode out of the castle and surrounded the prince. Mercy stamped down her guilt at the way Tamriel's face contorted in surprise and outrage when she pulled her hand out of his, moving back to join her family. The guards stepped into place between them, cutting off his path to her. She had known Tamriel would insist on following her into battle—that was why she had asked Nynev and the others to help her keep Tamriel safe. She couldn't let him die—not when he was the prince, the *king*, his people needed.

"You and your father are going to get in that carriage and flee the city," Nynev informed him. "We'll send word when the war is over. If you try to fight, the guards will drag you into the castle by force."

"They will do no such thing!" Tamriel hissed. "I am their prince—"

"And they have an obligation to protect you. I promised Mercy that if Firesse made it to the capital, I'd see you to safety. Come inside—your father's waiting."

He ignored her and looked at Mercy, the betrayal in his eyes burning her like a brand. "You'll get yourself killed. Let me fight with you. We'll fight together, or not at all. You chose me, and I chose you, remember?"

She shook her head and started down the stairs, Cassia and the others falling into step behind her. *I've been living on borrowed time since I killed Aelis,* she wanted to tell him. *If I am to die today, let it be in saving your life one last time.*

"Mercy!"

She didn't look back, but she could hear Tamriel fighting

the guards, trying to get to her. Nynev continued talking over the sounds of the prince's struggle. Their voices faded as Mercy and her family made their way toward the castle gates, gravel crunching under their boots. Dayna shuddered when they passed through the wrought iron gates where her daughter's body had hung nearly eighteen years earlier.

Mercy sucked in a tight breath when they stepped onto the cobblestone road, taking in the sight before her. Beyond the city walls, the flames had begun spreading from the infirmary tents to the cramped houses; alarm bells clanged, begging for help the city guards could not afford to provide. The fire would rage on, devouring everything in its wake, because the real threat was standing somewhere among the Cirisians and undead soldiers fighting for control of the city. No—not for the city. Firesse had made it clear she couldn't care less about conquering their land. She was marching for Ghyslain, for Tamriel, and she wouldn't rest until they lay dead at her feet.

"We're together now," Cassia murmured. Mercy glanced back to see her sister grab her mother's hand. With her other hand, she peeled off the black silk scarf covering her head and dropped it in the dirt. Dayna gasped at the sight of her daughter's shaven head, the mangled mess of her ear. "Nothing will ever tear us apart again. *Nothing*."

"You can't promise that, Cass," Ino said, stopping beside Mercy. His body was rigid, his eyes hard as flecks of obsidian, as he unsheathed his daggers and flipped them over in his palms, testing their weight and balance. "But we'll fight like hell to keep it from happening."

"Damn right we will," Matthias agreed.

"And we'll be right by your side the whole time," Ino vowed, nodding to Mercy. He touched the crest over his heart. "From today until our last."

Gratitude and love—love for these near-strangers, who

had fought every day of their lives to survive, who had accepted her without question, who would walk beside her into a battle unlike any in the history of Beltharos—swept over Mercy. She wished she could tell them to run, to save themselves from a war they couldn't possibly win without massive casualties, but she knew without a doubt that they would refuse. Tamriel was right—they would fight together, or not at all. If he were anyone but the prince, he would be standing here with her, as well.

Mercy unsheathed her own daggers and twisted the pommels together to form that terrifying double-bladed staff. The orange and red gemstones of the hand guards gleamed almost as brightly as the flames blazing before them. Over the crackling of the fire, the booming of the cannons, and the far-off clashing of swords, she could hear the shrieks of Tamriel's people as they scrambled to flee their burning homes—rats abandoning sinking ships. Their chance of victory was growing slimmer by the second, but for those innocent people, for her prince, for the city that had become her home, she would fight to the death.

40

TAMRIEL

The guards waited only long enough for Tamriel to watch Mercy and her siblings walk through the castle gates before herding him through the great hall and into the throne room. Upon his arrival, Tamriel found Ghyslain and Master Adan glaring at each other in the middle of the room, countless guards and soldiers surrounding them. The king and his Master of the Guard were clad in thick plate armor, and each looked mere seconds from drawing his sword. Seren Pierce and the other courtiers were nowhere to be seen—likely home with their loved ones to wait out the battle.

Master Adan's tight expression relaxed when he spotted Tamriel and Nynev. "The prince has arrived. Now please, let us take you and your son to safety. Your chance of escaping without drawing the Cirisians' notice diminishes each second you waste standing here arguing."

A shadow passed across Ghyslain's face. "I will tell you one last time, Adan, that I will *not* abandon my subjects to be slaughtered like cattle. Firesse will not rest until I face her in battle, so the only thing we should be discussing is why *you* think it is acceptable to keep me trapped here while Firesse burns my city to the ground around us." The king whirled around and glared at one of the guard-commanders. "Osiris, why hasn't a horse been armored and prepared for me to ride out to battle?"

The commander opened his mouth to answer, but Adan cut him off. "Your Majesty, you and your son will board that carriage and ride to Ospia if I have to bind you and throw you in there myself."

Ghyslain went still. "Was that an order, Adan?" Slowly, ever so slowly, he turned to his Master of the Guard, his rage rolling off him. He unsheathed his sword and leveled the point at Adan's throat. "You would dare order your king?"

Wisely, none of the guards made a move toward their king or their commander.

"As I understand it, you answer to me," Ghyslain continued, his icy voice filling the throne room. That razor-sharp blade didn't waver. "Your guards answer to me. I gave you an order, which you chose to ignore. Do it again, and I won't hesitate to put this blade through your throat. It won't be difficult to find a man willing to take your position. I doubt he'll make the same mistake when he sees your blood staining the floor at my feet."

Adan didn't move—didn't even acknowledge the sword at his neck. "My duty is to keep you safe, Your Majesty. Whether you like it or not, you serve this country, just as I do. You cannot rule it from a grave."

Ghyslain glared at him for a long, charged moment, then lowered his sword. He did not sheathe it. "I've been a terrible king, Adan. I know it—I've been too preoccupied chasing ghosts to rule properly, isn't that what they say?" A ghost of a smile passed across Ghyslain's lips. Tamriel's heart ached at the self-loathing he saw within it. "Firesse is coming to kill me. No matter how valiantly your soldiers fight, this war won't end until one of us is dead. If you spirit me away to Ospia, you'll only be prolonging the destruction. Creator knows how many innocent lives will be lost. Help me save my subjects, Adan. Help me be the king I should have been all along."

The Master of the Guard hesitated. Ghyslain offered him a hand—not a gesture from a king to his subordinate, but from one soldier to another—and, after a moment of thought, Adan clasped it and nodded. "And what of the prince, Your Majesty?"

"He'll take the carriage to Ospia as planned. Send as many men as you can spare to guard him." Ghyslain crossed the room and grasped Tamriel's shoulders, pain and devastation shining in his eyes. He lowered his voice so only Tamriel could hear. "Should I fail to defeat Firesse... You will run to Rivosa, or sail to Feyndara or Gyr'malr or one of the northern continents, and forget about this place. Do you understand? Forget about me, forget about your throne, and live. I have no idea what Firesse will do if she takes hold of the capital, but she will not be a friend of humans, especially not one of royal blood. Promise me, Tam. Promise me you'll survive."

Tamriel stared up at the king, the man who had always been a father to him in name only. For so many years, Ghyslain's grief-filled wails had haunted his sleep, had trailed him down once-bustling halls, had echoed in his ears whenever he'd caught the eye of some nobleman's pretty daughter. For so long, he'd seen his father as nothing but a coward and a broken husk of a man.

Recently, though...Ghyslain had been trying. He was trying to be the king he should have been all along, the king he hadn't been afraid to be with Liselle and Elisora at his side. Now, his father's dark eyes were more lucid than they'd been in years, his grip on Tamriel's shoulders tight and unwavering. Selfish as his father's request seemed, Tamriel knew Ghyslain was offering him more than just his life—he was offering a chance to give up the throne he'd never truly wanted, to escape the court and forget the pain he'd endured within these walls.

Tamriel shook his head and shrugged off his father's hands. "I won't promise you that, and I won't flee to Ospia. I'm staying here—with you—to fight. We'll defend our people together."

"If you die—"

"He won't." Nynev stepped forward, lifting her chin. "I'll protect him."

"As will I."

All eyes swung to Niamh, who was standing in the doorway in one of her simple muslin dresses. Her hair was plaited back from her face, her Cirisian tattoos peeking through her makeup, and her knuckles were white around the grip of a sword. She smiled at Tamriel as she stepped fully into the room. "You're lucky you have a bodyguard who cannot die."

"Is Adriel alright?"

"Resting. Whatever Mercy gave him did the trick. The rest of the Strykers are in the armory, preparing to fight."

A loud boom rocked the castle, the force of the blast reverberating through the stone bricks underfoot. It hadn't come from one of the cannons on the city walls—it was much too close. It had come from—

"The tunnel." Master Adan let out a string of curses. "Calum must have known about the secret exit. He—er, Drake—must have told the Cirisians. My men were ordered to only fire the cannons if the elves tried to enter the castle through the tunnel. If necessary, we will hold our position here."

Ghyslain nodded, drawing himself to his full height. With his dark hair neatly tied back and his sword in hand, he looked like one of the warrior-kings of old. That broken, grieving man of Tamriel's nightmares was nowhere to be found. "Ready our horses for battle," he commanded, his voice ringing out and silencing the murmurs of the guards. Immediately, they started filtering out of the throne room. Ghyslain strode toward the door, Adan and Tamriel trailing behind. The Cirisian sisters fell into step behind them, whispering to each other in their strange, lilting tongue.

"I do hope you're experienced with a sword, Your Majesty," Adan said with forced lightness.

"We'll soon see if my training has held up all these years. Tam, be on your guard at all times. The Cirisians have allied with the Daughters, and they still have a contract on your life." Ghyslain's eyes drifted upward, toward the heavens. "By the Creator, I hope I'm not making a mistake in letting you come along."

"Letting me come along? I'm not some stray dog yapping at your heels. I can fight, and I'll gladly do it to save our people from that monster outside our gates. After all," he said, smiling faintly, "I'm my father's son."

Ghyslain looked at him, surprise etched on his features. They slowed as they reached the front of the throne room, the bottleneck into the corridor leading to the great hall. He shook his head. "You may look like me, but you have your mother's heart. She would be so proud to see you today."

A lump formed in Tamriel's throat, but he refused to let them fall. He could count on one hand the number of times he had heard Ghyslain speak about his mother. "Thank you, Father."

His words were drowned out by another cannon blast, this one strong enough to crack the tiles beneath their feet. The ground trembled, and the candles overhead guttered out as the chandeliers began to sway wildly. Distant crackling echoed down the hall, the sound like shattering bones.

"The soldiers sealed off the tunnel," Adan said with a breath of relief as they stepped into the great hall. "The only ways in now are the servants' entrance and the main doors, and both require making it past the castle gates."

"They've breached the castle! The Cirisians have breached the castle!" someone shouted.

Tamriel reached his father's side just in time to see the young guard run into the room, his arms pinwheeling wildly, his eyes wide as saucers. He was younger than Tamriel—little more than a recruit. "The Cirisians have breached the castle!" he screamed. His head snapped back toward the hall from which he'd come, his breath catching as he spied something out of Tamriel's line of view. "They've—"

A spray of blood flew from his lips as the blade of a spear punched through his open mouth. He slumped to his knees, then fell face-first onto the floor, the shaft of the spear sticking straight up from the back of his skull.

A Cirisian woman stepped up behind him, her face, hair, and armor coated in blood and a strange gray powder—dust, Tamriel realized belatedly, from the tunnel's collapse. She cocked her head as countless elves walked out of the hall and formed a half-circle behind her, every one of them grinning with murderous delight. "They've breached the castle?" she asked in her soft, melodic voice. Her fingers curled around the shaft of the spear. She braced her foot on the boy's head and yanked the spear out.

The guards let out roars of rage and sprinted toward the Cirisian soldiers. Tamriel's heart leapt into his throat as they collided with a crash of steel, blood spraying. The Cirisians were outnumbered, but only barely. Adan had sent as many soldiers as he could afford to search for Firesse.

Someone grabbed Tamriel's arm.

"Out through the main doors," Adan hissed, jerking his chin toward the other end of the hall. Already, Ghyslain and some of the guard-commanders were running toward the exit. Tamriel made a break for the doors, Niamh following hard on his heels. Nynev fired off arrow after arrow, hissing curses, as Adan unsheathed his sword and leapt into the fray.

"The bastards just keep getting up!" the huntress cried. Tamriel risked a glance over his shoulder to see that the dead soldiers—Cirisian and Beltharan alike—had indeed continued fighting, some bearing massive holes in their armor from the Cirisians' spears, others with Nynev's arrows sticking from their flesh.

"Tam, duck!" Ghyslain yelled, just as someone tackled him. They went sprawling on the stone floor as something hard thudded against the wall and clattered to the ground.

"It's me," Niamh wheezed in Tamriel's ear. She clutched her side as she stood, then offered Tamriel her free hand and pulled him to his feet. She pointed to the spear lying on the floor at their feet, then at the bloody mark it had left on the wall—at the exact height of his chest. "That nearly hit you."

"Then let's go before they can throw another one." Tamriel scooped his sword off the ground—it had slipped out of his grasp when he'd fallen—and grabbed Niamh's arm, dragging her toward where Ghyslain and the commanders were waiting near the exit. "Nynev! Adan!"

The huntress and the Master of the Guard were fighting side by side in the middle of the room, facing off against four Cirisians who had broken off from the main group. Three of them were alive; the undead one bore a gaping gash in its stomach, its intestines hanging out around its knees, but it did not fight with any less ferocity than the rest.

"Go!" Nynev called without looking back. "We'll buy you time!" She slammed the butt of her hunting knife into the dead elf's nose. The bone broke with a sick crunch, but the elf did not so much as blink. "GO!"

Niamh choked on a sob as she and Tamriel ran for the

castle doors. Ghyslain and the guard-commanders were shouting for them to hurry. Then—

"What the hell?"

They stumbled to a stop just beyond the castle doors, nearly slamming into the king and the others, who stood gaping at something across the manicured lawn. Osiris pointed at the closed gate and the people clinging to it, reaching through the gaps in the wrought iron.

Niamh's breath caught. "Are they sick?"

"How did they get out of the End?" another commander demanded, turning on her.

"The gates were closed when I left an hour ago!"

A dozen guards stood at the end of the gravel carriageway, blades drawn and leveled at the sick as the gates creaked and groaned under the weight of so many bodies. At first, Tamriel assumed they were begging for help, for healing or protection, but as they descended the stairs and drew near enough for Tamriel to make out the individual voices, he realized the sick were *taunting* the guards. When one of the guards stepped too close to the gate, a hand plunged through and clamped down on the man's arm. He dropped his sword and began screaming, dropping to his knees on the gravel. The rest of the guards jumped back in alarm.

"Osiris, see what's happening," one of the commanders said, his voice wobbling. "You, too, Healer."

Tamriel and the others waited in tense silence as Osiris and Niamh approached the man, the sounds of the fight in the great hall spilling out behind them. As they neared the gate, the cries of the sick grew louder, more frantic. Niamh's shoulders hunched as she bent down to examine the writhing, shrieking guard. She shook her head, and Tamriel's mouth went dry as he watched Osiris plunge his sword into the guard's chest.

"Surrounded," Ghyslain muttered, shaking his head. Even

if they were willing to abandon the city, there would be no escape. The lake, with its churning waves and massive, sharp boulders, would be too treacherous for any but the most desperate to attempt to cross.

A yelp drew their attention back to the gates. The guard —the one who'd been sick moments ago—had begun to twitch, reanimated by Firesse's otherworldly powers. Niamh didn't hesitate before bringing her sword down on the guard's neck, cleaving his head from his body. The man immediately fell still and did not move again.

"At least we know how to kill them now," Tamriel said, frowning, as Osiris and Niamh started toward them. "Or...re-kill them."

"The plague was upon him in seconds," Niamh panted upon their return. "He was covered in a rash, his eyes blind, his mind gone. Kept talking nonsense to people who weren't there." She braced her hands on her knees and shuddered, still gulping down air. "Those people out there—they're elves, and they didn't have the tattoos. I think they're the slaves Firesse liberated. She sent them into the city to infect everyone."

"Impossible," one of the commanders scoffed.

Her eyes flashed. "She knew they wouldn't be skilled fighters, but that they'd be useful for spreading the plague, weakening your people." Her throat bobbed as she swallowed. "Adriel told me Firesse's powers control the plague, but I didn't think it could consume someone so quickly. Her strength..."

Tamriel's heart pounded as his gaze returned to the gate. Mercy was out there somewhere. Possibly dying. Possibly dead. Possibly one of Firesse's undead minions.

He shut out the thoughts. Death would not claim either of them today. "How did they get in the city?" If her soldiers had already breached the gates...

Osiris shook his head. "I have no idea."

Tamriel turned back to Niamh. "Can you combat her magic?"

"I don't know the spell she used. Even if I did, the amount of power such a spell would require is massive. Our best hope"—*our only hope*, she didn't say—"is to kill Firesse and pray that puts an end to her magic."

"Then it's up to Mercy and her family now." He tried to ignore the way his stomach clenched at the words.

"No. Firesse is coming to us." Ghyslain jerked his chin toward the inferno blazing outside the city, and Tamriel at last realized what the fire and the battle beyond really were— a distraction. A trick to divide their soldiers and their attention, just as the Cirisians had done their whole march across the fishing sector. Firesse really had been a dozen steps ahead of them this entire time. "She raised an army and led them all the way here to kill us, and she won't let anyone else take that opportunity from her. She's coming, and we're going to be ready when she arrives."

Master Adan burst through the doors of the castle, breathing hard. His silver armor was splattered with so much blood Tamriel couldn't tell how much was his and how much was the enemy's. Adan's gaze went to the gates, groaning under the weight of the sick elves, then back to the castle. "The throne room. It's the most defensible part of the castle. Bar the doors," he ordered Osiris and another commander.

The massive doors slammed shut behind them as Adan led them through the great hall, keeping well away from the fighting on the opposite side of the room. Nynev and the guards were holding their own, but they were tiring, and the undead soldiers showed no signs of slowing. They were all covered in so much blood it was hard to tell who was alive and who was another one of Firesse's puppets. The floor was slick with blood, and the tang of copper hung heavily in the air.

"Guards, to us!" Adan shouted as they sprinted down the hall to the throne room. Nynev slashed at one of the elves with her hunting knife, then ran after them, slipping and sliding on the floor. The guards followed close behind her. A bloody spear sailed over Tamriel's shoulder and glanced harmlessly off the wall. "Quickly, *quickly*," Adan urged.

They spilled through the double doors of the throne room, and Adan slammed them behind the last guard, sliding the heavy bolt into place. Through the wood, Tamriel could hear the elves mutter to one another in Cirisian. He doubted it would be long before they found something with which to break down the doors.

"I'm okay, I'm okay," Nynev was assuring her sister as she leaned against the wall, her skin shining with sweat, her eyes bright with the adrenaline of a fight. A nasty purple bruise blossomed across her jaw and blood leaked from a gash across the bridge of her nose, but otherwise, she looked no worse for wear.

Behind Tamriel, Ghyslain snarled, "You have the nerve to show your face here after all you've done?" The hatred in his voice sent a chill down Tamriel's spine.

He turned to find his father standing in the middle of the room, the remaining guards in a half-circle around him. Of the sixty men they'd had, only forty or so were still alive. The king was glaring up at the dais, and Tamriel followed his father's gaze up to—

Calum, lounging on the throne with his legs hanging over one of the arms, his chin propped on a hand. A lazy grin tugged at his lips. A dozen stunning, blood-splattered Assassins flanked him, bows in hand. "Hello, cousin," he drawled.

"Drop the charade, Drake," Ghyslain snarled. "We all know you're the real monster behind these attacks."

The creature wearing Calum's skin ignored the king completely and straightened, his eyes roving over Tamriel with fiendish delight. That lazy grin turned into a full-on beaming smile when Niamh and Nynev stepped forward, directly into the path of the arrows the Daughters had trained on Tamriel's heart. Calum lifted a hand, and the Daughters lowered their bows.

"I've come so far to see you, Tam," he said. He rose, unsheathed his sword, and stalked down the steps of the dais. The guards tensed, drawing closer to Tamriel and the king, but Calum stopped at the foot of the platform and cocked his head. "Won't you honor me with a duel, princeling?"

When Tamriel didn't respond, Calum frowned. "No? You don't want your father to have to watch me gut you?" He shrugged. "Oh, but it would be so much fun. Very well, then. We can do it the hard way."

"Where is Firesse?" Ghyslain called. "She sent her minion to do her killing for her?"

At last, Drake's eyes flicked to the king, a sneer tugging at his lips. "She knew you'd be waiting here for her, so she offered me some time to play. She'll be here soon enough. Now," he said, grinning, "Make sure you're paying attention, Your Majesty. I would hate for you to miss your son's slaughter."

He gestured for the Daughters to attack. They leapt into motion, half of them loosing throwing knives so quickly all Tamriel could do was blink as six guards fell to the ground around him. Adan shouted a command, and the guards surged to protect Tamriel and his father as the Daughters unleashed themselves on the nearest soldiers, laughing as their blades rent flesh and bone. Nynev elbowed Tamriel out of the way, a hunting knife in each hand. "Stay back, Your Highness. Let us deal with Firesse's puppet."

Across the room, Calum strode toward him with his

sword and dagger in hand, a cat stalking its prey. His eyes lit up when he saw Nynev and Niamh standing protectively before Tamriel, as if this whole battle was nothing more than a game. He touched one of the Daughter's shoulders as he passed, a girl with blue-black hair that shone like an oil slick under the light streaming in through the windows.

"You still want to complete the contract, Faye?" he asked, loudly enough for Tamriel to hear over the clanging of weapons and cries of pain. When she nodded, he jerked his chin toward Niamh and Nynev. "Rid the prince of his bodyguards, and the killing blow is yours—but only after we've had our fun." Drake didn't flinch when another Assassin's blade arced and sent a splatter of blood across Calum's sharp, angular face. He grinned, something dark and evil dancing in his eyes, and said, "Let's teach the king what a grave mistake he made in having me killed."

41
CALUM
ONE HOUR EARLIER

Drake's lips curled into a smirk when he saw the unmarked carriage waiting beside the rocky shore of Lake Myrella, half hidden behind the enormous boulder that concealed the castle's secret exit. He pressed a hand to the smooth brick of the city's exterior wall and waved Kenna and Farren over. The fifty other elves and Assassins under his command lingered just beyond the curve of the wall, waiting for a signal.

"Four dozen," Drake murmured to Kenna and Farren, nodding toward the guards surrounding the carriage. Then he gestured to the men standing atop the boulder, crossbows in hand. "Three lookouts. Take them out."

Calum watched in silent horror as the twins pulled the bows off their backs and sent three arrows arcing toward the guards. The second they hit their targets—the guards' bodies teetering, then falling and landing in a bloody heap on the pebbled shore—Drake pushed away from the cover of the wall and sprinted toward the shocked guards, his soldiers streaming out behind him. Before the humans could react, his blade plunged through the stomach of one and slit the throat of another.

By the time the last guard fell, the shore was drenched in blood and bodies. Faye crouched beside the water's edge to clean her dagger. "Some of the guards retreated to the castle," she told Drake, jerking her chin toward the entrance to the tunnel, nearly invisible through the artfully placed vines creeping up the boulder and the city's outer wall. "They're going to warn the king."

"Then they'll be expecting us," Kaius said, joining them by the water's edge. He plucked an arrow out of the carriage driver's chest, wiped the arrowhead off on a clean section of the man's tunic, and dropped it into his quiver. "We'd better not keep them waiting."

Once they'd finished gathering their weapons and tending to some minor injuries, Drake led the Cirisians and Daughters into the tunnel. The passageway was so narrow he could spread his arms and touch both sides. He trailed a hand along the damp walls, navigating the pitch blackness purely by touch. They didn't dare use a torch to illuminate the way; the guards stationed at the other end would see them coming from a mile away. For a long while, their only companions were the dank, earth-scented air and the occasional scrape of a weapon or armor against the jagged stone walls.

Then, a faint light appeared up ahead, bleeding from around a bend in the tunnel. "Go on," Drake murmured to Faye and Giovanna. The Assassins crept forward and loaded the small crossbows they'd brought from the Guild—each no longer than their forearms. They darted around the corner, slipping out of sight, and the Beltharan guards let out cries of alarm and pain as the bolts thudded into flesh. Drake and the others followed hard upon them, rounding the corner to find the Assassins locked in combat with four guards. Their blades sent sparks flying every time they glanced off the walls. The girls made quick work of the guards, using the close quarters and low light to their advantage.

"Well done, my darlings," Drake crooned as he stepped between Faye and Giovanna. Several yards ahead, countless royal guards stood at the mouth of the tunnel, gaping at the force Drake led. Calum could imagine how terrifying they looked—blood-splattered and hungry for vengeance, their Cirisian eyes glimmering in the darkness. Drake grinned. "But our work's not finished yet."

Like the breaking of a dam, the Cirisians and Assassins pushed forward, crashing into the waiting guards in a rush of steel. Together, they poured out of the tunnel and into one of the castle's underground corridors, forcing the Beltharan guards to yield precious ground. The floor soon grew slick with blood and gore, and twice Drake tripped over a body slumped across the middle of the hallway. The corpses weren't an obstacle for long, though. Within moments, Firesse's blood magic drew them to their feet and turned them against the dwindling Beltharan numbers.

"Fire it!" one of the commanders shouted, his voice raw with pain and fear. Calum watched through the chaos as a guard ripped a torch from its sconce on the wall and pushed through the fighting, ducking around slashing blades and flashing steel. The man Drake had been fighting threw himself to the side, and a second later, Calum saw why:

A boy, not much younger than Calum himself, was kneeling beside a strange black box, holding a torch to the box's fuse. It was a small cannon, Calum realized, and it was pointed straight at the mouth of the tunnel. Cirisians were still emerging from the narrow passageway. The guards were going to seal it off with half of Drake's forces still inside.

"Watch out!" Drake bellowed, sprinting for the boy.

They collided in a crunch of metal and bone. The torch flew out of the boy's hand, but Drake hadn't been fast enough. The fuse was short—and lit. Before Drake could reach up to snuff it out, the boy and another guard grabbed the collar of his breastplate and dragged him backward. His hands scrabbled for purchase on the slick stone tiles, and he could do nothing but watch as the cannonball hurtled into the tunnel and collided with one of the walls, in the process taking out a few Cirisians who had been too slow to move out of its path. The walls of the tunnel groaned, shuddering under the impact, but they held.

Drake flipped onto his back and kicked the boy in the face, breaking his nose with a sharp *crack!* He screamed and released Drake's breastplate, blood bubbling over his lips. Drake grabbed his dagger and jammed it into the eye socket of the other guard who had pulled him away from the cannon. He jumped to his feet just in time to see Faye and the other Daughters drop to their knees, another cannonball flying over their heads. There was a loud *boom* when it crashed into the stone, then...

Rumbling.

The roof of the tunnel collapsed, the impact nearly throwing Drake off his feet. He braced a hand against the wall as a cloud of dirt and pulverized stone filled the hall. The entire castle shuddered. When the broken bricks finally ceased falling and the cloud of dust settled, Calum gaped at the destruction they'd wrought.

Half of the Cirisians had been trapped in the tunnel, waiting for Drake and the others to clear the way into the castle. Where they had stood was now a mountain of rubble, broken bodies and shattered limbs peeking out from between massive hunks of stone. One of the Daughters let out a sob and collapsed beside the body of an Assassin. The dead girl's eyes stared unblinkingly at the hole where the roof of the tunnel had once been. Now, they could see straight up into one of the castle's twisting, labyrinthine halls.

At a snapped order from their commander, the dazed Beltharans turned and bolted down the corridor, off to report to their king and Master of the Guard.

"Get up," Drake snapped at the remainder of his force. About three dozen had survived, including all the Daughters save for the one in the tunnel. Slowly, groaning with pain, they rose and dusted off their armor. Drake waved Kenna and Farren forward and pointed down the hall in the direction of the Beltharans' retreat. "Take all the surviving Cirisians and go after them. They'll lead you straight to the king. Assassins, you're with me."

Once they had disappeared around the corner, Drake reached down and pulled Faye to her feet. She winced, shifting her weight off her right ankle, but did not balk when he instructed her to gather her Sisters and follow him to the throne room. Thanks to Calum's childhood in the castle, Drake knew of the small hallway that led directly to the throne room dais. With the city besieged, the infirmary tents burning, and the escape tunnel destroyed, that was the likeliest place Tamriel and Ghyslain would be. With the Cirisians approaching from the great hall and Drake from the throne room, the king and prince would be trapped with nowhere to run.

Make sure you're paying attention, boy, Drake whispered as he walked down the hall, the Assassins falling into step behind him. Hatred filled Calum at the smooth, smug sound of his father's voice. *This is the moment we've been waiting for. This is what you put into motion when you forged that contract on Tamriel's life. Now, we reap the benefits.*

❦ 42 ❦
MERCY

Mercy and her family hadn't made it more than two blocks from the castle when a lone guard appeared at the other end of the street, shouting something indecipherable as she hurtled toward them. She pointed at something over her shoulder, then collapsed to her knees in the middle of the road and began to retch.

"What in the Creator's name?" Matthias hissed, brows shooting up.

The woman wiped her mouth with the back of her hand as Mercy and her family approached. "Run," she panted, shuddering and gasping. "Run, before it's too late—she's coming to kill us all. Warn the prince. Warn—warn the king."

"Where is Firesse?"

"The End."

"The End?" Mercy frowned, stopping short. "That's impossible. How did they breach the city walls?"

The guard's head snapped up, and that was when Mercy saw the bright red rash covering half the woman's face, the glistening blisters across her flesh, the feverish gleam in her eyes. Mercy took a step toward the guard, but the woman fell back onto her heels and scrambled out of her reach.

"Don't touch me. Don't— You can't touch me." She wrapped her arms around her armor-clad knees and hugged them, trembling. "They're coming. They're coming to make you sick."

"Who?"

"This way." She pushed to her feet, swaying unsteadily, and shuffled to a narrow alley between two massive houses. She squeezed in far enough for Mercy, Cassia, Dayna, Ino, and Matthias to all file in behind her. For a few moments, the only sound was her ragged, uneven breathing. Then, they watched in horror as several dozen sick elves stalked down the street, their sallow faces drawn with pain. The horde— there was no other word to describe it—passed without a single glance in their direction. Every pair of glazed eyes was trained straight ahead.

"I freed that woman in Graystone," Dayna whispered, nodding to a blonde woman at the rear of the group. "They were all slaves."

"They're marching for the castle," Cassia murmured. "But how the hell did they make it out of the End?"

"Gates." The guard leaned her head back against the cool brick of the house and swallowed. "The elf sent them here. Used her magic to infect them—infect *us*."

"You mean you weren't sick before the attack?" Ino asked, horrified.

She shook her head. "I was perfectly healthy. They got my husband, too. He didn't make it out of the End."

It felt like an eternity passed before the sick elves shuffled out of sight. Even after Matthias peered out and gave the all-clear, they waited two full minutes before slipping out of the alley. Mercy turned toward the battle raging beyond the city walls. Behind her, Cassia kept murmuring the same thing—

You're all right, you'll be okay—to the guard. Cannonballs sailed through the columns of black smoke rising from the inferno, blasting Cirisians and undead soldiers to bits. Despite that, it was obvious even from this distance that Firesse's soldiers had gained the upper hand. The Beltharan forces were dwindling. Mercy hissed a curse under her breath.

"We need to get her to a healer, Mercy," Cassia said, her voice high and strained. "We need to get—No. No, no, no, no, *no.* Stay— *Stay with me!*"

By the time Mercy turned, the guard was slumped against the side of the house, staring up at the sky with dead, unseeing eyes. Her pupils had gone a milky white—like Pilar's had been before she tried to claw them out—and a dribble of blood trailed out of the corner of her mouth.

Dayna gaped at the corpse, then slowly lifted her gaze to the opposite end of the street, where the horde of sick elves had marched toward the castle. Her face went slack with realization. "Th-That's what Firesse was going to do to Adriel and me. That's why she didn't kill us outright when we tried to escape."

Matthias let out a strangled sound.

A chill snaked down Mercy's spine. She nudged Cassia out of the way and stooped to pick up the guard's sword, being careful not to touch the woman's skin. If Firesse's magic had somehow strengthened the plague enough for it to kill the guardswoman in a matter of minutes, she wouldn't take any chances with her supposed immunity.

The woman's hand—which had been lying limp in her lap—slowly clenched into a fist. Firesse's magic, beginning to reanimate her. Mercy gritted her teeth and swung the sword, cutting through flesh and bone. The woman's head thumped to the ground, and the corpse fell still.

She tossed the sword aside in favor of her double-edged dagger and frowned at her elder sister, ignoring the blood pooling around her boots. "Let's go." They were soldiers now —they'd grieve their dead after the war was won.

Sure enough, the slums were in chaos when Mercy and the others arrived not fifteen minutes later. Beltharan soldiers and city guards alike poured into the End through the open gate, shouting to one another over the din of clashing swords drifting from inside. Mercy could see fingers of flames licking the blackening sky over the wall. How Firesse's forces had made it past the city walls remained a mystery they didn't have time to contemplate. Mercy splashed through a dark red puddle as she led the others through the old archway and into the End.

The first thing that struck her was the blood. It was everywhere—drying between the cracks in the cobblestone road, pooling along the curb, dripping down the sides of buildings. The sight reminded Mercy of the map she'd found in Seren Pierce's study so many weeks ago; Cassius, upon waking from a dream-vision, had painted the entirety of Beggars' End in blood red ink. She stopped short, ignoring Ino's murmured apology when he walked straight into her back. They'd thought that the vision was intended to show them where the plague originated, but could it have been a premonition of this battle?

They wended their way through the streets, passing soldiers and guards locked in combat with Cirisians and skirting derelict houses consumed in flames. The cobblestone grew slicker the further into the slums they moved. They passed several large pools of blood, but no bodies. Firesse's magic was too strong; it reanimated the soldiers as soon as they fell, and there were so many people crammed into the twisting, winding roads of the End that it was hard to tell who fought for which side. Between the cries of pain, the flash of blades, the spraying blood, and the unbearable heat of the flames, it was all Mercy could do to keep walking, to see past the injured and dying soldiers around her in hopes of catching a glimpse of flame-red hair. *Kill the magic wielder, kill the magic.* That was all that mattered.

She let out a breath of relief when they turned a corner and came face-to-face with Bas, one of the guards who had shadowed her after she'd been struck by Drake Hamell's arrow. "Have you seen Firesse?" she shouted over the sounds of fighting, her throat already burning from the smoke and soot in the air. The question had barely left her mouth when she noticed the blood dripping down his side, the dagger still protruding from his ribcage. A fatal blow.

Bas's dull, glazed eyes betrayed no hint of pain as he hefted his bloodied sword and swung it low, straight for Mercy's waist—a move that would have cut her in half had she not seen him train, had she not anticipated the move. Matthias let out a cry of alarm as Mercy leapt forward, deflected the sword with her own blade, then whirled the double-edged dagger around and sliced his head clean off. Blood splattered across her face. Mercy nearly gagged at the feel of it on her skin. It was ice-cold and putrid, as if he had been dead for weeks. She shuddered, wiped it away with the back of her hand, and gestured for the others to follow her.

Together, the five of them slashed and hacked their way toward the center of the slums, pausing only long enough to instruct the Beltharan soldiers they passed to behead the undead creatures. Mercy's heart thundered as she watched Cassia lunge out of the arc of a fallen elf's blade and plunge her own dagger into the monster's chest, distracting it long enough for Ino to step up behind it and slice straight through its neck. By the time they reached the square before the dilapidated warehouse-turned-infirmary, they were all coated in thick, foul-scented blood. The wounds in Mercy's chest had begun to throb so intensely she could feel each thump of her heart all the way down to her fingertips. Wincing, she clenched and unclenched her left hand as she surveyed the carnage before them.

More people than she had ever seen in Beggars' End filled the clearing—hundreds upon hundreds of Beltharan soldiers, Cirisian elves, and reanimated corpses—locked in a whirl of clashing weapons and splattering blood. Two wooden houses across from them had already collapsed from the flames. Thankfully, the warehouse Hero had worked so hard to maintain appeared unscathed.

"Mercy!" Matthias shoved her out of the way as a Cirisian lunged at her, the blade at the end of his spear flashing. Dayna grabbed her arm to right her just as four more elves burst out of the alley to their right, their teeth bared and eyes bright with bloodlust. Mercy immediately lifted her double-edged dagger to parry the nearest elf's attack as Dayna and her siblings fell into defensive positions beside her. Something let out a sharp *crack*, and Mercy risked a glance at Matthias to see the bladed end of his opponent's spear clatter on the ground and roll well out of reach. Before the Cirisian could pull the knife sheathed at his hip, Matthias plunged his blade through the elf's leather armor and into his stomach.

"Traitor," the elf nearest Mercy hissed. She ignored him and feinted right, hooking her leg around his ankle and pulling him off balance. He slipped in the blood coating the street and crashed onto his back, glaring up at her with fury in his eyes. "You fight for the wrong side, soldier."

She didn't bother to answer before cutting off his head.

Mercy barely had time to breathe before another Cirisian was lunging toward her, his blade angled for her neck. She killed him easily, but another one filled his place the second he fell. There was no end to them—not to the Cirisians, and not to the corpses fighting alongside them.

The distant booms of the cannons had ceased. The battle in the field had to be over; it was obvious by the staggering number of Cirisians flooding the streets of the slums which side had won. They'd set their sights entirely on breaching Beggars' End, which meant Calum—or Drake—must not have known about the secret tunnel leading out of the castle. If he had, Firesse certainly would have focused all her efforts there, not on the slums on the complete opposite side of the city. She was here, fighting somewhere in the chaos.

Ino seemed to sense her thoughts. He looked away from his opponent just long enough to jerk his chin toward the house to their right. "Up there," he shouted. "The second-floor window—see if you can see her." When she nodded, he slipped into her place, taking on two elves to buy her time to run.

Mercy burst through the door and scrambled up the rickety stairs two at a time, her chainmail armor jangling with every step. When she reached the landing, she swung herself around the banister and ran to the window Ino had pointed out. Halfway across the clearing, she spotted a shock of white hair by the warehouse's door—Ketojan. Hero was beside him, brandishing a Cirisian's spear at anyone who dared step too close. Neither of them wore armor, but the few wounds Mercy could see from this distance were minor; they seemed to be holding their own through sheer force of will. She tried not to think about how much their deaths would devastate Tamriel as she dragged her gaze past them, searching the clearing for Firesse.

The rushing in her ears went dead silent when she spotted the green-and-gold scaled woman slaughtering her way through the Beltharan forces.

Mother Illynor.

Mercy had never seen Illynor fight before. The entire time Mercy was in the Guild, Illynor had never touched any blade except her dinner knife—until the day she'd almost killed Mercy for cheating the Trial. With her preternatural stillness, her smooth, savage grace, those calculating slitted eyes, the Guildmother had never needed to resort to violence to ensure her apprentices stayed in line. She'd been terrifying enough without it.

But watching her now... She was no longer merely the headmistress of the Guild. She was a nightmare made flesh. She was Death incarnate.

Illynor cut through bodies as if they were no more substantial than air. She was a hurricane, a raging tempest, killing with such speed and dexterity that Mercy could hardly keep track of her movements. She blinked, and two soldiers were dead—two more bodies to join Firesse's ranks of reanimated corpses.

Watching the headmistress, Mercy finally understood why Illynor had always seemed faintly amused by her dream of becoming the best Assassin the Guild had ever trained—she could complete a thousand contracts, could practice every day for a century, could master every weapon, and she would still not be a fraction of the warrior Mother Illynor was. The headmistress fought like she had done every move a million times, like she knew every attack her opponent would make before he even thought of it. She was the greatest warrior Mercy had ever seen.

A heartbeat later, Firesse and several Daughters strode into the clearing. Mercy bit back a shout of warning as she watched a handful of Beltharan soldiers break away from the group they'd been fighting and barrel toward Firesse. They clashed with the Daughters in a whirlwind of steel and blood, and it wasn't long before the soldiers joined the undead. The Daughters disappeared into the chaos, leaving the young First completely unguarded—undoubtedly a trap. Mercy could swear Firesse smiled as she surveyed the bloodied clearing, daring another soldier to attack her.

Kill the magic wielder, kill the magic.

Right behind her, a floorboard creaked. Mercy ducked, twisting her double-edged dagger apart as she moved, and plunged the twin blades into her attacker's stomach. Cold, foul-smelling blood poured over her hands. Gagging at the stench—like carrion, meat rotting under a hot sun—she looked up into her attacker's face and met bloodshot blind eyes, the skin around them swollen and red. Milky pus leaked out of the boils across its cheeks. Not just one of Firesse's undead puppets, then—one infected with the plague.

And its fingers were clamped around her bare, bloody hand.

"Firesse is across the clearing," Mercy said to Ino when she hurtled out of the house minutes later, her daggers dripping the creature's foul blood. She pointed, and he followed her gaze. "The Daughters are here—Illynor, too."

He deflected his opponent's blade and slashed low, carving a gash into the elf's leg down to the bone. The Cirisian let out a scream of pain, which was cut short when Ino's other dagger arced up and plunged through his ribcage, piercing his heart. Ino grunted and staggered back as he yanked the blade out. "Where do you want us?"

"You and Cassia take the alley and fight your way to the other side of the clearing, behind Firesse. Find a crossbow or a bow and quiver and get to a roof. If you can find a clear shot, take it."

He nodded. "Be safe." He ran over to Cassia and Matthias, who were barely managing to hold back three of

Firesse's men. Mercy slipped behind the elf her mother was struggling to kill—he was a swift fighter, quick, lethal—and plunged her daggers under the edge of his ill-fitting breastplate, piercing his kidneys. He fell, dead, as three more bodies thumped to the ground behind her. Mercy scanned her mother up and down. Dayna was bleeding from one side of her jaw and a gash in her upper arm, but the rest of the blood coating her leather armor didn't appear to be her own.

"There are too many Cirisians here," Mercy shouted over the din of clashing steel. "You should find somewhere safe to go until the fighting's over. Let me handle Firesse and the others."

Dayna shook her head, sucking in deep breaths. "I'm not leaving without you, Bareea. Never again."

"We swore to fight alongside you," Matthias said as he moved to Mercy's side, swiping at the blood pouring from a cut over his eye. "Did you see Firesse?"

She nodded, her pulse thrumming in her ears, and pulled them into a nearby alley for a momentary reprieve from the fighting. Mother Illynor would soon spot them. She peered out and caught another glimpse of Ketojan's white hair amidst the chaos. Half of it was plastered to his head, matted with shiny blood. "I'm going to kill her. I need you to get to the warehouse and help Ketojan and Hero protect the people inside. If it becomes too much—if you can't keep fighting—run."

"And leave you to kill Firesse on your own?" Matthias hissed. "Are you insane?"

"I'm the only one who has a chance of making it past the Daughters. Besides, Ino and Cassia will be right there beside me, watching my back," she lied. Out of the way—she needed them out of the clearing, out of the fight. The only way they would let her save their lives was if they thought they were helping her. "Illynor is Qadari. If you see her coming, you run.

Do you understand? You take Hero and Ketojan and you run as fast as you can. Hide at the tailor's shop, and we'll meet you there. Promise me."

Matthias nodded, blinking through the blood dripping down the side of his face. Dayna reached a trembling hand for Mercy, but she stepped out of the alley before her mother could touch her. "We don't have much time. The End is already lost."

Before her mother could protest, Mercy drew her daggers and plunged into the clearing. She dodged slashing swords and struck at any outstretched, plague-infected limbs in her path as she crept along the houses lining the clearing, keeping well away from Mother Illynor and her deadly blades. She wasn't stupid or arrogant enough to engage the Guildmother in battle.

Her pace slowed as she made her way along the edge of the clearing, fatigue settling deep into her bones. She felt like she could curl up and sleep for a month. Beneath her black-and-silver armor—that beautiful, wonderful, perfect gift from Tamriel—her skin was slick with sweat. The wound in her shoulder pulsed with heat. She may have ripped the stitches.

When she spotted Firesse's flame-red hair through a gap between the fighting soldiers, Mercy backed into the shadow between buildings and scanned the nearby rooftops for Ino and Cassia. They were nowhere in sight—still fighting their way along the side streets. Mercy sucked in a deep breath, pushing past the pain and exhaustion in her limbs, and scanned her surroundings. The few Daughters who had accompanied Illynor and Firesse were scattered about the square, slaughtering soldiers and guards left and right. The rest of the Assassins must be fighting their way toward the castle. She prayed Tamriel and Ghyslain had made it to the carriage in time.

She took another breath and ran.

The second another gap opened between the bodies, Mercy darted through it, her eyes trained on Firesse. The First's back was turned, her attention on Mother Illynor and the Daughters. Now. *Now*. Mercy tightened her grip on her double-edged dagger and leveled the blade at Firesse's head, pushing herself faster. The Assassin within her sang with perverse delight as the distance between her and the young First rapidly diminished. *Kill the magic wielder, kill the magic.*

By the Creator, she hoped Niamh was right.

When there were no more than a few yards between them, Firesse turned. Her brows rose in surprise and she jumped out of the whistling arc of Mercy's blade. "I was wondering when you'd show up," she crooned as Mercy twisted, using her momentum to roll and spring to her feet behind the First. Firesse whirled, smirking. She did not pull the sword sheathed at her hip.

She didn't need to.

She murmured a single guttural word in ancient Cirisian, and Mercy's blood boiled.

A scream of pain wrenched free from her throat as flames danced under her skin, ragged and raw from breathing so much smoke and blood and ash. Her armor merely trapped in the heat; her flesh was being cooked from the inside out, her blood boiling and hissing, her eyes burning every time she blinked. Her heart stuttered, on the verge of failing completely.

Then Firesse repeated the incantation, and the flames disappeared.

The sudden relief sent Mercy to her knees. She sucked in air as she fought to see past the black spots clouding her vision. Firesse knelt beside her. "The tough Assassin can't handle a little fever?"

Mercy growled and pushed to her feet, her hands shaking as she lifted her daggers. Firesse rose, too. "It was a valiant effort," she said as she drew her sword and easily knocked Mercy's swing aside. It glanced off the First's armor, barely leaving a mark in the leather. "Giving yourself up to kill me, I mean. A valiant effort, but a foolish one."

A tremor shuddered through Mercy—but not from an incantation. No, her body was betraying her.

"You can feel the corruption, can't you?" Firesse asked. She didn't bother to go on the offensive. She was letting Mercy tire herself out. "You can feel the plague killing you."

"I'm immune," she snarled through gritted teeth, but her mind betrayed her, calling back the memory of the sick elf's blood pouring over her hands in the house on the opposite end of the square, the brush of his blister-covered palm against her skin, the hammering of her heart against her ribcage as she had felt—*felt*—the plague seep into her. She'd cut off his head not five seconds later, but that brief contact had been enough. She was not immune. She was going to die like that guard they'd encountered on the way here. The plague had ravaged that woman's body in fifteen minutes. How much longer did Mercy have? Five minutes? Ten?

"For a while, you were, but I made the disease more potent to weaken your prince's people and ensure a victory for my own. We aren't soldiers, after all. We needed every advantage we could find."

When Firesse knocked aside yet another clumsy attack, Mercy stepped back and desperately scanned the rooftops again for Ino and Cassia. Her sister was nowhere to be seen, but just as she turned her head, she spotted Ino scrambling across a nearby rooftop with a Cirisian shortbow in hand. *Please,* she silently begged. *Take her down. End the battle here.*

As Firesse turned to follow Mercy's gaze, an arrow punched through the armor covering her left arm, leather splitting around the arrowhead. The First grimaced, and Mercy watched through the spots clouding her vision as

Firesse snapped the shaft of the arrow in two and ripped it out of her arm. Not a single drop of blood fell.

"How is that possible?" Mercy breathed. She retreated a step, and the movement sent another tremor through her body, a jolt of pain through her skull. The plague—Alyss and Pilar had endured this for days. Her knees trembled, and it took all of Mercy's strength to stay standing.

"Anything is possible with the powers of an Old God," Firesse responded, dropping the pieces of the arrow onto the blood-slick road. "Now, if you don't mind, I have an appointment with the king. I'll send him your regards."

Agony raced through Mercy. Her dagger slipped from her grasp as she slumped to her knees, then fell forward onto the dirty, grimy, bloody cobblestones. Distantly, she could hear Ino's cry of alarm as Firesse picked up Mercy's daggers and stepped over her body. Her breaths came out as dry, ragged gasps. They slowed, and slowed, and slowed...until a thick, heavy blackness came and swept her away.

❧ 43 ☙
TAMRIEL

The throne room was the site of a massacre.

Shortly after Drake and the Daughters unleashed themselves upon Tamriel, Ghyslain, and the guards, a loud banging had echoed through the room, followed by the groaning and splintering of the doors to the great hall. The Cirisians had found a heavy marble pedestal to use as a battering ram, and as soon as the opening was large enough, they poured through the broken doors, blades and bows drawn. Tamriel's heart had nearly stopped when the sick elves he'd seen outside the castle gates came tumbling into the room, accompanied by the undead corpses of the guards who had been manning the gate. *That* was why the Cirisians hadn't immediately tried to break down the throne room doors; they had let the sick elves into the castle before coming to the Daughters' aid.

Drake had charged at Tamriel first, a dark, savage hunger glittering in his eyes. It was still hard to reconcile the fact that the man standing before him, trying to kill him, was not his cousin. Together, Tamriel, Nynev, and Niamh had been able to avoid Drake's and Faye's slashing blades long enough to land a few strikes of their own, but nowhere near a killing blow.

Now, chaos reigned in the throne room. Near the dais, Master Adan let out a cry as he leapt in front of Ghyslain, lifting his sword to meet a Daughter's before it could strike the king. Their blades locked, and the Daughter immediately ducked and pulled a knife from her boot. In one swift motion, she buried it to the hilt in Adan's thigh and jumped to her feet as Adan staggered back, blood pouring through the gap in his armor.

"Tam!" Nynev yelled, drawing Tamriel's attention. He turned to see a plague-infected elf racing toward him, his bloody dagger held aloft. Just as Tamriel lifted his sword, an arrow pierced the elf's throat. He went down, gurgling, crimson dribbling from his mouth. Out of the corner of his eye, Tamriel saw Nynev lower her bow.

"Thanks!" he yelled, turning to parry a blow from a snarling Cirisian. The impact of their clashing swords reverberated up his entire arm.

"How about you watch your own ass so I don't have to be the one to tell Mercy how you got yourself skewered?" the huntress tossed back. She lunged forward, her hunting knives whistling as they arced through the air, trying to keep Drake as far from Tamriel as possible. Niamh was somewhere nearby, but he couldn't see her through the fighting.

Drake chuckled, and Nynev's expression darkened. "Something funny, demon?"

He pointed at something behind them. Nynev didn't take her eyes off Drake's blades, but Tamriel turned, sucking in a breath at what he saw.

Firesse.

The First strode through the broken double doors, Mother Illynor and a sizable portion of her army behind her. Every one of them was soaked in blood. Firesse paused on the edge of the fighting and surveyed the chaos with a self-satisfied smirk. Tamriel's gaze dropped to the wickedly curved daggers in her hands, and his heart stuttered, dread and terror turning his blood cold. Mercy never would have parted with those weapons if she could help it, which only meant one thing:

Mercy was dead.

An inhuman roar filled the throne room, echoing off the stone walls, drowning out the sounds of swords clashing and people dying, and it took Tamriel a moment to realize the sound came from *him*. He charged at Firesse, fury blazing within him. Nynev shouted his name, but his blood was pounding so hard he could barely hear her. He didn't look back, but he knew she was pushing through the throngs of soldiers, sick elves, and undead creatures, trying to reach him.

Someone snagged his arm and pulled him backward. Tamriel's feet slipped on the blood-soaked floor and he slowed to a halt, instinctively lifting his sword to break free of whomever had taken hold of him. When he looked up, however, it was into Master Adan's grim face. "Get ahold of yourself," he snapped. "Do you not see you're running to your death?"

"She— She killed—" He choked on the words.

"I know. I can't let her get you, too. Take a breath and look around. This is not a battle you can win. Not like this."

Adan nodded to the king, who was locked in combat with a Daughter and a sick elf, Niamh beside him. Niamh took the brunt of the Daughter's lightning-quick attacks, grimacing with pain when the woman's blade cut her flesh. No blood fell from her wounds, but Tamriel could tell by the gashes in her clothes that she had been struck several times—and by the pain on her face that she could feel every single wound.

A few yards away, Nynev had gone on the offensive with Drake, slashing out so quickly he was forced to yield step after step away from Tamriel and the king. His hate-filled eyes kept flicking to Tamriel, and his distraction earned him a deep gash in the cheek from one of Nynev's blades. Even so, Tamriel could tell the huntress was tiring, and Drake was growing impatient. As he took in the scene before him, the stubborn hope to which Tamriel had been clinging withered. The tide of the battle had turned against him. His father's troops were waning. The battle would not last much longer, especially now that Firesse had arrived. They had minutes, at the most.

"Go through the door tucked into the wall beside the dais," Adan said, low enough for only Tamriel to hear. "Stick to the smaller halls and get downstairs. Try to leave through the servants' entrance and make a break for the gates. You must get out of this city."

"But Firesse—"

"We will do everything in our power to stop her. The most important thing is getting you and your father to safety. Understood?"

Tamriel nodded numbly, the hopelessness of this war rushing over him, crushing his heart in his chest. They had lost. What was there left to fight for? Mercy was dead, the infirmary tents lost to the inferno, the fishing sector in shambles, his people wasting away from the plague. Yet...perhaps they could still salvage something from this day. Perhaps Tamriel and the others could escape, take shelter in some far-off city, and figure out a way to defeat Firesse once and for all. This would *not* be the end.

Adan released his arm and roughly shoved him forward, not bothering to say farewell. There was no time. Tamriel ran for the dais, dodging blades and spraying blood, and his father fell in behind him. They scrambled up the steps and bolted for the unaccented door set into the wall, almost out of the sight. He ripped it open—then slammed it shut.

"What—" his father began, breathing hard.

"Assassins." They'd been halfway down the corridor, running toward them with predatory grins. Firesse had set guards on every exit. They were utterly, completely trapped.

Across the room, Firesse began stalking toward the throne, wading through the sea of blood and fighting soldiers. She didn't bother to use Mercy's precious daggers; Mother Illynor and the Cirisians did all the fighting for her, clearing a path through the carnage. When the First passed under the light of a chandelier, Tamriel noticed that her sun-tanned skin had grown sallow, that inky shadows hung under her eyes, that what little he could see of her hair through the blood lacked its usual luster. A small flare of hope rekindled within him. Expending so much magic was costing her, weakening her, leaving her vulnerable.

"We have to kill Firesse *now*," Tamriel hissed to his father. "Before she can regain her strength."

"Trying to flee, Your Highness? How very cowardly of you." Drake bounded up the steps of the dais, his sword and dagger dripping blood. His eyes flicked to Ghyslain, full of contempt. "Well, you are your father's son, after all."

With that, he launched himself at Tamriel.

Drake attacked him again and again, so fast Tamriel barely had time to lift his sword to block before Drake swung his dagger toward Tamriel's face, stomach, neck. Tamriel's arms began to shake with the effort of matching the speed and strength of his blows. He and Calum had trained together all their lives, but Calum had always had a natural talent for swordplay. Every time they had dueled, he'd been two steps ahead.

In his periphery, the side door opened, and the other Assassins rushed into the room. Tamriel's concentration broke when he heard his father's sword meet the Assassins' blades. Seizing the moment of distraction, Drake feinted right, lunged left, and swung his sword straight at Tamriel's head. The flat of the blade connected with his skull hard enough to make Tamriel's ears ring. He staggered back, blinking hard against the spots blooming and bursting in his vision.

Tamriel pressed his free hand to the side of his head, and his fingers came away slick with blood; the edge of the blade had nicked him. "If only you could hear your cousin right now," that monster wearing Calum's skin purred, lowering his weapons. Tamriel took a step forward, lifting his sword, and the room swayed. "If only you could hear his screams, the way he pleads for me to spare you."

Behind him, Ghyslain let out a grunt of pain. He was no match for the Assassins. *Where the hell are Niamh and Nynev?*

Just then, an arrow flew through the air inches from Drake's nose and shattered one of the glass panes behind the throne. A heartbeat later, two more thudded into flesh, and Tamriel whirled around to see the Daughters his father had been fighting slump to the ground.

"Cutting it a bit close, aren't you?" Tamriel said with a shaky laugh as Nynev and her sister hurtled toward the dais. Faye followed close on their heels, bleeding from her nose and a long gash in the leather armor on her arm.

"I prefer to think of it as a dramatic entrance," the huntress quipped as she stepped between him and Drake. She threw her bow and empty quiver aside and unsheathed her hunting knives. Before the steps, Niamh turned on Faye, keeping her busy and away from him and his father.

Ghyslain grabbed Tamriel's arm and tugged him toward the door, but Tamriel didn't budge, struck dumb by the sight of the people who had just walked through the broken double doors.

Cassia, Dayna, and Matthias leapt into the fray, arrows flying, blades slashing, and immediately took down two

Cirisians. Ino sprinted into the room behind them, a body in midnight-black armor in his arms. *Mercy.* Tamriel's blood ran cold at the sight of the bright red rash striping her flesh, the blisters dotting her face and neck. She'd been infected by the plague, but the fact that she had not joined Firesse's undead ranks meant they still had time. She could still survive.

"Help me," Tamriel said to Ghyslain, ripping his arm out of his father's grip. Together, they ran to Niamh's side to help her fend off Faye. "Mercy—she's infected," he told her between gasps for breath. "Save her. Please."

Niamh's eyes widened. She scanned the room and sucked in a breath when she saw Ino cradling Mercy to his chest, being careful not to let her skin touch his. "I'll do my best. Try not to die."

Tamriel watched her run toward Ino, and his gaze landed on Master Adan, sparring with Firesse in the midst of the chaos. He'd somehow broken through the line of Cirisians protecting her. Mercy's double-edged dagger gleamed in the light as the First parried strike after strike, until Adan's sword locked with one of her blades. He knocked her back and, while she was still off-balance on the slick floor, plunged his sword through her stomach.

Ghyslain made a sound of horror and shock as Firesse twisted the grip of the double-edged dagger apart and shoved one blade into each of Adan's eye sockets. He dropped like a stone. The sword, still clenched in his fist, slid out of Firesse's stomach without so much as a drop of blood. "She's made herself invincible," his father murmured in disbelief. "Just like she did to Niamh—locked herself out of the Beyond."

Sensing their eyes on her, Firesse's gaze lifted and met theirs. She braced her foot on Adan's forehead and yanked the daggers out of his skull, then started toward them. *No more games,* her expression said. She'd come here to destroy them, and she had toyed with them long enough.

44
NIAMH

Niamh and Ino hurtled through the empty castle halls, Mercy's unconscious form cradled in her brother's arms. Niamh's body ached, pain jolting through every wound she'd sustained during the battle, but she pushed herself to keep up with Ino's long strides. *The infirmary. Get to the infirmary. Save Mercy. Save everyone. Kill Firesse—kill the magic wielder, kill the magic.* Mercy let out a low groan as they careened around a corner and stumbled down the stairs to the underground castle corridors.

"Foolish, stupid, stubborn, selfless girl," Ino hissed through clenched teeth, his arms tightening around his sister. "If she had only let us help..." He trailed off, guilt and fear plain on his face.

"Left here," Niamh said, letting out a relieved sigh when the door to the infirmary came into sight before them. She had no idea where the entrance to the castle's secret tunnel was, but every step of the way, she'd feared the worst—that they would return to find the infirmary buried under rubble, collateral damage from the sealing of the escape tunnel.

Adriel awoke with a start when they barreled through the

door. Ino gently set Mercy on the cot next to their father while Niamh searched the cluttered desk for Pryyam salt and a vial of the cure. She cursed under her breath, her blood-covered hands shaking violently. Fighting in the throne room, watching men die and come back to life, had dredged up the terrible memories of the night she had nearly died—the night she *should have* died.

"What happened to my Bareea?" Adriel asked, his voice tight with panic. "Is that the *plague?*"

Ino explained what had happened as he ripped off Mercy's armor, exposing the tunic and pants underneath. Niamh continued searching until—at last—her fingers closed around a cool glass vial. She found the jar of Pryyam salt a second later and nearly tripped over her own feet in her haste to get to Mercy's bedside.

"Stand back." *Save her. Save her. Save her.* Niamh rolled up Mercy's sleeve and immediately began rubbing the salt into her tender, blistered skin. The flesh shredded into ribbons at the slightest touch, milky pus oozing out and dripping onto the bedsheets. Mercy's agonized scream was so loud it made Niamh's ears ring. Niamh choked back a sob as she opened the vial and massaged the cure into the raw flesh, repeating the ancient Cirisian incantation over and over. *Save her,* she begged the Creator, the Old Gods, anyone who would listen. *Save her.*

Adriel and Ino watched in anxious silence as Niamh continued to work, treating Mercy's skin until there was not one inch of plague-infected flesh left. When all that remained was healthy, sensitive pink skin, Ino pulled the sheet over his sister and tucked it gently around her shoulders. Mercy had slipped in and out of consciousness while Niamh treated her, the pain almost too much to bear, but now she slumbered.

"Is she going to live?" Ino asked softly, his voice ragged.

Niamh nodded and slumped against the side of Adriel's

cot, exhausted and aching. She could be wrong; with Firesse so close, her magic so strong, the cure and the incantation might not be enough to bring Mercy back from the brink of death. Niamh had done everything she could. Now, all they could do was wait.

Kill the magic wielder, kill the magic.

"Thank you," Adriel whispered, laying a hand on her shoulder. She let herself lean into the touch, into that little bit of comfort, for only one second. Then she straightened and pushed to her feet. Firesse was still upstairs. Tamriel's people were still dying.

Ino's eyes rose to the ceiling. "Back to the battle, then."

She nodded again, but when she turned to follow him out of the infirmary, her gaze snagged on the corner of a paper peeking out from below a box of vials—the notes she and Lethandris had made while they'd been studying that ancient Cirisian book. One word caught her attention:

Aitherialnik.

The thread that linked the powers of the Old Gods of a single gens together.

Niamh froze, realization and dangerous, dangerous hope sweeping over her. Ino turned to her with a confused expression, his gaze following hers to the paper.

Whatever unnatural ritual Firesse had performed the night Niamh should have died had created a link between them, a thin, tenuous string binding their souls together. Niamh had tried to ignore it, had tried to bury it alongside the memories of that night and the strange sense of *otherness* that had haunted her since, but it had never vanished completely. She closed her eyes and reached for it.

It was there, so faint she nearly missed it—not a series of thoughts or emotions, but...a presence. A darkness, as if Firesse's soul had been irrevocably tainted by her abuse of Myrbellanar's powers. Niamh let out a sharp breath. Firesse had locked her out of the Beyond. Perhaps she could find an incantation to force her former First into it.

She ripped the paper out from under the box, sending the glass vials tumbling to the floor at her feet, shattering on the stone. She didn't bother cleaning the mess up. "Come on," she ordered Ino. "Quickly."

Niamh scanned the notes as they raced through the halls and bounded up the stairs, the strange words swimming before her. She and Lethandris had transcribed every passage that had related to Myrbellanar and his gens, but they'd only managed to translate a fraction of it. *Which one?* That slender, glittering thread hung between her and Firesse, mocking her.

"What are you reading?" Ino asked between puffs of breath.

"Spells—I'm trying to find one to kill Firesse."

"Well, can you hurry it up? We're in a bit of a rush, in case you couldn't tell."

She ignored the sharpness of his tone. "I can't just pick one at random. For all I know, I could bring the castle down on our heads."

"Maybe you should."

She scanned the paragraphs of text again, and her pulse picked up as her eyes swept over a short phrase in the middle of the page. *This one.* She wasn't sure how, but she knew it was the right one. She mouthed the words, not daring to give voice to the incantation until she was certain of the pronunciation. Myrbellanar only knew what hell she could unleash with the wrong spell. As she tested the words on her tongue, the magic flowing through her veins sang in response. *This one.*

She screamed the incantation—screamed the words over and over until her voice was raw. Beside her, Ino flinched, but he kept running, dragging her along when she began to fall behind. They pushed through the broken doors of the throne room and skidded to a stop on the bloodied floor. The guards were severely outnumbered—surrounded by undead creatures and Cirisian soldiers and Daughters of the Guild. The remaining guards stood in a line before the dais, trying in vain to hold off Firesse's remaining forces. Behind them, Cassia, Dayna, Matthias, Nynev, and a few more guards were locked in combat with Firesse and Drake, fighting to keep them away from the prince, who was kneeling beside his father, pressing his hands to a gash in the king's stomach, just below the edge of his breastplate. A steadily-growing pool of blood seeped out from Ghyslain and trickled down the steps.

A roar of rage and pain filled the hall, and every single person turned to Firesse as dark red blood began to spill out over her armor—from her face, her neck, her arms, from the gaping wound in her stomach. Mercy's double-edged dagger slipped out of her grasp and clattered to the floor. She swayed, shock written across her face as her body slackened, and she crumpled to her knees.

"Help the prince," Niamh hissed to Ino, never taking her eyes off the dying First. He sprinted toward the dais as the fighting slowed. One by one, the undead soldiers dropped to the ground, lifeless once more.

Something warm and wet trailed down Niamh's arm. Blood. It started as a slow trickle, collecting at the tips of her fingers and falling to the ground in fat droplets, but soon the entire left arm of her tunic was soaked, as well as the left side of her torso. The wound she had received the night she should have died had begun to bleed. She closed her fingers into a fist and cradled her arm close to her chest. At the front of the room, Nynev's full attention was trained on Drake, who stood frozen beside the throne, watching Firesse die. Niamh's heart swelled with love and pride and sorrow as she watched her sister, the woman who had given up so much for her.

Her thoughts drifted to Isolde as a shudder rolled through her, and her knees gave out. Sweet, wonderful, fiercely protective Isolde, who had spent two long years dragging her out of the darkness of her mind, two years cradling and soothing her when she woke up screaming. Beautiful, cunning, gentle Isolde, her first friend in the Islands, her first and only love. Niamh had never learned if her beloved had survived the wound she'd sustained after *Ialathan*, but she would find out soon enough.

I'll see you in the Beyond, my love, she thought as her heart pumped its last few beats. *Hopefully many, many years from now.*

✤ 45 ✤
CALUM

The First was dying.

Drake froze in shock, gaping at the blood pouring down Firesse's leather armor as she staggered, pressed a hand to the gaping hole in her stomach, and slumped to her knees. Between them, half hidden from view by the royal guards who had taken the opportunity to surround their prince, Tamriel knelt beside his father, his hands shaking as he alternated between trying to remove the king's breastplate and keeping pressure on the wound in Ghyslain's stomach. Firesse's face paled. She sucked in a shuddering breath, the light in her eyes fading, and crumpled.

Dead.

Distantly, the thump of bodies hitting the ground reached his ears, but still he did not move. People swarmed the dais and surrounded the prince, shouting over one another to go after the Daughters, to hunt down the rest of the Cirisians, to find a healer for Ghyslain. Someone roughly grabbed Calum's arm. *Calum's* arm. The prison around his mind and the icewater in his veins were gone; every last trace of his father's corrupting presence was absent, save for the memories. As the person gripping his arm dragged him backward, away from the chaos, he turned his head and met Faye's wide, terrified eyes.

"Don't make a sound," she whispered.

Together, they skirted the people clustered around the wounded sovereign—where Nynev, Dayna, and several other elves were now shouting commands, sending soldiers to pursue the retreating Assassins and Cirisians. Calum caught a glimpse of Mother Illynor's green-and-gold scales just as she stepped through the broken, splintered doors, her Assassins close on her heels. They weren't fleeing; their employer dead and unable to pay, they were likely intending to take advantage of the chaos they'd unleashed by pillaging whatever valuables they could carry.

Faye ripped open the side door and shoved him through first, silently shutting it behind her. Before he could react, she pinned him against the wall, the blade of her little oyster-shucking knife pressed to his throat. "It's you in there, isn't it?" she hissed, pricking him with the knife. Pain flared in his neck, and the accompanying wave of relief nearly sent him to his knees. It had been so long since he felt anything beyond the ice-water in his veins, beyond the shackles around his mind. The few brief minutes he'd managed to overpower Drake and take control were nothing compared to what he felt now, knowing he was truly, inexplicably, miraculously free.

It was through lips wholly his own that he said, his voice wobbling, "It's me."

"Can you run?"

He nodded.

"Get us out of here."

They sprinted down the narrow corridor and skidded around sharp corners, Calum hissing directions through labored breaths. He kept them to the smaller halls, the ones he had explored for hours as a child, and they arrived at the servants' exit without crossing paths with a single guard. He entered the password into the complicated combination lock, but the lock didn't budge. He cursed under his breath. Of course they'd changed it since the last time he was here. With Faye's help, they slammed into the door until the aged hinges snapped. *Those* hadn't been changed in a long, long while.

They stumbled out into the bright sunlight. Faye grabbed his hand and pulled him toward the open castle gates, using the tall hedge mazes as cover from the soldiers rushing in and out of the castle. "Stay here," she whispered. Before he could say a word, she slipped out, two throwing knives in her hands, and launched herself at the soldiers. A few heartbeats later, she reappeared at his side, her face flecked with fresh blood. "Come on."

"Why did you save me?" he asked as they passed under the gates and ducked into an alley between two massive manors. It opened up to a large courtyard with a gurgling fountain at its center. Faye jerked her chin toward it.

"Remove your armor and wash off the blood."

Without another word, the Assassin turned on her heel and walked back out onto the street. Calum obeyed her command, and a few minutes later, she returned. Faye tossed a clean shirt and a pair of trousers at him, then stepped up to the fountain and began to scrub the blood off her hands and face, her hair, and her weapons while he changed. When Calum turned back, she was dressed in a simple cotton tunic and leggings, her weapons hidden under the bulk of her oversized shirt. She perched on the edge of the fountain, the water behind her tinged pink, and began to braid her wet hair.

"When I was six, my twin brother fell deathly ill," she finally said, her voice so soft he could barely hear her over the gurgling of the fountain. "It was a long, slow, painful process. Every night, I slept beside him—my other half, my first friend—and prayed to the Creator that he would get better, that the healers Papa brought in from all over the country would find a cure for whatever was ailing him. They never did. They treated him with every manner of medicine, with leeches, with bloodletting, but nothing worked.

"One day, later that year, Papa opened our door to find a rich nobleman on our stoop, asking about Fredric. He said he'd heard the story from the people in town and wished to offer the services of his healer, who was on his way back from treating the queen of Rivosa of a wasting sickness—the same one the nobleman suspected Fredric had. All he asked for in return was my hand in marriage." She shuddered, tied off the braid with a strip of leather, and pushed it behind her shoulder. "Mama and Papa refused, but, fool that I was, I begged them to reconsider. I would do anything to save Fredric, as he would have done for me. I would not live in a world where he did not exist. And our parents...they were heartbroken and desperate. The nobleman and I were betrothed the next day, and he sent for his healer immediately...or so we thought.

"The healer arrived too late. I was lying beside my brother when he took his last breath, and I found out later that it wouldn't have mattered if the healer had arrived sooner. My betrothed didn't care about our family. He had only wanted a pretty young wife to warm his bed, to fulfill his filthy fantasies, and he had preyed upon our desperation to get one. He liked the power it gave him.

"When my father tried to break off the engagement, my fiancé sent men into our home to shatter his legs so he could never work the fields again. They masked it as a robbery gone wrong, and to the guards, it was the word of a poor farmer's family against that of a respected nobleman. So, on the day we were to be wed, I slipped out of the bedroom Fredric and I had shared, laid some fresh flowers on my brother's grave, and walked for two and a half days to find the Assassin it was rumored was staying in the next town over." Faye stood and gestured for Calum to follow her through an alley opposite the one through which they had come—one that would lead them away from the castle and, if they continued south, to the city gates.

"Illynor's contact heard that there was a child inquiring about the Assassin, and she knew that the Guild would never turn down a new recruit. She sent out one of her barmaids to find me. When she presented me to Llorin," Faye continued as they darted across the empty street, "I handed her the ten aurums I'd scrounged up in the market, told her my story, and asked her to kill my betrothed for what he did to my family. She took me up to her room, bought me food and drink, and walked out of the inn. Later, she returned with his head in a basket, and I asked her to take me to the Guild with her. I wanted to be able to rid the world of monsters like him—like your father." Faye glanced over her shoulder at him, frowning. "That's why I saved you. Sometimes, I could see you through his eyes. I could see you screaming. I wanted to be the person to free you from your demon, just as Llorin was for me."

"First Mercy, now me," he mused. "You seem to have a soft spot for broken things."

She didn't respond.

They shrank back into the shadows as a contingent of guards ran past. He spotted Kova and Tobias, two of the recruits he'd helped Master Oliver train not three years ago, in the middle of the group. The clanging of their armor faded as they rounded the corner, no doubt heading for the End.

He grabbed Faye's arm, stilling her, as she made to step out of the alley. "I need to see someone."

"You're the most wanted criminal in the country, the city is crawling with guards prepared to kill anyone who aided Firesse, and you want to make a *house call?*"

"Please. I just— Please. I can't leave for the last time without seeing her."

She sighed sharply through her nose. "Fine. Fine. Lead the way. But when I say we're leaving, we're leaving."

A stone pinged off Elise's window. Then another. And another.

"That's the fifth one you've thrown," Faye hissed from her lookout at the mouth of the alley. "If she hasn't answered by now, she's never going to."

"She will," he snarled through clenched teeth. Another stone went sailing through the air, glancing harmlessly off the glass. No answer. Not even a whisper of the curtains.

"Maybe she's found a new lover to warm her bed while you've been away."

Calum shot her a glare. She merely rolled her eyes and turned back toward the street. "Two minutes," she warned.

He stomped around to the back of the house and retrieved the key hidden in the planter beside the door. His heart pounded as he cracked the door open and peered inside, then slipped into the dark, empty kitchen. *Fool*, he cursed himself as his ears strained for the sound of footfalls. *Pathetic, lovesick fool.* Faye was right—they should be fleeing now, putting as much distance between them and the city as possible—but he couldn't leave Sandori without saying goodbye to the woman who had made it home for him.

The house appeared completely empty as he crept into the hall. Every room was dark, the curtains drawn, the candelabra unlit. Wherever they'd gone to weather the attack, they'd even taken Liri, their slave, with them. His heart sank as he turned to leave. He couldn't risk leaving a note, couldn't risk someone finding out that he'd come to visit her, for fear that they would dig deeper, discover the crimes they had committed together. No—better to disappear, to let her think he had forgotten about her. In that one small way, at least, he could protect her one last time.

"Calum."

His fingers—a mere inch from the doorknob—froze at the sound of Seren Pierce's voice. He turned to find Pierce bearing down on him, his face twisted in wrath as he grabbed the front of Calum's shirt and shoved him against the door. Over the seren's shoulder, Calum spied Nerida lingering in the doorway, a trembling hand over her mouth.

"You have the *gall* to come here after what you've done?" Pierce roared, slamming him into the door again, so hard the cabinets rattled. "You dare show your face in my home after you took her from us, you lying, traitorous bastard?"

"Took her from you? What do you mean, took her from you?" Calum winced as Pierce's fist pressed against one of the arrow wounds he'd sustained in Xilor. Faye began pounding on the opposite side of the door.

"It's all your fault," Pierce hissed, his eyes filling with tears.

Panic consumed him, closing a vice around his throat as he choked out, "What do you mean, took her from you? Where is Elise?"

"Lying at the bottom of an unmarked grave," Pierce snarled. Behind him, Nerida began to sob.

Calum's blood ran cold. He managed to stammer a weak, "What?" as Pierce's hands dropped from his shirt. The seren took a shuddering breath and stepped back, his expression raw and wounded, his shoulders slumped. A broken man.

"Elise is dead. The prince found the letters."

"No."

Faye shoved the door open. "Calum, we need to leave *right*

now. I'm pretty sure half the neighborhood heard the shouting."

He didn't move.

Elise.

Dead.

"I had to watch my daughter, my baby girl, die because of you," Seren Pierce said in a low voice, every word hitting him like a punch to the gut. Calum would have preferred yelling. He would have preferred death to the cruel, cold truth rolling off the seren's tongue. "Because of your greed, because of your plotting, my Elise is rotting in a traitor's grave. It should have been you."

Behind him, Nerida sobbed even harder.

Faye grabbed his shoulder. He hardly felt it. Everything within him had gone numb. "Calum, we need to *go.*" She pulled a dagger and leveled it at Pierce, but the seren merely crossed the room and wrapped an arm around his wife's shoulders.

"Take him away," the seren said to Faye as tears rolled down his cheeks. "Take him somewhere far, far away, where he can live the rest of his life knowing he was the one who sent my daughter to her grave. Take him somewhere the guards can't find him, where he can live every day with the guilt of her death on his shoulders." His gaze slid to Calum, full of pure, unadulterated hatred. "That's what he deserves for stealing our daughter from us. Death at the end of a noose is not a good enough punishment."

"I'm sorry," Calum finally managed in a reed-thin, wavering voice. "I'm so sorry—"

He kept saying it, over and over, as Faye dragged him out of the house and out of the city.

The next thing he registered was a fist meeting his face. He reared back, his hand flying to his aching cheek, and blinked at Faye as she shoved a horse's reins into his other hand.

"That was the only way I could get you to snap out of it," she said matter-of-factly. He brushed his tongue across his teeth. "Nothing's broken. You'll have a nasty bruise and a black eye for a while, but you'll be fine."

They were standing atop a grassy knoll, staring at the dark shadow of the city in the distance. How she'd managed to get him—numb, half-delirious with grief—out of Sandori, he had no idea, but he didn't bother to ask. Faye didn't seem at all in the mood to answer questions. He looked her over, taking in the fresh blood splattered across her shirt and crusted along the cuffs. She scowled and picked at it, wrinkling her nose. "I killed the guards. I couldn't very well saunter through the gates with you blubbering like a baby beside me. I contemplated leaving you in an alley somewhere to choke on your own tears, but even I'm not that cruel."

He didn't say a word. He simply turned to the chestnut stallion at his side and peered into the saddlebags. There wasn't much inside—a few changes of clothes, a dagger, a map, and a pouch of coins. The other one held a couple pieces of bread, some fruit, and strips of dried meat. He looked back at her. "Thank you," he finally managed.

"You really loved her, didn't you?"

He nodded and climbed onto the saddle, eager to leave the city, the memories of everything he had done and watched his father do, behind. They would never truly leave him, though. His sorrow was a living thing, a serpent coiled around his heart, squeezing tighter and tighter with each beat. Those words—*It should have been you*—would not stop echoing, clanging around in his head. Pierce was right.

It should have been me.

He shoved the grief somewhere deep, deep down, locking it away in that mental prison where Drake had kept him for so long.

"You're free now. Where will you go?" the Assassin asked.

"Rivosa, maybe. Or Feyndara. Perhaps I'll buy a boat and sail so far I'll fall off the edge of the world. Let the darkness take me." Just as it had so many times in the week leading up to the battle. Even though his father was gone, banished to whatever hell awaited monsters like him, the shadows, the scars on his soul, remained. "And you?"

Faye huffed a sharp, humorless laugh. "If it were just me, if Illynor and the rest of the Guild wouldn't hunt me down wherever I went, perhaps I'd go with you. I fell out of love with them the day Illynor ordered me to kill an innocent person." Her gaze drifted back toward the city, to the castle's tall spires, flecks of obsidian and gold shimmering under the sunset. "But I have someone else to save first."

"Mercy?" His brows rose. "You don't want to kill her?"

"I did, but...I can't anymore. Not after that day in Xilor, when she screamed as she watched Lylia's arrow fly toward the prince. I've known her for ten years, and I've never heard her sound like that—like someone had reached into her chest and ripped her heart clean out. Until that day, I didn't even think she had a heart." Her lips spread into a half smile, but it quickly disappeared. "I hated her for cheating me out of the Trial, but now I think she unwittingly gave me a gift. I'm going to free us both from the Guild."

"Good luck."

"I'll need it," she responded with a grim nod. "Before you disappear, I need you to do something for me."

"Do what?"

Her eyes flashed with warning. "Can I trust you?"

"Absolutely," Calum breathed. He was finished creeping

about in the shadows, plotting and cheating and lying. "Tell me."

She did. As they stood there, watching the sunset paint the sky over the charred ruins of Sandori, she explained exactly what she needed him to do. When she finished, Calum cast one last look at his city, at the homes of the people he had betrayed so grievously. Tamriel would never forgive him. *He* would never forgive himself. He dug his heels into his horse's sides, and it broke into a trot. He would do Faye this favor, then disappear. Perhaps if he rode fast enough, he would be able to outrun the demons prowling his mind. Perhaps he would one day forget the sound of Elise's laugh, the way her eyes lit up when she grinned, the speckles of paint that had always seemed to stain her fingers.

Perhaps—but not likely.

"Calum," Faye called when he reached the bottom of the small hill. He tugged on the reins, and his horse slowed to a stop. The Assassin cocked her head, a strand of blue-black hair falling free of the braid and into her face, and studied him with a piercing, unwavering gaze. "Everyone deserves a chance to start over. Mine was going to the Guild. Mercy's was coming here. This is yours. Don't waste it."

46

TAMRIEL

Tamriel forced himself to his feet as the guards hoisted his father onto a stretcher, one of them pressing a handful of bandages to the king's stomach, and carried him out of the room. Someone had managed to find a healer; he could hear the man shouting orders in the great hall.

Tamriel sheathed his sword and ran his hands down his face. Everything had happened so fast. He still couldn't make sense of it all. He'd been fighting Drake. Nynev had leapt in front of him, Mercy's siblings at her side, and held off his cousin's blade long enough for Tamriel to turn and search for his father in the chaos. Instead, he had found Firesse sprinting toward him, Mercy's double-edged dagger in her hands, her eyes glimmering with victory and bloodlust.

Then something had crashed into his side, sending him tumbling down the steps. When he had looked up, blinking away the stars in his vision, his father was on his knees, a hand pressed to the wide gash Firesse had carved in his stomach.

Everything after that was a blur.

Somehow, he'd ended up at his father's side. The king lay on his back, coughing and sputtering as hot blood spilled out of his stomach and coated Tamriel's hands. Firesse had stood over him with those Creator-damned daggers, ready to plunge them into his heart.

The next moment, she was dead.

Nynev grabbed his arm, drawing him from the memories. "Are you injured?"

Dayna and her children were gathered behind the huntress, bloodied and exhausted, but alive. Matthias clutched a gash in his arm, and a nasty bruise had begun to bloom on the side of Cassia's face. Ino's expression was impassive, unreadable as always.

He shook his head. "Mercy?" he asked Ino, hardly daring to breathe.

"Now that Firesse is dead, she'll live."

He let out a sharp breath. "And the rest of you?"

"Nice to see where your priorities lie, Your Highness." Nynev tried to smile, but the gesture fell short. She shook her head as if to clear it. "Nothing a few strong drinks can't fix once the war is won."

It was not over yet, and they all knew it. Firesse was dead, but every Cirisian soldier who had survived the attack had either fled or sought shelter somewhere in his city. Maybe they would lie low for a while, build up their strength, before striking again at the humans they hated so vehemently. Or maybe they would take advantage of the chaos and destroy as many of his people's lives as they could.

They turned to the room, to the sea of bodies and the thick, dark blood coating...everything. A few guards were walking around the room, turning bodies over to see who among them had fallen. Tamriel's stomach clenched. So many of his people had lost their lives today, Master Adan among them. Calum might be one of them. His father was somewhere in the castle, barely clinging to life. Tamriel shot a hateful look at Firesse's body. In death, her delicate features were smooth, relaxed—the face of a girl who was old enough to see how cruel the world was, and young enough to believe she could change it.

"Where is Calum?" he asked, his voice a low growl. He had no idea what he would say when he saw his cousin, but he needed to speak to him, to understand what had happened since *Ialathan*. When no one responded, he repeated, "Where is Calum?"

"The... The guards are looking for him, Your Highness." Dayna finally answered. She flinched at the anger that sparked in his eyes. *The Creator-damned traitor escaped?* "An Assassin helped him flee. They left a...a trail of bodies outside."

Tamriel's hands curled into fists. "I want every spare guard patrolling the streets for the coward. Have messengers sent out to every major town and city—I want him caught and brought to the city for trial. Whoever brings him in will receive a title and lands in the city."

Mercy's mother nodded and hurried toward the doors to the great hall, stepping carefully through the blood and around the dead. Before she had even made it halfway, she stopped beside a body and lifted a hand to her mouth. "N-Niamh. Niamh is—"

Nynev was gone before she could even finish her sentence. The huntress leapt off the dais and hurtled across the room, slipping and sliding on the slick tile. When she reached Dayna, Nynev dropped to her knees and cradled her sister's body, heaving, wracking sobs shuddering through her.

Tamriel and the others approached silently. As they surrounded Nynev and her sister, Dayna leaned down and kissed the huntress's brow before leaving to deliver Tamriel's orders. The small act of comfort only made Nynev cry harder.

Cassia knelt beside her and slipped an arm around her waist. Niamh's body was covered with blood from the countless blows she'd taken during the battle. Her shirt clung to the deep, horrific gash in her left arm and across her stomach —the one that, long ago, had nearly cut her in two. If not for that, she might have lived to see the other side of the war.

Ino crouched down and pulled a soggy, bloodstained piece of paper from Niamh's fist. He gently unrolled it, and shock flickered across Nynev's face when she saw the ancient, swirling script. "Your sister found the spell to stop Firesse's magic," Ino said softly. "She gave her life to save us all."

Tamriel laid a hand on Nynev's. "We will never forget her sacrifice," he vowed when her bloodshot eyes met his. "*Never*. The people of this city, this country, owe their lives to the Savior of Sandori."

Nynev nodded numbly, and a somber silence fell over them. For a few long minutes, the only sounds were Nynev's sniffling and the quiet sounds of the guards moving throughout the room, examining the bodies of the dead and dying. Finally, Matthias whispered, "She's smiling."

Indeed, the corners of Niamh's pretty rosebud mouth were curled up in a faint grin. With her eyes closed, her dark lashes fanned across her high, delicate cheekbones, she looked like she had finally found the peaceful sleep that had eluded her since her near-death. She looked...serene.

"She finally got the death she had sought for so long," Nynev breathed. She brushed her sister's hair back from her face, pressed a soft kiss to her cheek, and gently set her on the floor.

"I'll have the undertaker prepare her for burial," Tamriel said gently.

Nynev took a shuddering breath and pushed to her feet,

ignoring the blood soaking the front of her pants. She shook her head. "Have him prepare her for the journey back to Cirisor. She would have wanted a pyre among what remained of our clan."

TAMRIEL STRODE THROUGH THE CASTLE'S DIM, underground corridors, trailed by Ino and Matthias. They'd lingered in the throne room for about an hour, helping to drag out bodies and gather precious arms and armor. In that time, a servant had arrived bearing the news that the king was still in critical condition. The healer tending Ghyslain was doing all he could, but Mercy's precious daggers had cut him deeply. They had no idea how much longer the king would live.

A pang of sorrow struck Tamriel's heart. Ghyslain had been the monster of his childhood, a creature of nightmares, but the king had tried—in his broken, twisted way—to take care of him. He had sat beside Tamriel's bed the entire night after Calum attacked him, had warned him about the death awaiting him on the journey to Cirisor, had tried to shelter him from the vipers in his court. And now...he was dying.

Tamriel swallowed his grief as he turned the last corner and approached the door to the infirmary at the end of the hall. Mercy had needed time to rest and recuperate, so he'd waited as long as he could stand before visiting her. Now that the battle was over, he needed to see her. He needed a reminder that Firesse had not destroyed everything good in his world.

He turned the handle, and the door swung open with a whisper of well-oiled hinges.

"By the Creator," Matthias breathed.

The infirmary was a mess—the shelves toppled, bottles

and jars lying broken on the floor; half-burned papers and books smoldering in the hearth; and the bodies...

The guards who had been stationed outside lay in a bloody heap on the floor, their throats cut from ear to ear, their faces contorted in terror. Tamriel climbed over the broken shelves, his throat tightening. This was the work of the Daughters, without a doubt—and if they had butchered a few nameless guards so ruthlessly, he didn't want to imagine what they had done to Mercy, their Sister who had drifted so far from the fold. A ragged breath escaped him when his eyes landed on the cots lining the other end of the room.

They were all empty.

Steel scraped against leather as Ino unsheathed his dagger. "Where have they taken them?" he snarled, his eyes bright with fierce protectiveness.

They all whirled as a low groan sounded from the little alcove in the far wall—the closet where Alyss had slept. Tamriel hurdled over pieces of wood and shards of broken glass, Mercy's brothers right on his heels as he shoved the blood-splattered curtain aside.

Adriel blinked up at him groggily. "You— Is it over?"

"Where is Mercy? The Daughters took her, didn't they?" Tamriel could hardly force the words out past the lump in his throat.

Adriel frowned, the glazed look in his eyes fading a bit at the sound of his daughter's name. His nose was broken, dark blood crusted around his mouth and down the front of his shirt, and a large bump protruded from the side of his head. "I—I think so." He shook his head. "I can't remember much. Mercy was still unconscious. The Guildmother—she came down here. The guards tried to hold her off—tried to protect us. She slaughtered them without even batting an eye."

"Why did she let you live?" Ino asked.

He frowned again, his face paling. "She said—she said the

trade I made for my daughter's life seventeen years ago still held true, and that she had come to reclaim the girl who had run away. I-I tried to fight, but...she knocked me out." He grimaced and pushed to his feet. Tamriel reached out and grabbed his arm when he swayed dangerously to one side. Adriel reached into his pocket. "These were lying beside me when I woke up."

He extended his fist and opened his fingers to reveal two small trinkets sitting in his palm: the infamous gold mark of the Guild, a teardrop stamped into the front of the coin, and—

The sapphire ring Tamriel had given Mercy.

A TENTATIVE KNOCK CAME AT THE DOOR OF HIS FATHER'S study a few hours later, startling Tamriel out of his tumultuous thoughts. He drew the curtains over the window and turned to find Nynev easing the door open, her face red and splotchy from crying.

"You dismissed your guards," she said in lieu of a greeting. She quietly closed the door and sank into one of the high-backed chairs before the desk.

Tamriel slumped into the desk chair. "They're needed elsewhere." They still had not found Calum, or any of the Daughters. It was as if they'd merely vanished.

"How is the king faring?"

"I don't know." He'd gone to visit his father an hour ago, only to be shoved out of the room by the healer, guards, and servants who had been enlisted as assistants. They had told him only that the bleeding had begun to slow, but their expressions had not been especially hopeful.

"Once this mess is cleaned up, you're going to turn the

army on the Guild, are you not? You're going to get Mercy back."

"Damn right I am," he growled. It was easier said than done. Half of the army was scattered across the fishing sector, trying to repair the damage Firesse and her soldiers had wrought, and those in the city were injured and battle-weary. It would be an eternity before they were ready to march again —it would feel like that, at least. He reached into his pocket and closed his fingers around the sapphire ring. He would carry it until Mercy was once again by his side. "My only comfort is that Mother Illynor doesn't want her dead yet. If she did, she wouldn't have bothered abducting her. She still sees Mercy as a weapon—an unpredictable one, but a useful one—and she'll keep her there as long as it suits her."

Nynev lifted her chin and studied him, her expression unreadable. "And if you're wrong?"

"Then I will burn them to the ground."

She nodded and rose. "If I did not have a duty to my clan, I would be right by your side when you did it. Fortunately, I know some elves who would be more than happy to help you get their sister back."

He stood, too, and followed her to the door. "I'm grateful for your help, Nynev. Yours and Niamh's." Agony flashed in the huntress's eyes at the mention of her sister, but he continued, "My promise to Niamh didn't die with her, you know. When my army is ready, when the reconstruction is complete, I will help you take control of the Islands. We'll stand together against Feyndara and give the Islands independence."

To his surprise, the huntress stepped forward and embraced him. "Thank you," she breathed, "for everything." She leaned back and smiled at him. "You'll make a great king, Your Highness. I am honored to call you a friend."

He smiled, the gesture not quite reaching his eyes, and pressed a hand to his heart. "The honor is all mine."

Nynev turned to leave and, right before the door swung shut behind her, glanced back and winked at him. "Next time I see you," she said, "it had better be with an elven queen at your side."

47
MERCY

Jostling, swaying movement dragged Mercy from unconsciousness. She stirred, her body aching, and her eyes opened to the dim interior of a covered wagon. Terror coursed through her when she saw the green-and-gold scaled woman sitting on the bench across from her, watching through dark, slitted eyes.

Mother Illynor.

Mercy jerked upright, reflexively reaching for her daggers, but they weren't there. Neither was her armor. Her wrists were shackled together with heavy iron cuffs, chained to a link on the floor of wagon. A glance at her hand—her unblemished, plague-free hand—revealed that Tamriel's mother's ring was gone, too.

She swallowed her fear and forced herself to meet Illynor's cool, steady gaze. "Is Tamriel alive?"

Illynor regarded her for several long moments, then nodded. Mercy let out a sharp sigh, but her relief was short-lived when the Guildmother added, "For now."

"The contract is void," Mercy said, a note of desperation slipping into her voice. "Calum Zendais and Elise LeClair forged it with the king's signature. Tamriel's life is not yours to end."

"Have you any proof?"

She hesitated, knowing Illynor wasn't inclined to believe anything she was about to say. "The smudging on the contract. Elise was left-handed; if Ghyslain had signed it, the ink wouldn't have smudged. And—the execution. Elise confessed to the crime and was beheaded for it. There are official records in the capital."

The Guildmother leaned forward, bracing her elbows on her knees. "Well, we aren't in the capital now, are we? And seeing as you claim to love this prince of yours, you're not exactly the most reliable of sources." Her lips spread into a smile, the gesture unsettling on her sharp, reptilian face. "But I shall keep what you said in mind. Perhaps we can come to some arrangement when we return to the Keep."

"Why not just kill me?" Mercy hissed, her anger sparking. "Why bother taking me back?"

"You still belong to me." Illynor's slitted eyes narrowed, hard and black as flecks of shining eudorite. "What, did you think killing a couple of my Assassins would free you? You're *mine*, Mercy. My weapon to wield as I see fit."

"Why? I'll never be as great an Assassin as you. We both know it. So why not kill me back in the capital?"

"Because you fascinate me."

"I—" She frowned, faltering. "I what?"

"Llorin brought you to my Keep seventeen years ago out of the goodness of her heart. She saw a helpless babe in that rundown shack your parents called a home and could not bear to leave you to die. That same weakness is not what compelled me to let you live. I beat Llorin within *an inch of her life* for that weakness." Illynor reached forward and grabbed Mercy's arm, trailing a rough, scaled finger over the bumps and ridges of her old, faded scars. The skin there was pink and raw from the Pryyam salt Niamh had ground into her flesh. Every brush of her sleeve was excruciating.

Illynor's voice betrayed no emotion as she continued, "I let you live because I wanted to see what sort of creature would emerge from a lifetime spent only at the Guild, what sort of weapon my tutors and I could craft. We'd never raised a child before. We'd always been a home for runaways and strays. You were the first—an orphan elf, sister to the king's infamous mistress—and it was fascinating to watch you grow, to see you react to the hatred the other girls harbored for you. Sometimes you would lash out with violence. Other times, you would shut yourself up in your room for days and refuse to eat, refuse to speak, refuse to leave." Her fingers curled around Mercy's wrist, her sharp nails digging so deeply into the tender skin that Mercy had to bite back a cry of pain. "Do you want to know why I named you Mercy?"

Mercy nodded slowly. Her mind was already reeling, trying to piece together what had happened since her fight with Firesse in the End. The First must be dead, the plague along with her. The Assassins wouldn't be leaving the city so soon after the battle if the Cirisians had been victorious. Illynor had claimed that Tamriel was alive, but Mercy had no idea if Ghyslain, Nynev, Niamh, and her family had survived. And Calum—Calum could rot at the bottom of the Abraxas Sea for all she cared.

"I named you Mercy because I knew it was the one final way I could alienate you from the others. Personify the one thing an Assassin should never be, the one weakness she could never indulge, and the others were sure to despise you for more than just your elven blood. We forced you to rely on yourself, and yourself only, and merely sat back to see what came of it." She released Mercy's arm and leaned back in her seat. "If you rose up against them, fought to survive, to be worthy of the Guild, you'd be inducted and allowed to serve as a full-fledged Daughter. If not..." she shrugged. "Then we'd bury you and forget you ever existed."

"So my entire life has been a sick little *experiment?*" Mercy demanded, rage flushing her cheeks. "You let the apprentices torture and maim me for *entertainment?*"

"You were wonderful," she responded with a sly smile. "You did everything you were supposed to—and some things we never expected, like the Trial. You *surprised* me. I haven't been surprised in centuries. You were one of the best apprentices we have ever trained, Mercy."

The words made Mercy sick to her stomach. She'd been a fool to ever want to serve this despicable woman. She bared her teeth. "Don't say that."

"You were. Which is why it was so interesting when you betrayed us for the prince you were sent to kill." A glimmer of cruel delight passed through Illynor's eyes, and a shiver danced down Mercy's spine. "My ruthless apprentice went to the capital and found herself a heart. How could I kill you after that? How could I kill you when it is so intriguing to watch you and that little prince together? It seems my experiment, as you called it, has taken quite a drastic turn, and I'm interested in seeing where it goes. That, Mercy, is why I haven't killed you yet."

"I'm not your puppet," she snarled. "I'm not yours to manipulate as you please. You don't own me."

Illynor's hand moved so fast Mercy didn't even have time to react before the headmistress's palm connected with her cheek. Her head flew back from the blow, cracking against the wooden post supporting the canvas top of the wagon.

"You have belonged to me since the day Llorin carried you through the gates of the Keep. I have owned you since you were one week old, and I will own you until you draw your last breath," Illynor hissed. She stood and pushed aside the fabric flap behind her, reaching up to pull herself onto the bench beside whichever Daughter was driving the wagon. "It is up to you whether you spend the rest of your days serving me or rotting inside the Keep's dungeon." With that, she climbed onto the bench and let the fabric flap fall shut behind her.

Mercy let out a roar of frustration and slammed her fist into the post beside her. She tugged at the chains, at the shackles, at the link in the floor between her feet, but the metal did not so much as groan.

She reached up, chains jangling, and lifted the bottom of the canvas covering high enough to peer out into the star-flecked night. They were riding through a plain, but exactly where they were, she had no idea. Perhaps a detour along the edge of the fishing sector; Illynor wouldn't be stupid enough to take the straight route to the Guild. The main roads were probably crawling with guards.

Out of the corner of her eye, she could see another half-dozen wagons riding along behind them. The Assassins had disguised themselves as a caravan of traveling merchants. As long as Illynor kept her scales hidden under her heavy cloak, they wouldn't attract suspicion from any fellow travelers on the road, but the guards wouldn't be so easily tricked. Tamriel would have them searching every wagon and carriage moving south for weeks. Even so, Mercy knew that if it came to a fight, the Daughters would emerge victorious every time. Mother Illynor would die before letting Mercy slip out of her grasp again.

She turned her gaze back toward the horizon, wishing she could see the dark silhouette of Sandori in the distance. Her prince was waiting for her. Her family was waiting for her. She would be damned if she lost them again.

Someday, Mercy vowed, letting the canvas fall back over the side of the wagon, *I will return to you*. She held the image of Tamriel's face in her mind—his lips parted in a smile, his eyes shining with love and desire—and sat back against the bench, letting her lids fall shut. *I chose you, my love, and you chose me. Whether it is a month or a year from now, I will return to you.*

And when I do, we will cleave the world in two to find those who have wronged us.

FEARLESS
A BORN ASSASSIN, BOOK 4

Beltharos may have won the battle against the Cirisians, but the true war is yet to come.

For the first time since breaking the Guild's sacred oath, Mercy is a prisoner of the woman who has manipulated and tormented her all her life—and Illynor has no shortage of punishments awaiting Mercy for her crimes. All will be forgiven if she repents and dedicates herself to the Guild, but doing so means losing the family and life she left behind.

Chained and half-starved, she vows to never give Illynor the satisfaction of seeing her break, but her resolve weakens every day she must endure the Guildmother's torture. She can only hope Tamriel finds a way to free her before it gives out entirely.

Turn the page to read the first chapter of the fourth book in the Born Assassin series, Fearless.

1
MERCY

The first thing Mercy registered when she awoke were the shackles clamped around her wrists and ankles. The cold metal bit at her skin and sent goosebumps prickling up and down her arms.

The second thing she registered was the feeling of cotton on her tongue.

She'd been drugged.

Her eyes flew open to a pitch-black room. Panic closed its fingers around her throat, tightening, twisting, cutting off her air. Her hands were coated in dried blood—even though she couldn't see it, she could smell it, could feel it crusted to her skin. She squeezed her eyes shut, wading through the haze of her memories until flashes of the attack on Sandori flooded back:

Fires raging outside the city walls.

Blood coating the uneven cobblestone streets and ramshackle houses of Beggars' End.

Her vision fading as the plague devastated her body and mind.

She'd nearly died. She *should* have died, and she'd bet

anything Ino and Cassia were the only reasons she had not. They must have fought their way to her and taken her to Niamh to be cured; when she had awoken in the Guild's wagon after the battle, she'd found her skin clear and unblemished.

She shuddered, the jangling of her chains shattering the heavy silence of wherever the hell Illynor had imprisoned her. The dungeon, most likely. It was obvious she was underground; the stone tiles beneath her were damp and icy, and the scent of dirt hung in the air. A sliver of fear slid into her heart. If Illynor had been planning to kill her for her betrayal, she would've done it in the castle. She never would have bothered to drag Mercy all the way back to the Keep. No, Illynor had a special plan to make her pay—one Mercy was certain would make her wish she had died of the plague.

A swath of light cut across the room as a door in the opposite wall swung open. Mercy hissed in pain, squinting against the sudden light as a dark silhouette—two—filled the frame. She couldn't make out their faces.

"So you've finally decided to join us," Illynor said in her harsh, rasping voice. The Guildmother swept into the room with no sound but the swish of her heavy cloak against the floor. The Daughter accompanying her lingered on the threshold, watching them. "I was wondering when you'd wake up. Sorin's sedative was far stronger than I'd anticipated."

"How long have I been here?" Mercy mumbled, her tongue clumsy and thick from the drug.

"What do you remember?"

"Waking up in the wagon. Riding through the plains. A—A box." She stumbled on the last word, her throat tightening once more. The Daughters had driven their wagons for two days without stopping in an attempt to outrace the soldiers Tamriel and Adan had sent after them. When they'd finally allowed the horses to rest, Tanni and Sienna had grabbed

Mercy and shoved her, chains and all, into the false bottom of one of the wagons.

It was the first of Illynor's punishments.

The compartment had been barely large enough to fit Mercy's body. She had spent the remainder of the ride to the Keep in that little box, her knees pressed into her chest, her breaths shallow and labored from the stifling heat of the midsummer days. After what had felt like an eternity, she'd been so desperate to escape the confines of that boiling compartment that she'd clawed at the trapdoor until she'd broken her fingernails down to the quick. Illynor had kept her in that box without food, without water, for *two days*.

She looked down at her feet, trying to pretend the memory of those long, excruciating hours didn't make her heart hammer against her ribcage, but it was no use. The walls of the dungeon pressed in on her, drawing closer and closer until she was back in that cramped little box, until every breath she took wasn't enough to fill her lungs, until terror began to fray her nerves. She clenched her fists, needles of pain shooting down her still-sore fingers, and forced out, "Nothing else until now."

"We returned three days ago."

Mercy looked at Illynor sharply, unable to hide her surprise. It had already been a week since the Guildmother abducted her. "And how long do you plan to keep me here?"

Illynor cocked her head, her scales glittering in the light seeping in from the hallway. "As long as it takes you to beg my forgiveness."

"Your *forgiveness*?" Mercy repeated incredulously, her voice a broken rasp. "You want me to beg your forgiveness for not wanting to spend my life slaughtering people for coin? For not being grateful to you for shoving a sword into my hands the day I learned to walk? For being angry that you *manipu-*

lated me and treated me like your own little *experiment* my entire life?"

"How about for giving you a home when your own parents didn't want you? For offering a starving elven orphan a place in my Guild?" Illynor growled, stalking closer. Every step made Mercy's stomach twist. Even though she knew what Illynor was saying wasn't true, the sheer authority behind the Guildmother's words made the affection-starved apprentice within her want to drop to her knees and spout apologies. "Or for allowing you to live after you made a mockery of the Trial, and for being so kind as to give you a *contract* for it?"

She stopped a foot away from where Mercy was slumped against the wall and grasped her chin with a hand, her sharp nails digging into Mercy's flesh. Her slitted eyes narrowed. "You should be grateful I didn't gut you the moment I laid eyes on you in Sandori."

Mercy jerked out of Mother Illynor's grip, turning her face away.

"Hm. Very well. We'll do it the hard way." Illynor turned to the woman standing in the doorway and snapped, "Get her to her feet."

The Daughter strode toward a wheel set into the wall on Mercy's right, her black clothing rendering her nearly invisible in the darkness. The sound of metal scraping on stone echoed through the room as she began to turn the wheel. It was connected to Mercy's cuffs through a long series of chains and links set into the floor and ceiling.

"Kismoro Keep predates the Year of One Night," Illynor explained as the slack in Mercy's chains slowly disappeared. "This room was used to torture enemy soldiers for information. As that is what you now are to us, it seems only fitting to keep you here."

The Assassin continued turning the wheel until Mercy was forced to stand, her limbs spread-eagled and her back pressed to the wall behind her. Her legs, weak from so many days without food or water, quivered under the weight of her body.

Illynor's eyes were hard as chips of obsidian. "I have told you all your life, Mercy, that you belong to me. You are *mine*—my pet, my project. My perfect killer. That does not change because you ventured into a human city and fell for the first boy who looked twice at you. I have spent seventeen years training you and I am not letting that investment go to waste."

"You're centuries old. Seventeen years is nothing to you."

"But it is everything to you, my dear."

"I'll never give in."

"You say that now. Tomorrow, or the next day, or a month from now, I will break that spirit of yours. You will fall to your knees before me, repent your crimes, and give yourself fully to the Guild." She smiled, a flash of white in the darkness. "I would not wait too long if I were you. You do want your prince to live to see his coronation, don't you?"

Mercy went completely still. "His coronation? Was the king killed in the battle?"

"He sustained a mortal wound. It is only a matter of time before he succumbs to it and his handsome son takes the throne. A single word from me, however, and your dear prince will follow his father to the grave."

"*No*—the contract is a forgery. It's void. I told you that," Mercy said quickly, desperately. Tamriel couldn't die. She'd do anything to keep Illynor from laying her hands on him. "His life is not yours to take."

"The evidence is in the capital, you claimed. Well, child, we are not in the capital now, are we?" Illynor lifted her chin. "Consider his life as hostage until you comply. Pledge yourself to my Guild and Prince Tamriel will live. Resist, and I'll have the Daughter who kills him bring back his head to keep you company."

"You're *lying*," Mercy snarled. It was a bluff. It *had* to be a bluff.

"I am many things, but a liar is not one of them," Illynor responded coolly. It was true. Like the rest of the Qadar, the Guildmother had always been painfully, brutally honest. She was conniving, cold, and manipulative, but honest. "This is the deal I offer you: the prince's life for your loyalty. Now what do you say?"

Say yes, a little voice in Mercy's head whispered. *Say yes, and save Tamriel's life.* Fear had turned her blood cold. She wouldn't be surprised if Illynor could smell it rolling off of her.

She shook her head. "No."

"No?"

"No," she repeated, firmer this time. She met Illynor's eyes and summoned all the courage she could. "You won't kill Tamriel because you and I both know that if you do, I will *never* submit to you. You can try to break me, but if you harm him, I will never, ever swear the vow."

"I think you underestimate how persuasive I can be," Illynor responded, a warning in her voice.

"I think you underestimate the depth of my loathing for you. I'll fight every day to be free of you, and if I cannot achieve that, I will turn my blade upon myself. Your perfect little killer will be no more."

Mercy's heart pounded against her ribcage, but she did not let her gaze stray from Illynor's. She had no power, no cards to play, except to turn Illynor's obsession against her.

"Maybe whatever punishments you dream up will be enough to make me submit," Mercy continued. "Maybe they'll convince me to swear the vow. But I will never give myself to the Guild if you kill Tamriel. That is the line you may not cross."

To her surprise, Illynor let out a low chuckle. "Oh, you're going to fight me with everything you have, aren't you? You think you're going to make it difficult for me," the headmistress purred, relishing the idea. "Then I shall play your little game. I swear to you, Tamriel will not meet his end at a Daughter's hand." She waved a hand to the Assassin—who had been standing so still and so silently Mercy had forgotten she was there—and the Assassin let go of the wheel. All at once, the slack returned to the chains, and Mercy dropped to her hands and knees.

Illynor leaned down and tipped Mercy's chin up. "I will see you again soon, my dear."

With that, she straightened and strode out of the room, her cloak swishing behind her. The Daughter, still cloaked in shadow, trailed after the Guildmother. When she stepped into the hall, the torchlight gilded her blue-black hair.

Mercy went rigid.

"Faye," she breathed.

At the sound of her name, Faye stilled, then slowly, slowly, turned to face her. Mercy's first friend—her only true friend—glared at her with such hatred it hit her like a physical blow. "What do you want, traitor?"

"Just...I'm sorry." She'd needed to say it for a long time. Even after everything—even after Faye tried to kill her in Xilor and in Firesse's short-lived war—Mercy owed it to her. Faye had shown her nothing but kindness, and Mercy had betrayed her. "I'm so sorry...for everything."

Her former friend's lips curled as she reached for the door handle. "You should be," she snarled as she slammed it shut behind her, plunging Mercy back into darkness.

ABOUT THE AUTHOR

Jacqueline Pawl spent her teen years trapped between the pages of books—exploring Hogwarts, journeying across countless fantasy worlds, and pulling heists with Kaz Brekker and his Crows.

But, because no dashing prince or handsome Fae has come to sweep her off to a strange new world (yet), she writes epic fantasy novels full of cutthroat courtiers, ruthless assassins, unforgettable plot twists, and epic battles. She is a Slytherin, and it shows in her books.

She currently resides in Scotland, where she can be found chasing will-o'-the-wisps, riding unicorns, and hunting haggis in the Highlands.

For news about upcoming books, visit her website at:
www.authorjpawl.com

instagram.com/authorjpawl
amazon.com/author/jacquelinepawl
bookbub.com/profile/jacqueline-pawl
goodreads.com/Jacqueline_Pawl

ALSO BY JACQUELINE PAWL

Defying Vesuvius

A BORN ASSASSIN SERIES

Helpless (prequel novella)

Nameless (prequel novella)

Merciless

Heartless

Ruthless

Fearless

Limitless

A Born Assassin Series Omnibus

THE LADY OF INNISLEE SERIES

Court of Vipers

Printed in Great Britain
by Amazon